# EXILE FROM REALITY

The great djinn waited in the hearth fire, ready to carry them across the void, but Kestrel hesitated.

Then there was a sudden commotion. Four wizards in sweat-dampened robes burst into the room. "There they are!" one shouted. "The ones who conspired against the august council. We've caught them at last!"

Kestrel saw them rushing toward Phoebe and made up his mind. Closing his eyes, he pushed her forward toward the great djinn's chest, moving to join her. He felt the wings close around them and Astron's demon elbow pressed painfully into his side. Reality vanished. The last thing he remembered was hearing the archimage's words:

"If they escape, broadcast the word across land and sea. There is to be no place safe for them in all the realm of man!"

# Riddle of the Seven Realms

## Lyndon Hardy

**CORGI BOOKS**

# RIDDLE OF THE SEVEN REALMS
A CORGI BOOK 0 552 13440 6

First publication in Great Britain

This edition published by arrangement with Ballantine Books, a division of Random House Inc.

PRINTING HISTORY
Corgi edition published 1989

Corgi Books are published by Transworld Publishers Ltd., 61–63 Uxbridge Road, Ealing, London W5 5SA, in Australia by Transworld Publishers (Australia) Pty. Ltd., 15–23 Helles Avenue, Moorebank, NSW 2170, and in New Zealand by Transworld Publishers (N.Z.) Ltd., Cnr. Moselle and Waipareira Avenues, Henderson, Auckland.

Printed and bound in Great Britain by
Cox & Wyman Ltd., Reading, Berks.

*To my daughters, Melinda and Jennifer*

# CONTENTS

## PART FOUR: *The Two Realms of Symmetry*

## PART FIVE: *The Realm of the Aleators*

## PART SIX: *The Ultimate Precept*

# THAUMATURGY

The Principle of Sympathy —— like produces like

The Principle of Contagion —— once together, always together

# ALCHEMY

The Doctrine of Signatures —— the attributes without mirror the powers within

# MAGIC

The Maxim of Persistence —— perfection is eternal

# SORCERY

The Rule of Three —— thrice spoken, once fulfilled

# WIZARDRY

The Law of Ubiquity —— flame permeates all

The Law of Dichotomy —— dominance or submission

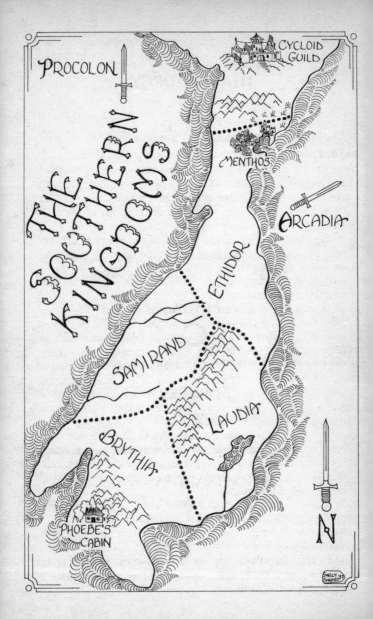

# Prologue

KESTREL looked past the flame toward the cabin door and estimated his chance of escape if something were to go awry. Like the lairs of most wizards, there were no windows in any of the walls; the distractions of the outside could well be done without.

He glanced back to the center of the room at the figure standing in the chalk-drawn pentagram that surrounded the firepit. Phoebe was not reputed to be a wizard of prowess and it was no simple devil that she was trying to summon.

If only she had been as greedy as the rest! The price he asked for an entire wagonload just like the branches he waved in front of their faces was usually low enough to hurry all of their thoughts away from testing what they were to receive. Some stored it all in their larders without even bothering to examine any of the leather sacks. Usually he was well into the next kingdom before they learned that a simple woodsman had gotten the better of the bargain rather than they.

But this one chose even to doubt that the sack he brought inside contained only anvilwood and nothing else. She had insisted upon a test to see that more than just the merest of imps was contacted through the realms, once the fire was lit.

Kestrel looked around the cabin. Thick beams bridged stout walls of white plastered mud. On the left, a bed of straw with room for only one stood underneath a shelf sagging with rolls of parchment. Behind Kestrel and extending along the wall on the right were tiers of wood-framed cubbyholes rising to the high ceiling, a

1

scrambled collection of nailed-together boxes and wide-mouthed bins.

In most of the openings Kestrel could see the contents stuffed nearly to overflowing and spilling onto the wood-planked floor with goat-bladder sacks, vials of deeply colored powders, dried lizard tongue, sunflower seeds, licorice, and aromatic woods; this was as well stocked a wizard's larder as Kestrel had ever seen.

Kestrel looked again at the wizard staring intently into the flame. He had sought her out because of the tales of her wealth. All the practitioners in the Brythian hills, though they thought little of her skill, admitted that she was the richest. But if not for that, his interest might have been piqued anyway. Rather than in ratted tangles, her well-groomed hair fell in a cascade of shiny black down the back of her robe. The broad and youthful face was clear and unwrinkled. It carried the open simplicity of an unspoiled peasant girl, rather than the somber broodings of one who dared to thrust her will through the fire. The sash of the robe, adorned with the logo of flame, attempted to pull tight a waist a bit thicker than the current fashion. But at the same time, it accentuated curves that would otherwise be hidden. Despite her caution, her manner had been quite warm. She did not display the disdain that vindicated in part what he did.

Kestrel ran his hand down the back of his head, feeling how well the thinning hair still covered the beginning of a bald spot. He imagined how he must have appeared to the wizard when he had knocked on her door barely an hour ago—brown curls on top, what there was of them, deep-set eyes about a long slash of a nose, and wide lips in a sincere-appearing smile. His clothing was plain but still fairly new. The road dust on tunic, leggings, and boots had just been applied around the bend from the cabin, rather than being the result of a three-day journey, as he had said.

How much had his ease in gaining entrance, Kestrel wondered, been because of other thoughts in Phoebe's mind, rather than the possibility of acquiring some of the rare anvilwood that peeked from the rucksack on his back. He savored the mental image which suddenly sprang into his mind. What would it be like to offer a wagonload of true potency instead of the disguised snags and rotten branches and to ask a fair price, rather than display an apparent ignorance of the value of what he possessed, or not to hurry away before his deception was discovered?

No. He shook his head sadly. He could not take the risk. He had to take advantage of the base impulses of others. It was his only defense. Long ago, he had trusted—and the scars still remained.

Phoebe suddenly stiffened. "I am yours to command, master," she said.

Kestrel immediately sensed that something was wrong. The air above the flame shimmered and danced. A hand emerged from nowhere, and then a head with features more plain than bizarre. The demon was no towering giant with menacing fangs and crackles of lightning, but Phoebe's jaws went slack and her hands fell to her sides all the same. She had not won the contest of wills; the demon had done so, instead.

Kestrel made a step to the left and then hesitated. The demon might be content with domination of the wizard and pay no attention to him as he slowly glided past. It was still morning. He could be well away before nightfall and anyone else suspected. On the other hand, he would be abandoning what little anvilwood he had remaining with nothing to show for it.

In mixed fascination and fear, he watched as the demon continued to tear apart the fabric of reality and emerge into the realm of men.

# PART ONE

## *The Realm of Daemon*

CHAPTER ONE

# Astron's Trek

ASTRON ran his tongue over the stubs of fangs he had filed away. In the palm of his fist, now clinched with tension, he felt nails ground short in the manner of men. Only two small knobs protruded from his back where one would expect the powerful wings of a splendorous djinn. Unlike his clutch brothers, Astron had no real weapons with which to fight.

The broodmothers' talk was that Elezar's mood was most foul. Only the foolish or those consumed by the great monotony would elect to be near a prince of demons when his disposition was less than ideal. Far more pleasing were the thoughts of the cozy contours of Astron's own den where he could spend eons rearranging the small collection of artifacts he had managed to keep for his own. If hints of boredom did begin to grow, he could catalogue more of the names that the skyskirr gave to their lithons or even start his investigation of what men called love. The summons of his prince easily could have waited until the next scheduled time.

Astron looked about the outer perimeter of Elezar's domain. He was standing on a thin plane of matter which hung suspended in the black expanse that constituted the realm of the demons. On the flatness were massed the splendid domes of his prince, mighty structures that soared into the blackness and blazed with color. In the distance other pinpoints of light shone against the background of ebony, some steady and pure, beacons of the princes who did not choose to hide. Others flickered at the edge of visibility, lures for the unwary or perhaps evidence of the enormous weavings of warring djinns.

Astron glanced down at his feet and the smooth surface of the plane. It glowed with a soft iridescence, pleasing to the eye. Pathways to the various domes were subtly marked for those who knew the signs. Behind him, the plane ended abruptly not far from where he stood, the edge sculpted in a graceful pattern that encircled the entire periphery. If he peered over the side, Astron knew, he would see a scene very similar to the one above—glimmering lights in a pitch-black sky.

Astron picked out a trail and followed it into the midst of the domes. The ones near the periphery were squat and ornate, no more than simple hemispheres encrusted with arabesques and intricate designs, lairs for brood-mothers and little more. Behind them towered the true marvels of Elezar's domain, stiletto spires that soared to heights far beyond what their delicate walls would seem to support. In clusters and splendid isolation, they sat atop broad vaults and fluted ellipsoids; over a sea of juxtaposed and intersecting bubbles they pierced the emptiness of the void. Fierce lights of lavender and orange upwelled from ports cut into the roofs of the domes. Intense beams ricocheted from shiny mirrors on the spires and scattered from curves and planes glittering with twinkling jewels. Elezar did not hide his domain from others who hoarded their meager store of matter in the blackness of the realm.

Astron quickly threaded his way between the outer domes and then entered an archway that opened into one of the larger central vaults. He paid no attention to the small devils huddled around the lump of rock in the first chamber, nor to the manner in which the stone jerked and bobbed above their craned necks. Levitating a boulder was beyond his abilities, even if aided by the will of others.

He passed sleeping lairs resonating with deep snores, treasure vaults crammed with artifacts from dozens of realms, quiet rooms of dark contemplation, and weaving alcoves shimmering with half-finished constructions. Finally he entered the grand rotunda itself at the very center of the domain.

Astron saw that the great hall was nearly empty. Except for Elezar, in the pit at the very center, sitting on a pillow of silk and down, and a swarm of imps buzzing about his head, no other demons were present. The prince was clothed in a glittering robe of deep sea-green, covering all of his slender body, except for his fingertips. Delicate features, an upturned nose, thin lips, and ears that were barely pointed sculpted a narrow face. Straw-pale hair ran over a brow flecked with gold, and half-closed eyes glowered under long curving lashes. No great scales or hair-pierced warts marred the smooth skin. Like Astron himself, Elezar could pass unnoticed in the realm of men if he were not too closely regarded.

Astron saw the discontent smouldering behind Elezar's eyes and felt his limbs begin to tighten. Slowly he started down tile-covered steps toward the prince, barely bothering to notice if any weavings had altered the shape of the rotunda since his last visit. As before, the ceiling was a large inverted bowl with a span greater than the outstretched wings of a hundred djinns. Sprays of soft colors caressed its glassy-smooth surface and glowing crystals throbbed with light all around the periphery.

A dozen entrances pierced the circular wall which supported the dome, each framed with fluted columns and interspersed with sculptures of heavy metal or artifacts wrested from other realms. The flooring was a series of concentric circles, each one a step lower than the last and converging on the pit in the very center.

"You are late, cataloguer." Elezar's soft voice floated upward from the hub. "Surely even one whose only concern is the making of lists must know the folly of displeasing a prince."

Astron's arms and legs tightened further. Even his stembrain stirred from its slumber. The broodmothers had been right; the prince was troubled and did not care if his irritation showed. With eyes discreetly averted, Astron descended the remaining distance to the pit and squatted uncomfortably on a small cushion at Elezar's feet.

The prince waited a long moment before he spoke

again, eyeing Astron with a cruel smile. "If I had not watched the hatchings myself, I would not believe that the demon that huddles before me is no less than a splendorous djinn," he said.

Astron kept his head down and said nothing.

"And what of the broodmothers, mighty cataloguer?" Elezar stepped forward and thrust his toe into Astron's ribs. "What of the carriers of our seed? Do they tremble with anticipation in your presence? Does their skin grow moist at your touch?"

The prince paused and then kicked forward a second time. Astron felt a stab of pain in his side, but did not move. It was but a mere token of what Elezar could do if he unleashed his great power.

"Or perhaps, instead, they merely confide their whispers, as if you were one of their own," Elezar continued. "Yes, as if you served no more purpose than they. Why should you not retire to their dens and prove your worth by becoming a warmer of eggs?"

Despite the iron-tight bands of his will, Astron felt his stembrain stir. Eggwarmer indeed. Only the deformed and slow of wit were charged with such a task. His value to the prince was far greater, as he had demonstrated dozens of times before. Who else had deduced the meaning of the cakes of congealed fats that mortals called soap, the purpose of the forged metal they thrust into the mouths of horses, or, the most perplexing of all, why their warriors grasped right hands in greeting?

He opened his mouth to speak, feeling the words rush upward sharp and cutting, but at the last moment he slammed his teeth together, biting off the sound. Deliberately he pushed the hot thoughts away and concentrated instead on visualizing the safe and comfortable contours of his own lair. Let the prince say what he would, Astron would not be provoked like some minor devil.

For a long moment nothing more happened. Then Astron saw Elezar's shadow retreat and heard the swish of silk as the prince sat back down on his cushion. Cautiously Astron raised his head upward and judged that finally he must speak.

"I have been of use to my prince in the past," he said. "Perhaps there is some additional service that is to be performed as a result of this summons."

Elezar took another moment before answering. "Any of your brothers would have replied with bolts of power, even though it would have surely meant their death," he said. "How could even one such as you retain clear thoughts after what has been spoken?"

"I am not like my brothers," Astron said quietly. "I am different in more ways than those that you have chosen to notice."

Elezar grunted. "And it is those very differences upon which I am now forced to depend," he said.

Before Astron could reply, the prince looked up into the cloud of imps above his head and gestured rapidly with his left hand. Instantly the swarm began to twinkle rapidly with a kaleidoscope of color, each sprite brightly glowing in a vivid hue. Their lazy hovering changed into a complex tangle of loops and dives. Astron saw a pattern suddenly emerge from the random motion. Arcs of fiery red imps, like droplets of molten lava, soared upward in a central column and then cascaded over onto waves of emerald-green that seemed to dance in empty air. Blues and yellows threaded through the rest, knitting complex tapestries that pulsated and changed in subtle ways that one could not quite follow.

Then, as suddenly as it had begun, the synchronized display winked out. The cloud of imps returned to their aimless hovering above the prince's head. The membranes retracted and Elezar's eyes refocused. His brow wrinkled with a scowl.

"More than three eons it took to train them all." Elezar waved at the swarm. "Three eons for that one clutch alone." The arc of his arm continued around the expanse of the rotunda. "I will not give them up, cataloguer. Not them or a single dram of hard matter in my domain."

"You are among the mightiest of princes," Astron said. "And the djinns who obey your commands number more than those of any other. What demon could possibly challenge you for possession of—?"

11

"Your skill is supposed to be one of making lists," Elezar interrupted. "Your knowledge of the other realms is the most profound of any in my retinue. Tell me quickly then, what are the seven laws that govern the affairs of men?"

Astron wrinkled his nose, puzzled. Such knowledge was widespread throughout the realm. Even the prince himself would have at least a casual acquaintance with the seven laws. Why would Elezar choose to exercise him through a memory drill like a broodmother instructing her scion? Astron started to ask the reason for the question but then saw the frown deepen in Elezar's face.

"The first two laws are the concern of wizardry," he said quickly, "the law of ubiquity—flame permeates all, and the law of dichotomy—dominance or submission. It is through fire that the barriers between our realm and the others are broken. And when, through it, we contact a dweller on the other side, one must end up the controller of the other; there is no middle ground.

"Of all the realms, ours is unique. The fires of the other universes connect them only to us and never to each other. If ever men, the skyskirr, the fey and all those who exist elsewhere interact it is because we have brought them together.

"And although these others can coexist side by side with no threat from one to another, our own involvements are much more tightly bound. Whenever one of us leaves our realm to sojourn elsewhere, it must be as the master of the one who has summoned or else as his slave.

"But you know all of this quite well, my prince. None less than you organized the great plan to conquer the entire realm of men and bend it to your will but a tick in time ago. Had it not been for the one that the mortals call the archimage—"

Elezar's hands clutched spasmodically and Astron veered back to his original course. The prince did not like to be reminded of his defeat by a mere human. "The next is the rule of three," Astron rushed. "Or as it is commonly cast—thrice spoken, once fulfilled. The

12

proper chants intoned three times over give men the power of sorcery and illusion to cloud the minds of one another.

"The maxim of persistence is the fourth. As the magicians in the guilds like to state it—perfection is eternal. If certain precise rituals are enacted flawlessly, then items can be produced that will last as long as the life of any demon.

"The fifth is the doctrine of signatures—the attributes without mirror the powers within. Based upon closely guarded secret formulas, those that men call alchemists brew strange concoctions that sometimes produce remarkable results. Far more powerful would be the craft if chance did not play a role in every successful brewing."

Astron again glanced at Elezar's hands but saw no change. Somehow the listing of the laws of magic was bound up in whatever was vexing the prince.

"The last two are the principles of sympathy and contagion," Astron hurried to finish. "The thaumaturges who use them speak of 'like producing like' and 'once together, always together,' but sympathy and contagion are what they mean. By taking a small part of a whole and exercising it in a simulation, the rest of the bulk is forced to act correspondingly. It is the craft by which men build their walls and transport heavy burdens."

"My prince," a deep voice suddenly rumbled from one of the rotunda entrances, "the signal lights have been blinking. Gaspar with his retinue is now on his way. There are twenty-two djinns of lightning and lesser devils as well."

On the rim of the rotunda, the entrance was darkened by the massive form of a colossal djinn, his folded wingtips scraping the archway as he entered. Powerful black muscles rippled across his chest as he moved. Slitted eyes of piercing yellow glowed in a face of darkest jet.

"What is your command, my prince?" the djinn asked. "Though we are fewer, my clutch brothers and I can make his landing one that will cost."

Elezar turned to answer, "No, no, Delithan. To

13

meet Gaspar on his own terms is surely a strategy of defeat. Invite him in unchallenged. We will use the time to our advantage."

"A djinn lives to fight, my prince," Delithan rumbled. "He exists only to rip matter asunder and drink deeply of its dying shrieks. If that is denied, there is little that restrains surrender to the great monotony."

"There will be many more battles in the epochs to come, Delithan," Elezar said. "Do not deny yourself the opportunity to engage in them by a miscalculation now. Push aside thoughts of the brooding doom. As you have in the past, trust in your prince."

"An epoch ago, none could call himself master of my lord," Delithan said. "But now there is indeed one who can so claim and he is only a man. Perhaps Gaspar too is mightier and the coming struggle is the last."

With a sharp crack, a spark of blue light suddenly arched from Elezar's left thumb to his forefinger. His arm swung out from his body in the direction of Delithan, a mask of anger etching the fine lines of his face. The huge djinn brought an arm up over his eyes. The pale outline of a shield began to materialize in front of his chest.

For a moment the two demons stood frozen, the crackle of ionization covering any words that they might have spoken. Then, as quickly as it had sprouted, the arc of energy in Elezar's hand winked out of existence. His face softened. He rotated his palms upward in Delithan's direction.

"Gaspar has grown so bold as to attack me in what all the princes acknowledge as my strength," Elezar said softly, his sudden outburst back under control. "It is a foolish boldness for him to do so and I will not reply in kind. There may yet be the thrill of battle for you against his djinns of lightning, Delithan, but as long as I am your prince, it will be a time of my own choosing. Now take your clutch brethren into the void as I have commanded and escort him here without incident."

Delithan's shield disappeared before it completely formed. He hesitated a moment and then dipped his head

14

in acquiescence. Stooping to clear the archway, he turned back the way he had come. "A djinn lives to fight," he rumbled as he left.

"Gaspar," Astron blurted as Elezar turned back to face him. "Gaspar of the lightning djinns. Though his numbers are large and mighty, he would not dare to challenge you without due cause. None of the other princes would permit it. They would rally to your aid and against all he has no chance."

"His attack is not one of djinn against djinn," Elezar said. "Instead it was something quite unexpected, although, of course, I showed no surprise." Elezar paused. His eyes flared. "He has posed a riddle, cataloguer, a riddle to test the prince most noted for cunning of all those who rule.

"The stakes are familiar, the ones I have accepted from demons with far keener minds. If I answer correctly, then Gaspar and all who follow him are mine to do with what I will. If not, then I and my domain are his."

"A riddle?" Astron said. "Then surely there is no threat at all. The likes of Gaspar could not formulate a puzzle that would long give pause to one such as you, my prince. And if you were—were too busy to answer yourself, then many in your domain would have sufficient wit to formulate the solution."

Elezar ignored Astron's words. "You were telling me of the laws that govern the realm of men. What of the metalaws which lie behind them?"

"Of the three of them I know far less," Astron said. He felt his stembrain again begin to stir. Elezar was moving on to things with which he was far less familiar.

"Three of them," Elezar repeated. "So you state that there are ten laws rather than seven?"

"No, the three metalaws are quite different from the rest," Astron said. "Each of the other realms, that of men, the skyskirr, the fey, and the others, is governed by seven laws of magic out of infinitely many. The metalaws govern which ones are active and how they are changed."

15

Elezar looked over Astron's head to the far side of the rotunda. Translucent membranes flicked down over his eyes to remove external distractions as he defocused in thought. "The metalaws were known by some of the most ancient princes," he said. "Even if we could not use them ourselves, we understood their manipulations well. And in the realm of the skyskirr, they are all-important; compared to them, the laws themselves pale into insignificance."

Elezar stared back at Astron. "But in the realm of men, for epochs none realized that such things as meta-laws existed. For the mortals, there were only the seven laws of magic as you have stated them, constant and unfailing. Humankind spent their brief lives entirely ig-norant of the greater powers that slumbered all about them."

The prince paused. "So you see, it is indeed possible. Gaspar's riddle might be a valid question, one with a definite answer. Ah, for the answer." Elezar looked away. "The answer that would give me victory over yet another who thinks his power greater than mine."

The prince ran his slender tongue over his lower lip, apparently savoring an imagined victory. He smiled and waved to the hovering imps for another display. But as the complex pattern formed. Elezar shook his head and motioned them to return to stillness. He looked back at Astron. "But I have no ready reply, cataloguer," he said. The words were forced and came with difficulty. "I stall for more time and Gaspar guesses at my weakness. He even taunts me with clues, so sure is he that I will fail."

Astron felt his thoughts suddenly boil and tumble. Elezar, Elezar the one who was golden—of all the princes, he was the one with the keenest mind. The others might wage their games of power by mustering great arrays of djinns into eye-blinding battles, but Ele-zar time after time bested them all with deft strokes of high strategy or bound up the outcome in riddles for which only he could unravel the answer in the end.

And if this time Elezar could not provide the solution, then there was great peril for all that he commanded as

16

well. The barely controlled rages of Gaspar were well known throughout the realm. None without an equal appetite for ripping things asunder could hope to survive for long under the rule of a prince of lightning. Astron looked down at his short nails and flexed the wings on his back that were never there.

But mixed with all of that, the surprise and the fear, there was something else that churned with the rest—a riddle, a riddle that even Elezar himself could not solve, a mystery that led perhaps even to the realm of men. What new and wonderful things might then be learned by one sent to observe or by one tasked to record the labors of those questing to find the answer? What increase in power could come to one who catalogued rather than fought?

Elezar apparently did not notice Astron's momentary inattention. The prince stood up and waved his arms in the air. "As you have stated, cataloguer, for every realm that we can contact, fire is the medium that breaks down the barrier between us. And for each of those connections, we are at the mercy of those who dwell on the other realm to build the flame and send their thoughts through it. We must wait for the call, the tugging at our own being, before we can begin the struggle that matches our wills against theirs.

"How much more powerful we would be if we could initiate the interaction, to go forth into the other realms at our own choosing rather than await events of chance. That is the essence of Gaspar's riddle, cataloguer. He states that the power of the laws and metalaws pale for the one who has the answer. It is the ultimate precept, he says, the underlying principle upon which all else is built."

Elezar brought his arms back to his chest. "The riddle is quite simply stated: In the realm of daemon, how does one build a fire?"

Astron saw the eyes of the prince again widen. He felt a rush of questions but knew better than to speak.

"We have great control over the little matter that has been brought back through the barriers to our realm,"

17

Elezar continued. "We can weave and transform it into exotic shapes that please the eye for eons. But somehow, in all the epochs that I can remember, no one in our realm, whether mighty prince or lowly sprite, has ever created a flame. None have been able to form the dance of ions that signify the combination of air with other things. The answer indeed must be the ultimate precept, cataloguer, and Gaspar's riddle or no, I, among all the princes who rule, will be the first to find out how it is done."

"But how will you learn?" Astron asked cautiously. "Is it perhaps in the realm of men that the answer would lie?"

"None in my personal domain have any hint to the solution, cataloguer," Elezar said. "I have decided that it is elsewhere I must look." The prince paused and intensified his stare. "But there is little time for undirected and random search. First, I must ask the one who might have a greater chance of knowing the answer to the riddle than even I."

Astron's interest suddenly vanished. Cataloguing in the relative safety of the realm of men was one thing. Dealing with others of his own kind was quite another. And if it was the one he suspected that the prince had in mind—

"Not old Palodad," he said. "The broodmothers say that even mighty djinns cannot return from his domain unscathed." He looked in Elezar's eyes and saw the prince nod slightly.

"Yes, Palodad," Elezar said, "the one who reckons."

Astron felt his stembrain begin to struggle harder to free itself from his rational control. Knowledge was power, it was true, but the risk must be commensurate with the reward. Even with a well-disciplined phalanx of splendorous djinns, Astron would not care to enter the domain of the demon reputed to be maddest of all. Besides, his specialty was in the other realms. It would not make sense to send to the domain of another prince one without the ability to weave or fly. Surely it must have

18

been for something else that Elezar had summoned him before the scheduled time.

"Which of your phalanx have you selected to dispatch?" Astron managed to say through jaws drawing suddenly tight. "How have you balanced between the need for strength in a far domain as well as here to impress Gaspar when he arrives?"

"You are the emissary, Astron, you alone, the one I have selected above all others in my domain."

"But I am a mere cataloguer." The protest rushed from Astron's lips. "Far more do I know of the workings of men than the traps in our own realm. I serve better helping to unravel what information another might bring back from such a trek than braving the perils myself.

"Look at my fangs," Astron said as he spun quickly around. "See again the stubs on my back. My role is to observe and record. It is the calling of the devils and djinns who can weave to perform actions for their prince."

Elezar shook his head slowly. "The broodmothers are most likely correct; Palodad's lair will be dissimilar to any other in the realm. But it is because you cannot fight that I have chosen you, cataloguer. The unfamiliar will not provoke you to rage. You above all else will keep your stembrain under control, because you must."

Astron looked beyond the prince to the cool serene walls of the rotunda, familiar sights that he had viewed many times before. He thought of the comforts of his own lair with the artifacts whose purposes were yet to be discovered. Even the realm of men with the strange customs and exotic structures was to be preferred to the dangers that lurked for the unwary in his own realm. He felt the tug and pull of his stembrain straining to be free, to run amok and control his limbs in a frenzy of chaos and self-destruction.

"There is more at stake than the rule of my domain," Elezar said. "Gaspar will treat my own djinns with dignity, grant them a final battle that would satisfy even their lusts for destruction." He paused and bored his sight into Astron. "But as for you, my wingless one, a

19

nimble wit and knowledge of arcane lists will have little value for him. At best, your torture would serve as a moment's distraction. You might hope that the process would not be a lingering one."

Astron looked into Elezar's eyes, searching for even a hint of indecision, but saw only the resolve of a prince. His shoulders slumped. The last thoughts of his den faded away. For a moment, he did not speak, but finally he willed his tongue to move. "Arrange for the djinn who will transport me," he said softly. "I will perform my duty as the prince commands."

CHAPTER TWO

## The One Who Reckons

As the dimly flickering light grew brighter, the overwhelming emptiness of the realm began to fade. Astron craned his head upward at the djinn who carried him, each shoulder tight in a unflinching grip. The demon showed no change in expression as they closed on their destination, the boredom of flight just another indication of the encroachment of the great monotony into its mind.

Looking over his shoulder, Astron could no longer distinguish the shine of Elezar's domain. It was lost in the sparse scatter of glowing dots that gave a feeble hint of pattern in an otherwise featureless expanse. Despite countless eons of slowly wresting matter through the flame from the other universes, the great vastness was still the true character of the realm. Only in the small confines of one's own lair or in the everchanging patterns of the domain of a prince could one temporarily forget the meagerness that enshrouded imp and djinn alike.

Endowed with the power to cover great distances almost without effort and the ability to transform whatever

20

one saw into unlimited other shapes, the cruel jest of it all was that there was so very little on which those powers could be exercised. It did not take long before the farthest corners of the realm had been explored, all the interesting weavings formed and destroyed, and the bizarre mysteries of men and those of the other realms sampled and discarded. Ultimately all that was left was to sit and wait, contemplating the curse of an immortal lifetime—sit and wait until the great monotony drove one to surrender to the stembrain and self-destruction in a new and interesting way.

Astron shook his head free of the brooding thoughts as the features of Palodad's lair became more clear in the darkness. Just as the other domains, the domain of the one who reckoned hung in space. Unlike Elezar's, however, it cast forth no shafts of brilliant light. Only the glow of a single imp marked the entrance to a long, sloping tunnel that led to Astron knew not what.

After he was deposited at the entrance, Astron bade the djinn to wait and cautiously entered. He felt the smooth surface of time-worn stone beneath his feet— true stone of condensed matter, rather than a web of fleeting energy that merely hinted at substance. Around his head and shoulders, the gnarled tunnel walls squeezed downward in the total darkness. The solidness of the steps was a surprise and the darkness too much a reminder of the cold and depressing emptiness of the realm. But there was no other choice. Astron clasped his fingers into fists and began descending as rapidly as he could, each step less than a heart beat.

Images of what could come to pass if indeed he did not succeed flitted through Astron's mind—Gaspar's rasping laugh, the small mites that crawled in the greasy stubble on the prince's chin, his minions ripping asunder the delicate columns and domes that Elezar had taken eons to weave, demigorgons crushing the skulls of the imps in their massive hands and degutting the larger devils with searing bolts of flame.

Astron tightened the coils of his fists. He for one was not ready for such a fate. His hatching had been less

21

than an era ago. The great monotony did not yet dampen his will to live as it did for some of the others, who had sampled a dozen times over all that Elezar had to offer, others who would have to be goaded out of a jaded lethargy even to die. No, if and when they came for him, surrounding his slight body with stares and gloats, it would be far too soon.

Astron grimaced. If and when they came, he hoped that for once he would have the strength of his clutch brothers, strength to deny to Gaspar any satisfaction, strength to be able to look back with unblinking eyes and stand silent, even though they pulled away his fingers and toes one by one.

It was all because of arrogance, Astron thought. His prince had been too proud not to accept Gaspar's challenge on the terms with which it was given. Elezar should have denied the fairness of the riddle. But he was too concerned about what the other princes would think if he refused a test in which, after all, he was supposed to be the strongest of all.

The tunnel turned sharply to the left without warning, and Astron banged his head against a jutting overhang. His thoughts jangled back to his immediate concern. "More than a million steps in total darkness," he muttered. "This Palodad constructs an approach of more than a million when a few hundred easily would do. Even a sublime devil guards his lair with only fifty. Fifty steps, though he might weave the essence of a rose."

Astron rubbed the throb in his temple with one hand while he cautiously extended his other forward. "There must be some truth to the accounts," he said to himself. "What sane demon would dare to be so wasteful? To squander his wealth on stride after stride of featureless rock when he could occupy himself for epochs building intricate sculptures instead."

His question echoed unanswered down the dark tunnel and Astron paused a moment more, trying to will himself into placid composure. To approach in a state of visible apprehension would place him at an immediate disadvantage. He was, after all, the emissary of a prince.

He squeezed his fists all the tighter and set a grim mask on his face. In silence, he trod the last ten thousand steps, not even bothering to count.

Finally he reached the entrance barrier and pulled it aside. The tunnel suddenly blazed with light. Translucent membranes flicked over his eyes as he stared into the brilliance. The drone of tiny wings mixed with the slur of countless curses, creating a din that assaulted even the most insensitive ears.

He saw the walls expand outward from where he stood to form a giant sphere, dotted with smaller globes of incandescence that banished all shadows from its interior. He stood on a ledge that circumnavigated this globe, a small pathway that gently curved and finally disappeared out of sight on both sides behind the massive constructions that filled the enclosed volume.

Directly in front, a causeway arched from the ledge to link with the nearest of the structures. The edifice looked like some gigantic gameboard, a collection of tightly packed cubical cells built of rusty iron spars with row upon row of repeated patterns forming an immense vertical plane. Thousands of cells were stacked into a single column, and thousands of columns ranked together from left to right.

Each cell was occupied by an imp, mostly rock gremlins with pale green skin, warted eyelids, and thick leathery wings. But here and there, Astron saw other types, waterwisps, smouldering fifenella, and pigmy afreets almost as tall as the span of his forearm.

Every imp, regardless of type, was collared with iron and linked with short pieces of chain to the lattice. The inhabitants of each row were joined together by lengths of rope that draped from cell to cell and looped around right wrists outstretched rigidly above slumbering heads. The end of each rope terminated on a separate shaft of steel at the edge of the lattice that ran to other constructions farther back in the sphere.

More cords dangled from shafts above each column, connecting the left wrists of the demons positioned in the same vertical line. Although all seemingly were asleep,

23

about half had their mouths open and long dangling tongues oozed a drool onto those confined below.

As Astron watched, a shaft on the side suddenly twitched away from the lattice, joggling the arms of the row of gremlins to which it was connected. They all sprang alert. An instant later one of the rods on the top also lurched from its resting place, waking a column as well. Another moment passed with the aroused demons tensed and eyes open wide. Then, almost as quickly as they had wakened, they returned to their rest, facial expressions the same as they had been before. They all returned, that is, except for one, the one who had been common to both row and column, the one who had had both arms tugged.

The selected imp waited restlessly until another gremlin, free-flying and unfettered, buzzed into view to position itself in front of the lattice.

"Bad news, mintbreath. It's a tongueout," the newcomer squeaked. "And from the way things are cycling, I doubt another change will come for an eon or so."

"Gimme a break," the awakened imp answered. "I'm way ahead on tongueouts. I had to drool for over an eon just a few cycles ago. My jaw still aches from the effort. And I can remember my state in my head just as well as you. Wake me in an era and I will still recall whether I had been set to be in or out."

"Tongueout," the hovering gremlin insisted. "Or do you want me to report you stuck? If the upkeep crew replaces you, then you will be sent to the register pit. At least here you get to sleep most of the time."

The imp in the lattice grimaced and then finally spat out its tongue at the messenger. With a growl he pitched his head forward on his chest, letting his body dangle from its fetters. The fluttering gremlin then flew away just before another tug on the rods aroused a fifenella and the cycle started again.

Astron shifted his attention to other lattices nearby the first. Some were identical in construction, giant arrays of sleeping imps. In others, tall columns of sprites were bound spread-eagled with a limb stretched tight toward each corner of its cell and the fetters running from the leg of one to the arm of another. In spasmodic waves the demons twitched and shuddered, jiggling the left leg if only one arm were tugged and the right if both were stretched instead.

In yet other cages, mighty djinns flipped from being erect to standing on their heads in response to the jabs and pokes of their neighbors next in line. Back into the recesses of the cavern the jumble of imprisoned demons filled the span of the eye, islands of symmetry joined in a chaotic web of lines, shafts, and darting imps. All of it was alive with jerk and tug, great rolling waves of activity that coursed and pulsed in patterns that could not quite be followed.

Astron's mind whirled. He had been prepared for strangeness. If nothing else, his many trips into the worlds of men had accustomed him to the unusual. But the expanse was too great. Never before in his own realm had he seen so much matter concentrated in one place. Countless numbers of fetters and chains, cell placed upon cell, lattice after lattice, receding into the distance. Elezar was reputed to be among the richest of the princes, but all his fanciful domes would be lost among the massive constructs in the sphere.

"With no matter for payment? One dares to come with no matter?" A raspy voice sounded over the noise.

Astron looked upward and saw a platform that jutted from the wall of the sphere some hundred spans above where he stood. Descending from it in a rope-hung bucket was a demon of about his size although certainly not his shape and form.

The posture stooped; a long curved neck cantilevered from the deep valley between bony shoulders. The scales of the face were cracked and peeling. Near the gnarled ears, some scales were missing altogether, revealing a pulsing underlayer that quivered like freshly flayed flesh. Eyes squinted out from grimy hollows, one rheumy with phlegm and the other jerking in erratic directions, independent of its mate. Emaciated arms terminated in three-clawed hands, one wrapped permanently

25

about a crystal of some polished metal, the webbing between the fingers spread like a threadbare cape over the gleaming surface.

"And no wings as well, I see," the voice continued as the basket descended to eye level. "Quite presumptuous to come without wings to get you from here to there."

Astron stared at the demon as it slowly swung a spar from the basket over to the ledge and hobbled across. "I am unfamiliar with the tradition of this domain," he said slowly to the advancing figure. "This is the first time I have come. I act upon the request and demand of my—"

"What did you say?" The demon cupped his free hand behind his ear. "This is the first what?"

"The first time," Astron repeated. "The first time that—"

The rest of his words were drowned in sudden laughter. The approaching demon tilted back his head and boomed with a repetitious grate, each rasp more dissonant than the last. Astron opened his mouth to speak again, but then thought better of it, waiting instead for the other finally to lapse back into silence.

"Time," the demon repeated with his last rasp. "Not only time but the first time. Here, hatchling, look at this."

The good hand reached into a small pouch hung over a pointy hip and produced a curiously shaped glass, two bulbs, one above the other with a small constricted passage between and grains of sand slowly draining from top to bottom.

"This is time, hatchling. See it flow incessantly. In a continuous stream. Eons, eras, epochs, one after the other without seam, without division, apparently without start and finish. There is no first time, there is no last. There is only time and it is one."

Astron retracted his membranes and stared at the figure before him. The awe for the surroundings gnawed at his resolve. "Palodad?" he asked cautiously. "Are you the devil, Palodad, the one who reckons?"

"I am indeed he." The demon straightened his back slightly, his demeanor suddenly sober. "And you no doubt are the messenger of some prince who cannot see his way out of a problem. This may be your first visit, but across the eons it is but one of countless others."

"I come by the command of Prince Elezar," Astron said. "He strives against Gaspar of the lightning djinns for the right of supremacy."

Palodad's good eye brightened. He put away the sandglass and looked over Astron far more carefully than he had before. "Ah, Elezar, Elezar, the one who is golden," he said slowly.

"Yes, and as you say, I come with a riddle that is in need of its key."

"If Elezar cannot answer, then it must be a puzzle indeed," Palodad said. "I have advised him once before on matters of great weight. If this is of like proportion, then a mere fistful of iron will not suffice for payment."

"Nevertheless, the answers the prince must know."

Palodad grunted. For a long moment he stared unblinkingly at Astron. Then he put away his glass and turned to hobble slowly back onto the spar. "Come," he called over his shoulder. "Come and tell me what exactly perplexes the great Elezar so. I will elect to be flattered by his attention, even though it has been slow in coming. It certainly is about time he again has decided to ask for my aid."

Palodad suddenly jerked to a halt and smiled. "Yes, it is about time," he repeated with a rasp. "About time. It could be for nothing less." He tilted his head back and opened his mouth into a great circle. His laugh filled the air and echoed from the wall. For a dozen cycles of the nearest lattice, the demon clutched his arms to his sides, rocking back and forth, oblivious to everything around him.

Then, as abruptly as he began, Palodad stopped and resumed his shuffle toward the bucket. "I had instructed you to follow," he called back as he entered the basket. "Or did your prince send just an imp still afraid of its broodmother?"

Astron looked again into the interior of the sphere, at the bound and jerking sprites. He heard again the howls

of pain and maledictions. The scene troubled him
greatly, far more than any mystery in the realm of men.
A reluctance coursed through his stembrain, putting
stiffness into his limbs when he commanded them to
move.

"I will remain untouched," he muttered to himself. "I
need only stay until I have information for the prince."
With a pace no swifter than Palodad's he moved toward
the waiting bucket.

## CHAPTER THREE

## Lore of the Listmaker

ASTRON lost track of the number of pulley baskets he
rode before he finally reached Palodad's destination,
deep in the interior of the sphere. As the last bucket
whisked from view, he found himself in an open-top box
of stone as solid as the steps that had led to the entrance
of the old demon's lair.

To his immediate left, in front of one of the four confining walls, a continuous belt moved on rollers and
creaked off through a dark recess into the sphere
beyond.

Directly in front stood a collection of glass jars,
densely packed with swarms of swirling mites. Behind
them were stacks of what looked like shallow baking
sheets, some piled in precarious columns and others only
two or three deep littering the floor. Through an archway
in the distance, Astron saw a small devil brushing a
sticky glue onto the surface of one of the sheets and
adding it to another stack. A cloyingly sweet odor drifted
from the glue and hung heavy in the air.

On the right, the wall was covered with tiny glowsprites, each one crammed between the limbs of his

neighbors, but somehow arrayed in precise lines. The small demons winked on and off with random bursts of light across the spectrum. All the colors of the rainbow stirred in motley patterns, each imp no larger than a thumbnail, but with thousands of neighbors producing a pulsating and almost hypnotic glitter.

"It is here that questions are composed," Palodad said behind Astron. "Here I affix the mites to the matrix and send the instructions to my minions who await beyond."

"But to what purpose?" Astron turned and shook his head, unable to contain himself any longer. "Why the million steps? How can so many submit to such an existence?"

"These are the questions of your prince?" Palodad asked.

"No, no, not these. His is much more profound." Astron regretted the words as soon as they had left his lips. They revealed that Elezar's messenger was not totally unimpressed by what he saw and hinted therefore that Palodad's power might be the greater. The prince would not be pleased.

"But nevertheless I am a cataloguer," Astron added quickly. "It is my nature to ask so that I can observe and record."

"A cataloguer. Indeed." Palodad paused and squinted. "No doubt the lack of wings and protruding fangs gives you greater satisfaction with your amusement."

Astron turned away his eyes. Things were not starting well at all. "I am, in fact, a splendorous djinn," he said softly. "At least my clutch brethren were. But I was hatched without wings and grew in stature no greater than you see me now."

He hesitated a moment and looked back at Palodad. "But no matter that I cannot weave great cataclysms or burst assunder condensed rock with the wave of my hand. I am a cataloguer and a good one. I filed my fangs myself so that the effect would be complete. With hood and cape I have passed among men, raising not a modicum of suspicion. And yes, I even managed the domination of a strong-willed one or two."

29

"No doubt," Palodad said. "Even the smallest imp declares he has a few wizards under his spell."

"What I say is true. I have no need to speak otherwise."

"It does not matter." Palodad waved the words aside. "I have little use for the boasts of others in any case. The workings of my domain tell me far more of what has happened and what yet will come to pass." He paused and stared at Astron. "Perhaps, as a cataloguer, you might appreciate that more than the others. Tell me your name. We will see what I know of the followers of Elezar the prince."

"It is Astron—Astron the one who walks."

"Ah, Astron. It will be easy enough," Palodad said, turning to pick up one of the metal sheets from the floor. "Not thousands of syllables that record all of your exploits like some who have come."

He placed the sheet on the belt and pulled a lever to stop it moving. Then he turned the lid on one of the jars at his feet, releasing a cloud of mites. Moving with a quickness that surprised Astron, the old demon began plucking the tiny imps from the air one by one and affixing them to the sticky surface of the sheet. With the metal ball in his other hand he smashed them flat so that they would stay. In what seemed like an instant he had immobilized several precise rows of mites, some with their heads aligned along the lines and others perpendicular to it.

Palodad surveyed his handiwork for a moment and then kicked the empty jar aside, waving the unused mites away. He hobbled back into the stacks behind them and returned a moment after with several more sheets, these already filled with imprisoned imps. He formed a chain of the trays on the belt. With one final grunt, he pulled the lever to start them moving toward the slit in the wall.

"Pay attention to the glowsprites," Palodad said. "It will take awhile for the framing instructions to be obeyed. After that the images will unfold quickly enough."

Astron looked at the random dance of lights on the far

wall. For a moment nothing happened; then suddenly the pattern changed. The glowsprites began pulsing in unison, creating bands of color that seemed to move across the wall. Kaleidoscopic shapes formed and dissolved; scenes of other parts of Palodad's lair exploded into sharp focus and then faded away. Faces of great djinns snapped into view, one after another, faster than Astron could follow. Then the flickering stopped. A single image remained for him to view.

Astron stared at what he saw. A slight demon somehow familiar seemed to frown back from the plane of the sprites. About the figure was a clutter of trays and jars. In the apparent distance stood a gnarled old devil that looked exactly like Palodad. He saw the second demon scratch absently at a pockmarked cheek with a hand clutching a metal sphere and he whirled to see Palodad do the same.

Astron spun back to look at the vision, took a step forward and extended his arm. The image on the wall copied his motions. He touched his forehead and bared his filed-down fangs in a grotesque grin, watching in fascination as the face staring at him responded in kind.

"How is this possible?" Astron asked. "For all of demonkind, none of us cast a reflection."

"Truly not." Palodad smiled. "Light is altered when it is scattered from our bodies. It subsequently can be adsorbed but not reflected again." He waved his arm at the wall. "What you observe here is merely what I have instructed my sprites to do. They watch how you move and then each glows in the required hue and intensity to form an image that mimics exactly. They form a precise copy so that you see yourself as you appear to others."

Astron looked back to the wall. He straightened to full height and squared his shoulders, staring intently at what he had never seen before. His head was oval and symmetrically formed, with the small knobs where the horns of his brothers would be. No tufts of hair grew from the delicate swirl of his ears, and on the supple pale flesh only a hint of scaling was visible in the glow of the sprite light. The eyes were deeply set and the nose and lips a trifle large, but as he had said, without close scrutiny he could pass for a native in the realm of men. It was for these features that he had found favor with Elezar, he knew. The prince himself was unlike most demonkind and, rather than minimize the difference, he flaunted it.

"Evidently in the grand scheme of things," Palodad said, "there was need to collect more than just superficials about you, cataloguer. That is why the image is so sharp and clear. Look to your left. There is more that can be displayed than physical form."

Astron watched a second pulsing of color next to his reflection. It quickly distilled into the image of a broodlair, with pieces of broken shell littered among the coarse grasses. Four tiny djinns, tufts of down still clinging to rapidly flapping wings, danced above the lair, while one smaller demon cowered in the straw. With a shock, Astron realized what he was witnessing. No sound accompanied the animation, but he remembered the shrieks an era ago as his brothers had swooped down upon him, claws gleaming sharp. Even worse, he recalled, was the laughter as they turned aside at the last instant, barely avoiding contact. The two more precocious of his brothers already had felt the first intuitive grasp of weaving and formed bolts of crackling pain that they sprayed upon Astron's back as they sped by.

Astron clinched his long, slender fingers as the memory of impotency flooded through him. Four brothers, all splendorous djinns, and he with no more power than a lowly sprite, able to convert the air he breathed into food and water and nothing more.

But before Astron could dwell further on the memory, the image formed by the glowsprites shimmered and shifted. He saw himself half grown, eyes wide with membranes pulled back as he examined the object he delicately cradled in his hands. The devil who stood next to him in the image had his arms folded across his chest and a face showing uncompromising pride. Astron remembered that he had not cared.

Acknowledging the magnitude of the feat that brought

32

condensed matter of such quality through the flame had not been in his thoughts at all. Slowly he had leafed through the delicate sheets that were stitched along one side, studying intently the rows and rows of markings and occasional drawings of other objects equally strange. Some he had recognized—coins, belt buckles, forks; a random sampling of things retrieved by other demons on their journeys through the flame. And for some of these he suddenly had understood their use and meaning from the context in which they were drawn.

Astron nodded his head as he watched. He remembered the electric thrill that had arched down his spine. Who among all of demonkind would have guessed that the cylindrical fingercap guarded a human's fingertip against pricks from the tiny sword and trailing thread that bound together two pieces of cloth.

There was more merit than mere mass in an object fetched from beyond the flame, he had realized. There was knowledge as well, knowledge that might be of use to a prince who wished to astound his peers. And with knowledge came stature and regard, even for a djinn without wings or the ability to weave.

"All the artifacts that I possess," he remembered he had said, looking up quickly at the devil at his side. "The web of the spider, the pollen of a flower, everything in exchange for this."

As the trade was made, the image dissolved. When it refocused, Astron recognized a scene of only months ago as measured in the realm of men. He stood in his hood and cloak beside a cottage hearth; only the last embers remained of the evening fire. At a table across the room, a human serving girl stared in Astron's direction, her eyes wide and unblinking, totally under his command.

"What are your instructions, master, while I wait for you to return," she had said.

Astron remembered his hesitation. He knew full well what would happen to her when she was found after his departure. Men professed to feel compassion, but they dealt with demon possession with a zeal that was hard to understand. And she was not a wizard, boldly reaching into the flame to test her will against Astron or his kin. Only by accident had she looked too long into the hypnotic dance of the fire and allowed Astron to pass through the barrier between the realms.

Elezar would be satisfied enough with what has been learned, Astron had decided. The purpose of the little orb attached to the side of the door had been perfectly explained. None of the other princes would guess that it was to be rotated before being pulled.

"Return to the way you were," Astron had said. "I release you from my control. The prince cannot care about one mind more or less. Besides us, who in the two realms would know?"

The scene began to fade. Astron turned away to face Palodad. "How did you find out?" he asked. "I have told no one of what I did. Indeed, why even bother to record my affairs, rather than the lives of the princes that rule?"

"I have the relevant information on them as well," Palodad said. "Do not prejudge your role in the scheme of things. I am, after all, the one who reckons."

The old demon squinted his good eye at Astron. "The more interesting question is not how, but why. Why did you release the human female when you had no need? Even without wings, one would not expect such behavior from the clutch brother of a splendorous djinn."

"I—I do not know," Astron said. The vividness of the memories was unsettling. The impact of all he had seen began to numb his mind. His thoughts started to go off balance. He felt his limbs tighten. Was his the madness that came with the visit to Palodad? Was his lair so overwhelming and knowledge so great that one could not hope to keep his own clear thoughts in the old devil's presence?

Astron flicked down the membranes over his eyes and concentrated on the comforts of his own den. He had not one book by now but three. Some of the strange symbology that accompanied the pictures he was beginning to understand. Of all of Elezar's cataloguers, he was held in the highest regard. He had pledged to his prince and had

34

a mission to perform, regardless of the great powers exhibited by the old demon at his side. And the results were needed quickly, before Gaspar lost his patience and it was all too late.

Astron firmed his resolve. He would not waver. Digging his shortened nails into his palms, he slowly, deliberately retracted his membranes and looked at Palodad.

"Questions concerning Astron, the cataloguer, will be for another time," he said. "I am here now by demand of Elezar, the prince."

Palodad did not immediately answer. He pointed silently at the imaging screen indicating that he could show more, his lips curved in the hint of a mocking smile.

But Astron held his determination. The urgency of his visit locked firmly in place. He willed his thoughts to calmness and waited for the devil to speak.

"Questions concerning the one who walks will be for when?" Palodad asked at last.

"For another time," Astron said.

"Yes, for another time, another time," Palodad echoed. He kicked one of the metal trays aside and again dissolved in a fit of laughter. "There is no getting away from it," he gasped. "It is always a matter of time."

The devil clutched his sides and crumpled into a ball at Astron's feet. Rolling about on the hard stone slab, he flailed his spindly legs and bellowed incoherently, giving no signs of ever stopping.

Astron waited patiently for a moment and then scowled in annoyance. Now with his focus away from his own personal safety, the pressure to obtain results felt all the greater. He looked about for the presence of a broodmother who might give aid to the stricken devil, but saw none. He hesitated a moment more. Then with a shrug copied from the humans he turned and began to walk toward the doorway behind the stacks of trays.

But Palodad stopped laughing before Astron had gone two paces. "You have not yet told me the question of your prince," the devil said calmly.

Astron paused. Now there was no hint of madness in Palodad's tone. It was as if the devil was totally unaware of his actions moments before. Astron shook his head, trying to toss off the behavior as he had all the rest. Slowly he turned back to face the devil and waited until the old one was erect.

"Gaspar's riddle is most unusual," Astron said finally after Palodad had finished smoothing his pouches and straps. "It is most unusual that the likes of a lightning djinn would even conceive of one of such difficulty."

"But nevertheless, apparently he did," Palodad said. "How unlikely the conundrums, the agreement is no less binding."

The old devil paused and a faraway look came to his eye. The corners of his mouth rounded in the beginnings of a grin. "So quickly now, state what it is that your prince wishes to know. You already have wasted enough of my precious—"

Palodad's cheeks lifted further. The hint of a giggle started in his throat.

"How does one start a fire?" Astron interrupted quickly. "On the worlds of men, in the 'hedron of the skyskirr, and in all the universes that we know, there is fire and flame."

"It is the means by which the barriers between our realms are overcome and mind is linked with mind," Palodad said. "Elezar does not need the one who reckons to tell him that."

"In every realm there is flame except for one," Astron said. "Except in the realm of daemon itself. We have pulled through the barriers artifacts that are solid and ones of liquid and gas. But never in all the epochs that any can remember has there been fire in the domain of any of the princes."

Astron stopped. He looked at Palodad intently to judge the old devil's response. For a long moment neither moved; the only sound was the background cries echoing in the confines of the sphere.

Then Palodad shuffled to the jars on the stone floor and released another swarm of mites. For many cycles of the lattices, he grabbed them from the air and affixed them to one metal sheet after another, feeding the com-

36

pleted trays through the slot in the wall. When he was done he turned his attention to the glowsprites, watching closely the random blink of colors and form. This time they did not shape coherent images, but Palodad nodded and smiled, mumbling to himself when he seemed to distinguish one particular pattern from another.

For how long he remained waiting, Astron could not tell; but finally, one by one, the sprite lights winked out, leaving only a surface of muted gray.

"There is the matter of the payment," Palodad said at last. He rubbed the metal ball he carried in his hand against his leg and then looked absently at the shiny surface. "Did your prince delegate to you the bargaining as well?"

"Then you do know the answer," Astron exclaimed. "You have calculated it with your strange devices even as we waited."

But Palodad held up his hand before Astron could say more. "As you have said, the riddle is most profound. It is no wonder that even the likes of Elezar could not fathom the direction in which to proceed."

The devil paused and fingered the pouch containing the hourglass at his side. "In fact, even I do not bargain with the solution to the conundrum," he said. "I can only indicate where it is the most—the most profitable for Elezar to look. As for the details of the answer, he will have to find it on his own."

The sudden buoyancy of Astron's hopes drained away. Despite all the tales of the broodmothers, the old devil knew little more than his prince. Elezar already suspected that the answer lay outside of the realm of daemon. Merely being told where to seek would be worth far less than the answer itself.

"You speak of payments," Astron said cautiously. "Surely a mere hint carries little value at all."

"Many others have found my prices reasonable enough." Palodad waved his arm out across his lair. "With each riddle I solved, I obtained a few more spars, stone for another trio of steps, cages for one or two more imps. Each exchange in itself has not amounted to much, but over the eons I have managed to build all that you have seen. And, rather than waste my wealth on trivial amusements for the senses, I have focused it on increasing my ability to compute, to collect and store even more of what happens in the realm, and to predict with greater and greater accuracy what the future will bring."

Palodad smiled and tapped Astron's chest with the ball he clutched in his fist. "Elezar chose his emissary well," he said. "I get no great amusement spending eons maneuvering through complex negotiations for the last dram of mass. Your prince merely has to fetch for me something from the realm to which I will direct him. That will be payment enough."

"If what you desire is more than base iron, then it will not be so easy for any of Elezar's retinue to wrest it back through the flame," Astron said. "The prince will not care for an agreement that carries such a complication."

"I am fully aware that the living residents of the other realms can transport objects through the flame far more easily than can any of our kind," Palodad said. "Elezar will have to enlist help from men, skyskirr, or some other beings, it is true. But I have faith in his ability to figure out a way."

"It is a complication," Astron repeated. "As Gaspar presses for an answer, my master will have less ability to comply."

Palodad scowled. He pressed the heavy orb of metal to his chest. "Tell him that I will validate his answer," he said. "Whatever he discovers, he can bring to me before he risks exposing it to Gaspar. I will weigh the plausibility of correctness with the computations that are at my disposal and no one else's in the realm. In exchange for a modicum of matter, he will know not only where to look but be certain that what he finds is correct.

"Tell him, cataloguer. Tell him what I offer. He will ponder and then finally acquiesce. It is only a question of time."

Astron grimaced, but Palodad took no heed. He slapped his arms about his waist and staggered back into the conveyer belt, howling in apparent glee. "Time,

38

time, time," he gasped. "The focus always returns to time. When will it ever end?"

Astron slumped to the stone slab in frustration. He felt the beginnings of doubt that his journey had accomplished anything at all. Perhaps all the talk of computations and hints were no more than the ravings of madness, a perverted defense against a growing presence of the great monotony.

He shrugged his shoulders. But if there were anything else to try, surely his prince would have so directed him. Palodad represented the last hope, as slim as it was. In resignation, he watched the old devil flail on the hard stone, waiting for the seizure to end.

Eventually Palodad stopped and righted himself, wiping away a mucus-filled tear as he stood. "You should now go," he said, waving to a bucket descending from a level above. "Repeat to your prince the offer I have made. Come again and tell me when he has agreed. Then I will instruct in detail where it is you are to search and what you will bring back for me in exchange."

Astron nodded and rose to meet the descending basket. The outcome of the meeting was far from satisfactory. He doubted that the duty to his prince was yet quite completed.

CHAPTER FOUR

## Princes of Power

THE domes of Elezar were just as Astron had left them. He felt the talons release their grip on his shoulders and dropped the last few spans to the decorated plane on which the structures stood.

"Until the prince gives me cause to return to Palodad's lair, I will have no further need," he said to the djinn still hovering above him. "Return to your own den and await command."

The mighty demon gave no acknowledgment. With one beat of his wings he soared rapidly upward. Soon he was but a speck vanishing from sight. Astron watched him go and for a moment more followed the flights of others as they transported objects and smaller devils to and from Elezar's domain.

He was a cataloguer, Astron thought, the best in all the retinue of his prince. He understood the value of knowledge and traded it for power far beyond what one would expect for one of his size and lack of ability to weave.

He was a cataloguer and yet... He flexed his arms trying to imagine for perhaps the millionth time the sensation of darting between the uppermost spires of his prince's towers, of swooping down into the dark abysses, or even of visiting distant lairs without the assistance of a djinn dangling him from great talons and protecting him from danger.

Astron closed his eyes, wiggling his fingers in exaggerated slowness, straining for the feel of the matter about him, trying to caress its form and texture, molding it into the shapes that he commanded, and transforming even its innermost structure and bonding so that it became as he desired.

But as always, the feelings did not come. His weight pressed all too firmly on the soles of his feet. His palms and the tips of his fingers felt no more than the tenuousness of air. He was only Astron, the one who walked. Besides, there was no time for such reverie, he decided angrily. He must report to the prince.

Quickly Astron navigated through the maze of peripheral domes to the main rotunda. The slight give of the thinly stretched web of matter to each stride reminded him of the firmness of Palodad's crude steps of true stone. The outer passageways were empty; the flitter of imps and bustle of messenger devils had stopped. When he burst into the central rotunda, Astron found that every demon in the domain had gathered. In concentric

40

circles, they hovered and squatted; all eyes were focused on the hub in which were conversing no less than two princes of the realm.

Astron felt his limbs stiffen. He might already be too late. Gaspar and his minions had arrived. Astron saw Elezar sitting on the same pillow of silk and down. Ignoring the other cushions, Gaspar stood with arms folded across his chest, his massive torso rippling with muscle that seemed just barely under control. Deep-set and cruel eyes brooded under an overhanging brow, shadowing a face that never smiled. With a wave of irritation, he brushed aside the mites that swarmed about his chin. Small bursts of unwoven energy crackled from his fingertips, arching spontaneously from joint to joint. In the dreams of men, it was demons such as Gaspar that they feared the most.

Astron hesitated. One part of his mind willed his legs forward to tell the prince what little he had learned. Another bade him to remain still; it would not be prudent for Gaspar to hear the extent of Elezar's ignorance. In nervous anticipation, Astron waited for some indication of what he should do.

"I have come to settle our wager," the lightning djinn's voice rumbled throughout the dome. "Either you know the answer to my riddle or you do not. There is nothing to be determined by delay. Submit to your doom as you have agreed."

The guard of colossal djinns behind Elezar, six in all and each identical to the tiniest scale to his brethren, tensed and bared their fangs, but the prince motioned them to remain calm.

"Your haste hints of weakness," Elezar replied. "How bored has your following become?"

"There is no trace of the great monotony in a single one." Gaspar waved at the brace of lieutenants he had brought with him, now standing off to the side. He glanced about the dome and eyed the web of vaults and spars that held the expanse of the great roof aloft. "Every one of them looks forward with anticipation to when they can reduce all of this to base iron."

41

"And even if your challenge should prevail," Elezar said, "after the few brief moments of destructive fury, what then? What new amusements will you promise? How can you hope to keep alive their will and allegiance for even an epoch more? In the end, you will lose, Gaspar. The eons and eras stretch before you farther than you dare imagine."

Elezar paused and lowered his voice to a whisper, although all present could still hear. "Are you not already weary, Gaspar? Does not the futility of it all begin to gnaw? Will one more orgy of destruction be that much different from the last? Submit, submit to me, and at least the ending will be amusing for all."

"No," Gaspar thundered. He unfurled his wings and rose a span above the floor cushions. The air around his shoulders began to crackle and hiss. Sparkles of color pulsed into existence above his head.

The guard djinns quickly interposed themselves between Elezar and the other prince. Gaspar's lieutenants vaulted over the smaller demons between and formed a rank alongside their leader, their synchronized wing strokes creating a wind that whistled through the rotunda archways.

"Are these the actions of a prince secure in his command?" Elezar continued his questioning as the djinns maneuvered. "Why do the images I propose prick at your stembrain so?"

"I will have your existence to do with what I will," Gaspar roared back. "It has been promised. Agree to the conditions of the challenge and surrender. If you do not, it will not only be the lightning djinns that you must face. All of daemon will aid my just cause."

"And if you hurl one bolt at what is mine before that surrender is made, what then of the agreement?" Elezar said. "If a single atom of my domain is disturbed before I accede you the right, on whose side will the realm render succor and aid?"

Pops of thunder exploded from Gaspar's hands. For a moment, the intensity of the arching between his fingers increased. Then the demon curled one hand into a fist

42

and smashed it into the other, smothering the pulsating energy. He roared an incoherent bellow of frustration and waved his lieutenants back to their positions. Sullenly he drifted to the rotunda floor, again folding his arms across his chest.

Elezar's guard djinns resumed their positions behind the prince. For a long moment there was silence throughout the vast dome.

"I will illustrate my point in a less destabilizing manner," Elezar said at last. He motioned to an archway and four devils responded by carrying in a sculpture on a stand of marble.

Astron saw that it was molded in heavy bronze, a cluster of bubbles popping from a viscous broth, a copy of an artform prevalent in the realm of the fey. As the devils positioned it between Elezar and Gaspar, six more demons waddled forward, each one squat and broad, with eyes that squinted from between deep folds of flesh. They positioned themselves directly behind Elezar and gazed at the sculpture from expressionless faces.

"Now pick one of your lieutenants," Elezar said. "I give him leave. He may do with this matter as he wishes."

Almost in unison, Gaspar's djinns expanded their chests. Crackles of energy began to dance from their fingertips and eyes. Their alertness for possible battle moments before was a mere shadow of the excitement that gripped them now. Gaspar grunted irritably and motioned one near the middle forward. The selected lieutenant quickly arched across the intervening distance and landed with a heavy thud near the sculpture. His eyes widened. He wiggled his fingers, letting short arcs of piercing blue jump from one hand to the other.

"Wait a moment until the shield demons are ready and then you may begin," Elezar said. "I wish to minimize the effect of your craft upon the dome and the others who watch."

Gaspar's lieutenants nodded. Astron heard the shield demons begin to hum in a six-voice harmony. Simultaneously he saw the lightning djinn start to fade. On the top, bottom, and each side of the demon, a plane of haziness began to form, six sheets of growing opaqueness that intersected and confined him and the adjacent sculpture into a box.

As if they were filling with fog, the surfaces grew less and less transparent, finally hiding the djinn totally from view. The glow of imp light around the rotunda walls reflected diffusely from what looked like a solid cube. The shield demons had constructed a confining barrier, Astron knew. Little energy could penetrate it from either side.

But then the interior of the cube pulsed with light. In a heart beat, Astron saw a searing bolt of yellow rip from the djinn's hand and strike the sculpture with a devastating force. The power released was so immense that even the small fraction that trickled through the barrier was sufficient for all to see what was happening.

The sculpture ripped asunder where the bolt struck it at mid-height. Globules of molten metal sputtered from the point of contact. Two jagged halves ricocheted from the walls of the confining box. Before the image faded, the djinn struck a second time with two quick bolts that hit each of the tumbling pieces. Again the metal shrieked and tore; four fragments bounced about the cube.

With increasing rapidity the djinn aimed strike after strike at the fragments, ripping them into finer shards and filling the confining volume with light. Astron flicked his membranes over his eyes. The outwelling residue of the destruction was too painful to watch directly, even with the shield demons' barrier in place. Between spread fingers, he watched the djinn begin to froth and gesticulate wildly, barely in control of himself as he sought to rip the cloud of scrap into even smaller rubble.

The onslaught continued unabated until only a hazy dust filled the cube. No recognizable part of the original sculpture remained intact or any of the metal of which it was composed. Only motes of transmuted matter bathed in the glow of the careening light.

With no more targets on which to focus his power, the djinn finally stopped, slumping exhausted in one corner of the box. Elezar motioned to the shield demons. The side of the confinement nearest to Astron dissolved away as quickly as it had formed. Amidst pulses of escaping light and heat, the djinn tumbled out to lie at Gaspar's feet, limbs scattered haphazardly and with a smile on his face beneath glazed eyes.

"Such is the amusement that you offer to those who would follow you," Elezar said, "and to any who has not tasted the pleasure of total destruction, the allure might be strong indeed."

The prince looked down at the djinn slowly regaining his composure. "But I wonder, Gaspar, now that the experience has been savored, what more can you promise that will not be repetition of the same. And after the second, the dozenth, perhaps the hundredth time, what then will be your hold over this mighty djinn?"

"You speak of events that are in epochs yet to run," Gaspar said. "None of my lieutenants, nor any of the legions that they command, have tastes so jaded that they do not look forward to repeat for all your lair the small sample we have witnessed here."

"My point is not yet complete." Elezar raised one robed arm to cut off the other prince. "Let us see first the principle upon which the allegiance to my domain is founded."

As Elezar finished, a small devil came forward, barely larger than Astron himself. He entered the box from the open side and immediately sank into a deep contemplation of the still swirling dust. For a long moment nothing happened. Then a tiny spark of light blinked into existence before the devil's eyes and, following that in rapid succession, a series of others.

Gaspar rumbled with impatience but Elezar and the concentrating devil paid him no heed. For a long while more, there was no visible change in the haze, but then Astron saw a sparkling precipitate begin to fall to the bottom of the box.

"A significant fraction of the matter has been lost to light and other rays," Elezar said. "But it is of no concern. The weaver will work with what is at hand. He will first reassemble the basic particular components back into copper and tin, reversing the transmutations of your lieutenant. Then he will reconstitute the sculpture, coalescing the particles together one by one, if need be."

The prince paused and looked at Gaspar. "It took this one an era to make the first sculpture, staring from a hoard of bronze another of my minions had obtained from the realm of the skyskirr. It will take him eras more to reconstitute it and restore what he had before or perhaps craft something of greater beauty still. Eras, Gaspar, eras, not mere heart beats, and then it is done. He will be constructing, weaving, paying attention to painstaking detail to ensure that each little mote is in its proper place. It is a matter of rational control of the stembrain, not surrender to its lust.

"Eras and not heart beats, Gaspar—that is why princes such as I will endure long after djinns of lightning have long since surrendered to the great monotony."

"The stronger shall endure the longer," Gaspar said. He motioned his lieutenant to resume his position in line. "And there is little doubt between the two of us as to which it will be."

Gaspar unfolded his arms and stuck a bulbous thumb toward his chest. "My will has forever been my own," he said, "but in cold reality, Elezar, you can make no such claim." The djinn paused and looked around the assembled demons in the rotunda. "It is no less than another riddle. How can any here choose to ally themselves with one who has been enslaved by a mortal?"

"It was no common man," Elezar shot back. "No less than the archimage did I contest in wills. And I am not ashamed of the result. No prince of the realm would have fared any better than I. Certainly not a coarse djinn who has not even dared to answer a single call when it has come through the flame."

"So you assert," Gaspar said. "Such is your interpretation of the events. But if this mortal is so great that even princes bend to his will, why are there no others who also call him master somewhere in the realm?"

"I have spoken with accuracy," Elezar said. "The archmage knows quite well the folly of too much interaction with our domains. It is a mark of confidence in his power that he has no compulsion to exercise it wastefully."

"Spoken like a true slave of a dominating master." Gaspar laughed. "A lowly imp could not have put it better. Come, Elezar, Prince Elezar, submit to me now before my followers discover that the victory does not represent that great an accomplishment."

"I will not be distracted by your words." Elezar beat his right arm against his chest. Astron saw the agitation billow in his prince's face. He stirred uncomfortably. Against Gaspar, Elezar's strength lay in his wits, not the plasma that glowed about his fingertips.

"If dominance by a man is of such little consequence," Gaspar continued, "then why does it upset you so much that I discuss it openly in front of those who blindly follow? Perhaps there is more to the story that you have not told."

"Begone!" Elezar stood and shouted. "Flutter back to your rough stone lairs and await the answer to your riddle. I will reveal it to you when the time is proper."

"I have come for it now," Gaspar growled, unfurling his wings.

"I said begone." Elezar clapped his hands together. The air above his head hissed. Traces of blue sparked about his ears.

Gaspar flexed his fingers, letting small tendrils of light race up from the webbing near the palms to the fingertips. "You warned of the consequences that would accrue from the rest of the realm if I struck outside the bounds of our agreement," he said. "Do you not think that the other domains would judge with equal disfavor one who professes to know what in fact he does not? Admit the truth, Elezar. You might once have been a prince, but now you are nothing more than the dimwitted doll of a man."

Elezar snarled, baring fangs that he seldom showed to others. With a flick of his wrist, a bolt of ionizing blue arced between the two princes, striking Gaspar on the shoulder and spinning the djinn to the ground. Gaspar swooped into the air, a small rivulet of smoke wisping from where he had been touched. A glaze of pain clouded his eyes. Sparks showered off his knees and elbows into the air.

"The prince of lightning djinns does not submit to such insult," he yelled. "If you are so foolish as to test the strength of me and my lieutenants, then so shall you meet your doom."

With an ear-shattering roar, the djinn unleashed a huge bolt in Elezar's direction that slammed past the weaving devil and into the midst of the shield demons. One was hit directly in the chest and exploded in a spray of bone, sinew, and gore. Those on either side were hurled from their feet, colliding with Elezar's guards, who scrambled airborne to get out of the way.

Astron saw Gaspar's lieutenant rise in reply; then almost instantly the upper expanses of the rotunda filled with brilliant bursts of light painful to see. All of Elezar's followers who had surrounded the hub arose in a mass confusion, some scrambling for exit tunnels and others surging forward to aid their prince.

For a moment, Astron hesitated, shouldering aside the imps and sprites lesser than he who raced past. His stembrain said to run but he knew that his duty was to help Elezar as best he could. He heard the air implode in a great clap of thunder and then the crash of falling matter from somewhere across the rotunda. Shrieks of pain blended with the crackle of ionization; one of Elezar's guards plummeted to the floor a wingspan away, the odor of charred flesh bubbling from a smoking hole in his side.

Near the apex of the dome, two more djinns converged on one of Elezar's lesser devils who had soared forward into the fray. One methodically countered strokes of crimson with larger bolts of his own, meeting the thrusts of energy head-on and dissipating them harmlessly into the air. The other unleashed his power unimpeded, each stroke blasting asunder a limb or wing.

The prince must withdraw, Astron decided. Elezar's

48

guard demons were too few. Despite their battle lust, they would not prevail against massed lightning djinns in the confines of the rotunda. The prince must retreat to a position where he could direct all the demons at his command—draw Gaspar's minions into separate battles where superior numbers could harry each one singly.

But how to withdraw safely? Astron's thoughts raced. Even though his membranes were down, he had to squint his eyes against the fierce glare as he looked in the direction of the hub. He saw the arcs of energy, his prince, the master weaver, the scattered shield demons, and Elezar's guards trying to form into some sort of protective array.

Then, with a sudden flash, Astron realized what must be done. He whirled about, looking for a devil to carry a message to the prince but saw only chaos. There was no one to listen. He squeezed shut his eyes for an instant, picturing the smooth walls of his den in which he stored his artifacts and the comfort of leafing through his books and deciphering their meanings.

"Duty," he muttered at last. "Without duty there is no purpose—only surrender to the impulse of the stembrain and the great monotony."

Wondering if he would ever see his treasures again, he waved aside a cloud of imps winging past and headed for the hub. A blob of plasma from a fallen djinn roared by his left, hitting a small devil in the back as he ran, incinerating the tiny wings and burning its way through to the chest.

Astron ducked away from the searing rays, scrambled over the body of another fallen demon, and reached Elezar's cushion that had been hastily kicked aside. Out of the corner of his eye, he saw the figure of the prince, outlined against the fierce glow, blocking bolts of energy with his own and yelling commands to his guards above the din.

Astron scrambled around the periphery of the hub to where the shield demons sprawled in disarray. Their opaque screens had dissolved but the squat demons were

49

too slow-witted to do more than move a few feet from where they had originally stood.

"Form your barriers," Astron shouted to the one closest. "The prince commands and needs your aid."

The nearest shield demon grunted. The space between him and Astron began to fog as it had before.

"Faster," Astron commanded, looking over his shoulder to verify that Elezar and his retinue still stood their ground. "And make it horizontal, directly on top of your head."

The forming barrier began to tip toward the ceiling and Astron scrambled aside to instruct the next in line. As he did, one of Gaspar's lieutenants saw the activity, broke off his engagement with four lesser demons, and dove to the attack. Astron saw the djinn fold his wings and dive. As pulses of energy leaped from outstretched fingers, Astron sprawled flat on the rotunda floor, feeling waves of heat roar past his head. He looked up to see the djinn swoop on by and then turn to attack a second time. Astron rose to his knees and scrambled beside the shield demon constructing his screen. The next volley spattered harmlessly from the thickening barrier as the djinn roared overhead.

Astron quickly instructed the other three shield demons that remained alive. Before the djinn could attack again, he was safely inside a box with an open bottom resting on the rotunda floor. The attacking demon released three bolts in frustrated fury, then turned his attention back to Elezar and the few remaining guards that still stood hovering over their prince.

With the attention temporarily diverted, Astron rearranged the positions of the shield demons, rotating their opaque planes until they too were inside the protective enclosure they had created.

"Now, in unison, toward the hub," he commanded. "First the left foot and then the right." The strange mechanical way that men used to move in synchronization was proving to be a most useful piece of information.

The shield demons lumbered forward, their barriers

bouncing and banging against one another as they moved. The seals between the edges did not remain perfect and backwashes of energy spilled inside to carom about the interior. Astron danced about to avoid the stray ricochets while he directed the demons forward, concentrating intently on how many steps to take before he reached the vicinity of Elezar and his guards.

After a dozen steps, he commanded a halt and then directed the demons controlling the shield nearest the hub to rotate his barrier floorward. Astron threw his arm in front of his eyes and looked out of the enclosure. He saw Elezar down on one knee, his right arm grasping the other near the elbow. The prince's face was frozen in a mask of pain as he steadied himself among the dead and dying at his feet. Two remaining guards stood on unsteady limbs between Elezar and three towering lightning djinns. Behind them all, Astron heard Gaspar's booming laugh as he urged his minions on against the other devils who flitted about the huge hall.

"Quickly, my prince, you need shelter to compose your thoughts," Astron shouted as he darted out from the protecting shields. He side-stepped a spent pulse of energy and stumbled over smoking cushions to Elezar's side.

Elezar turned slowly as he approached, released his injured arm and prepared to defend against the new attack as best he could.

"No, it is the one who walks," Astron said. "Command those that you can into the shelter."

Three more bolts of plasma screamed overhead. One of the remaining guards reeled backward, clutching his shoulder and vainly trying to stop the flow of green ichor from a gaping wound. Astron shoved away the reluctance coursing up from his stembrain and did what he had never dared before. He touched Elezar's extended hand, wincing as much from the thought of contact as from the prickles of pain created by the sparks that ran along the prince's palm.

Elezar's eyes flared momentarily at the familiarity,

51

but then in resignation stumbled backward with the tug. With his injured arm he somehow waved others to follow. In a rush, all of the nearby imps, sprites, devils, and demons abandoned their defenses and scrambled after the prince.

Astron heard Gaspar's roar as he realized what was happening. "After Elezar," the lightning djinn shouted. "Ignore the lesser devils; we can make game with them at our leisure. Focus your energies. Stop the one who dares to call himself prince."

Bolts of plasma lanced into the protective enclosure as Astron and the others tumbled under the upraised barrier. Shouts of agony echoed through the air. Astron felt sprays of wet stickiness on his back as he directed the shield demon to drop the open side back into place.

When the panel sealed with the others, the scene momentarily plunged into near darkness. Except for a rumble transmitted through the floor, the sounds of battle faded away. Then, just as suddenly, the top of the enclosure blazed with light, a diffuse glow that spread outward from a focus and slopped over the edges of the plane. The pulse decayed, but it was immediately followed by a pair and then a half dozen or more as Gaspar's djinns converged to attack.

The shield demons inside of the protection were undisturbed by the onslaught, however. The plane pulsed and glowed, but except for the inwelling light, they deflected the energies away.

Astron saw the bursts of energy move methodically from the top panel to the one nearest the hub and then around to the others. Gaspar was testing each one in the hopes of finding a weakness in the defense. But all the shields held, each as well as the next.

Astron felt his stembrain retreat backward from his conscious thoughts. Elezar could not hold out forever within the confines of the box. Eventually Gaspar would think to attack from underneath the thin flooring upon which there was no shield. But at least it bought some time for the prince to think and plan a counterthrust in conditions that were more favorable. In the diffuse darkness, he groped to find Elezar and tell him of what he had learned in Palodad's lair.

## CHAPTER FIVE

## Through the Flame

"So even Palodad did not know the answer," Elezar whispered through pain-clenched teeth when Astron had finished reporting on his trip to the old one's domain. "All that he can offer is the direction in which to look and verification of what is found in exchange for some exotic form of matter. It makes how the likes of Gaspar came upon the conundrum much more a riddle of its own."

Astron shifted uncomfortably. He had little room, sandwiched between the legs of a stonesprite and with his back pressed against the barbed wings of a messenger djinn. Elezar's ability to force aside the distractions of pain, the bursts of light, and what was happening outside of their enclosure might indeed be the necessary talent of a prince, but it was disconcerting, nevertheless.

The assault of energy against the barriers of the shield demons had continued unabated while Astron had informed the prince. In dim outlines, he caught glimpses of the destruction of the rotunda and several of the other domes beyond. Muted cries filtered through even the thickness of the woven walls as more and more of Elezar's followers were routed out of their hiding places and made the sport of the lightning djinn's lust for battle and destruction. Soon all the rest would be gone, and the attention of every demon that Gaspar commanded would be turned to the box that sat on the rotunda floor.

53

"How Gaspar possessed the riddle is of little enough consequence," Astron said quickly. "And since you struck the first blow, the lightning djinn will feel justified in his destructions, whether you can solve his puzzle or not."

"The key is the disposition of the other princes who rule." Elezar weakly shook his head. "If I can get word to enough of them undetected, then sufficient might can be marshalled to drive Gaspar from my domain. And once he is removed, the others will judge what he has already done to be sufficient compensation for my momentary indiscretion. He will be able to unleash his will again only if I indeed fail to present to him a satisfactory solution to the riddle."

All four sides of the enclosure flashed in unison. The flooring shook with a great spasm. Astron heard a prolonged rumble and images of falling spires filled his mind.

"All that you suggest will take time," Astron said. "The aid I have rendered is at best only temporary." Already his feeling of accomplishment was fading. The baser emotions of his stembrain had begun to reassert themselves again. "Would it not be better now to focus on Gaspar's immediate threat to your well-being?"

"I must go by stealth to another node in the realm." Elezar ignored Astron's words. "One that is dark and not the lair of any demon of power. From there, I can dispatch my messengers while Gaspar dissipates his energy with fruitless destruction here."

"But how will you journey there?" Astron asked. "Not—not all of your present retinue are winged. The few djinns here cannot carry us all."

"Do not despair, walking one," Elezar whispered. "You still possess value. I would rather you not be wasted as some lowly imp. Look at those crowded about you. You are the only one with more than a feeble bulb of pulp riding atop his stembrain." The prince paused and then reached out and squeezed Astron's wrist. "Your mission is a different one, cataloguer, and I bid you to begin it now. It is with you that I must entrust the quest for the answer to Gaspar's riddle. You are the one to bring true flame into the realm of daemon."

Astron's feelings bubbled. It had been quite enough to visit Palodad's lair once. He had returned with what he could and had saved, at least temporarily, the prince as well. What more reasonably could be asked of one such as he?

His stembrain forced him to look through the translucence of the barriers, to estimate his chances to skitter away while Gaspar and the others concentrated on more important targets. But even if he escaped safely, what if Prince Elezar then fell? What then would be the demands of duty? What reason would there be for the existence of a cataloguer? Would there be any other prince who would appreciate the value of one who only studied the puzzling details of other realms?

The shriek and tear of matter from outside the barriers pushed its way into his thoughts. Astron shook his head. The speculation was not the substance of a true riddle. There could be no other choice.

"When Gaspar finally breaks through, be sure to command a djinn to return me to Palodad's lair," Astron said at last. "I will tell him that you agree and find out in which realm the search is to be conducted."

"No, no, not Palodad," Elezar whispered hoarsely. "As the old one said, you will need the aid of a being from outside of our realm. A strong one with great will and equal to the task. You must find him first so that you will be ready."

"But where—"

"From the realm of men. You must go through the flame first to the realm of men. Dominate whomever you contact and instruct that one to carry you to Alodar, the archimage. Only he will have the wisdom to decide and choose among his minions the one best for the quest. Have the archimage contact me back through the flame so that we can agree on his succor and aid."

"The archimage," Astron said. "He is the one among men who has mastered all five of the mortal magics—indeed the only one to bring a demon such as yourself—"

"That is why you must link minds with another mortal," Elezar said, "someone with lesser strength or will whose mind you can control. Use the one you dominate to guide you to the archimage. Then you can converse with him with your own faculties intact, rather than wrestle to speak freely while under his power."

Astron started to say more, then thought better of it. The groan of twisting matter and flashes of crackling plasma had intensified rather than abated. It would not be long before Gaspar, even in his rage, deduced how to renew his attack on Elezar. His decision had been made. No time must be wasted to ponder it more. If Elezar commanded him elsewhere, then he would go. He must make contact with a mind that at that very moment was probing into the realm—make contact and hope that his will would be the stronger.

Astron twisted into a comfortable position as best he could and fought to push the light and sound out of his thoughts. He breathed deeply—a curious practice he had noticed in the realm of men—but it helped no more than it ever had before. With his membranes down, he tried to image the emptiness of his own surroundings, vast expanses of black desert sprinkled with rare oases of matter.

His thoughts soared as his body could not, past glittering lairs swarming with imps, feebly glowing fortresses of devils who no longer cared, and dark nodes unclaimed by any prince. Astron imagined himself in total darkness, undistracted by anything in his realm, his mind blank and open to the tendrils of thought that pierced through the barrier from beings on the other side.

He willed his mind to stillness, but even his stembrain knew that he must be careful, avoiding the lures that were the most tempting. As Elezar had said, he could ill afford a struggle with a wizard of great strength. The law of dichotomy admitted no middle outcome. When contact was made, one of the beings would dominate and the other must submit.

And yet it would serve no purpose for the battle to be

an easy one. Control of the likes of a mere serving girl did not provide the means to gain audience with the archimage of men. No, the linking of minds must be chosen to be precisely correct, a grapple with a being of some will and hence possessor of power, a being of consequence but not so great that Astron would find himself the one dominated as the final connection was made.

Astron gingerly tested one probe and then quickly flitted to another. For a mere instant, he saw a vision of dancing flame and behind it some gnarled wizard pushing with his thoughts and daring mighty djinns to accept his challenge. Astron felt his way past a dozen more, retreating from most with haste and discarding the rest as not worthy of even such a demon as he.

Finally he touched upon one different from the rest— a being of inner strength, but also with a softness that perhaps could be molded to his desire. Astron tentatively let his own mind engage the tendrils of beckoning thought. He felt the essence of his being coil like smoke and intertwine with the wisps reaching out for him. First at a single point, then rapidly with many others, the two minds meshed and flowed into one another, preparing for the struggle that was soon to come.

It was a female, he realized with a shock as the intimacy increased—a female and yet a wizard nonetheless. He felt her flow of will begin to stiffen and push back against his own thoughts as he tried to maneuver them so that they surrounded and confined. Astron increased his concentration, imagining strong sinewy vines looping through a flimsy trellis and pulling it to ground. His hands tightened into fists. The muscles in his back bunched in bulging contractions on his slight frame.

He perceived more of the universe that was joined through the flame, a pentagram of chalk, the wizard in dark robes staring into a firepit cut through a planked floor, and the strong odors of aromatic woods. Behind her was another, a dark-headed man with deep-set eyes of gray, his furrowed brow beaded with sweat as he watched the struggle unfold.

Astron felt the interlocking thoughts lose all their

pliancy, congealing first into stiff ropes and then bands of steel. At every juncture where they crossed his own, there was a sudden tugging, an urging to push through the barrier and travel from one realm to another.

Astron set his teeth and pushed out with his arms against the protecting walls of the shield demons. He wanted to vault through the flame into the other world, it was true, but only as he willed it, a master of the one who beckoned, rather than as her slave.

The floor suddenly buckled and then spattered upward sprays of molten metal. Two of the lesser imps a few feet away from where Astron struggled screamed in pain as a ball of pulsing plasma tore through from underneath and bathed them in its destruction. A gaping hole fizzed and steamed where moments before had been a plane of matter.

"Demons, surround your prince," Astron heard Elezar call out. "Guard the portal so that the lightning djinns do not pass."

"Let none escape," Gaspar answered. "We will catch and then fry them all. Pursue them no matter where they flee. I will boil Elezar and his minions, even if they vanish to another realm."

Astron was only dimly aware of the scramble among the devils and sprites who had sought the refuge with his prince. He struggled to concentrate on his own battle and strained to buckle the resistance to his thoughts.

He heard another loud crash that shook all of Elezar's domain with a shudder. The flooring split asunder, disintegrating into disconnected platelets of twisted matter. Astron felt the support of the shield demons tumble away and then a sense of falling into the emptiness of the realm.

"Yield," he shouted across the barrier as he fell, "yield to him who is the stronger." In desperation he pounded his clenched fists to his chest and strained with a final gasp to end the struggle with the wizard.

The inky blackness exploded with painful light. A stab of singeing heat rolled across his back. He heard death cries barely a span away. The panic building in his stembrain pushed against its restraints. If Elezar lost now, what could his quest matter? It would only be a question of time before Gaspar's lieutenants hunted him down for a far more ignoble death.

But just as he prepared to relax his straining will and submit to his fate, he felt a reduction of the tension and then a sudden collapse of resistance to his thoughts.

"I am yours to command, master," a voice said in his head. Astron did not bother for one final look to see how those around him fared. With single-minded dedication, he thrust himself through the barrier into the realm of men.

# PART TWO

# *The Realms of Men and Skyskirr*

## CHAPTER SIX

# Wizard's Wood

KESTREL shifted uneasily as the demon materialized above the flame in Phoebe's cabin. In barely a dozen heart beats, the creature stepped from the flame, apparently as solid from head to toe as the wizard he had just subjugated.

"I am Astron, the one who walks," Kestrel heard the demon say. "I command you to take me to Alodar, the archimage of all men, so that the message from my prince to him can be made known."

"I am a wizard of Brythia, the hindermost of the Southern Kingdoms," Phoebe answered in a slow monotone. "The great Alodar resides in Procolon far to the north, beyond Samirand, Laudia, and even Ethidor." She turned her hands palms upward and shrugged. "The petty squabbles of the princes have closed the border between us. Unless you are willing to wait for several months more, you will need the service of men-at-arms to cross it, not the skills of a master of the arts. Give me some other task, one for which there is some hope of success."

Astron looked around the room. "The rate of time is never quite the same among the realms," he said, "but several of your months will be far too long." The demon's eyes fell on Kestrel as he finished stepping clear of the fire that was fading into glowing embers and curls of smoke. "If not you, then perhaps your lackey. Why can not he lead me to the archimage by your command, just as you must obey my wishes as your own?"

"Ah, pause for a moment," Kestrel said. "There is a slight error in your logic." His mind was suddenly made up. More anvilwood he could obtain somehow. Getting entrapped by a devil was another matter altogether. "I am but a simple woodchopper, not a hero from the sagas. I was just stopping by to show my wares. If the lady is not interested, then there is no obligation I have to her."

Kestrel stepped quickly to the side, aiming to place Phoebe between him and the demon. He glanced at the door and calculated how many more glides it would take to be safely away.

"The task is as I have stated it," Astron persisted. "My control of your mind, wizard, is not so great to smother all thought. Perform what I command and I shall set you free. Let your creativity be the key to your release."

Kestrel slid two more steps to his left. He kept his head down and avoided looking at the demon. Catching a demon in the eye was to be avoided at all costs, he remembered.

"Acting together, the wizards of my local council might successfully petition for a writ of safe passage," Phoebe said slowly. "But it is difficult to get them to agree on anything so concrete, especially if there is no gain in it for them."

"What then is the motivation that would prod them to act in haste?"

"The wizards of my kingdom are enamored of the tangible rewards from their craft," Phoebe said. "It is to the golden brandels of Procolon or the magic tokens of Pluton across the sea to which they listen the most."

"What of these things do you have?" Astron asked.

"My wealth is the greatest of any on the council, it is true," Phoebe said. "But divided and spread among them, the enticement would not be all that strong. There are ten of them and each has at least three-quarters of what you see here."

Kestrel stopped in midstride. Ten times three-quarters, he thought quickly. More than seven times the potential gain of what he had hoped for from Phoebe alone. If there were only a plausible story with which to approach the entire council, something that would appeal to their individual greed but force them to act collectively, some dealing with the realm of demons that no wizard could afford to let pass by. The allure would have to be quite spectacular, something that would withstand the scrutiny of not one but half a score.

Kestrel almost involuntarily jerked up his head and looked at Astron. The demon did not appear all that ferocious. Perhaps, with Phoebe under his command, he had no lust for another. Perhaps, in fact, the sagas were distorted and the risks far less than the babblings that had been recorded. It would be just what he expected of wizards—concocting a great peril to enchance their own importance and the magnitude of their fees.

Kestrel had hoped for ten brandels from Phoebe's purse. If he could get the devil to agree, he might leave these hills with over a hundred. And besting not one but ten so-called masters in one stroke would be all the more satisfying as well. The more he pondered it, the more the risks dissolved away and the rewards grew increasingly tempting.

"Your first instincts were correct," Kestrel called to Astron as he returned to Phoebe's side. "I am the key to getting the necessary petition from the wizards' council. Just do as I say, and we both shall be compensated as we desire from our efforts."

Astron wrinkled his nose. "As you say? It is I who have asserted the more powerful will in coming through the flame. I control the wizard who called me and, through her, any of those bound to her own command."

"This is not like that," Kestrel said quickly. "Your command of the wizard is part of the plan I have in mind, but between you and me, it is more of a mutual agreement." He stretched his face into a smile. "A contract between partners that we both swear to uphold—like the formal exchanges between alchemists and apothecaries for rare ingredients and tested formulas."

"If not the wizard, then who is your prince?" Astron asked. "And what do you mean when you speak of contracts and swearing to uphold?"

"I am a free man and have obligations to no one, neither king nor master," Kestrel said. "My will is my own." He saw the demon's face distort further and he rushed on. "The important thing is that we agree to act in each other's behalf—on our honor, not by threat of penalty but by being true to our innermost values of being."

Astron did not speak for a long while. He looked from the placid face of the one he controlled to Kestrel's sudden enthusiasm. "In my realm, one serves a single prince and no other," the demon said at last. "Breaking allegiance is such a personal shame that the will to resist the great monotony is shattered as well. Is that what you mean by contracts and honor?"

"Why, exactly so," Kestrel said. "I could not have explained it better myself."

"And if I follow your instructions, you will arrange my audience with Alodar the archmage?"

"Yes, that will be our agreement—on our honor."

Kestrel saw Astron's face relax. The demon stuck out his right hand toward Kestrel. "I do know some of the customs of the realm of men. I agree, human, to what you call a contract, working to mutual benefit upon our honor. Here, clasp my hand to seal the agreement and then let us begin."

Kestrel grasped the offered hand and shook it slowly, hardly noticing the coarse texture next to his own skin. "Listen carefully then. Here is my plan," he heard himself say, but his thoughts were elsewhere. Something about the demon was strangely disturbing. He had agreed all too quickly—too soon for Kestrel to figure out what his real motives were. An agreement on their honor—it sounded as if the devil actually meant it.

Kestrel clapped his hands for attention. Several hours had passed swiftly since he outlined his plan to Astron. Now it was nearly noon, and nine wizards had gathered in the small garden outside of Phoebe's cabin. The eldest three sat on a long wooden bench next to a small pond lined with smooth stones. Behind them stood the rest, all robed in black and wearing faces heavy with the seriousness of their craft.

Kestrel stood next to Phoebe on the other side of the pond, next to a tier of dove cages and neatly trimmed bushes that flashed waxy leaves at the high sun. He glanced once at the small scroll of parchment he had tossed into the pond before the wizards' arrival and smiled. As yet none of them had called attention to it; it would serve its purpose well.

To the left, Kestrel's wagon stood hitched and ready, his mare nibbling contentedly on a bed of flowering hornweed. The birch-framed canopy over his pinewood-filled sacks fluttered in a quickening breeze. The last of the doves dispatched with a summons circled overhead, apparently building up the courage to return to its roost just beyond Kestrel's reach.

Kestrel ignored the hovering bird. The message tied to its leg probably stated only that the last wizard in Phoebe's council would not come. Enough were already present to make the production worthwhile; judging from the pleasant jingle of their purses, the effort would be worthwhile indeed.

Kestrel took a moment to study the masters seated in the front. Undoubtedly they were the ones to convince; then the others would follow. The one in the middle, Maspanar, appeared the most bloated with self-importance. Any revelation of facts would have to be his; monetary aspects were of less concern.

On Maspanar's right sat Geldion, a shriveled hulk that stared back with piercing blue eyes. He seemed to dare Kestrel to speak, to commit some error that immediately could be pounced upon and exposed to the others.

The last of the three, Kestrel decided, was his primary target. Benthon's black robe was a trifle newer than all the rest. Golden rings adorned slender fingers not smudged by charred embers or sooty ash. The eyes danced about the confines of Phoebe's garden, searching for an opening, an opportunity for gain that would continue to feed his expensive habits.

"Masters, if I may have your attention," Kestrel said after he had satisfied himself that he could predict how the assembled wizards would react. "Your colleague in craft apologizes for the lack of words of greeting and sweet wine." He waved his hand in Phoebe's direction. "But her startling discovery is of such great importance that she dare not break her concentration for trivial amenities. When you have witnessed what she has to demonstrate you will understand why."

"Who is this that speaks for the wizard Phoebe?" Geldion demanded. He looked over his shoulder and spoke to the masters standing behind the bench. "He wears no robe with a logo, nor have I heard her talk of any bondsmen in her service."

"I have interrupted my studies merely as a courtesy," Maspanar said. "I doubt greatly that the youngest of our council—and a woman at that—has found anything not yet well known to most of us." He shrugged massive shoulders beneath a robe that had been patched more than once. "If the dabbler has found a means of amplifying our powers as her note indicated, then let her explain her alleged discovery and be done. There is no time for the smooth tongues and empty thoughts of others."

Kestrel forced his smile wider. Years ago when the opinions of other mattered, such rude manners would have hurt and given him pause. But now he was as hardened as the rest. He would give them what they deserved, matching their insensitivities with a disdain of his own. Kestrel looked out for himself and no one else. Let the masters beware.

"A simple flame." Kestrel pointed back through the open doorway into Phoebe's cabin, totally ignoring the challenges. It would serve no purpose to spar with Maspanar or Geldion until after Benthon was securely hooked. "You can all see it burning within the pentagram on the floor. Perhaps the keenest among you, even from the distance, can guess what fuels the blaze."

"Simple pine logs," Maspanar shot back. "The height of the yellows, smoke with little soot, and the lack of intense blues mark it as nothing else."

"Yes, dried pine it is," Kestrel said. "The tunnel between the realms for small imps and sprites and little else. For demons of true power, more exotic woods and powders must be consumed to bore through the barrier that keeps them from us."

Kestrel paused, replacing his smile with a serious mask. "More exotic woods are needed for demons of true power," he repeated, "or so one would expect."

With a sudden thrust of his arm he reached into the cabin and grabbed the door by the knob. In a blur of motion he repeatedly opened the door a crack and then slammed it shut, a staccato burst of sound filling the small garden. After perhaps a dozen slams he flung the door all the way open, again permitting the wizards to view the interior.

Kestrel's smile returned as he saw Astron stride forward from the flame, exactly as he had planned. The decorum of the wizards dissolved into babble of excited voices.

"Impossible," Geldion said. "No demon of that size could come through such a simple flame."

"Some trace element, perhaps," Maspanar replied. "A substance of great power so that merely a small amount was necessary."

"But what of the control?" Benthon spoke for the first time. "That is indeed no small imp of little will. Our voices distract too much and place Phoebe in great peril."

"I am yours to command, master." Astron bowed to Phoebe as he exited from the cabin. "Give me your instructions so that I may serve."

Phoebe frowned as she heard the words, mouthing them silently for a second. Then she suddenly shook off her lethargy. "Do not concern yourselves with the risk, my colleagues," she said. "Observe, I need devote merely a fraction of my attention to control."

She turned and looked at Astron as he emerged. "Go among them, devil," she said. "Let them examine you at will. Perhaps the experience will be of interest." Then, with a flourish, she turned her back and began picking a bouquet of flowers from a bed near her feet, her features totally hidden from the others.

Kestrel saw Phoebe's face relax to a lifeless stare as

her hands mechanically groped for nearby stalks. He looked back at the wizards, but their attentions were all focused on Astron as he came forward. Things were going well. He would be far away before anyone deduced that Phoebe's words were merely the ones the demon beforehand had commanded her to say.

"Not an imp but neither a mighty djinn," the talk of the wizards continued.

"But if from simple flame and with no great struggle of will, the phenomenon does deserve some investigation."

"This is indeed most surprising, I admit. My respect for the woman must climb a notch. She may become a credit to us yet. Tell us, Phoebe, what is the name of the one you have so effortlessly summoned? How was his domination achieved?"

"I am called Astron, the one who walks," Astron said. "But that is of little matter. I have done my part. Now I wish you to perform yours with haste. Surrender to the man whatever it is that provides my audience with the archimage. It is the agreement that we have sworn on our—"

"Masters, your attention, please," Kestrel cut in. "Surely your interest is more on how Phoebe was able to perform her feat rather than its result." He frowned in the direction of Astron. He had been so busy beforehand explaining how Phoebe should be controlled that he had neglected to tell the demon to keep his own mouth shut as well. "I have been instructed by your colleague to explain her discovery while she keeps the devil under control," he said. "But be advised it might take several hours, and any attempt to rush could completely destroy what is being demonstrated."

"Several hours," Astron said. "How curious. It must be a ritual I have not witnessed before. Under any other circumstances, I would be most eager to add the details of its performance to my catalogues."

"Masters, if you please," Kestrel persisted. He flexed his shoulders trying to dislodge the tiny burr of apprehension that had suddenly made its presence felt under the smooth blanket of confidence in his scheme. "The key insight that Phoebe exploited in her experiment was the willingness of the demon to come. It is true that mighty djinns, virtual kings in their own realm, are ill-disposed for the journey through the fires. Only with exotic woods to reduce the barriers and great struggles of will have you been able to woo them.

"But consider instead another approach—an approach in which you provide a bait, an enticement for the devil to journey on his own accord. Phoebe has shown it to be true; simpler flames are all that is needed, and the demons' spirits are more docile when they appear in our realm. One must provide in addition only the cadence of sounds that sends notice of the lure to the realm where they live."

Kestrel paused and looked at the assemblage carefully, one by one. "Think of it," he said. "Mighty djinns at your beck and call. No more costly expenditure for rare powders and woods."

"Another example," one of the wizards behind the first row called out. "Although this one before us is no simple imp, he seems to have little more value beyond his increased size."

"Little value?" Astron said. "But I am a cataloguer. I know perhaps more of your realm than any other of my kind. My prince values me highly. Because of that I am here rather than any oth—"

"Exactly so, a cataloguer." Kestrel scowled at Astron again. "He was enticed here by the scroll that Phoebe laid out before the flame. See it there in the pond. It was the lure that made possible a transition even in the fire of pine."

"That is the second time you have looked at me that way," Astron said. "What message are you trying to convey?"

"What is this that the demon is asking?" Geldion said. "Phoebe, have you given him leave to speak of his own free will?"

"No, no, pay him no heed," Kestrel said. "Focus instead on the second experiment. The key is to assemble a lure from your possessions that will entice another demon here. I will manipulate the door as before and you will see."

"What kind of lure; what do you mean?" Benthon asked.

"Anything," Kestrel said. He felt his apprehension lessen. Benthon speaking now could not have been more nearly perfect. "Anything at all. It seems the greater the quantity, the mightier is the demon that responds."

He paused a moment and rubbed his chin. "I guess there is one thing, however, that you of course will not attempt to employ. I have heard the jingle of your purses and could not help thinking of it. A brandel from Procolon will fetch a gold imp, a sackful, a bigger devil of the same bent. Their only interest is in hoarding. About the only useful command you could give them is to go and find it in the ground where it is not yet discovered by men."

Kestrel stopped and shrugged. "Of course I realize that you are all men of ethics and would not use your powers for such base gain of a few nuggets of metal."

"You stated that the bigger the lure, then the more powerful the demon which would respond and the more able he would be to perform his special talents?" Benthon asked.

"Yes, that is the fact of it," Kestrel said. "Why, I would imagine that a gold *djinn* would not even have to look. He would transform the metal out of baserock, as much as was commanded."

Benthon's eyes widened. He opened his purse and thrust it at Maspanar. "Then such an experiment it will be. Empty what you have into mine and we will share in whatever is gained in return."

"I think that we proceed without sufficient caution," Geldion said. "I am not yet satisfied with the explanation of what little we have seen transpire."

"Then do not participate," Benthon said. "Only those who take the risk shall benefit from the returns as well." He turned back to Kestrel. "What would it take to fetch the likes of this gold djinn to do our bidding?"

"From what Phoebe has instructed me, I would say about eight or nine times the amount in your purse alone. And with such a demon in your power, he should be able to produce tenfold that amount in less than a day."

"What do you say, Maspanar?" Benthon persisted. "If you decide to join, then surely the others will follow."

Maspanar grunted, looked at Astron and then back at the dying fire in Phoebe's cabin. He shrugged and reached for his belt. "What is the harm?" he said. "The worst that can happen is that the claim is not true. And with woman's work, I suspect that somehow that certainly is the case."

"But if she is correct?" one of the masters in the second row asked.

"With ten of us here, surely we can dominate whatever comes through the flames." Maspanar shrugged a second time. "If it proves to be small, we can command it into a magic bottle for study at our leisure. If something of greater size appears, we can call forth clouds of imps on our own that will harry it until it too is subdued."

For a moment no one moved. Then, in a flurry of jingles and flailing straps of leather, the six wizards who stood behind crowded around Benthon and added their contribution to a growing store. Finally Benthon himself held his bulging purse in front of Geldion, gently waving it to and fro.

Geldion scowled once and reached for his own pouch. Showing no pleasure, he emptied his coins in with the rest and then folded his arms across his chest.

Kestrel tried not to let his excitement show. The wizards had all come better prepared than he had dared hope. Now for a little more maneuvering and it would all be done.

"But, but your ethics," he said. "If you get too much gold, then even the economy can be altered—just as it was on Pluton across the sea some two decades ago."

"A wizard indeed is entrusted with a most solemn trust." Benthon stepped forward, thumping his chest with his free hand while his sack hung heavy in the other.

"Therefore, we judge the risks and take only those that are prudent." He turned and waved back at the others. "And here our judgment is unanimous. What Phoebe has apparently discovered must be verified with all expediency. Any reward that is possible for our efforts will be administered with discretion." He stopped and looked Kestrel in the eye. "There might even be a brandel or two for the lackey who made the process all the quicker rather than throw up objections that are of no real concern to one of his station."

Kestrel looked down at the sack and ran his tongue over his lips. "I guess there is only one more thing to be aware of, and then my conscience is clear," he said. "Whichever one of you actually controls the demon will have some advantage over the others. And, as Phoebe has explained it, the closer you are to the flame, the greater your chances of being the most likely to grab the demon's will. But then, of course, the closer you are, also the greater the danger. In good faith, I recommend that you all stay outside as did the woman, rather than try to crowd around the flame inside the cabin."

"One side," Benthon said. "My will is the strongest and I am not afraid."

"Wait, drop the gold here in the pond," Kestrel said as he rapidly stepped aside. "By the scroll that lured the first demon to Phoebe. You must be between the lure and the flame for the connection to work."

"Watch this for us, Phoebe," Benthon said as he gathered up speed. He tossed the sack into the water. It fell with a plunk satisfying to Kestrel's ears. "We will be back for it in a few moments, and, if you indeed are correct, for a good deal more."

Maspanar and two more wizards followed Benthon. Then, in a mass of elbows and shoves, came the others.

"The cadence of sound for a gold djinn calls for fifteen immediate slams and then a wait of some twenty minutes for the last," Kestrel said. "If the door is opened before then, the connection is broken and the entire effort wasted." He looked with satisfaction as Geldion started

74

to join the rest. Mentally he measured the strides from the pond to his waiting wagon.

"I have pondered the existence since you first mentioned it," Astron interjected suddenly, "and I cannot think of a single example. No, I am sure of it. None in Elezar's domain nor any of the princes who hang in the void near him have ever known of such. It is an extraordinary occurrence. I devote my life to cataloguing the mysteries and surprises of other realms and find that there is still much I cannot know of my own natural surroundings. Gold imps and even djinns of gold. Yes, it is extraordinary. There is no other word for it."

Geldion paused in the doorway and turned around. "What did he say?" he asked. "It sounded as if he is questioning the existence of what we are about to seek. Phoebe, make him explain what he meant."

Kestrel scowled. He ran forward and grabbed for the doorknob, blocking the wizard's exit with his body. "There is time for that later," he said smoothly. "Wouldn't you rather I get the cadence started right away? You know I won't be able to begin until you are inside and the door able to hit the jamb."

"Phoebe, answer me," Geldion persisted. "Stop denuding that flowerbed and answer me."

"Go ahead and speak, Phoebe," Astron said. "I am anxious to get things concluded as much as anyone."

Phoebe rose slowly and turned toward Astron. "What shall I reply, master?" she said. "You have not instructed me this time as to what you wish me to say."

"Wait a moment," Geldion said. "Who is the master and who the slave? Maspanar, step back here for a moment. Now that I think of it, Phoebe has been acting most strangely. She should be examined at once to verify the freedom of her thought."

"The gold djinn! Look, he comes now through the flames." Kestrel pointed back into the cabin. It was an act of desperation, but things were unraveling fast. He pressed against Geldion's side but the master did not yield.

"But if not Phoebe, then who is manipulating the

75

devil?" Geldion continued as his eyes danced about the garden. He looked from Phoebe to Astron and then to Kestrel at his side. He glanced at the wet sack of gold resting on the bottom of the pond, his eyes suddenly wide. With a strength surprising for his size, he pushed through Kestrel's restraint and staggered back into the garden. "Guardsmen," he shouted, "guardsmen, attend at once."

Kestrel heard the squeak of leather and rattle of steel in a clump of trees near a bend in the road a small distance from the cabin. He scowled at his bumbling, first with the demon and then not checking the environs to ensure a path of escape. Evidently at least one of the wizards was suspicious enough not to come by himself. The size of the treasure had been too great and he had dreamed too much on how it would be spent, rather than ensuring its capture.

Kestrel saw perhaps a half a dozen men-at-arms emerge from their hiding place and begin jogging toward the cabin, their swords drawn and shields rigidly in place. With a sudden surge, he pushed Geldion to the ground and bolted over his sprawling body. In a single fluid motion he leaped to the edge of the pond and scooped out the bulging sack of gold. He glanced a second time at the approaching warriors and back at the wizards now spilling out of the cabin. It was going to be close, he thought, but, considering his mistakes, no less than he deserved.

Kestrel ran to his wagon and started to fling the sack into its interior; but as he did, a well-aimed rock cracked painfully into his shouders, forcing him to release his grip. Like a ripe melon spewing its seeds, the wet leather pouch hit the ground and burst apart. Circles of gold flung in every direction, some rolling under the wagon and others arcing all the way back to the pond.

Kestrel bent to the ground and then hesitated. The first of the wizards was almost upon him. He would be an easy target once he crouched over. He watched the last of the coins stop their spinning and settle to the rough ground, sparkling in the sunlight. It was more than he had ever seen at one time. With an almost painful regret, he pulled himself up into the wagon, empty-handed, and grabbed for the reins.

"Block his escape! Don't let him get away!" the wizards shouted to one another.

"We have the woman. They should be punished together."

"A barrier across the road. Quickly before he bolts!"

Kestrel slapped the reins against the hindquarters of the horse. The wagon jumped into motion. He grabbed his whip and increased its pace, all the while looking down the road and trying to judge on which side to try to run past the converging men-at-arms. He saw the upraised hands that were grabbing the side of the wagon wrench away as he gathered speed.

The wagon surged forward and Kestrel leaned to his left, looking back over his shoulder past the covered awning toward Phoebe's cabin. Only one wizard ran after him in labored slowness; three more were sprawled on the ground where they had fallen away. Most of the rest fluttered around the spilled sack like feasting blackbirds fighting over the coins in the sand. The last two held Phoebe in tight grips on each arm, pulling her forward uncomprehendingly toward the rest. Perhaps the demon mingled among them, but in the confusion of black robes, he could not be sure.

Kestrel's eyes lingered on the woman. With him safely away, the wrath of the other wizards would all fall on her, even though she bore no responsibility for what had happened. He recalled his feelings when they stood together inside her cabin and then shook his head at the sudden impulse that welled up within him.

Madness, he thought. The only course was to be safely away before the men-at-arms could organize sufficiently to block him. But the impulse remained. He looked again at her blank face and remembered the sweet smiles it once bore, even when it carried her own caution.

"It may as well be three errors," he muttered to himself as he suddenly pulled the reins to the left, circling the wagon just before the road narrowed to a single lane. Without reducing speed he raced back toward the cabin, aiming directly toward the wizards who held Phoebe in their grasp.

## CHAPTER SEVEN

## The Would-be Sorcerer

KESTREL turned the wagon around well before the men-at-arms could reach him. He slapped the reins across the mare's hindquarters, urging her back toward the cabin. The master who had chased him down the road immediately scrambled to the side and let him pass. The others, busily intent on scooping coins from the ground, took no heed until he was almost on top of them. Then they too scattered in a flurry of flapping robes and tinkling coins.

Kestrel aimed his wagon directly at the wizard on Phoebe's left. As he expected, the master dropped his grip and jumped out of the way. The horse slowed and Kestrel leaned over to the side as he passed. He extended his arm around Phoebe's waist, and she flopped against the rough planking of the wagon like a rag doll as it careened by. Even though the mare was slowing, the momentum was too great for the remaining wizard. He let go of Phoebe's arm with a protesting cry.

With his free hand, Kestrel pulled the horse to a stop. Dropping the reins, he lifted Phoebe up beside him. Her eyes were glazed, totally oblivious to what was happening. He let her sag into a heap, then leaped from his seat onto the mare's back and jerked the beast's head to the left. There was too little time to back up slowly and turn.

Hoping that the front wheels had sufficient free play, Kestrel started the horse forward, pulling it to the side as much as he dared. The mare whinnied in protest and

78

started to rear, but Kestrel kept his grip firm and kicked her onward. Stepping into the flowerbed, the horse bumped the wagon wheels over the low boundary stones that separated the garden from the walk. Stomping the small bushes and spring blooms, they barely edged by the cabin on the right, the hub of the rear wheel scraping as it passed.

Just as the wagon bumped out of the garden and back onto the path that led to the road, the men-at-arms ran forward, shield and sword arms blocking the way. Kestrel did not falter. Focusing on the shield of the man on the far left, he dug his knees into the mare's sides. As the troops converged, he circled the horse's neck with both arms and swung from its back in a giant arc. With feet stiffly extended, he hit the upraised shield with a jarring blow, sending the man-at-arms sprawling before he could strike.

The impact sent Kestrel swinging backward. He raised his feet as high as he could to avoid the stomping hooves of the mare, now thoroughly frightened and running as fast as it could. He saw a sword's-length distance open between him and the men-at-arms who were nearest and then two lengths more. The warriors rallied to run after; but weighted down by shield and mail, they quickly realized that they could not keep up. In an instant, the clatter of pursuit and shouts of anger started to fade.

Kestrel clung to his precarious hold while the mare raced onward. The occasional clump of trees at the roadside grew into more frequent groves and then finally merged into the beginnings of true forest. Stately elms crowded the pathway, enfolding a canopy over Kestrel's head. From above, the sunlight alternately burst through unabated or was totally blocked from view. A gentle breeze swirled away the dust thrown up by the wagon's rapid passage.

Finally the mare spent her wind and slowed to a gentle walk. Listening between the hoof clops, Kestrel could hear no sound of the wizards or men-at-arms. He dropped to the ground and grabbed at the reins as they passed, pulling the horse to a stop.

Kestrel gave himself the luxury of a long deep breath. He was getting too old for such theatrics. And now he probably would have to move on to the next kingdom to practice his skills. He could not count on the shame of the masters in being outsmarted to keep his presence secret. Soon every wizard within the flight of doves would know to watch for a woodcutter and his wagon. He would have to change his tale altogether and probably target another of the five arts as well.

And what of Phoebe? She might not think that snatching her from the other wizards was much of a rescue. Of course, in her present state, she might not think much of anything. Kestrel looked up into the wagon. What was he going to do now?

Suddenly there was a movement from within the awning. A figure stirred. Kestrel dropped his jaw in surprise.

"Why did you turn back?" the demon Astron called down from where Phoebe still slumped. "Even more than the location of the lair of the gold djinns, that is the part I most want to understand. Why did you return to fetch the woman?"

Kestrel recovered his senses and shot back. "What are you doing here? How did you follow where no one else could?"

"I climbed in the back of this—this conveyance while you were pulling the female wizard in through the front," Astron said.

"But why?" Kestrel slowly inched back from the wagon. He looked quickly up and down the tree-darkened road. He and the demon were alone. Astron looked no more menacing than he had when he had first appeared in Phoebe's cabin with his almost human face and muted scales, but the apprehension Kestrel had felt then returned swiftly to his thoughts. And now there was no lure of gain to distract him from the risks of dealing with demonkind.

"I doubt control of my will would be that interesting," he said quickly. He brushed off some of the road dust from his arms and straightened his tunic and rucksack, trying to look as imposing as he possibly could. "Probably it would be better for you now to find some convenient fire and vanish back to whence you came," he said.

"The law of dominance or submission applies only when one of my kind transits between the realms," Astron said as he vaulted from the wagonbed to the ground. "Once I am across, there is no need to wrestle any further. I will do you no harm. Besides, there is the matter of the contract. I have yet to meet with the archimage. You have sworn on your honor to provide the means."

"That was merely half of it," Kestrel snapped back quickly. "I was to have received something to line my purse in exchange for my efforts. Thanks to you, I have nothing to show. The contract is balanced on both sides. We each entered the agreement with nothing and now neither is any the better because of it."

"That is not quite so." Astron stepped forward and opened his fist. "In the confusion that followed the bursting sack, none of the wizards seemed to mind that a demon was scurrying over the ground with them. This is perhaps not what you fully anticipated, but it is far from the nothing of which you speak."

Kestrel looked down at the offered palm. There arrayed in a neat row were more than two dozen brandels, glinting with the light that filtered through the canopy of trees shading the road. A dozen brandels—less than he had hoped but as much as he had expected from convincing Phoebe to buy his wagonload of wood in the first place.

He reached out to grab the coins as Astron slowly tipped his hand. "This is compensation for the errors you made by speaking out, is it not?" he asked. "A settlement and then we can be on our separate ways?"

"This is payment in full," Astron said. "I have honored my part of the bargain; now you must honor yours."

Kestrel shook his head in disbelief. The devil was indeed serious!

Or so he professed to be. The doubt immediately fol-

lowed in Kestrel's thoughts. Honor, contracts, and trust
—such things were mere abstractions. They did not
really exist—not for him anyway, not since he had
trusted too much and paid the price. Could it really be
any different for the demon? Kestrel stared at Astron's
unblinking expression, trying to fathom the true motives
that lay behind it.

Astron did not speak. Kestrel looked away, noticing
almost absently the foam standing on his mare's withers.
He reached into the wagon for a coarse rag and began to
wipe the moisture away, his mind churning with what he
should say next.

Kestrel finished rubbing down one side of his mare
and then started on the other. "Do you not understand?"
The words burst forth at last with more bitterness than
he would have liked. "Understand what it means to bargain with one such as me. I am no hero from the sagas,
performing great deeds for kings and masters of the five
arts.

"No, my satisfaction comes from motives much less
lofty. I prey upon these so-called heroes; the masters
most highly regarded give me the greatest thrill. I tempt
them where they are the weakest and appeal to the baseness in their characters that is easily as great as mine.

"Was Phoebe truly interested in the properties of anvilwood or the fact that the price I seemed to offer in
innocence was merely a tenth of what it would fetch
from Procolon to the north? Did the wizards care about
the effect of gold nuggets common as pebblestones on all
those about them or merely wonder which one would
end with the greater share?

"Honor, heroes, the masters—each time that I succeed, each time that they reveal the rotten core beneath
their masks of righteousness, it piles proof upon proof.
There are no such things as heroes, only men, and not
one any better than I."

Kestrel stopped and slumped his shoulders. Why had
he said so much? His values and how he acted were his
business alone, certainly not the concern of a being from
somewhere beyond the flame. It was best to end things

quickly so he could be on his way. He stared silently at Astron, waiting to see how the devil would react to what he had said.

"You speak with great passion," Astron replied after a moment. "A passion that I never before have observed." He reached into the wagon and grabbed a second cloth. Eyeing Kestrel's work critically, he dabbed at an apparent wetness on the mare's hindquarters that had been missed. The horse whinnied and backed away, but Kestrel patted her neck and calmed her back down.

"I wish that I had the time to pause and understand it more fully," Astron continued, "but for now we must continue. Tell me, what is your plan for gaining the attention of the archimage?"

"Didn't you just hear what I said?" Kestrel flung his rag to the ground. "The merging of our paths was an accident, an alignment of the random factors, as the alchemists would say. Now that the business at Phoebe's cabin is done, there is nothing more to bind us together. Here, keep the brandels. But look elsewhere for a hero with honor, if one you must have."

"I do not know as much as I must of the realm of men," Astron said. "For that, I must rely on you. But of sprites and wizards my knowledge is perhaps the deeper. For the foreseeable future that will be your greatest need."

"What do you mean?"

"Wizards are most proud. Their wills are not easily diverted, once they have set upon a goal." Astron stepped around the mare, thrusting his face into Kestrel's, his eyes glowing with intensity. "Do you really think that every master who visited the woman's cabin will forget what has happened and let you continue unimpeded on your way?

"Or will they call forth from my realm the most powerful devils that they dare and send them searching— searching until you have been found and cast in some dim dungeon as punishment for your deed?"

Kestrel felt a chill race up his spine. Maybe Astron was right. Simply disappearing and starting over might not be so easy. And years in a dark cell he could well do without.

"We are cleanly away," Kestrel said. "Once we reach the juncture, the road will be one well travelled. Demon-aided or not, I will be able to fade successfully from sight."

"It will take time." Astron shook his head. "But eventually you will be found. At first they will dispatch hundreds of small imps or perhaps even thousands if their ire is truly great. Tirelessly, these will dart throughout every corner of your world, examining the features and actions of you humans as closely as they dare. Those who match the descriptions given them will become the subject of a more intense investigation by devils with greater capacity above the stembrain. Even though, to ones of our realm, you all look very much the same, in the end all the possibilities will be eliminated except one."

Astron halted. Kestrel saw him flick transparent membranes down over his eyes. The demon's face seemed to take on a distant and preoccupied look.

"Now that I think of it," Astron continued after a moment, "our urgencies are closely intertwined. The same imps and devils called forth by the wizards could most likely have a second mission as well. If Gaspar has already triumphed, then the visitors to your realm will be instructed in addition to search for Elezar's missing cataloguer so that he can be returned to his fate.

"Yes, woodcutter, I need your help to navigate through the realm of men just as you need one such as me—one who knows the signs of the presences of my kind." Astron held up the rag in his hand and tossed it to Kestrel. "My eyes see reds that men cannot, especially when my membranes are in place to filter out the distractions of the blues. That is how I can so easily detect the areas of moisture that you missed on this creature's back. In like manner I will notice the imp glows far sooner than could the finest wizard in your realm. I can alert you of the danger while we pursue our common goal."

"What common goal?"

"Why to find the archimage, of course," Astron said. "If he stands to these wizards as a prince does to the djinns of my realm, then only he will be able to turn aside their anger and tell them to desist."

Astron paused. The hint of a smile crept onto his face. "So you see, what we seek is the same, as well as what we avoid."

Kestrel felt the dampness of the cloth that Astron had thrown him and dropped it to the ground with the other. He patted his mare and frowned.

"You can detect the presence of these imps before they can get too close?" he asked.

"Far before what you might dismiss as a fleeting spark of light or a distant buzz of an insect, I can recognize it for what it truly is."

"And once detected, you can confine them as well?"

"They would bite my fingers just as surely as yours," Astron said. "It is the bottles made by your magicians that are best to keep them in."

"Such jars cost a great deal," Kestrel said. "Far more than a dozen brandels. I have—have dealt with a guild of Procolon to the north and know full well what one might bring."

"Then too there is the matter of the gold imp and others of its kind. For those I do not know for sure that I can even detect."

"If you have not heard of such, then they most probably do not exist," Kestrel said.

"But I heard you speak of them to the wizards."

"It was a lie." Kestrel shrugged his shoulders, dismissing the thought. He looked into the demon's unblinking eyes. Not being able to snatch even a glimmer of what he really was up to made him very uncomfortable. But what Astron had said made sense. Kestrel had bruised the pride of not a single wizard but almost a dozen. The archimage probably was the only one who could get him out of his fix. Only Alodar would have enough power to turn aside the masters' wrath once he somehow was convinced it was all a simple mistake. And

85

surely Kestrel could come up with a plausible explanation before he got to the capital of Procolon. Crossing the border would be the only problem.

Kestrel smiled. Now that he thought of it, being in the presence of the archimage might lead to other opportunities as well. The master of five magics was a man just like the rest. What satisfaction there would be in giving him the chance to outsmart a simple woodchopper. The archimage! Yes, it would be the greatest triumph of all!

"Very well," Kestrel said after a moment's more deliberation. If the demon had any ulterior motives, he would deal with them when they became more apparent. For now he would continue as he had been asked. "Our paths are still joined. I will get us to the archimage—as we, of course, have originally agreed."

"A lie," Astron said slowly, apparently ignoring what Kestrel said. "You spoke something which was not a reflection of the truth, or at least your interpretation of it."

"Of course," Kestrel said. "I explained to you already what I am about, what all men are about. Concern yourself about it no longer. The only difference is that some of us are more skilled in seeing through the words to what stands behind."

"You have this skill of observation?" Astron asked.

Kestrel sighed. The events of the past hour had already been too draining. He did not want to experience any more intense feelings. He shook his head and turned away.

Astron waved at the mare and wagon. "I understand," he said, "that you do not have the means of transporting us as swiftly as a mighty djinn. One is bound by his honor for no more than he is capable of giving." He reached out and tugged on Kestrel's sleeve. "There will be time, therefore, that can be most profitably spent with no hint of disgrace—time to tell me how you learned to discern the truth of things that are not."

Kestrel studied Astron's expression. He saw no trace of mocking judgment. The demon's words of honor and trust unlocked memories that had been suppressed for too many years. Unbidden, they bubbled up to be examined again. They would not go away until they had been acknowledged. And if only a being from another realm heard them, who would really care?

"I did not have such skills at first," Kestrel heard himself say softly. "Not at first, when perhaps they counted the most." He waved his arm up toward the wagon where Phoebe sat entranced. "In many ways the wizard reminds me of her—at least in the way she speaks and smiles."

Kestrel looked down at the brandels he clutched in his hand and ran his fingers over the bust of the old queen. "Evelyn was a wandering sorcerer, so she said, unaffiliated with those on Morgana across the great sea. The logo of the eye on her robe was plainly stitched and unadorned. A sorcerer of great beauty she was as well, as fair as Vendora, the ruler of Procolon, in her prime.

"Her love for me knew no bounds, she told me. Anything that I asked that was in her power would be mine. And who was I to believe otherwise, a lad barely out of his teens.

"The request was simple enough—to go with her among the townspeople I knew, add credence to her tale, and hold the pledges for safekeeping that each of them subscribed. When the total was sufficient she would add a matching amount of her own and then, while I waited outside the gates, negotiate with the Cycloid Guild for the sale of some properties that would aid in the enchantments. With them she would form great illusions of healing and relieve the deep-set pains that even sweetbalm could not touch. Our village would become famous for the soothing comforts the charms provided. Everyone would share in the fees that such wonders would bring. And I would learn the words of the spells and be second only to her in the eyes of the grateful.

"Three days I paced in front of the forbidding doors of the guild before some of the more suspicious townspeople came and asked to count again the contents of the sacks I so carefully guarded. When they were opened and iron disks instead of soft gold spilled out, I was as much shocked as they. Even when told how the switch must have taken place in a moment of intimacy, I would not believe. At any second, I knew, the gates would open and Evelyn would emerge with a satisfactory explanation.

"But she did not come; she left by another exit from the guild almost as soon as she had entered. No, she reappeared not then nor during any of the four years I wasted away in a dungeon in punishment for my part in the crime.

"So when I finally was set free, I started learning to look intently at the faces, to read behind the words and to serve to magicians and other masters some of the same formulas that they would brew for me."

Kestrel paused and shrugged. "It is not so difficult if you set your mind to it. Every man betrays his innermost thoughts with slight gestures and the tugs of muscles in his face, master as well as slave. You merely have to put yourself in his place and feel as your own what must be his driving desires. Each time you observe, the readings become clearer, the hidden motives behind them easier to read.

"And with that understanding comes the power to manipulate, to guide and channel according to your own desire. One can twist a master of the arts like a magic ring about his finger and show to the world, like Evelyn, how undeserving he is.

"So in the end I have become a sorcerer as much as any other. No, I know nothing of the incantations that are so hard to say but if spoken thrice bind the spells. I do not bend others to my will by force of magical art. The illusions that I spin are fabrics of the other's own thoughts, rather than my own. I merely encourage the impulses that are already there and enable them to flower for a brief moment for my own gain before they are subsequently smothered by shame."

The sadness in Kestrel's face tugged like a great weight. "Now I do have the skill of observation," he said. "I can see through men to their true worth. And unfortunately, I am among the best."

Kestrel stopped his rambling. He looked at Astron

88

with questioning eyes. "Now do you understand any better?" he asked.

"No," Astron said. "It is all very interesting, but in fact, I guess I do not. Why would this Evelyn say she would return and then change her mind without letting you know?"

Kestrel sighed again. At least for the moment, the bitterness was expunged. And it was far better for a demon to hear his confession than for someone who could manipulate the information against him. For a long moment there was silence; then Kestrel waved back to the wagon. "Climb inside and let us be going," he said. "I have some clothing that you should don so that you will not attract notice as we travel northward."

Astron nodded. "But you have not yet told me of the wizard. Why did you return for her at such great risk?"

"I do not know." Kestrel shrugged. "But it does not matter. Into the wagon, I say. Let us be gone."

"You had no real need," Astron persisted as he climbed aboard. "As I understand it, it could only be the act of a hero."

CHAPTER EIGHT

## Talk of the Thaumaturges

THE race across the Southern Kingdoms was swift. Kestrel pushed the mare as much as he dared, barely stopping for food and sleep. Astron had no requirement for nourishment and Phoebe in her entranced state needed little. In three days' time they crossed Samirand and Laudia and entered Ethidor, which bordered Procolon on the south. During their trek, Astron saw no sign of the searching imps, but the compelling sense of urgency did not abate. At any moment, the wizards could discover where they were and subject them to their wrath. The tale of what awaited Astron back in his own realm, if he did not succeed in time, Kestrel could scarcely believe, but the demon remained steadfast in urging the wagon onward.

Toward dusk of the third day, they arrived in the port of Menthos as the onshore breeze blew thick plumes of dark smoke from foundries across the isthmus. Kestrel pulled his horse to a stop at the head of the main street of the town. He glanced back at Phoebe, who appeared to be sleeping on a rough bed under the wagon's canopy. The branches and snags meant to be foisted off as anvil-wood had long since been discarded. Astron sat at Kestrel's side, wearing a long cape and hooded like a master, although no logo was displayed. A worn tunic, leggings, boots and gloves covered most of his faintly scaled skin.

On the left side of the main street, behind a sidewalk of rough planking, stood a long row of apothecaries, wooden-faced structures mainly of one storey. Some were brightly painted and prosperous-looking, others were dull with isinglass windows scratched and hazy. "Galena and cinnabar," some of the placards over doorways proclaimed; "Fresh vacuum of all quantities, created daily," said others.

On the right, steep stairways led down a short cliff to docks and quays. Riding gently at anchor were broad-beamed galleons, all lying high in the water, though some had their decks filled with closely packed bottles, their sails unfurled, ready to weigh anchor.

At the other end of the street, behind high fences, large smokestacks towered into the sky, belching dense black clouds. Even from the distance, one could hear the roar of huge bellows feeding air into furnaces and smell the hint of metallic fumes.

The traffic on the street was the usual mixture of scurrying messengers, maids hawking fruits and material from simple carts, merchants in animated conversation, and an occasional litter bearing someone of importance. Mixed with the rest were men-at-arms in groups of twos

90

and threes, wandering aimlessly, apparently looking for something to spark their jaded interests.

"An alchemist's town, no doubt about it," Kestrel said as he pointed to the rising smoke. He had decided it best to explain things to Astron as soon as something new was seen by the demon. It would reduce the chance of questions at inappropriate times, like those that had been asked at Phoebe's cabin.

Kestrel shook his head slightly as he spoke. He had become quite used to the physical presence of the demon. The oddity of his bizarre origin had long since faded away. A wrinkled nose, Kestrel now understood, indicated puzzlement, the flicking of the eye membranes a retreat into the deep logical thought. But beyond these simple signs, he still could not fathom any motives behind those that the devil professed. Hopefully, they would become more apparent as they drew closer to the archimage.

Despite his statements about experience as a cataloguer of the realm of men, Astron was totally ignorant about some of the simplest things. Abstract concepts beyond what one could see and touch took a good deal of explaining. But the demon was an eager and attentive pupil, asking questions until he was sure that he fully understood.

"If this is the lair of alchemists, then what formulas do they work?" Astron asked. "The chance for success must be quite high, judging from the number who are congregated all in one place."

"Vacuums," Kestrel said. "By melting metals, the alchemists of Menthos can produce the hardest vacuums on the great sea. They are in demand by magicians and thaumaturges for their own rituals and simulations."

"But a vacuum is the total absence of matter. How can that have any value at all?"

"I do not understand the details," Kestrel said, "but by connecting one of the bottles produced here to another vessel, the air can be removed far better than by any pump. Lids can be sealed with greater force than that provided by the finest waxes. Huge pistons can be

91

made to move along long cylinders, raising bridges over navigable rivers."

"The absence of matter," Astron mumbled, "and in the realm of men great effort is put into its creation." He wrinkled his nose. "Another fascination. If only there were more time."

Kestrel started to say more, but he suddenly spotted what he was looking for on the crowded street. Half a block down from where they had stopped, three brown-robed young men were performing their services for a queue of men-at-arms standing on the sidewalk, waiting their turn. Kestrel pointed out his destination and started the mare slowly forward.

"Thaumaturges," he said, "a journeyman and two apprentices. See, one wears but a single wavy line on his sleeve; the other two are unadorned. But no matter that a master is not present. They will know what is happening by the nature of their trade better than most."

Astron leaned forward to watch the activity as the wagon approached. One of the apprentices deftly clicked short shears through the long hair of a sergeant who sat in a portable chair set up on the sidewalk in front of the line. The second scooted about on his knees sweeping up the locks as they fell and passing them on to the journeyman seated at a table a little distance away.

The last of the three carefully extracted a single strand of hair from the rest of each tress and dipped it into a pot of glue at his side. With a smooth motion, he aligned the sticky hair along the length of a piece of twine directly in front of where he sat. The men-at-arms chatted among themselves and the apprentice who wielded the shears, apparently totally oblivious of the other activities about them.

"I recognize the craft," Astron said as they approached. "The one with the doubled blades is called a barber. In exchange for a coin he removes hair from the head and face."

"In the Southern Kingdoms, there is no fee." Kestrel pulled the wagon to a halt directly in front of the line of waiting men. "The hair itself is payment enough."

92

"Something new for sale?" one of the men-at-arms called out, jingling the purse at his waist as Kestrel vaulted to the ground. "It has been a fortnight of staring at the fires across the marsh. This is our first day of leave."

"How much for an evening with the wench?" A second poked his head into the interior of the wagon and spied Phoebe's reclining form.

"Although she is mine to command, such base use is not—" Astron began before Kestrel reached up and laid a hand of warning on his arm.

"A fortnight without rotation." Kestrel smiled. "A long time without distraction. Tell me, how have things fared on the border for those who might wish to pass?"

The two men-at-arms turned suddenly silent and resumed their place in line. Kestrel noticed the glower of the sergeant who sat in the apprentice's chair. "My business is with the journeyman," he said. "What he has learned from all who have sat here certainly is not the fault of your own fine squad of men."

Kestrel watched the sergeant relax back into the chair as he walked down to where the journeyman worked his craft. As he approached, he noticed the hatchet-sharp nose that split the thaumaturge's elongated and melancholy face and how, with eyes furrowed with concentration, he arranged more than two dozen pieces of twine in front of him, each with a hair glued down its length from the head of a different man. The journeyman mumbled something that Kestrel could not quite catch and then began deftly to weave the strings into a stout rope the thickness of a man's thumb.

Simultaneously a second hair from each of the clippings before him disentangled from the rest. Like worms on a hot griddle, they danced toward one another and then began to intertwine. In a perfect mimicry of the weaving of the journeyman, the hairs wove into a tiny replica of the rope but with a diameter smaller than the shaft of a pin.

"What is your greatest length?" Kestrel asked as he approached.

"Over ten times the height of a man but with a carrying strength for its size greater than anything but the strands of a spider's web. You have no need for bulky ropes of hemp or cotton when you can possess such compact beauties as these braids."

"Only ten times? Oh, then it is a pity." Kestrel backed away. "I was hoping for something more the distance from here to the quay."

The journeyman looked up from his work. His eyes ran over Kestrel's rumpled tunic and he frowned. "Even with the aid of thaumaturgy which weaves the tiny strands as quickly as if they were readily handled twines," he said, "what you request would take much effort to produce. Each short length must be knotted together. You speak of something measured in golden brandels rather than the mere coppers of Ethidor. Are you sure you do not waste my time?"

Kestrel paused a moment before answering. Then he shrugged and smiled. "Perhaps you are right. There are probably others who have what I want directly on hand." He turned to go and, with what looked like an afterthought, tossed a brandel onto the table amid the braids of hair. "For your trouble," he said.

The journeyman eyed the coin as it spun to rest on the rough surface. He looked at Kestrel a second time and then apparently made up his mind. "Luthor, to the master's den," he commanded. "Fetch the other braidings with length of ten. I will knot them all together for a price that would be most fair."

As the apprentice scampered off, the journeyman called out to Kestrel, who was halfway back to the wagon. "Here, I will show you how it is done while we wait," he said. "Watch as I join together the short length I have just made with another of similar size."

Kestrel hesitated a moment but then continued toward the wagon.

"You ask of the border," the journeyman continued. "Perhaps there is something of interest I can tell you to pass the time." He waved his arm at the remaining apprentice, now working on the next who stood in line.

"There is much that we learn from those with whom we trade."

Kestrel turned slowly and shrugged. "I have heard that many are the numbers who mill about in the bogs."

"And for no real purpose," the journeyman answered quickly. "Our own Prince Rupert's troops are there merely because his alchemists could not abide by each other's agreements with the miners of Procolon—ambushing and waylaying each other's shipments of galena and other lead ores as they came south to the foundries. When Celibor rips his mind from lusting after some wench, he is the worst, and his rivals little better. It is no wonder old Queen Vendora dispatched a garrison to guard the way.

"Then Rupert's pride could not stand the presence of Procolon's banners on his soil. So his own legions were dispatched to ensure that none remained on this side of the border. And now they sit staring at each other, with no traffic at all going either way."

"None at all?" Kestrel asked.

"A month ago, a small wagon about the size of yours attempted to run past Procolon's lines, after bribing some squad on this side of the marsh." The thaumaturge shrugged. "Their archers gave him no chance to speak before everything was consumed in flame."

"And writs of safe passage?"

"A profitable business." The journeyman laughed. "I can point you to a dozen scribes who would gladly write the most impressive documents for a suitable fee. The trouble is that the men who walk the Procolon line are as testy as ours. They swing their swords first and then ask their sergeants if it was the proper thing to do.

"But never mind all of that. Let me show you how I will make the length of braid that you request." The journeyman positioned two lengths of woven rope in front of him, the strands in each one cemented to individual hairs. He grasped a single twine from the end of each and with nimble fingers knotted them together. Then he selected a second pair, interwove them with the first and joined them together as well. Proceeding methodically, a pair at a time, he spliced the ends in a strong bond.

Kestrel did not follow the motions of the two corresponding braids of hair but he knew what was happening. They too were becoming knotted and bound in exactly the same way as the easier to manipulate ropes in the hands of the thaumaturge. The laws of "like produces like" and "once together, always together" were being used to perform a perfect simulation.

Instead, Kestrel was looking in the direction in which the apprentice had sped away. When he saw a blur in the distance that indicated the young man's return, he suddenly reached out and tapped the journeyman on the shoulder.

"The sergeant seemed a little perturbed that his men might talk of the border," he said quickly. "What do you suppose he thinks when he hears the same words come from you?"

"What I have said will cause no harm," the journeyman answered. "He is concerned only about the regulations laid down by his captain."

"Still." Kestrel pointed at the brandel lying where it had fallen. "How would you explain that a stranger was willing to pay gold for what he has heard?"

"But you said that is for—"

"I see his frown deepen." Kestrel smiled back to the sergeant waiting for his men. "Perhaps the two of us should go over together and explain."

"No, the braided—"

Kestrel reached down and deftly scooped up the coin. "On the other hand, perhaps it is best for everybody if this transaction never took place."

Before the thaumaturge could say more, Kestrel glided back to the wagon and climbed aboard. Just as the apprentice came panting up with coils of the tiny rope about both his arms, Kestrel motioned the mare to start away. The only problem was merely getting across the border, he remembered thinking. It looked as if it was not going to be quite so easy.

\* \* \*

The afternoon faded into darkness while Kestrel pondered how to proceed. He had slowly navigated the wagon up and down the streets of Menthos a dozen times, looking at all the shops and factories, but no inspiration had come. With a growing fatigue, he studied in the encroaching dimness the last of the foundry fires as they winked out for the night. Somehow, the solution to getting past two lines of armed men and into Procolon had to involve the large works of alchemists, but he could not quite put all the elements of a solution together.

Kestrel glanced at Astron, sitting patiently at his side. The demon had halted all his questions when he had been told that interruptions would not be appreciated for a while. Kestrel glanced back into the interior of the wagon at Phoebe's still slumbering form. He sighed. He was bothered about that little detail as well.

What good had it done to rescue her from the other wizards, if she remained in a semianimate state under the control of a demon? Sooner or later, someone would get suspicious about a woman in a trance, wearing the robe and logo of a wizard. Word would surely get back to her peers. Crossing the border would be difficult at best, and Phoebe in her condition was an added complication.

On the other hand, if Astron were to release Phoebe from his domination, Kestrel was not sure what would happen. She might immediately try to contact her council and aid in Kestrel's apprehension as well. How easy would it be to convince her to keep quiet about her travelling companions?

"What about the wizard?" Kestrel asked out loud after a moment's more thought. "Is it harmful to keep her in such an unnatural state?"

"Eventually, yes," Astron said. "The muscles atrophy and the thoughts turn sluggish, even after one is released. In time, she would become no more than a vacant doll with drool on her chin."

Kestrel jerked the horse to a sudden halt. "I still do not know quite why I brought her along," he said, "but certainly not for a fate such as that." He wavered for a moment in uncertainty and then thought of the warmth of her smile. "Perhaps it is better to release her now."

"By eventually, I meant a long passage of time," Astron said. "As for the present moment, do you really think it wise? I have held her to avoid more struggle of the wills, but if I were to set her free, she might not be similarly inclined. Most likely she would try to dominate me instead. The first contest was hard enough. I do not wish to undergo it again."

"No, somehow, I will take care of that," Kestrel said. His thoughts raced as he spoke. Now that he had decided, it was important that the deed be done. "She is the key element of the exchange. A countess is what we need. Yes, a countess to impress one of the alchemists with the possibility of a very large reward."

"A reward? In exchange for what?" Astron asked.

"Transport across the border in exchange for—for a mine," Kestrel said. As he spoke everything fell into place. Phoebe was the missing element that he had been searching for! By posing as a countess, she would give them the credibility that was lacking in his half-formed plans. Never mind about the risk of letting her decide for herself. He would work out something when everything could be explained. Kestrel turned the wagon into an alleyway and halted.

"Quickly," he said. "Release her now so that we can purchase some clothing appropriate for her station. At dawn tomorrow, we must be ready to start."

"Your motives regarding the female I still do not understand," Astron said. He wrinkled his nose and for a long moment nothing happened. Then abruptly his face cleared and he turned his attention to studying the tackle of Kestrel's mare.

"Awake," he said simply. "I release you, wizard, to command your own will."

Kestrel watched Phoebe's eyes flutter and then spring open. She looked up at the wagon's canopy in the darkness and then at the two figures hovering over her. Her eyes widened further and she clutched her fist to her mouth, preparing to scream.

Kestrel reached down and stroked her arm. Gently he placed an extended finger on her cheek.

Phoebe's eyes flashed in the gathering darkness. She drew a deep breath and slowly returned her hand to her side.

"Where am I?" she asked in a controlled tone after a moment. "What is it that you want?"

"Remember the anvilwood?" Kestrel tried to make his voice soothing. "I am the woodcutter who brought it to your cabin. You summoned a demon more powerful than you could control."

Phoebe's eyes shifted from Kestrel to Astron. "Yes," she said in sudden recognition. "The demon. His will was too strong. I could not resist. I am his to do with what he will." She shuddered and snapped shut her eyes. "The council was right after all. Their barbs and jeers are true." She tugged at the folds of the robe about her hips. "I wear the logo of a master only because of my father's wealth, not because of skill. Go ahead, devil, do with me what you will."

"No, you do not understand," Kestrel continued. "Test your thoughts. They are free. The contest is finished and you are dominated no more."

Phoebe cowered in silence for a long moment but then Kestrel saw the tension gradually fade away. The wrinkles vanished from her brow. Tentatively she sat up and shook her head, as if trying to toss away thoughts that did not belong.

"Free-willed I am, woodsman," she said cautiously. "Thank you for your aid." She reached down in confusion to her waist and patted a purse that was not there. "Your product is as good as you bragged it to be. You need not show me the contents of each leather sack as I originally intended. Let us go back into the cabin and I will pay you your price, though I must say that I am getting the better part of the bargain."

"Ah, things are not quite that simple," Kestrel said. "You see, we are not outside your cabin, but in Menthos, near the border to Procolon."

99

The tension in Phoebe's face returned. "Menthos! I do not understand."

"Your council of wizards has become enraged," Astron said. "As we speak, they no doubt have many imps scouring the countryside looking for—"

"You," Kestrel cut in. "Yes, you are the one they seek, a wizard in flight from what they construe as the justice that is your due."

"Yes, the council and their hidebound ways," Phoebe said. "But Menthos? I still do not understand."

"Well, this is the way of it," Kestrel said. He looked into Phoebe's questioning eyes. He should have thought things through a little more thoroughly before having Astron release her from his control.

"Yes," Phoebe said. "What indeed is the way of it?"

"The council of wizards think that—" Kestrel began but this time Astron interrupted.

"We need your help," the demon said, "to cross the border and see the archimage. Kestrel sees you as the key element of the plan. Despite what he has done to your reputation back in Brythia, we need your help here and now."

Kestrel grimaced, expecting Phoebe's face to knot into one of displeasure. Next time, he just had to get the demon to understand and follow his lead, rather than cut in on his own. Not that there would be a next time, if Phoebe decided to rectify what had happened to her good name. He shook his head, awaiting the outburst. Why had freeing the wizard been such a good idea?

But the hard words did not come. "You need my help," Phoebe repeated, "the service of a wizard, and you have come to me."

Kestrel blinked at the unexpected tone. "Wizardry, why no," he rushed to say. "It was something rather different from that." He looked into Phoebe's eyes and found the words of deception harder and harder to get out of his throat. "We must get to the archimage," he said at last, "and for that we must first cross the border. I think that I have a means of accomplishing it. We need an impersonation of a countess, one who is the seeker of thrills, one who can convince an alchemist to grant favors in exchange for profit to be received later." He hesitated and then added in a mumble, "The archimage will be able to set things straight between you and your council as well."

"Then it is true," Phoebe said. "I was indeed dominated by the demon. If it is skill in wizardry that you desire, elsewhere is where you should look."

"No, no, if wizardry is called for along the way, you are the one to whom we will turn," Kestrel said. "It is just that there are other requirements as well."

"You need me?" Phoebe questioned again.

Kestrel just nodded, trying to fathom the motivations behind the pretty smile. He was having difficulty reading the wizard, just as he did with the demon, but for a different reason. The emotions were on her face well enough; but when he looked at her, distracting thoughts warped the logical cadence of his thought.

"And it will help you with the council," he repeated weakly.

"The council." Phoebe shook her head. "I have little doubt that they have found some way to give me censure." She smoothed the folds of her robe and shrugged. "It has not been such an easy struggle. Without the largess of my father, I would never have been able to pay the triple fees the masters charged to initiate me into their art. The stocking of my larder comes less from the few payments I receive for my craft than the continued openness of his purse.

"Far better for all concerned, it has been made quite clear more than once, if Phoebe behaved more like her cousins and sisters, lounging in the dresses of brocade and attending the balls of the prince."

"What do you mean?" Astron said. "I cannot yet follow when men speak in such abstraction."

"Men, indeed," Phoebe said. "I suspect the realm of daemon is much like what you see about you here." She narrowed her eyes and looked piercingly at Astron. "Tell me how it is that only the males answer the summons through the flame and grapple with the wizard's will.

101

Why no females? What have you done with them?"

"Why, that is not the purpose of the broodmothers," Astron said. "They serve one function and no more. It is unthinkable for it to be any other way."

"And you, Kestrel, how many wizards of my sex have you encountered in your peddling of woods?"

"Ah, you are the only one."

"Yes, the only female wizard in Brythia, perhaps in all the kingdoms that border the great sea. Despite all the regulations thrown in the way, the unapproving stares, the whispers behind my back, I became a master—an equally accredited master in a local council, whether they liked it or not."

"Then, if your council does not look with favor on you at the moment—" Kestrel began.

"It can only be an intensification of what already was felt. I am an embarrassment to them because I am so different and do not assume their stately airs. But no matter, I have won the robe and they cannot take it away."

Phoebe paused and looked at Kestrel. "What is important to me now is not their thoughts, woodcutter, but yours. What do you think of a master who happens not to be a male? Would you use me when you could elect to choose a man instead?" She glanced over at Astron and her voice softened to a whisper. "Use one who has already proven that a demon such as that is her better in a battle of wills?"

Kestrel blinked again. "I have considered you a master, no different from the rest," he said. The question went deeper than that, but his answer was a truthful one. She had been chosen for the anvilwood because of her greater wealth, not anything else. As for the rest, he felt the old barriers sliding strongly into place. No good could come from raising the innermost feelings and trying to strip away the scarred layers of pain.

"Well said." Phoebe smiled faintly. "Perhaps my instincts in the matter were correct from the first. Stand in the light so I can see you better. No, not you, demon, only the man."

Kestrel climbed back down from the wagon and into the brightness of the street.

"Yes, it is all coming back now." Phoebe's smile broadened. "I remember why I invited you in. And as for now, wizardry or something else of equal value, it does not really matter. Just so I am a full partner, and not a tool to be manipulated like a sorcerer's slave."

"You will not try to continue our struggle for dominance?" Astron asked.

"No, why should I?" The smile vanished from Phoebe's face. "If you still desired to control my will, I do not see how I could resist a second time, knowing I had lost the first." She turned her eyes away from Astron and lowered her head. "I have already proven myself worthy to wear the logo of the master. Perhaps in the end, that will be sufficient."

"There is no more to it!" Astron exclaimed. "Kestrel, you are most remarkable. I apologize for my doubt. When there is more time, you must explain how you achieved such an agreement of wills."

Kestrel lightly touched Phoebe's arm again. Despite the inner warnings, it felt good to do so. "Things are not always what they seem, demon," he said slowly. "I have already told you that."

Astron wrinkled his nose and his membranes slid into place. For a moment he stared off into the distance and did not speak.

He suddenly burst out of his contemplation after a moment. "Then let us get on with your plan. The flickers of light that I now see at the end of this alley—I do not believe that they are the simple fireflies of your realm."

CHAPTER NINE

# The Alchemy of Air

KESTREL hit the tapper against the brass door with authority. The gong seemed to reverberate all along the high metal-plated fencing that ran around the foundry. Even though it was barely dawn, smoke was already spilling out of the stack on the other side of the enclosing barrier. The wheeze of the bellows was quite loud, like the moan of a great djinn with nothing to destroy.

Astron had not been sure how much longer it would be before the wizards became certain of their location, but they had little time for additional delay. They had to get over the border and to the archimage soon, or it would all be too late.

Kestrel cupped his hands to his mouth and spoke directly at the demon, the noises within the foundry masking his words more than a few feet away. "Now remember, Astron," he said. "You are the consulting alchemist for the countess. You will observe the process and say nothing. Occasionally shake your head slightly in disapproval after an explanation. Under no circumstances ask any of your questions. Just be on the lookout for more of your kind."

"But an alchemist I am not," Astron said. "I cannot speak that which does not reflect reality."

"That is just the point," Kestrel said. "Do not say a thing. Let those inside draw whatever conclusions they will. For what they think, you are not responsible."

"To stand and shake my head is not very interesting, Kestrel. At least I should be able to find out something to add to my catalogues."

"I will see to it that you are suitably amused," Kestrel

104

said. "Just keep quiet while you are about it."

Kestrel turned his attention to Phoebe. The gown they had purchased the previous evening with eight of the dozen brandels suited her well; she carried herself as one would expect of the nobility. She returned his approving look with a smile, but he pulled his eyes away. She had enthusiastically taken on the role he had outlined to her and did not even bother to ask any more about what had happened at her cabin or even the reason he was originally there.

So long as she did not ask, Kestrel decided, there was no reason for him to explain more. He darted one more furtive glance in her direction. And yet his logic did not quite ring true. For the first time in a long while, he was somehow uncomfortable about what he was hiding from someone else.

The door suddenly opened and Kestrel turned to meet the gateman. "The grand countess of Brythia, second cousin to the king, is here to discuss terms for the shipment," he said. "Show us to the head alchemist without delay."

The gateman puckered his prunelike face into a mass of wrinkles. With studied disapproval, he looked up and down Kestrel's own plain clothing and Astron, hooded by his side. "I have received no instructions about a visitor," he said. "You will have to wait until I check with master Celibor."

"Surely we can wait inside, rather than here on the street," Kestrel said. "Perhaps even a chair so that my lady can sit. The purse she carries is most heavy. And from what I hear of master Celibor, he will be most anxious to meet her."

The gateman glanced at Phoebe, hesitated a moment, then snatched at the brandel that Kestrel waved in front of him. "You may use my stool." He waved as he headed off across the interior of the foundry yard.

Kestrel and the others stepped inside. Quickly, he surveyed the enclosure from one end to the other. The fencing formed a huge square, each side the length of a sprinter's race. In the rear corner of the left stood dumps of ore, huge boulders ripped from deep running mines, glinting with crystals of gray in the morning sun. A dozen laborers swung hammers at the larger ones, reducing them to smaller chunks and dust that were shoveled onto a belt squeaking over a long row of wooden rollers. Spinning flywheels and convoluted belts moved the rock into massive grinders and then through acrid chemicals dripping from glazed retorts. At the terminus of the conveyor, a fine powder fell into a chute leading to a huge brick-lined anthanar in the center of the square. On the backside of the furnace, barely visible from where Kestrel stood, two three-man bellows alternately expanded and shot air into the burning firepit.

A tall shed spanned the opposite side of the square, covering loads of sand that fell from hoppers into a red-hot cauldron. There a dozen glassblowers dipped long hollow tubings into a transparent slag. With bursting cheeks, they blew huge flat-bottomed bottles with tiny necks. These too were conveyed to the furnace and entered on the side opposite from the processed ore.

Near the front of the anthanar stood two alchemists, each furiously writing on parchment, giving life to the formulas that formed the basis of their craft. They stood on either side of a third conveyor, this one discharging a sequence of lead-capped bottles that were collected and arrayed in designated squares throughout the yard. Behind the back of the second master, in a cast-iron trough, a river of molten metal ran into an array of molds, presses, and rollers.

A bright lead foil extruded from the last of the rotating cylinders. Intricate objects that Kestrel did not recognize dropped from the presses into a hopper. Some of the molds were simple ingots, conveniently shaped for resale elsewhere. The rest formed struts and geometric figures, evidently destined for a vast array of dull gray structures beyond the cooling area.

Among the distant sprawl were skeletons of icosohedrons in three different sizes. Nestled with solid-sided cubes, small spheres clustered like grapes on long cylindrical stems. Beyond the smaller structures, giant pylons soared twice the height of a man. Hollow balls of lead fully ten arm-lengths in diameter shone dully in the morning sun. To the left of the completed spheres stood one in midconstruction, the bottom of a mesh-covered skeleton sheathed in a foil of lead, while laborers heated and fused additional sheets above its bulging equator.

"Somehow, in the final step of the formula that the alchemists guard in their grimoires, the smelting of the metal produces the vacuum," Kestrel explained to the others. "The lead is used as a seal only because it is conveniently there. As you can see the bulk of it goes into the molds and presses for resale elsewhere as a by-product. I think the geometric shapes are used in magician's rituals, although some of the foundries make small statuary to sell to the nobility as works of art as well.

"But beyond that is where our interest lies, where the vacuum is tested to verify its quality. As you may know, not a single formula of alchemy can be guaranteed to succeed each and every time. Indeed, the more powerful have the least chance of all. Each product must be verified to ensure that the process has produced what was desired."

Astron and Phoebe turned to look where Kestrel pointed. They saw two workmen drag one of the larger bottles from a square and place it adjacent to what looked like a stitchery of cured hides lying on the ground. One connected a bellows to the collection of hides and began pumping. In a few moments it inflated into a perfect sphere. Then the second workman thrust the neck of the vacuum bottle into the bellows opening and broke the seal.

With a powerful hiss that the three could hear even from where they stood, the sphere buckled and warped, although not back to the flattened shape it had before. Like a lumpy pillow, it sagged on the ground at the workmen's feet. The first bound off the opening at the bottom and the other set it apart from the rest of the gear so that it received the full glare of the rising sun.

"Yes, what is it?" A master wearing the logo of the inverted triangle had emerged from a hut near the glassworks and followed the gatekeeper back across the foundry yard. He was short and swarthy with small quick eyes that squinted in distrust. His jaws hung heavy like a bulldog's. Kestrel wondered whether, if he got his grip on something, he would ever let go.

"If it is a large order, you had better place it quickly." The alchemist waved toward the pile of rock waiting to be crushed. "When that is gone, there will be no more for vacuum for a goodly while, at least until the border to the north is once again open."

"Master Celibor, I presume," Kestrel said. "This is Countess Phoebe and she indeed is most anxious to buy." Kestrel paused and forced a smile. "Her mind as yet is not totally made up, however, between dealing with you or the establishment across the street."

"What—Iliac!" Celibor exploded. "He is no less than responsible for the blockade in the first place. You should be blaming him for the rise in prices, not giving him aid by favoring him with trade. If he had not persisted in trying to divert ore wagons rightly meant for me, then none of this confrontation at the border would have happened. Even the archimage would be visiting our fair kingdoms rather than wasting his good time entertaining the ones who call themselves skyskirr from some forsaken place or another far away."

"Nevertheless, he has the reputation for a splendid product," Kestrel said.

"Lies of the market place," Celibor spat. "He turns out great volume of glassware and at less cost, it is true. But how many prove to be nothing more than jars of clear air rather than vacuum of prime hardness, answer me that? Why, look you at the pains we take to ensure that each batch has indeed run its course, rather than randomly failed as is sometimes the case."

Celibor paused to catch his breath. The ruddiness of his cheeks began to fade. He waved in the direction of the hide sphere. The crushing indentations had vanished; the sun had warmed the air that remained until the skin was again tight and firm. As everyone watched it began gently to rise from the ground and tug at the single fetter that held it in place.

"Elsewhere along the street," Celibor said, "they merely let the balloons rise to their maximum heights and do no more. Those batches that produce the highest they label as premium grade vacuum, no matter that they might be half as good as the ones produced the day before.

"Here we do more than that. We actually calculate the degree to which the jars are empty from measuring the balloon's ascent. Nowhere else are such quantitative tests made, not in a single foundry along the street. We know the volume of our balloons; the hides have been cured so that they no longer stretch. From the height to which they rise and equilibrate with the lesser density of air outside, we can compute the mass that rides within. From these numbers we then determine precisely how well the test bottle extracted some of the original contents and thence from that how good was the vacuum it originally contained."

"That is most interesting," Astron said. "A quantitative calculation aimed at showing nothing as the result."

Celibor looked at the hooded figure and frowned. "Not every batch produces a balloon which rises so well," he explained. "Some bottles extract only half the air because only half was removed from them by the random perturbations of the creation process. Some draw no air at all: total failures the likes of which you are much more likely to find across the way."

"How high do these balloons rise?" Phoebe asked.

Celibor looked at Phoebe as if he were noticing her for the first time. With a deliberate coolness he ran his eyes over her body. "A most interesting question, my lady," he said. "We usually test only a single bottle in a batch; so, like the one you see there, they rise only perhaps as far as the top of the anthanar's stack or a little higher."

Kestrel noticed Celibor's reaction to Phoebe, but surprisingly the satisfaction of a plan going well did not come. Rather than being pleased that she had excited the alchemist's interest, he felt irritated by the degrading way in which he showed it. It would indeed be soon enough when they were well away.

"And no gondola attached for one to observe?" Phoebe asked as Kestrel tried to draw back Celibor's attention.

"Why no, not every time, my countess, it would be a great waste." Celibor did not take his eyes from Phoebe. "Although we have baskets and the necessary riggings obtained from the thaumaturges up the street, the purpose is to test, not to lift a considerable weight. And with the onshore breeze, there is risk as well. A parted tether would mean the occupants would sail right over the encamped armies and deep into Procolon itself."

"But then think also of the thrill of it," Phoebe said in a bored tone. "If only for a part of an hour, floating like a cloud and looking down on the coastline as far as one could see. So much more exciting that all those dreary teas and receptions. Yes, Kestrel, see to it. Do business with the one who will offer a balloon ride as part of the bargain."

"You are talking a considerable expense," Celibor said. He finally looked from Phoebe back to Kestrel and Astron. "And although I have been most free to point out details of my trade, I know nothing of you other than what you profess." He motioned back the way he had come. "Visit me in my chambers, my lady; I will ask more of you there." Celibor again looked up and down the length of Phoebe's gown. "Never mind the clutter along the way. It is quite safe, since we keep it well away from the flames. Just lift your hems a trifle and they will not be soiled as we walk."

"The countess and I will gladly follow," Kestrel said quickly. "But consultant Astron's time is perhaps better spent in evaluating more of what takes place here. Pair him with someone who talks well and fast. He is the best of listeners."

Astron opened his mouth to speak, but Kestrel grabbed him by the arm. "There, the man with the pen and quill—perhaps you will be amused by learning more

110

of these calculations. Or even the sculpturing—see, look at that scaffolding going up on which they are hanging those foils of lead. Surely those will be of more interest than standing around listening to the countess and the master exchanging pleasantries."

"The calculations and the structures, why yes," Astron said. "The sculpturing is akin to what I call weaving and, for one who cannot do that, it would be interesting indeed. I need feel no guilt. While I wait I can no better serve my—"

Kestrel squeezed Astron's arm tighter and the demon stopped. He nodded and slowly started to move in the direction Kestrel had indicated. Kestrel whirled to catch up with Celibor and Phoebe as they walked to the hut. The alchemist had his arm around her waist while he pointed out other aspects of his foundry. Curse it, Kestrel thought. She permitted it just as he had instructed her to.

Kestrel watched Phoebe try to shield from her eyes the afternoon sun streaking into the hut through a low window. He shifted uncomfortably on his stool, kicked at cracked and discarded parchments that cluttered the floor, and looked out the doorway into the foundry yard. He saw Astron with some sort of sextant sighting the top of the huge lead spheres and then the pylons at their side. Throughout the yard the bustle of the activity continued as if the border blockade did not exist. The bellows whooshed. A blistering heat radiated from the openings of the anthanar.

Kestrel frowned at the lengthening shadows. Despite Celibor's other interests, his first concern turned out to be for his profits. For most of the day they had argued, and no agreement was yet in sight. Soon the sun would be setting, and they would have to come back the next day, something that Kestrel definitely did not want to do. He would have to play through the last part of his plan, whether the alchemist gave him an opening or not.

"But do you not see?" Celibor waved his hands around the confines of his hut. "This is no palace with

111

rich furnishings paid for by the profits of my trade. Iliac across the way has seen to that with his low prices and inferior products. I need the coin to pay the workers as the effort is done. I cannot afford to await until the order is complete no matter how alluring is the bounty I would receive."

The alchemist looked at Phoebe slyly. "Besides, I cannot really believe that a few moments aloft is the primary reason you are so anxious to do business with me. Why the concern, my lady, about pretending you are a bird?"

Kestrel became immediately alert. Celibor's statement was what he had been waiting for. "You drive a hard bargain." He laughed. "And this day grows long." He looked at Phoebe. "With your permission, my lady," he said.

Phoebe nodded slightly. Kestrel watched Celibor lean forward from where he sat.

"There is the matter of the new mine," Kestrel continued smoothly. "One not in the mountains of Procolon to the north, but in the very hills of Ethidor itself."

"There are no such mines," Celibor scoffed. "Our own hills have been scoured many times over."

"But not from a height, not from a vantage point no other has taken." Kestrel lowered his voice to a whisper. "And not with a sketch of what to look for drawn by a sorcerer while under a far-seeking trance." Kestrel pulled a tightly rolled parchment from his belt and waved it quickly in front of Celibor's face.

The alchemist reached for it but Kestrel pulled it away with a nod. "You understand how critical it is that word of this reach no one else. Your craft can ill-afford a repetition of what has caused the impulse to the north to occur."

Kestrel waited for Celibor to withdraw his hand and then continued. "Of course, our original plan was to find the location and then keep it from all, offering our ores to the highest bidder." His smile broadened. "But you deal with such skill that a direct share might be more in order. Enough perhaps so that you see the raising of the balloon as much in your interest as in ours."

Celibor glanced at Phoebe and then back to Kestrel. "How do I know that these are not more words, perhaps as empty as the rest?"

"You do not." Kestrel shrugged and rose. "There is a risk here that must be taken—a single balloon ride for half share in what may be the only source of ore while the blockade continues. Perhaps those across the street would indeed be more receptive."

"No, wait," Celibor said. "In good faith, I have made investments as well. Come outside and see what I have instructed the workmen to do while we talked. If we can agree on a fair price, then even today the deed can be done."

Kestrel looked over to Phoebe and she tilted her head slightly a second time. He shrugged and turns his palms upward to Celibor. "Evidently, she likes you," he said. "A few hours more she has graciously granted."

Celibor grunted and scurried past where they sat into the afternoon sun. He squinted his eyes against the harshness and motioned for them to follow over into the testing area.

Kestrel and Phoebe left the hut with regal slowness and stepped out into the daylight. They walked past the cooling lead ingots, lattices, and polyhedra and through the shadows cast by the great spheres and pylons. Astron looked up from what he was studying and motioned but Kestrel waved him away. The hook was nearly set and he could not afford to be distracted.

Kestrel noted the contents of other huts as he passed. One on the left was piled high with cured animal hides and beyond it were seamstresses lashing them together into a growing pile of balloons not yet used. On the right, knot makers tied lengths of braided hair into canopies that would fit over the balloons when they were inflated and tether them to the ground.

When they caught up with Celibor, he was pointing at a long row of bottles all connected to a hose of some rubbery fiber. Like a giant centipede the construction

113

wandered through the open area where the tests were performed.

"More than one bottle will be needed to remove enough air so that the three of you can be borne aloft," Celibor said. "My craftsmen have labored long and hard to connect all of these bottles in parallel so that the evacuation can quickly be done."

Kestrel looked down the snaking line. "Then we are almost ready," he said. "Why haggle over details when we can be at the task right away."

"It is not quite as you make it seem," Celibor said. "Two more bottles must be connected to the chain. That is no easy matter if one wishes not to lose all the vacuum in the process. Then we have to bind a valve to the balloon itself, one that will not leak once it has been removed of its air." Celibor waved to one of the leather spheres resting on the ground. It was partially inflated and tugging slightly against the beginning of a breeze. "And the heating arrangement I have not yet contemplated. Much air will be extracted for this ride, not just a little amount. Heating what remains to regain the original volume is an intriguing challenge all in itself."

Kestrel studied Celibor's expression, trying to judge the truthfulness of his words. He resisted the impulse to grab the end of the hose nearest him and hurry the process along. Then suddenly as he wrestled with what to say next, there was a loud pounding on the metal doors that led to the street.

"Open the gates," a voice sounded over the fence. "In the name of the wizards of the Brythian hills. You house the ones we seek."

Celibor glanced at his gateman in annoyance and then back in the direction of his hut toward a pile of shields and swords. Kestrel spun around to look at Astron and saw the demon pointing frantically into the air. Though it was not yet dusk, a swarm of lights could be seen dancing along the fence line in a confusing buzz. The demon had been right; the wizards had caught up with them and far sooner than Kestrel would have thought. Now there was no time left for subtle maneuvers. Every second would count.

"Defend your property rights," Kestrel shouted at the puzzled alchemist. "A direct attack from your rivals across the way. They strike in desperation to prevent the ascent of the countess into the air."

Celibor continued to hesitate and Kestrel turned his attention away. He had to get the foundry workers to act. "You, and you with the sextant," he directed. "Back to the weapons store and arm yourself against the entry. Delay them as long as you can." He waved at the apparatus directly in front of where he and Phoebe stood. "Never mind the last two bottles. Quickly affix the valve." He looked at the blank stares of the workmen and tried not to think how much more must be done.

With a sudden crash, the doors sprang inward and a squad of men-at-arms burst into the foundry yard. Behind perhaps twelve warriors, each clad in mail, came a quartet of wizards, shaking their fists and urging those in front forward.

"Benthon and Maspanar," Phoebe said, "and others of my council. What you said was true. They pursue me with great vigor."

"To the weapons." Celibor evidently shook off his indecision when he saw the men-at-arms. He picked up the hems of his master's robe and ran for his hut. "The visitors speak truly. Iliac seeks to get my share of the mine for himself."

Kestrel looked from the gates and back to the master's hut. Perhaps eight of Celibor's workers would arm and provide some resistance. He glanced at the two struggling with the valve and saw that they were now working as fast as they could.

"What of the devils?" he asked Phoebe quickly. "Where are the ones bigger than the imps on the wall?"

"Benthon is quite conservative," Phoebe said. "He will use demons of as little power as he can. Perhaps the imps are all that they have under their spell."

"Then help with the balloon," Kestrel decided. "I will aid in the defense to give us as much time as I can."

115

Kestrel bolted to Celibor's hut and pushed two of the slower workers aside. He reached for one of the shields and grabbed the sword that was closest of the lot. The blade felt heavy and not balanced to his liking but there was no time to choose.

Swinging his arm back and forth in what he hoped were menacing arcs he advanced with Celibor and four others to meet the first of the attacking men-at-arms. Six of the wizards' men raised their shields to meet them. With a ringing clang, steel crashed onto steel. Kestrel lunged forward, trying to get around his opponent's guard, but the man who faced him was skillful and dodged nimbly to the side. The rest of the wizards' men moved quickly behind the first and spread to outflank Kestrel and Celibor on both sides.

Kestrel retreated a step backward and darted a look back to the gate, sucking in his breath at what he saw. Another dozen men poured through the opening, lancemen and archers who fanned out across the yard. The limp balloon that was to be passage over the border made an ideal target and in a heart beat three arrows pierced the hide as if it were paper. The sphere crumpled and sagged to the ground. The lancers ran to the ore heaps and glassworks, pushing all resistance in front of them into a disorganized retreat.

"Another balloon from the storage hut," Kestrel shouted in desperation. "Start the bellows while there is still a chance." He tore his gaze away from the scrambling workmen at the shouts to his adversaries and barely ducked a swipe at his unprotected neck.

Kestrel retreated another two steps and stumbled backward over a fallen workman, trying to block out the growing sense of futility that hammered at his thoughts. He heard a crash behind him and then a clatter of metal. A hot blast of air roared from the anthanar and almost blistered the back of his head. Flames shot up from the glassworks. Globs of molten slag arced over the yard, starting small fires in the debris wherever they landed. One hit the stack of uninflated balloons, and Kestrel groaned. In a moment, their remaining means of escape burned along with the rest.

Kestrel looked around for Phoebe or Astron, but acrid smoke was beginning to obstruct his view. He saw one of the pylons fall and then a second. The huge lead sphere seemed to lumber from its pedestal and lurch his way. Kestrel staggered backward and felt the wall of Celibor's hut. The alchemist had dropped his sword and was on one knee begging for mercy, a trickle of deep red running from his forehead.

The smoke thickened. Kestrel took a deep breath, plunging into where it was densest, just missing another swipe at his side. The fumes hurt his eyes. He squinted into the dirty grayness, just barely able to make out the menacing forms pursuing him and the indistinct objects toward which he ran.

Kestrel staggered a dozen steps forward and burst back into clear air. Tears clouded his vision. He shook his head in surprise, trying to understand what he saw. Almost directly in front were Phoebe and Astron, standing in the gondola Celibor had planned to couple to the balloon. Frantically the two were waving their arms and beckoning him forward.

Kestrel took one step, puzzled. The gondola was made of straw. Soon it, too, would be in flame. It was better to run as best one could. But while he pondered, the box lurched in his direction, scraping along the ground. A shadow passed over Kestrel, and he looked up, astonished. The gondola lifted from the ground and started to climb over his head.

Stunned, Kestrel watched Astron reach out over the edge of the box while Phoebe held him by the waist.

"Grab my hand, mortal," Kestrel heard Astron shout. "This is no time for your stembrain to assume command."

Kestrel nodded blankly. He raised his arm and felt a surprisingly strong grip about his wrist. Then, with a stab of pain in his shoulder, he was lifted clear of the ground, just as a man-at-arms made one last stab at his dangling feet.

Kestrel looked down at the foundry. With gathering speed, it seemed to move more and more rapidly away. He heard the ping of an arrowhead on metal and glanced skyward for a second time. There was no mistake about it. The gondòla was tethered to a sphere of lead.

## CHAPTER TEN

# The Magic Bottle

"What wizardry is this?" Kestrel said as he climbed into the basket. "Balloons of lead cannot fly."

"There was no other choice," Astron said. "The ones of animal hide were all rendered useless by the minions of the wizards."

"It is not a matter of choice." Kestrel shook his head, still slightly dazed by what had happened. He looked over the edge of the gondola and saw the foundry yard shrink into toylike smallness. To the north, the camps of the two armies began to take shape into recognizable forms. The green wetness of the border marsh faded into the dark shadows of the setting sun. The low hills that led to the mines of Procolon grew closer with each passing moment. The onshore breeze was pushing them in exactly the direction Kestrel wished them to go.

"It is not a matter of choice," he repeated. "The metal is too heavy to be borne aloft."

"The calculations shown to me by the alchemist were most interesting," Astron said. "It seems that the force carrying a balloon aloft is proportional to its volume. The greater the size of the sphere, the more it can lift."

"One need not study one of the five arts to understand such a fact," Kestrel said. "The key point is that the weight of the balloon itself must be included in the total."

118

"And so it is," Astron said. "The mass of a balloon increases as the square of its radius while its volume and lifting power increase with the cube. Regardless of the density of the material, eventually there is a size large enough that it can be buoyed aloft."

Kestrel watched Astron pause, and what might be a smile of pleasure crossed the demon's face.

"I was fascinated by the concept of the vacuum," Astron continued. "And once I understood the principles, it was easy to perform the calculation for the lead sphere to which you directed my attention. Not only was it large enough to carry the skeletal structure inside which gave it shape but, as you can see, the three of us as well. I connected the gondola harness and the bottles of emptiness as soon as I saw that it was the last balloon remaining."

"It never was intended to be a balloon." Kestrel started to protest again, but then he stopped. Of course, he understood finally. For him, or any other man for that matter, connecting the vacuum bottles to the lead sphere would never have occurred as a possibility. But Astron was not blinded by the obvious. The demon merely thought it fortunate that the great ball was large enough to carry the three of them. There really was nothing of the five arts involved at all. Kestrel let out a deep breath and looked groundward. They were safely away and soon would be visiting the archimage.

But as he scanned the scene, a twinkle of light near the foundry wall caught Kestrel's eye. The feeling of relief immediately vanished. He studied the dancing pattern until he was sure, a scowl deepening on his face all the while. He pointed the light out to the others, and Astron nodded in confirmation. The cloud of imps that had tracked them to Menthos still pursued their flight. The buzzing sprites would have to be dealt with immediately, or they would have gained only a little respite from the wizards' wrath.

"Perhaps a magic bottle." Phoebe pointed at the trailing swarm. "Others of my council have spoken of them frequently. They use them to confine the imps that they summon through the flame. If we can capture them all before any returns to report where we are, then we will be cleanly away."

Kestrel stared out at the imps and pondered what Phoebe had said. His thoughts raced, pulling together the elements of another plan. "I think the wizard is right," he said after a moment. "We certainly have nothing to aid us in this empty gondola. And there are so many that we must find a way to deal with all of them at once. Let us land while there is still a bit of light and continue on the ground." He looked to the north, trying to judge their rate of motion. "If we are lucky, it will be far enough north that we quickly can reach a guild that I know of which specializes in the making of those magic jars. Perhaps, if we can intercept a single magician on the road, the odds might not be all that great."

Kestrel began constructing the details of what to do next, but stopped suddenly in midthought. The urgency of the moment was as great as ever, but somehow he still felt slightly puzzled. Despite the explanation about the balloon, something else was bothering him just under the surface of his thoughts.

Kestrel looked over at Phoebe and saw her smile. He put his arm around her waist to steady their stance as the basket began to rock in the quickening breeze. Phoebe did not protest. Instead she brought her pleasing softness to press against his side.

The full realization of what had happened thundered into focus. First the demon, and now the wizard. By his own cunning, Astron had managed to secure a means of transport over the border. Phoebe had joined him in the gondola. She alone would have been sufficient to see him the rest of the way to the archimage. There was absolutely no reason for them to pull him into the basket as it ascended. No reason at all—and yet they did.

Kestrel bargained with the baron whose crops had been damaged by the descent of the balloon and the metal sphere was traded for another horse and wagon.

Soon the trio were on the main road leading to Ambrosia, the capital of Procolon.

While Kestrel guided the steed, Phoebe and Astron held torches aloft on the moonless night. The swarm of imps that tracked their progress would not be deterred by lack of light, and the increased speed was worth the illumination.

They were on the road but for a fraction of an hour when, as Kestrel had hoped, he caught the reflecting glint from a huge bottle on the shoulder of a cloaked traveller on the crest of the hill ahead.

As the wagon grew closer to the solitary figure, bent far to the side by the weight of his load, Kestrel smiled with satisfaction. The cloak was turned inside out, but his trained eye could make out the stitching for the ring logos sewn to the other side. The man was a magician on the way back to the Cycloid Guild.

"Do you care for a ride, stranger?" Kestrel called out as the wagon drew abreast. "Your load looks heavy and you in the need of a rest."

The magician looked up with eyes dancing with suspicion. He was short and broad like a plowman, rather than shallow-shouldered like so many practitioners of the arts. "I can manage my own way," he said. "There is no assistance that I need."

"Not even if you carry an imp bottle?" Kestrel said. "I recognize the shape, straight sides of wide diameter and the narrow neck."

"What do you want?" the magician growled. He stopped and gently set the bottle on the ground. With his free hand he reached for a small dagger strapped to his belt.

"Why, to buy, of course." Kestrel pulled the wagon to a halt. He reached back under the covering and pulled out the wizard's robe Phoebe had abandoned for the dress of the countess. He pointed at the logos of flame. "We travel simply to avoid notice, just as you do. What is the price that you would set in your guild? We will pay double—double provided that it can be proven to be truly impregnable to the weaving of simple imps."

121

The magician examined Kestrel critically and then Astron at his side. His eyes widened as Kestrel pulled away Astron's hood and he saw the fine network of scales.

Kestrel reached into his pocket and pulled out the remaining brandels of the Brythian wizards. With a flourish he flung them at the magician's feet. "Double the price, and three pieces of gold more for the trouble of the demonstration." He paused and smiled. "Just think how satisfied the other masters of the guild will be when you report to them that you have sold the bottle, not for the going price, but one and a half times that amount. Twice for you but only one and a half passed on to the coffers of your guild. It would serve them right. You are the one who has had to toil in the blackness while they wined and dined in anticipation of the fruits of your labor."

The magician looked down to his feet at the gold coins sparkling in the torchlight and grunted agreement. He stooped to his knees, rapidly retrieved the brandels, and thrust them into a purse next to his knife.

"That the bottle is a true prison of imps there can be no doubt," he said. "Magic rituals lead either to perfect results or else to nothing. And I have performed the last step myself—alone in a flat field when the moon was at nadir. I completed the square of numbers precisely in the order prescribed. The cymbals were struck thrice and then buried.

"And then the glass hummed of its own volition, sucking strength from the cosmic spheres and forming unbreakable crystal. It would not have rung unless my actions were the perfect last steps to a perfect ritual, producing a jar like the imps it will surround, one that will last eternally."

Kestrel watched the magician draw the dagger from his side and flip it over in his hand. Pommel first he crashed it down onto the side of the bottle, causing it to ring the seductive harmony of the finest bell. A second time he banged on the glass and then a third but the bottle wall held firm and did not shatter.

"See," the magician said. "That is no ordinary con-

122

tainer but one that has been transformed by the skills of my craft. You cannot break it or its stopper. More proof than that surely you do not need."

"Nevertheless, this purchase is not one of little consequence," Kestrel said smoothly. "Surely you cannot deny us the assurance of putting imps in the bottle and seeing that they cannot escape."

"Well, if I were the buyer, then perhaps I would want to know for sure that—" the magician began.

"Wait a moment," Astron said suddenly. "There is the matter of volition. Only the wizards that command the cloud that pursues can will them into what they know to be a trap."

"I have thought about that," Kestrel said. "We will just have to hope that the motives that drive your kind are not so different than those that push upon men."

"What do you mean?"

"Are not imps noted for their curiosity?" Kestrel asked.

"Except for their vanity, it is the strongest of traits," Astron said. "They are always chattering that their abilities are the equal of the mightiest of djinns. But their inclinations have nothing to do with control of their will. There is no—"

"Such is what I have heard from the writings in the sagas," Kestrel said, "and such I will use. The only other thing I need is a lure. What is it that would attract them the most?"

"In the realm of men? Why, vinegar, I suppose. At least it is said you can catch more imps with it than with honey."

"Then vinegar it is," Kestrel said. He motioned the magician into the wagon and grabbed the large bottle as it was pushed upward. "We will hasten to the next village and buy a few coppers' worth." He looked at Astron's wrinkled nose and his smile broadened. "Observe carefully, cataloguer," he said. "We will see if there might be another power that operates among the realm of demonkind, another power than what you call your weaving."

* * *

Kestrel shifted uncomfortably in the tree and pushed Astron slightly to the side. It would have been better if the demon had not come, but his curiosity could not be thwarted.

Astron looked down at the bottle directly below them in the nearly empty field and whispered in Kestrel's ear. "In the first place," he said, "this is no hiding place at all. Surely they will spot you to be here as if you were on the ground. In the second, even if one were in the bottle, you could not spring downward and insert the stopper quickly enough before he flew to safety."

"I know," Kestrel whispered back. "Those are exactly the things I am counting on. Now be quiet and watch. The sooner we settle down, the quicker they will come."

He looked back to the road in the distance where the wagon was parked. The magician leaned against one of the wheels talking to Phoebe and seemed totally distracted. Quickly Kestrel glanced out over the field. In a perimeter perhaps the span of a dozen men, small fires burned at each of the corners of a pentagram under bubbling pots of lilac water that scented the air with a sweet fragrance. Imps hated it, Phoebe had said, and oftentimes wizards used bouquets of flowers to keep them away when they probed for more powerful demons through the flame.

Kestrel sighted the distance between the fires for the last time and judged that they were properly placed, enough of a nuisance to make approaching the bottle under the tree a challenge but not so close together that the imps could not do so if they strongly wished.

For a longer time than Kestrel could judge, nothing happened. Then a single twinkle of light swept in from the distance and hovered for a moment over the open mouth of the bottle. The imp circled the glass jar twice and then darted up to within a few feet of where Kestrel and Astron hid in the branches of the tree.

The small demon hovered with his wings buzzing. Kestrel could see the tiny eyes staring into the foliage. Then abruptly it abandoned its scrutiny and plunged in a straight line to the ground. With tiny hops, each about the span of a man's stride, it measured the distance to the bottle.

The imp looked back up into the tree and then along the path it had traversed on the ground. Kestrel saw it rub a bony hand along a pockmarked jaw and its eyes squint shut, apparently in thought.

A second imp appeared near the top of the tree, buzzing within inches of Kestrel's back. With a shrill cry it dropped to the ground and hopped toward the bottle as had the other. The first sprite soared skyward as soon as he heard the shriek, shouting what sounded like insults as the second laboriously jumped along the ground.

The second imp stuck out his tongue at the first. He turned his attention to the bottle at his side. Cautiously, he paced around the perimeter, extending each foot lightly and testing the firmness of the ground. He reached forward, placed a palm on the smoothness of the glass, and then immediately jumped backward as the first imp dove within a wingspan of his head, laughing raucously.

The second imp waved some gesture that Kestrel did not recognize and glared at the first until it stopped and hovered at the height of the tree. Apparently satisfied, the second vaulted up to the open mouth of the bottle and peered inside. He hesitated only a moment, extending first a finger, then an arm, and finally his entire head into the smooth walls of the mouth. All he would see, Kestrel knew, was the large cup of vinegar that had been carefully placed inside.

The sprite lowered himself to the bottom of the bottle and repeated the same slow approach to the small bowl. Squinting in the dim light to make out the detail, Kestrel saw him stick a finger into the cup and then touch it to his lips. A moment passed and then the imp abandoned his caution altogether. He plunged his head into the liquid and began loudly slurping.

The first imp apparently saw what was happening as well. He dove into the bottle, knocking the other one aside. Like two children fighting over a single toy, they began pushing each other away from the tasty prize. Al-

125

most instantly, a half dozen more sprites appeared from
the distance. In a rush, they raced into the bottle one by
one, bowling those that preceded into the hard glass
walls and lunging for the cup of vinegar for themselves.

"Do you see any more?" Kestrel tensed.

"None at the moment," Astron said. "But—"

Kestrel did not wait to hear more. He dropped from
the tree to the ground with the stopper in his hand just as
the imps had decided he would. One that had been
knocked the farthest from the cup of vinegar spotted his
motion and shrieked a warning. In unison the imps
stopped their fighting and took to flight. Like bees discharging from a shaking hive they buzzed up the height
of the bottle into the neck.

Kestrel sprinted to the jar as fast as he could, but, as
he had guessed, he did not have to hurry. The buzz of the
imps died in the grunt of crashing bodies. In a tangled
mass they wedged into the neck and could ascend no
further. The ones underneath the first cursed and pushed
against those above but to no avail. Kestrel dropped in
the glass stopper before a single one could escape.

"Why, that is most remarkable." Astron jumped to the
ground after Kestrel. "They are trapped just as surely as
if you were a wizard who could command their will."

"As I told you earlier," Kestrel said, brushing his
hands in satisfaction, "knowledge of the push and tugs
that compel one to action can indeed be a great power.
Evidently, beings are the same everywhere, whether
they are men or demon."

Astron started to say more, but instead suddenly
pointed at the jar. Kestrel's satisfaction evaporated. A
single glow of light flittered in from the south, made two
circles of the bottle, and then with a burst of speed raced
away in the direction from which it had come.

"A straggler," Astron said. "One that was distracted
and did not fly in formation with the rest. Imps are well
known for their lack of discipline. Perhaps that is a fact
that you should have utilized as well."

"Never mind that," Kestrel snapped. "He has seen
what has happened. You can bet that he will streak back

and tell the wizards where we are without fail."

Kestrel began running back to the wagon. "Come! At least I know the thinking of my own kind better. I suspect there is very little time before some of your more powerful cousins will be visiting us on this very spot."

Kestrel waved to the magician as he passed the master running into the field. "We do not want it after all," he called out, "but you can keep the imps to demonstrate to the next buyer in exchange for your trouble."

Kestrel pushed past the openmouthed magician without bothering to offer any more explanations. He clambered onto the wagon and lent an arm to help up Phoebe. He whipped the back of the horse. In a sudden cloud of dust, the three again were on the road.

Kestrel pushed the horse recklessly, not bothering to make sure of holes and ruts before he chose his path. The more distance they put between themselves and the field, the longer they would have before rediscovery by demons who would not so easily be fooled.

"I do not deny it, mortal," Astron said, after they had bounced along for more than an hour in silence. Kestrel glanced sideways in the torchlight and saw the demon's nose relaxing into a straight line.

"You have shown me that there is more to learn in the realm of men than the things that can be described easily in my catalogues." As he continued, he looked Kestrel in the eye. "But also I wonder," he said. "I wonder if any amount of your tugging and pulling would have gotten the lead balloon off the ground."

## CHAPTER ELEVEN

# Archimage and Skyskirr

THE race up the coast was a blur. There was no time for
the luxury of sleep or even food for the horse. How long
it had taken, Kestrel could not recall. Through half-open
eyes, he spotted the simple sign that marked the turnoff
from the main road to the ward of the archimage. With
aching arms, he steered the wagon onto the narrow
gravel lane that wound into the low hills on his left.

After they had climbed to the pass between the nearest peaks, he could see down into the valley that lay
between him and higher buttes farther away. Birch and
aspen climbed partway up the hillsides. Tall green
grasses filled the valley floor, waving in the breeze like
ripples on a stagnant pond. One area was cleared of vegetation near the center. In it stood a dozen wooden
cabins arranged in a circle around a two-storey house of
stone. Pulsing bellows like those at the foundry spat
blasts of cold air near the closest. Curls of wizard's
smoke rose from chimneys of the next two in line. Three
spinning energy wheels of the thaumaturges whirled on
the far side of the compound. Next to them, magicians
slowly added spars to a complex latticework in step to
the intricate jingling of hundreds of tiny bells. A few of
the cottages were totally dark, sorcerers' lairs with even
the windows painted black to block out the sun. On the
grounds between the structures, knots of robed masters
argued and gestured as they walked quickly from one
experiment to another.

"I see no high walls or metal gates," Kestrel said.
"Anyone could approach the archimage with no resistance at all."

"There is a little hut at the foot of the road." Phoebe pointed. "I believe one states his reason for calling to a page therein, and he arranges an interview, if it is worthy. As for security, the power and reputation of the archimage is such that he has no need for walls and gates. If not for honorable means, it would be folly to approach."

Kestrel grunted and urged the horse onward. There was as yet no sign of imps or more powerful devils; but, even with having to reestablish the trail, they could not be far behind.

Phoebe reached out and grabbed Kestrel's arm as the wagon gathered speed down the last incline. "Before— before we meet the archimage and I am possibly questioned about my craft, Kestrel, I must understand all that has happened at my cabin." She lowered her eyes. "Perhaps it was something that would embarrass me," she said. "Yes, that is it. The demon made me do something quite unladylike in front of the other wizards. You are too much the gentleman to tell me about it."

Kestrel pulled his lips together in a grim line. He looked at Phoebe's attractiveness in the fancy dress. Despite the fatigue, he felt a great longing. Without the immediate rush, it would be easy to say the words that would result in another conquest of a master of the arts.

But the well-spun phrases would not come, not even ones that set the foundation for later. Phoebe's apparent trust was too overwhelming. How could he deceive her as he had done to all the others when what she wanted had so little value?

"The past cannot be changed," Kestrel said, "no matter how much one might wish it. If you were embarrassed, would you really want to know?"

"No, I would not," Phoebe said after a moment. "Not if it caused me to lock all that I am behind a barrier through which no one else can see."

"What do you mean?" Kestrel asked.

"You know full well," Phoebe said. "For the length of this headlong flight, I have been chattering away, telling you everything about myself that came to mind. Perhaps it took my thoughts from what would happen if we are caught, but I have said much nonetheless."

"I did not wish it otherwise," Kestrel said. "If you suspect that I was bored but just being polite, put your mind at ease. I enjoy your company."

"And so about the wizard you can now recite volumes," Phoebe continued. "About the woodcutter, what can be said other than that he indeed did at one time chop some trees?"

Kestrel slumped over the reins, wishing the entry hut all the closer. Mixed with everything else, he felt an onrush of discomfort. It was not enough that he refrain from further deception. Phoebe wanted more. She was asking no less than that he reveal things that long ago he had vowed never to share again.

"I can be only one of many possibilities," he said while continuing to look straight ahead. "Why me and not some other? One more suited to your station."

Phoebe tightened her grip on Kestrel's arm and pulled herself closer to him. "It gets to be lonely in the cabin of a wizard," she said. "Lonelier than you might otherwise believe. And at first, I admit my thoughts were for a brief interlude. You appeared far better than most that I had seen in the past year.

"But there was something else," she said. "Something I saw behind the eyes of one who professed to be a simple woodcutter."

"Do not probe too deeply," Kestrel said. "You might not like what you will find."

"No, my first impression has been confirmed." Phoebe reached up and turned Kestrel's face to hers. "I saw the excitement when you explained to me how we would cross the border. I witnessed the swordsman rushing to defend when he was outnumbered two to one. There is perhaps more to Kestrel the woodcutter than he dares admit even to himself."

"Does not the ritual prescribe that the male pursues and the female demurs?" Astron poked his head out from under the wagon's canopy. "Or does the fact that the woman is the one that wears the logo of a wizard alter

130

that? It is no wonder there is so much anguish and confusion in the matter. The variations are too many for one to keep track of them all."

Phoebe pulled back her arms, like a child caught in the fruit larder. She frowned at Astron as she dropped her hands to her lap. Kestrel felt a wave of relief and then a twinge of annoyance. He could work out his feelings without any help from the demon.

He darted a glance at Phoebe. No, perhaps it was best that Astron had come forward. What he would have said if he were forced to answer at this moment he did not know. A silence descended on the three. For the rest of the distance to the entry hut no one spoke.

When they arrived, Kestrel glanced over his shoulder and then back to Astron. The demon shook his head, indicating that he detected nothing. Kestrel vaulted from the wagon and into the hut. Soon all three stood facing an ancient page, bald-pated with splotchy skin, sitting behind a high desk. His folded hands rested on a huge appointment book bound in gilded leather.

Kestrel returned the page's stare and glanced quickly about the small room, trying to seize on the story that would get them immediately to the archimage.

"Elezar," Astron said before anyone else could speak. "I have a message from Prince Elezar for the archimage that should be heard at once."

The page looked at Astron through half-closed eyes. He leafed through the pages to the very front of the book and scanned a list of names. "Elezar," the page repeated, "Elezar." Suddenly he stopped and his eyes opened wide. "Ah, exactly what is the—the nature of this prince?"

"He is a demon," Astron said. "A mighty ruler of over a hundred djinns."

The attitude of the page immediately shifted from bored indifference to obsequious concern. He climbed from his high stool and motioned the trio to follow.

"It is the foremost of the archimage's instructions," he said. "Certain visitors are to receive priority over the others who come asking no more than a boon. But above

131

all else, master Alodar has written that he is to be interrupted on any news of Elezar the demon in the realm of men. Quickly, follow me."

In a moment's time, they were across the courtyard to the house of stone and ushered into a large library, brimming with scrolls and books of crackling parchment. A ladder was propped on each of the four walls to reach shelves that stood beyond the grasp of the tallest man. Three round tables were also covered with piles of paper. On a fourth stood a bubbling retort and convoluted paths of glass tubing. A model of a crane and small blocks occupied the fifth, next to a clump of bar magnets and needles of steel. Next to it, the light of a single candle worked its way through tiny slits and a series of lenses that alternately expanded and contracted its radiance.

Kestrel noticed Astron's membranes flick down when he saw all of the books. After the page left to find the archimage, the demon stood motionless for a long while. Then slowly, with a delicate reverence, he approached the closest table, reached out and touched the gilt letters that spelled "Practical Thaumaturgy" on the volume on top. Suddenly oblivious to the reason they had come, the demon gently opened the cover and stared at the penstrokes on the first page.

A doorway deeper into the interior of the cottage clicked softly. Kestrel turned to see who entered. His face stiffened in surprise.

"We are manipulants of the skyskirr," said the first of four thin beings who filed into the library. "We understand the astonishment that shows on your face. Many of the strange happenings of your realm affect us in a similar way. Be at peace. All that comes to pass is guided by the great right hand."

Kestrel shook his head. Astron looked almost human. The imps that had been captured in the bottle were no more than gross copies of a normally shaped child. But these four were distinctly alien, unlike anyone else he had ever seen. They were tall and slender, impossibly thin for a man. Large, puffy lips protruded from faces of bony

132

gray planes. Primitive jewelry hung from ears and noses. Each wore a simple loincloth coiled about his hips.

"You too are djinns from Astron's realm?" Kestrel asked. He backed into one of the ladders and pulled Phoebe protectively to his side.

"No, we are skyskirr," the first repeated. "On our lithons we sail through the 'hedron's sky. The wind whistles with our passage. With graceful arabesques, we circle the larger stones and from them scavenge what the great right hand provides.

"Our realm is self-contained, as distinct from that of the demons as you judge yours to be. We must use the might of a djinn and the intermediary of the flame to travel from our universe to here."

Kestrel ran his hand over his mouth. Not from the realm of demons but elsewhere beyond the flame, he thought. He glanced quickly at Astron. Yes, other realms, just as the demon had said.

"Besides those of men and demons there is a third?" Phoebe asked. "I have heard whispers of such a thing and of metalaws behind those that we know so well."

"Indeed, it is true," the first skyskirr said. "For us the laws of magic are different; we, in fact, change them all the time. Our visit here and now is to see if your thaumaturgy is a craft that will be useful besides the ones we already know."

"Of course, there are consequences in any such venture," the third suddenly said. "Perhaps it was the intent of the great right hand that such knowledge we were not meant to possess." The skyskirr pounded a shovel he was carrying against the floor and then touched the blade to the chest of the fourth, who slumped almost hidden behind the other three.

Kestrel looked at the last skyskirr for the first time. The deep-set eyes seemed not to focus but dart almost independently about the room. A thick drool ran from one corner of his mouth. With his hands, he picked at his loincloth, removing small pieces of lint that were not really there.

"Mortonzel has seen too much of gently curving horizons," the third skyskirr continued. "He has felt for too long the oppressive pull of the great lithon that binds all of you humans. Only occasionally are there winds to caress the full length of his hair." He turned and poked with the blade of his shovel at the chest of the first. "Now even the archimage dismisses us for something he says is of greater importance. It is a sign of the great right hand, I say. Let us begone. I feel the sickness of mind beginning to bubble within me as well. Build the flame, Purdanel, and summon the djinn that will return us to whence we came."

Purdanel looked quickly at the second skyskirr and then around the room. For a moment his eyes rested on Astron, who was slowly turning the pages of the book. "You may have the volume," he said. "It was to be a gift from the archimage but I think it will provide no value in the realm where the lithons fly."

Without waiting for an answer he grunted and pounded his own shovel twice against the floor. Purposefully, he marched out of the room. The other three skyskirr followed, the last being gently led.

Kestrel shook his head again. Lithons, the great right hand, soaring through the sky—it sounded most bizarre indeed. His intuition had been confirmed. If the skyskirr reacted so badly to the realm of men, then surely he would fare as poorly if transported to where they were from.

But before he could ponder more, a second door opened as quietly as the first. Someone else entered the room.

"I am Alodar, the archimage," the newcomer said. "Tell me quickly. What is the news of the sighting of Elezar the golden? Few know even the sound of his name. What is it that you have seen?"

Kestrel jerked his thoughts back to why they had come. He watched the archimage as he approached. Streaks of white ran through fine yellow-brown hair. Furrows of concentration had become permanently etched at the bridge of the nose. The purple robe hung simply over a slight frame. On one sleeve were the logos of all five of the crafts.

Kestrel looked most intensely at the eyes. They were alive with intelligence and a driving will shone through. He felt a surge of doubt about what he hoped to accomplish. The archimage was not one to be either easily fooled or tempted.

"It has been almost thirty years," Alodar continued. "Thirty years since our one and only encounter." The furrow above his nose deepened. "And the truth of it is that one is sufficient for any man. For all this time, I have hoped there would not be the need for another."

"There is also the matter of the wizards of Brythia," Kestrel said carefully. He pointed at Phoebe and her robe that she carried over her arm. "They are ill-disposed toward this master who has travelled a great distance to seek your aid in clearing her name. Ah, hers and the ones who accompany her as well."

Alodar stopped his rush into the room and quickly looked about. "Forgive my lack of hospitality," he said. "Find a chair to your liking. It is just that dealing with the likes of Elezar is so urgent that—"

Alodar stopped and his eyes narrowed. "What demon is this?" he asked, pointing at Astron. "Which of you have him under control and why is he dressed as a man?"

Astron looked up from the book he was perusing. He threw back his hood and tilted his head slightly in Alodar's direction. "My will is bound only to the service of my prince," Astron said. "I am Elezar's messenger, bidding that you contact him at once through the flame."

Alodar frowned. "Elezar can pass through the barrier only after many lesser demons have preceded him. Since our first battle, all wizards everywhere interact with great caution so that never do too many come through to our realm at any one time."

"Contact only, not passage, is what my prince desires." Astron stepped forward. "He is in great peril from his own kind and seeks out aid from the only one he acknowledges as greater."

135

"Few enough know even the name of the prince," Alodar said. "But perhaps you have somehow learned. If you are truly from the golden one, then you will have knowledge that others would not."

"His eyes are green but flecked with gold," Astron said. "His stature is but fingerwidths greater than mine. Hooded, he, too, could pass unnoticed in the realm of men. His—"

Alodar waved Astron to stop. He slumped into a chair at one of the crowded tables, then looked back at Kestrel with a a weary smile. "I would much rather handle a squabble among a dozen councils of wizards," he said, "or spend more time trying to squeeze one more secret from the lore recorded in this room." He arched his back and stretched. "But three decades of running from one crisis to another eventually take their toll. The glamor of being world-saver wears thin after perhaps the dozenth time."

Kestrel did not respond. He looked out of one of the high windows, but still saw no sign of any imps or djinns. There might be time enough after all. Soon he would learn which of Astron's words were no more true than the fancies that he himself wove. Hopefully from what he discovered he would be able to spin his own scheme to turn aside the Brythian wizards. He glanced at Alodar's intense expression, deciding how much his tale should dare.

"If you would assist," Alodar said to Phoebe, his reluctance apparently shoved aside without a moment's more thought. "I will light the fire in the hearth and attempt to see if what this demon says is true." He pointed to a well just outside one of the windows. "But if he has warped his words, be ready with a full bucket. I will want the flames doused before any great harm can be done."

Phoebe stepped forward cautiously. "I—I am not sure that I am worthy, archimage," she said. "Although I won the logo of flame fairly, even the small devil who is with us I could not command."

"I am the one who will challenge Elezar." Alodar

136

shook his head. "Such a task I would wish upon no other. I do not need your skills as a master, just a quickness of eye and arm."

Phoebe let out her breath. She scowled, apparently annoyed at herself for the image that she presented. With a quick nod she scurried to do the archimage's bidding.

Kestrel and Astron watched the archimage deftly bring a simple flame to life in the stone-lined fireplace along the north wall. Alodar left for a moment and then returned with some powder that he flicked into the blaze. The fire immediately billowed and flashed into a rainbow of color.

As Phoebe returned with the water, Alodar pulled his chair directly in front of the growing flames. Making himself comfortable, he stared into their hypnotic dance. For a long moment, nothing more happened and Kestrel shifted his weight from one leg to another. His eyes darted around the room. He wondered about the propriety of taking a second chair for himself.

Then, just as he had about made up his mind to move, the flames flashed green and an eerie voice whispered from out of the hearth into the room.

"Ah, master, you have come." Kestrel heard a gentle sighing. "Astron has done well for his prince."

"He is so weak!" Alodar exclaimed. "This is hardly the one with whom I wrestled so long ago."

The archimage paused a moment, then immediately shook off his astonishment.

"What is it you wish?" he said. "We have decided long ago, Elezar, that the affairs of the realm of men were no longer to be your concern."

"So they are not," Elezar replied. "But I am one prince among many. I maneuver to keep the interests of the others away by your command and have succeeded because of my own great power."

The fire spit and sputtered.

"My prince has not recovered from his wound." Astron took a step toward the hearth. "And by the weakness of his voice I would deduce that he has received another."

137

"But consider this, archimage," Elezar continued, apparently not hearing the voice of his cataloguer. "If my own power were to wane, who then would keep the other princes from coveting the realm of men as I did myself? And unlike creatures of my kind, you age, master. Are you ready again to undergo the test of wills that you undertook in your prime?"

"What other prince?" Alodar leaned forward in his chair. "Who else in the realm of daemon focuses his thoughts in a way that should not be his concern?"

"There is Gaspar," Elezar said. "He has proven far more potent an adversary than I did first suspect. My own domain he has ripped from the void. And before his attack a full dozen other princes he had previously allied to his cause. My hiding places in the blackness he has found one by one. The dark node I now occupy is the last. There is little time left before I am overwhelmed. Do as my messenger directs; you can fight to save the realm of men now or wait till later when the outcome will be more in your disfavor."

Kestrel shook his head. He could barely believe what he was hearing. Imps and sprites or minor devils summoned with anvilwood were one thing, but warring demon princes and archimages were quite another. And evidently Astron's story was correct, just as he had stated from the first. What had he got himself into?

"These events are all very sudden," Alodar said. "I find it hard to believe that one as crafty as you, Elezar, would be reduced to such straits. I will need time to verify if what you say is true."

"Time is the luxury that you do not have, master," the flame whispered with Elezar's voice. "Gaspar hunts not only me but all who serve as well. In the last few ticks of the eon, many imps have crossed the barrier between our realms. Some have been instructed, I know, to track down my cataloguer—track him down so that mightier djinns can pluck off his limbs one by one, just as surely as Gaspar wishes the same fate for me. Each moment you hesitate brings closer the time when you must confront not one demon passing through the flame but more

138

than a score. Discover what must be done before it is too late."

The flame sputtered. Elezar's voice faded into the glow of the hot coals. Kestrel strained to hear more but the whispers of the demon dissolved into indistinctness. Alodar frowned and then turned to look at Astron. "What then is the message of your prince?" he asked. "What would he have me do that would restore him to power and protect the realm of men as well?"

"The prince needs a transporter," Astron said. "One to carry matter between the realms. One whom he trusted you to choose."

"We have little traffic with the realm of the skyskirr," Alodar said. "Ever since the metamagician Jemidon restored our laws to their natural state, the path between the two universes has been opened but rarely. It is merely by chance that you have arrived while some manipulants are also here."

"I do not think it is to the skyskirr that we must go," Astron said. "Their realm has little more diverse matter than my own. It would be somewhere else instead."

Alodar's eyes narrowed. "There are others, are there not?" he said slowly. "It was of course obvious after I learned of the existence of the 'hedron, but I dared not seek the definite proof. Contact with one other realm was disruptive enough. It would have been folly to explore too far."

"Yet, just as the number of laws number more than seven," Astron said, "so does the counting of the diverse universes that populate the void, each with its own essence and rituals, distinct from the rest."

Kestrel stirred uncomfortably. The conversation was about things he could well avoid. He would have to divert its course into matters of more direct concern.

"The wizards of Brythia are responsible for the imps of which this—this Prince Elezar speaks," he said. "Restricting the masters from such reckless action might help with your other problem as well."

Alodar nodded absently but kept his attention on Astron. "What else then, demon," he said. "Of what other wonders should I know besides the multitude of realms?"

"There is the ultimate precept," Astron said. "That is what my prince seeks—the ultimate precept, a concept superior to the laws of magic, one transcendent to the metalaws behind them, the answer to the riddle that provides the greatest power of all."

"In which realm does one search for this ultimate of precepts?" Alodar asked.

"Only Palodad knows that," Astron said. "In exchange for bringing him some exotic matter from whence he directs us, he will tell us where to look."

"Palodad, additional realms, ultimate precepts." Alodar's frown deepened. "It is all too much to swallow at one sitting. Perhaps Elezar has constructed what we men call a fantasy and expects somehow to convince us that it is real."

"It is a chance for redemption," Phoebe interrupted suddenly. Kestrel saw that she had placed the bucket of water on the stone floor. Her cheeks were flushed with excitement.

"It came to me while the two of you conversed," she said. "I cannot continue through the rest of my life always blushing in apology for a single failure in my craft. I must strike out again and somehow prove a woman's worth. It is by accomplishment that I will yet show the wizards of my council the meaning of respect. By proven deed will I gain comfort, even in the presence of the archimage of all the crafts." She paused and took a deep breath. "And even though the archimage hesitates, then I will not. Tell me, Astron, is this Palodad strong-willed, like your prince?"

Kestrel bolted across the room. He put his hand on Phoebe's arm and looked over his shoulder at Alodar. "She has not quite recovered from the haste of our journey," he said quickly. "Dismiss her words as merely some nervous prattle."

He spun his head back around and looked at Phoebe intently. "This is no game with imps and sprites," he said. "Did you not hear the words from the flames and see the strange beasts the skyskirr were? Be careful or you will get us into a pit deeper than we presently are."

Kestrel stopped and studied Phoebe's expression. He did not like what he saw.

"Imps and sprites," she shot back. "Is that indeed all you think me capable of? If the need arose, despite your words, would you trust me with more?" She looked away for a moment and then disengaged herself from Kestrel's grip. "I know I stated when we began the journey that the adventure was all that mattered. But how can I be other than the demon's slave, if deep inside you cannot judge me to be your equal?"

Kestrel opened his mouth to speak, but he did not know what to say. For Astron to talk of other realms was his own business. No doubt at the root of his desires was the wish to return safely home, regardless of where that really was. And the affairs of demon princes were certainly the concerns of one such as the archimage. But Phoebe was another matter altogether. He glanced quickly at her sudden determination and shook his head. He must have been right when he first explained her words. It was the fatigue of the journey. In a calmer moment she would see the folly of dealing with such immensities just as clearly as he.

But Phoebe ignored his outstretched arm. She grabbed the sack of powder still at Alodar's feet and threw another handful into the dying flame. Thrusting the pouch into her cape, she took a deep breath as the fire roared back to life. "Palodad," she said. "Palodad, come forth. I command you to submit to my will."

"Who tugs and pulls at the one who reckons?" a deep voice suddenly boomed from the hearth in response. "He is no mighty djinn who can be commanded to burst asunder great rocks or wield bolts of awesome lightning. Begone! Let him be! Wrestle with someone else, someone more worthy of your mettle."

"If you are named Palodad, then you are the one I seek," Phoebe said. "Submit now to your master so that you might answer the questions that I have about realms other than my own."

141

"It is not the one who reckons whose tendrils of thought intertwine with yours. He is my prince. I speak on his behalf for all who come asking at the doors of his domain."

Kestrel hesitated, not knowing whether to rush forward and pull Phoebe away or let her be, so her concentration would not be disturbed.

Astron released one hand from the book he still clutched to his chest and tugged on Alodar's purple sleeve. "If the one that has been touched serves old Palodad, then it is just as well," he said. "He can learn from the old one and tell us in turn in which realm we are to seek—tell us what is to be brought back in fulfillment of the bargain to the one who has him duty-bound."

Kestrel saw Astron shudder. "In fact, the intimacy of mind is probably all the better with a minion than with the old one himself," the demon said.

Alodar's expression did not change for a moment, but then he nodded. He indicated for Phoebe to continue.

"Whose mind then do I touch?" Phoebe said. "Speak your name as token of submission to my will. Tell me how it will be that you will convey Palodad's thoughts. Be swift about it. There are many assembled here and the waste of time is great."

The flame flashed hotter. Kestrel felt a blast of warmth on his cheeks.

"I am Camonel, the one who carries," the voice rumbled deeply. "Prince Palodad has instructed that indeed I do submit to what you ask. We need not exercise the ritual of struggle. Feel my thoughts. I do not resist. He can speak through me as if my mouth were his own."

There was a brief pause while the fire danced wildly and then the demon behind the flames spoke again.

"Time, did you say time?" The words rolled out from the hearth. Kestrel heard what he thought was laughter and saw Astron take a cautious step backward. "Time—there is no way either to save or waste it." The flame spat and crackled. "It flows regardless, marching past to be lost forever. Do not speak to me of what even the most powerful of wizards cannot bend to his will." The laughter boomed again, this time more forceful, echoing from the stone walls and filling the room with sound.

"The riddle of the ultimate precept." Alodar forced his voice through the din. "Ask him if it is no more than a cleverly worded ruse on the part of Elezar the prince to seek again control of the realm of men?"

"Elezar, the one who is golden, is but a few time-ticks away from being but a memory," the voice answered through the flame. "His domain is gone, dissipated into a fine dust that slowly drifts in the realm. Only one dark node remains his to command and soon it too will be found. I will record in my domain his many exploits; but, except for that, he will soon be forgotten like the rest. His only hope lies in looking elsewhere—elsewhere in a realm for which I alone have calculated the identity."

"Then where is this place?" Alodar persisted.

"Will you agree to bring back to me the pollen of the giant harebell flower in exchange for what I will tell?"

"I will make no—" Alodar began.

"Yes," Phoebe interrupted. "Yes, tell us and we will go."

"No, you have no authority," Alodar cut back in. "Wait, Palodad. Only I am—"

This time the words of the archimage were put off by a second blast of radiation from the hearth. A billowing ball of orange flame rolled into the room, pushing Kestrel backward and to the side. A heavy black smoke coursed along the stone floor and an acrid smell stung Kestrel's nose. He saw a large brown djinn stoop to enter the room from the fireplace, thick scales covering limbs that pulsed with tight muscles. The tips of leathery wings scraped against the slope of the ceiling, the fire behind shining through between a network of blackened veins. A single row of coarse hair sat atop eyes deep-set in rugged and angular bone. Tiny nostrils flared with each breath above a mouth distorted to the side in a permanent sneer.

"I am Camonel." The demon's deep voice rumbled much louder than it had on the other side of the flame.

"Palodad instructs me to transport whomever you have selected into the realm of the fey."

"The fey," Alodar said. "What manner of place is that?"

Camonel's deep laugh again filled the room with sound. "You men know of it in your fantasies. Underhill kingdoms, trilling pipes with melancholy airs, creatures you think no larger than the smallest imps."

"Not the realm of the fey," Astron interrupted. "They are all wizards, every one. It is no place for a cataloguer who is merely striving to serve his prince. Why can it not be someplace gentle, as is the realm of men?"

"I am ready," Phoebe said. With her chin thrust high, she stepped forward to where the djinn stood in front of the hearth.

"Wait," Kestrel heard himself shout. "Wait, Phoebe, this is madness. Think of what you are doing. You cannot follow that monster, aided by no more than the likes of Astron."

"Why, I did not intend to." Phoebe looked back. "It is to be the three of us, just as from the beginning."

Kestrel lunged to a halt and stared. This indeed was madness. The affairs of archimage and demon prince might be of great importance to some, but they were no concern of his. Let some other so-called hero step forth for the honor and the glory. In the end, the rewards would turn to bitter ashes. The one who jumped through the hoops would find that he had been manipulated merely for the benefit of others who would not take the risks themselves. This was no role for Kestrel the woodcutter. There was nothing whatever in the bargain for him.

Kestrel looked at Phoebe as she slowly drew closer to the waiting djinn, her nose clamped shut to hold out the pungent odor. His thoughts tumbled in confusion. He was here only to clear his name and perhaps win a few pieces of gold from the archimage so he could boast of it in the tavern.

But there was Phoebe as well. Her life probably was forfeit as soon as the leathery wings closed around her willing frame. He thought of his rescue from the foundry of the alchemist, the pleasure when she had pressed against his side, and her insistence in seeing good in him when there was none to be found.

While Kestrel hesitated, there was a sudden commotion at the door. Four wizards in sweat-dampened robes burst into the room. "There they are," the first one shouted. "The very ones who conspired to cheat the august council of Brythia. Come forward, Maspanar and the rest. We have caught them at last."

Alodar looked sharply at the intrusion, but before he could speak, the high windows along the wall above the doorway shattered in a spray of tiny shards. Two demons almost as large as the one in the hearth plunged into the room, circling overhead with crackles of blue flame pulsing from their fingertips.

One of the wizards who rushed in added his voice to the commotion. "Please forgive the interruption, master archimage. Forgive the interruption, but we come to rectify a great wrong to our craft."

"Yes, and since I have had time to ponder it," another one said, "I recognize the one bearing the rucksack from before—some five years ago in Laudia to the south." He pointed at Kestrel, his face beet-red with anger. "A swindle then of my hard-won gold, just as it was at her cabin. Do not be deceived, archimage. Their words are smooth, but carry not a word of truth, not even the ones of the demons that they command."

One of the wizards raced up to Phoebe and tugged at her robe from behind. Kestrel slapped his arm away. He looked into her eyes and saw her bold composure begin to falter in the confusion. Stepping to the side, he barely missed a searing bolt of blue that crackled from above and sputtered the hard stone at his feet into a bubbly slag.

He saw Alodar move toward Phoebe as well and made up his mind. "It is because of her and no one else," he yelled above the noise of the others. "For her alone, do you understand. Not for the sake of great princes or the well-being of mankind. Only for Phoebe am I doing

145

this. The rest of you matter no more than you did before."

He grabbed Phoebe firmly about the waist. Desperately, he put the thoughts of what might be even worse than smacking lips and soaring lithons out of his mind. Closing his eyes, he pushed her forward toward Camonel's chest. He felt a smothering heaviness on his back as the wings closed around them and Astron's elbow pressed painfully into his side. Almost absently, he grasped the book the demon thrust at him and shoved it over his shoulder into his rucksack. He reeled from the dizziness. Reality seemed to spin. The last thing he remembered was the words of the archimage:

"If they escape, I want the word broadcast even across the sea. Apprehend them at all costs and bring them back. There is to be no place in the realm of men where safety will be theirs."

# PART THREE

*The Realm of the Fey*

CHAPTER TWELVE

## *Rings of Power*

ASTRON watched the djinn vanish back into the flame.
He glanced at Kestrel and Phoebe and saw what he more
or less expected. Both stood transfixed in wide-eyed
wonder. He remembered how his own stembrain had
seized control on his first visit and how he had barely hid
in time.

The trio stood next to one of three small fires, beside
a stream that flowed between the gently rising slope of a
rustic glade. The hillsides were covered with a carpet of
thick grass, each blade the size of Astron's legs. Scattered here and there were huge flowers of red and gold,
towering into the sky on giant stems from clumps of
thick foliage. The proportions were all wrong, but in the
realm of men they would be called foxglove, white-
thorne, primrose, and thyme. A ring of mushrooms, each
as big as a small hut, circled the hillsides in a single precise line halfway up the slopes. On the crests, the flowering bushes merged into a thick forest of glistening leaves.

No one else appeared to be present, but behind them
on the bank stood a large granite-gray boulder with what
looked like a wooden door in the side. The trilling of
distant pipes blended with the sigh of a gentle breeze.

Astron pointed to the hillcrest. Gently, he guided the
other two upward and into the shadowy cover. They
moved perhaps fifty steps and then ducked beneath a
low-lying leaf that was easily the size of the largest djinn.
The soft sky glow that was everywhere the same winked
out into inky blackness. The click of large insects in the
distance blended with the crunch of lichen underfoot.
Astron sniffed the fungal pungency of his surroundings

149

and waited for his eyes to adjust to the darkness.

The canopy of leaves was not complete. After a moment, Astron could see the diffuse light from the pale blue sky trickle between jagged edges and paint the thin spots between the huge, webby veins with an iridescent glow. Behind him perhaps some ten paces, Astron knew, was a coarse and woody trunk that soared as high into the sky as the tallest structure in the realm of men. Thick emerald branches cantilevered out into a shower of leaves that hung nearly to the ground. Between the stem and the circling umbrella of foliage was the shelter in which they hid. One had to proceed cautiously in the realm of the fey, much more so than in the worlds of men.

"Where are we?" Kestrel finally found his voice. "And look at the size of this—this ragwort! What kind of giants are we among?"

"We were lucky we arrived when we did," Astron said as he retrieved the book of thaumaturgy from Kestrel's rucksack. "From the looks of things, the ring has not yet begun to form."

He wrinkled his nose, wondering what to do next. Somewhere in this realm, according to Palodad, was the answer to the riddle. But beyond that, there was no clue. And from the tone of his prince's voice, what little time had been left was almost totally gone.

Astron felt the tug of his stembrain, but wrestled it into submission. All of the imps that had pursued him in the realm of men did not help matters. And in the ward of the archimage, two colossal djinns had appeared as well. With all the traffic between the realms, Gaspar could not help but be close behind. It would be a race to see if he or Elezar would be the first to fall.

And what of the humans? At least one would be needed to wrest the harebell pollen through the barrier when the time came, but what would happen after that? Their own realm had grown increasingly inhospitable, and his was no place for any other kind.

He saw Phoebe draw near Kestrel, and the woodcutter put his arm about her waist. The crease in Astron's nose deepened. He had been with these two far longer than with any other mortals and he had learned many things. But if he were asked to explain their behavior to his prince, he would not be able to do so.

The one called Kestrel could speak of things that had no existence whatsoever in the reality of any of the realms. After the flight from the cabin of the wizard, he had seemed reluctant to continue the journey to the archimage. Then, after the terms of their agreement had been satisfied, he had continued the quest through the flame, not in response to the command of any prince, but apparently of his own volition. Despite these contradictions, Kestrel had the skill to manipulate a half-dozen imps as if he were a practiced wizard. There was much more to be learned from this mortal and new experiences to be felt and tasted before their journey together was over.

Astron looked at Phoebe, who was smiling at Kestrel in the dimness. A bonding was growing between the two —perhaps even the one that men wrote so much about in their sagas. What could be so different from the duty to couple with a broodmother whenever a prince commanded?

"I knew you would come," Phoebe said.

"Yes, and evidently now we must see it to the end." Kestrel answered. "Instead of merely weaving a story for the archimage, all we have to do is solve a demon's riddle, discover the most powerful natural law of them all, transport harebell pollen, whatever that is, across a flaming barrier, and restore a prince to power, thereby saving the entire realm of men. Then we might have a chance somehow to return to the archimage and convince him that we were right all along."

Phoebe laughed. "You left out the part about a female wizard proving her worth," she said.

Kestrel snorted. "At least it does not appear quite as bad as I had imagined. Except for the size of things, this could well be a sheltered valley in any of the the kingdoms that border the great sea. Once we understand better what goes on here, we just might survive after all."

Astron looked out onto the glade a second time. The trill of the pipes was louder, and soon there was motion on the crest across the way. A row of flute players bobbed into view. Behind them, several rows of dancers were leaping in unison to the sad melody that wafted through the air.

The leaves rustled at Astron's side and he smelled a sweet fragrance as Phoebe drew near. "We must be dreaming," she said as she squinted up at the procession. "Look, Kestrel, besides the creatures of a childhood tale, what else could they be?"

Astron looked intently at the procession. The pipers and dancers were drawing close enough that rough features could be seen. The tallest would tower two heads above Astron, but a weighing scale would tip in the demon's favor. Slender limbs protruded from tunics of deep green, and long delicate fingers arched gracefully over the shafts of the flutes. Tumbling curls of gold bounced above delicate features that gave no hint of gender. They were lithe and thin, like the skyskirr, but somehow shrouded in a delicate beauty, rather than a repulsiveness that made men want to turn away.

The step of the pipers was light, and those of the dancers lighter still. In impossibly long glides, they darted from one point of the slope to another, hovering in midleap till they barely touched the ground.

"Men know of the fey?" Astron asked. "The words of the archimage lead one to believe that this realm should be as new to your kind as was that of the skyskirr some few time-ticks ago."

"Only in legend," Kestrel whispered back. "Tales for wee ones to send them to sleep. Strange beckoning music that one must at all costs avoid. Outwelling light from deep forest mounds. Tiny enough to hide in the bowl of a flower or under a curling leaf—not the size of a man; the scale is all wrong."

Kestrel stopped and darted a quick look around at his surroundings. Cautiously he reached upward and stroked the fine hairs that lined the underside of the leaf over-

152

head. "Legend," he muttered, "a coincidence. It can be no more than that."

Astron saw more ranks come over the crestline of the hill. He spotted the dull sheen of copper and felt the stir of his stembrain. Two more lines of pipers marched in precise step behind the dancers, their faces all grim and unsmiling, and with unsheathed blades attached to their belts. While those before them descended to the stream that transected the glade, the sentrymen fanned out to circle the shallow bowl. In a matter of a few moments, they were standing at attention, a sentry next to each of the toadstools that ringed the glade. One was barely a stone's throw from where Astron and the others hid.

The trilling of the pipes intensified. Astron saw a litter come over the crest of the hill. Surrounded by fluttering attendants, what could only be the equivalent of a prince's carriage jostled down the slope. The one inside was dressed in a tunic like the rest, but fancy embroideries of brilliant reds decorated a green deeper than that worn by the others. A garland of tiny blossoms crowned the brow where the yellow curls had faded to the color of pale straw.

Behind the first ruler came a second and a third, and then a disarray of others, some in clumps of twenty and others in twos and threes. The chatter of many voices began to be heard among the melody of the pipes. Occasionally what Astron thought might be tinkling laughter sounded with the rest. Finally, the litters came to a halt directly in front of the door into the rock. All the music faded away. The richly dressed occupant of the first rose to his feet and spread his arms to the sky. His face showed the first signs of age, and there was a cruel hardness in his eye. His melodic voice, barely deeper than that of a human woman, filled the air.

"What is happening?" Kestrel whispered. "Can you understand the tongue?"

"Yes," Astron said. "On my previous visit I learned it well from one kinder than the rest." He concentrated for a moment on the words coming from the stream side and began translating them for his companions.

153

"Come forward, high king Finvarwin, venerated judge. It is the season," Astron repeated. "Come forward, Finvarwin, and decide which creations have sufficient beauty, which will be granted the privilege of continued life. Tell us all who will receive the rewards for their efforts and who must render service as penalty for failure. I, hillsovereign Prydwin, speaking for all the others, request your presence."

The wooden door suddenly swung outward. A frail and stooped figure shuffled out into the light. The top of his head was totally bald, with a few long stringlets of bleached gold hanging to his shoulders. His face looked caved in, as if struck by a mighty blow. Squinting eyes sat atop a flattened nose. The chin jutted out from under a mouth long since vacant of teeth. Rather than a tunic of green, the newcomer wore a long robe of white, cinched at the waist with a rope made of vines.

"I am ready," Astron heard Finvarwin say. "I will judge as I have so many times in the past."

Finvarwin waved his hand out over the assemblage and then shielded his eyes. "Which one is Nimbia?" he asked. "Which one attempts to create without the aid of a mate?"

One of the fey standing somewhat apart from the rest came forward and dipped her head. "It is my creation that you have asked to inspect, venerated one. May your judgment be keen and fair."

"Look at that one!" Kestrel suddenly gasped in a voice almost loud enough for the nearest sentryman to hear. "I do not know how these creatures judge, but if she were in Procolon, men would fight for just one of her smiles."

Astron looked more closely at the one called Nimbia. She was a bit shorter than the rest, about his own height, and wore a plain tunic, with no added embroidery. Her face was slender, with soft angles, high cheeks, and a tiny upturned nose. Large eyes danced beneath a halo of gold. The way she moved was in some indescribable way different from the rest, a dancelike flow of smoothness, to be sure, but yet each step brought attention to the

154

bounce of her breasts. In the realm of men, she indeed would be judged a great beauty, Astron thought, and from what little he did know of the fey, in their underhills as well. He puzzled for a second time about the lust that went beyond the duty to couple and wondered if it affected those before him in the same way as it did Kestrel and his kin.

"You will be the last," Astron heard Finvarwin say to Nimbia. "I will judge first those more likely to prove worthy. Vastowen, prepare the ring for the use of all."

The occupant of the second litter, more heavy-set than the rest, bowed and then addressed the assemblage. "A dozen djinns," he said. "At least a dozen for I am confident that what I have started has begun to grow of its own volition."

The pipes again started their trilling. Everyone present focused their attention to the three fires burning on the streambank. Vastowen motioned to one of the females standing nearby. Shyly, she came forward and clasped his extended hand. Together they waded across the stream to the side on which Astron and the others hid.

Vastowen grabbed a handful of powder from a pouch at his waist. With a fluid motion he distributed the dust into the three fires. The flames roared skyward, each suddenly a brilliant purple of glistening heat.

"Come forward, djinns of the circle, I command you," Vastowen said. "Come forward and make the bridge so that we can see into elsewhere."

"He is a wizard!" Phoebe said. "A wizard, but evidently a foolish one at that. One djinn is sufficient a contest of wills for anyone; against a dozen no one can withstand."

"They are all wizards," Astron said. He felt his stem-brain stir at the thought. "The high king, the hillsovereigns, the litter bearers, even the sentrymen formed into the ring. It is what makes a journey here so risky for one of my kind. The struggle of dominance or submission could occur with each and every one that I meet."

Astron waved at the figures before him, now all concentrating on the three fires at Vastowen's feet. "And if a single one of them has insufficient strength, he can enlist the aid of another. In twos and threes or even scores, they can meld their wills as one. A solitary devil or even a prince is no match for the scores you see before you here. They can summon and control a dozen djinns with ease. It is no wonder that none of the princes who rule cast covetous thoughts toward a realm such as this."

As Astron spoke, a transcendent djinn materialized in the first of the three purple flames. In an instant after, the other two were populated as well. Vastowen waved his arm in a great vertical circle. Astron heard the great demons grunt acquiescence, bowing their massive heads to their chests.

The djinn from the second flame beat his wings. With one great stroke he vaulted onto the shoulders of the first. Wisps of purple plasma trailed along with his jump; when the third took position on top of the second, the slender column of flame rose to an unbelievable height. The air roared with bubbling energy. Astron felt the heat penetrate even the shelter in which he hid.

More djinns appeared in the two abandoned fires. Each after his display of submission placed himself on top of those who had preceded him. In a matter of moments, a column of twelve djinns encased in a sheath of dancing flame ascended high into the pale sky.

"And now the circle, I command you," Vastowen said when the last had taken his position. "A great ring of demonic flame from the realm of the fey to the one that I direct."

A terrible groan escaped from twelve mouths in unison. For a moment, nothing seemed to happen. But imperceptibly and then moving faster, the column bowed from the vertical and arced toward Astron's right. The djinns each gripped their hands upon the legs of the one above and the topmost of all extended his arms over his head, reaching out into the empty air.

Like a supple blade of steel, the column of djinns bent more and more to the right, the one at the base leaning farther and farther in the opposite direction in response to the lateral forces which pushed on his shoulders. For a moment, the topmost demon cantilevered parallel to the horizon; then, with increasing speed, he turned head downward as the curvature of the column increased.

The tower bent into a great hook and tightened further. All around the loop, what had been the topmost djinn touched ground a span away from the fire into which were still anchored the feet of the first. Now nearly horizontal himself, the last djinn in the line pulled himself forward with his hands until he was able to grasp the legs of the first and drag them onto his shoulders. The dozen djinns had formed themselves into a fiery ring that was four times the height of a tall man.

Astron felt Phoebe stiffen next to him. The power of twelve mighty djinns bent to a single purpose probably was something that she could not easily imagine. But in the realm of the fey, Astron knew, such feats were commonplace, a single element in their own complex rituals. As he watched, the pale sky that was surrounded by the ring clouded and darkened. The groans of the djinns intensified into shrieks of true pain. The air heaved and buckled, distorting the view of the hillside beyond the ring. Bolts of lightning materialized out of nothing. Rolling thunder echoed throughout the glen.

The scene within the ring dissolved into a blur of dull colors. The hillside appeared to melt into a formless slag that oozed outward to the edges of the ring. Eventually, the entire area of the enclosed circle was nothing but an indistinct gray that occasionally pulsed and twitched.

"Is this a sorcery?" Kestrel asked. "An illusion like the ones constructed on Morgana across the great sea in my own realm?"

"Of the five arts used by men, only wizardry is employed by the fey," Astron said. "They are using that single art now to command those of my kind to open a passage into yet another realm." Astron paused and squinted at the amorphous blandness contained by the ring. "But look how they accomplish it! Not a small path that flits an imp from one universe to another. Yes, I understand now that I witness the event firsthand.

157

Within the ring we can all see from one realm to another."

As Astron spoke, the grayness began to take on shape. Colors deepened. Bright lights started to shine through the gloom. Muted tones appeared first, and then saturated reds and yellows. In sunbursts of color, tiny, bright, spinning balls came into sharp focus. Moving in complex yet graceful trajectories, what appeared to be intricately carved spheres spun rapidly on randomly aligned axes and darted in and out of sight within the boundaries of the ring. Occasionally two would pass close by one another and alter their velocities, revolving for a moment about a common center before dashing on.

"Ah, the music of the spheres," Vastowen said. "Look at the vibrancy of the dance, Finvarwin. I included no friction so they will orbit about one another forever. I—"

The female next to Vastowen pulled on his hand. He stooped forward to listen to what she had to say. For a moment they exchanged animated whispers, then he nodded and reached into a second pouch at his belt.

"And there is yet more, Finvarwin," he called to the high king. "My soulmate's inspiration soars beyond the richness of what has already been revealed. Look, we cast in more pollen and with our combined effort cause there to be more."

A cluster of small nodules sped from Vastowen's grasp and through the ring of djinns. The scene wavered and trembled, returning back to a muted gray. Astron saw the female fall to one knee with a gasp, although she did not release her grip on the hand of her mate. Beads of sweat popped into being on Vastowen's smooth brow. Wiping away the salty drops that streamed into his eyes, he stared at the opening, straining until his arms and legs began to tremble.

In silence, everyone around the glen watched the opaque grayness of the disk. Then, as quickly as it had formed, the indistinct fog retreated to reveal once again the whirl of the brightly colored orbs. Only this time Astron noticed there were more of them rushing among one another with trajectories tightly packed. In an instant, two collided with a burst of brilliant light. In the wake of the collision, dozens of even smaller spheres, as bright and complexly decorated as their parents, popped into being and exploded outward in wild arcs of their own.

"It is not rich enough." Finvarwin waved his arm at the display. "I need not waste time by seeing more. A multitude of such dim fuzziness soon becomes tiring. I suspect that eventually all of those tiny blobs will dissipate far from one another, devoid of interest. No one will want to watch. Everything that you have shown will all fade away."

"No!" Vastowen shouted. "The creation has volition. I know it does. I can feel the energy of its life forces pulsing inside. Suspend judgment if you must. Let the patterns intermingle and produce new variations. We can all wait and thrill in its blossoming richness, which will be all the greater when we gather the next time."

"You know the rules as well as any hillsovereign." Prydwin stepped forward to stand next to Vastowen. "Once shown to the high king, a creation cannot be withdrawn and substituted with another."

"But we added to the basic premise even as you watched. Surely that—"

"Enough," Finvarwin said. "You have presented fairly, and fairly have I judged."

Vastowen opened his mouth as if to say more, but he looked around the glade and stopped. Even the retainers that had come with him had backed away from his litter and did not return his glance. Vastowen dropped his mate's hand to his side. The scene within the ring of djinns returned to a muted gray. With hushed expectancy all of the fey awaited Finvarwin's next words.

"To Prydwin," he said. "Yes, to Prydwin. The entire underhill in its entirety. To dissipate Vastowen's holdings among the rest, rather than grant a single boon, might encourage similar exhibitions of little skill."

"Thank you, venerated one." Prydwin quickly sank to one knee and tilted his head. "I will make great use of the resources that you have so generously—"

"Enough," Finvarwin said. "Who is next? What does he present?"

"But the disposition of your largesse." Prydwin rose to standing. "It is only right that everyone knows."

Finvarwin grunted. Prydwin's face broke into a smile. He turned to face Vastowen and his mate. "For you, hillsovereign, my mercy will be swift. You may choose which of my sentrymen will guide his dagger to your heart."

The expression on Vastowen's face did not flicker. "My sovereign," he mumbled. Glancing for a final time at his mate, he squeezed her hand and then pointed out randomly at the circle of mushrooms. "That one," he said. "That one will be as good as any."

"Not yet." Prydwin put up his hand to stop the sentry from leaving his post. "First there is the matter of the rest. You will probably want to hear."

Prydwin turned his attention to the litter bearers and the others of Vastowen's retinue. "For those who remained underhill and did not come, their penalty is to travel to my own domain and there begin service as I direct. You there, carry back the empty chair so that they will know that their hillsovereign is no more.

"As for the rest who were so bold as to accompany their liege." Prydwin's smile broadened. "Your yells and screams shall serve to inspire me to greater creations still. The pain may not be brief, but at least you will have the consolation of adding to the greatness of the art."

Several of the fey around Vastowen's litter suddenly started to run; but before they had travelled a dozen steps, the sentrymen cut off their escape and herded them back toward the stream.

The first two began whimpering softly as their hands and feet were bound with a vine bristling with thorns. Like slaughtered pigs, they were fastened to a beam that was placed between two pairs of crossed stakes. The oily contents of a plant bladder was spilled over their tunics. Then, without further ceremony, they were set ablaze.

The fires burned slowly, billowing up dense clouds of

160

pungent black smoke. Through a growing haze, Astron could see the march of the smouldering flames burning outward from where they were first lit, down each leg and arm and toward the head.

The death cries of the fey were high and piercing, so much so that even Kestrel had to release Phoebe so he could cover his ears. Astron saw the complexion of the two humans wash chalky white as they stared at what they saw.

"Let us be away," Phoebe whispered urgently. "They are so many. This is no place for us."

"We do not know where." Astron shook his head. "A moment more and perhaps something of value might be learned. See, the sounds have stopped and the hillsovereign Prydwin speaks again."

Astron translated Prydwin's words. "Those are the briefest. The rest I will save for later when there will be more time to enjoy."

He looked at Vastowen's wooden face and chuckled. "I have saved the best for last," he said. "Your mate, Thuvia, is a comely one. I think that my creations too will benefit from the experience of her pleasures."

Vastowen looked toward Thuvia, tears streaming from his eyes. "Do not be afraid," he said so that Astron could barely hear. "Perhaps he will be gentle."

"Gentle?" Prydwin suddenly barked with laughter. "To my underhill and remove her of her garments," he roared. "Prepare the pinchers and tongs. We will see if you judge me gentle."

"Enough of the unimportant," Finvarwin's reedy voice cut in. "Who is to be next in the judging?"

"I am, venerated one," Prydwin said. He turned his attention away from Vastowen's followers, their fates apparently totally dismissed from his mind.

The hillsovereign gestured to the females who stood by his litter, and one came forward to stand with him in front of the ring of demons. With an almost staged casualness, he waved his arms once, dissipating the muted gray in an instant. Splotches of color filled the disk, reds and yellows and vivid greens. Like an artist's palette left

161

in the sun, the hues flowed into one another, creating greater blotches still of purples and orange.

To Astron, the motion appeared to be quite random. Only the greater size and amorphous shape distinguished what he was seeing from Vastowen's spheres.

"I sense the power of your creation," Finvarwin said after a moment of watching the slow movement within the ring. "The massive forms transform with purpose and dedication. Yes, the creation is worthy—not as complex as those of the chronoids and reticulates that you have seen before, but vibrant nonetheless. There is no penalty, Prydwin. Instead you fairly may receive a boon."

"You have blessed me many times already, venerated one," Prydwin said. "Of material things I have little want. I ask instead that you give me knowledge, arcane knowledge of our own realm that only you remember, knowledge so that my own worth might grow."

"Very well then, the answer to three questions shall be your prize. Think of them carefully, Prydwin. When all ceremonies have been completed, then you may ask."

Prydwin tipped his head to the high king and retreated back to his litter, satisfaction wreathing his face.

"Who next?" Finvarwin repeated. "Who next to be judged by the high king?"

Astron heard a soft murmur run through the assemblage on the other bank of the stream, but neither the owner of the third litter nor any other came forth.

Finvarwin waited a moment more and then motioned toward Nimbia. "Then the time has come," he said, "the time for the reckless one who dares to create without a mate."

Nimbia waded across the stream and addressed herself to the ring of djinns. She performed no bold display, but the gray began to dissolve slowly away. Astron saw that, rather than into a riot of color, it transformed into a field of deepest black.

Astron squinted his eyes to shield them from the glare of the sparks that danced around the circle of djinns. He drew his membranes into place, and that helped even more. In the smoothness of the deep ebony he saw the beginnings of subtle movement and then a texturing that rippled across the field of view from left to right. An occasional glint of light, reflecting from an unseen source, gave a sheen to the surface, highlighting at first regularly arranged depressions and then ribs and furrows that oscillated in sinuous patterns.

With each passing moment, the texture of the surface changed from one form to another. Astron watched fascinated, not able to predict what would happen next, but delighting in each new variation as it emerged. The effect was totally unlike the presentations of either of the other two; the slow melodic pace soothed, rather than agitated with jerks and starts. Astron glanced at the high king, wondering what his judgment would be.

"Enough," Finvarwin said. "I let us view longer in order to give you the benefit of the doubt. But there is little there to distract one from a boredom greater even than the attempt of Vastowen. The punishment can be no less. To Prydwin with your underhill, Nimbia. It is for hillsovereigns who are proficient in their art to hold sway over the fey."

"Sentrymen, to your duty." Prydwin motioned from his litter. "Arrange an escort so that her honor might not be unduly tempted. Bring her with Thuvia. It will be a pleasure deciding which will be first."

"Never," Nimbia suddenly shouted in a voice almost as deep as that of a male. "I will not meekly submit like Vastowen, just because a few wish it so. Our traditions are ancient ones, but there are times when even they must be disobeyed."

She kicked at the dagger of the first sentryman who approached, sending the blade twirling to the ground. Then scrambling in front of him, she retrieved the knife before the surprised guard could react. With a wide swipe, she spun quickly about, waving off the others who had begun to approach.

She looked quickly at those who stood near the high king and then at the sentrymen converging from across the stream. "You all saw the images," she shouted. "You do not need the age of Finvarwin to search for small subtle differences. Be true to what your eyes have shown you. Mine was a true creation, a difficult balance of predator and prey. Prydwin's was no more than the bubbling flow of plasma, thick pastes swirling in convection in a heated pot."

Except for the closing sentrymen, no one moved. Finvarwin squinted at Nimbia, then shook his head.

"Your underhill is no better protected than all the rest, Nimbia," the high king said. "Against all the rest, eventually it will fall. You are dealing with the inevitable. Prydwin has offered to accept you as his mate. Go with him in peace. Perhaps together the two of you will combine to produce an imagination greater then either of its parts—just as the fourth dictum states."

"Prydwin!" Nimbia spat. "Never." She waved the dagger in the air. "Who among you has the courage to act as his heart tells him?" she called out. "The courage to aid a lady of the realm when she calls in distress?"

"The hillsovereign speaks with too much boldness for one defending herself alone," Prydwin said. "Fan out and cover all of the trails. She may have aid just beyond our view."

"That is the signal that we start to move." Kestrel tugged at Astron's arm. "I doubt it will do us any good to be mistaken for part of the losing party."

Astron shrugged off Kestrel's hand. "The one named Finvarwin is one that we need to interrogate further. Perhaps more than any other he would know of harebell pollen and even the ultimate precept."

"Yes, the old one certainly," Kestrel whispered back. "But at a time when not so many are about. Now we must be going, before it is too late. Being hunted in two realms should be enough, even for a demon."

Astron looked out at the ring closing in on Nimbia. He glanced over his shoulder in the dimness. Kestrel was right. There was a path leading through the dense underbrush and he should lead, because he was more familiar with what they would encounter.

Astron glanced a second time at Nimbia. His thoughts

164

took a strange turn. Kestrel also had been right about how to get the imps into a bottle. The way the human had planned to manipulate the wizards at Phoebe's cabin was something no demon would have conceived on his own. For the dozenth time he realized there was much about the mortal that Astron wished to learn.

But the words Kestrel spoke were sometimes so unexpected and peculiar that Astron could not fully comprehend the intent—duty to oneself rather than a prince, lures for gold djinns when none such existed, or travelling through the flame for Phoebe and no other.

Perhaps mere words would not be enough to unravel the mysteries of men; perhaps their experiences would have to be sampled before understanding could come. Astron looked one final time at Phoebe and Kestrel, standing close together with their arms about each other, and made up his mind.

He stripped away the hood and cape from his back. Gripping the book of thaumaturgy firmly in both hands, he suddenly sprang out from the cover of the heavy leaves. The sentryman standing nearest turned in the direction of the rustling sound, but grappled for his dagger too slowly to defend himself as Astron rushed forward. The demon swung the book high overhead and then crashed it down on the skull of the startled guard.

The fey crumpled to the ground. Astron staggered to retain his balance and somehow managed to tuck the bulky volume under his arm. He bounded down the hillock toward where Nimbia still waved a dagger of her own. A shout of alarm went up from the onlookers. Everyone seemed to freeze in their tracks. Astron felt the beginning of a compelling pressure in the depths of his thoughts.

He grimaced in resistance, pulling his face into a tight little ball, forcing the mental probes away. Through eyes half closed, he saw Nimbia dip her dagger cautiously as he ran up and extended his free hand.

"To safety, through the underbrush," Astron shouted as he closed. "If no one else will defend you, then I am the one."

Nimbia hesitated a moment, but then firmly clasped Astron's outstretched wrist. He felt a surprising tingling when the smoothness of her skin touched his, but pushed the sensation away. Almost jerking Nimbia from her feet, he reversed direction and began racing back up the hill.

The pressure against his thoughts increased. The fey dealt with a demon by force of will, not slashing blades. He felt the probes of many minds mold into one unifying whole. "Stop, desist," a voice inside his head seemed to say. "We are many and you are one. You cannot resist the combined will of us all."

Astron stumbled over a small rock, but continued his climb. His limbs began to stiffen. The panic in his stem-brain stirred from its slumber. As they reached the sentryman Astron had felled, Nimbia drew even with the demon. In half a dozen more steps she was tugging on the grip between them, pulling Astron forward into the cover of the bush.

"Why did you do that?" Kestrel shouted as the pair ducked under the leaf. "Have you gone mad? Has some wizard put you under his control?"

"I do not know for certain," Astron said thickly. He waved at Phoebe and then dropped his arm heavily to his side. "But then I would not have had to, if you had explained—explained why you rescued your wizard when you could have been safely away from her cabin."

## CHAPTER THIRTEEN

# The Paradox of Beauty

A dagger soared into the underbrush over Astron's head, entangling in the drooping leaves. Retreat deeper into the foliage was an immediate necessity or else Nimbia would not be the only one captured by hillsovereign Prydwin.

But Astron found his thoughts becoming much more sluggish. His limbs would barely move. It was difficult enough understanding the words of both Kestrel and Nimbia as they spoke in their respective tongues.

"There are only three of you!" Astron heard Nimbia exclaim. "And none from my own underhill as I had supposed."

Another dagger crashed into the canopy. Kestrel pushed Phoebe to the ground out of its path. "Well, what is the rest of the plan, demon?" he asked. "You know this place as we do not. In what direction do we proceed?"

"Only three," Nimbia repeated, "but then effective, nonetheless. Prydwin's kind are so used to his will being obeyed without resistance that his sentrymen have little chance to do more than serve as a frame for the presentation of his creations. As I think of it now, none of my kind would have succeeded. The daggers were too many. A bold action, demon, was precisely what was needed."

Astron felt her grip tighten in his hand. "Come," she said. "If we escape safely back to my own underhill, even though you are not one of the fey, you will be rewarded."

Nimbia turned into the darkness toward the huge trunk and pulled Astron after. He clutched the book of thaumaturgy to his chest and struggled as best he could not to stumble. Dimly, he was aware of Kestrel and Phoebe following behind.

The little light that filtered between the overhanging leaves vanished altogether. Astron saw Nimbia pull what looked like a gnarled root from her belt and, with her free hand, extend it overhead. The tuber glowed with a feeble yellow light that just managed to illuminate the obstacles that lay in their way.

The thick trunks that supported the overhang grew closer together. Aboveground, suckers caused more than one stumble as they ran. Grublike insects with bodies as big as the arm of a djinn scurried out of their way. Rasps and loud clicks blended with the stomp of their feet against the ground.

For how long they raced, Astron could not tell. Except for Nimbia's glowroot, the darkness was as deep as the void in his own realm. His chest began to hurt from the exertion. Sharp pains crackled through his knees. He was a demon of contemplation and not used to such stressing of his body. What little weaving he was capable of to supply his basic needs was being severely overburdened.

Then suddenly Nimbia stopped at the base of a particularly large trunk. She gestured upward and released her grip on Astron's hand. Like an acrobatic gibbon in the realm of men, she grabbed hold of a low branch and swung herself upward. Kestrel grunted in understanding. He cupped his hands to give Phoebe a boost. With Nimbia astride the limb and pulling, Kestrel pushed from below. Phoebe clawed her way onto the limb in a tumble of cape and long skirt. Kestrel followed quickly. Only Astron remained on the ground.

The pressure to submit grew in intensity. Astron found he could barely move. With agonizing slowness, he raised the book for Phoebe to grasp and then cupped the branch in his hand.

"Hurry," Kestrel whispered. "They cannot be far behind."

"It is the contest of wills," Nimbia said. "The followers of Prydwin command him to be still."

The thought that Kestrel and Nimbia had no way of understanding each other floated slowly across Astron's mind. He should serve as translator, but somehow he no longer cared. Perhaps it was hopeless to run further. Eventually they would be found anyway. Why not at least take a rest at the base of this bush, rather than exert himself any more?

Astron felt his grip on the branch loosen. With a feeling of peace, he began to slide to the ground. Slumped in a heap at the base, perhaps he would not be seen. Or even if they did see him, what really did it matter? Astron curled up into a tight ball. A crooked smile formed on his face.

But just as consciousness began to fade, a thought of piercing sharpness ricocheted through his head. Resist, it commanded. I am the closest and have the greater influence. Resist their wills because I wish it so.

Nimbia! Astron stirred from his dimness. She was a wizard like the rest. Her thoughts churned with the others. And somehow they were different—strong because of her nearness, to be sure. But the crushing drive to dominate was held in restraint. Her will was adding to his, repelling the others, giving his own consciousness room in which to function, time to construct barriers against the pressure to quit.

Astron vaguely became aware of many hands tugging on his body and of being lifted into the air. He felt the rough fiber of the stringy bark against his skin. He flailed past the first horizontal level of branches and then several tiers more. Finally he felt an embrace that held him firm. Nimbia's arms coiled around him. He smelled the exotic aroma of her closeness and heard the rustle of her tunic against his own.

"Do not fight me, demon," he heard her whisper. "Blend your will with mine. Cling to me and do not let go. When they pass below and do not find us, their command will be for you to come forth, and you must not."

Astron saw the dance of glowroots in the distance and a line of sentrymen fanning out along the crude path on which they had fled. He heard Phoebe suck in her breath and the three about him stiffen into nervous silence.

As Nimbia had predicted, the voices inside his head changed their direction. No longer was he implored to stop and freeze. Instead, he felt a growing urge for action, to bolt forth and run into the open, to flee the dismal dark cover to the gentle light of the glen.

Astron's limbs began to tremble. With all the concentration left to his command, he clutched Nimbia harder, willing his arms to stiffen. He must hold on.

Nimbia seemed to sense his struggle. Her grip tightened and her thoughts blended with his. He felt the strength of her inner being, like a vault of steel. He poured his own essence into it, molding to the contours of the container, pressing against her, like an annealing of the alchemists that could not be torn away.

Through barely open eyes, he saw the followers of Prydwin draw closer, peering cautiously into the inky darkness and listening for some sound of their flight. Some passed in the distance to either side, but three came close to the enormous bush in which they hid.

Come forward, the voices commanded. Come forward; it is the will of the fey. Astron slammed shut his eyes and crushed Nimbia to him. He heard the gasp of her breath from the force of his embrace. He felt her nails dig into his back, even through the thickness of his tunic. The trembling of his limbs shook his entire body in spasms. He ached from the effort to remain silent and still.

Mentally, he tried to keep the image of Nimbia's vault in focus, pushing against the surface of her being everywhere he could. He felt her accepting his struggle, welcoming the intertwining of what he was with her. He saw beyond the smooth strength that she projected into recesses of her existence that went beyond the immediate struggle—hints of great pride in her creations, the agony of defeat in competition with Prydwin, the frustration of the petty jealousies of her courtiers, and a deep-lying melancholy that perhaps even she did not understand.

Like the flickers of a dying flame, the images fluttered briefly in Astron's mind, then faded away. If he were struggling to dominate her across the barrier of the flame, he would have pursued them further, exposed them to view, analytically picked the one most painful, and then exploited it until her will was his own to do with as he chose.

But Nimbia was sharing his struggle. To meld the fullness of her strength to his she had to expose the foundations from which it sprang. She bared the innermost essence of her being in trust. He could do no more than accept the gift that was given.

The urge to howl in pain rose in Astron's chest. He clamped his jaws shut, feeling that his teeth would explode into fragmented shards from the pressure to remain silent. Every muscle in his body ached from the conflicting commands to remain immobile on one hand and to dance into fevered action on the other.

He felt the strong walls of Nimbia's mental vault buckle on the bottom and the band about the mouth wrench apart in a silent scream of ripping metal. Although he strained to resist, the top stretched wide and, as if pushed by giant thumbs, the bottom bulged upward toward the opening. Almost helplessly, he felt the container wrenched inside out, exposing his own being to the relentless will of the others.

But then, just when he could stand remaining silent no longer, the pressure lessened. Almost in disbelief, Astron darted a glance out of one eye to the ground below. Whistled commands sang through the leaves. The sentrymen were moving on through the brush.

As the searchers departed, so did the pressure in Astron's head. The trembling of his limbs slowed to random twitches and then stopped altogether. His own consciousness expanded to fill all of his being. Almost with a sense of reluctance, he felt Nimbia's presence within him withdraw as well.

No one moved, however. All four remained frozen, lest the smallest sound draw the attention of Prydwin's sentrymen back to where they hid. In silence, Astron heard the whistles and calls grow fainter until only the buzz and click of the insects remained.

171

Finally, after an immeasurable time, Nimbia shifted slightly and uncoiled her arms from around Astron's back. With muscles stiff from fatigue, he released her as well. Nimbia pulled the glowroot from her pouch and brought it up to eye level. Astron saw her look him in the eye and then quickly dart her glance aside. A hint of redness blossomed in her cheeks.

"Forgive me," she said softly. "When we struggled to resist the will of the others, I could not help but learn of things that you probably do not want to share."

"And I of you," Astron responded. "I sensed I should not but—"

"If those are thank-yous you are exchanging, they can come later," Kestrel cut in. "No doubt the others will return this way when they have convinced themselves they have lost our trail. Ask the nabob if she knows of a more permanent shelter we can reach before nightfall."

Astron shrugged and told Nimbia what Kestrel had said. Serving as the intermediary came easily now. The conversation flowed almost as swiftly as if they all spoke the same tongue.

"There is no nightfall," Nimbia said. "The soft blue that you saw in the glen remains eternally the same. Finvarwin and the old ones before him say that our realm is a globe centered inside a hollow sphere that radiates light and heat uniformly. There are no days, no seasons. It is the reason that we find such delight in our creations.

"And as to safety, we will journey to the hill under which I am the absolute ruler. Perhaps, before the other sovereigns decide on how they will combine their forces and attack, there will be enough time to create again— create before the next judging with something that even Finvarwin cannot deny is the best."

"Would not moving and staying hidden be better?" Kestrel asked. "To face again the pronouncements of your high king seems fraught with risk."

"I must," Nimbia said. "It is my duty, my duty to my people."

"Duty," Astron repeated slowly. "I know of duty— or at least I thought I did. I come to your realm in

172

search for the answer to a riddle because my prince demands—"

"Come." Nimbia touched her finger to Astron's lips. "The human is right. We must get underhill before Prydwin's sentrymen return."

For what would be hours in the realm of men, Nimbia led Astron and the others through the darkness of the brush. They encountered no sign of Prydwin's followers and eventually emerged on the edge of a clearing similar to the glen in which they had first arrived. Rather than slope down to a stream, however, the grass-covered ground rose from where they stood. From all sides of the open space, at first gently and then with increasing slope, the soft greenness underfoot tilted upward to form a high hillock in the very center. Like a great upside-down bowl thrust against the ground, the bulge dominated the landscape; its broad, flat apex stood higher even than the crest of the bushes which edged the clearing.

As Nimbia moved out into the open, the ground underfoot began to vibrate with a great rumbling. The music of pipes and lyres filled the air. Astron saw the hillock shudder slightly and then begin to move. The ground parted with a clean horizontal slit. On dozens of stout pillars, the central portion of the hillock rose slowly into the air.

Brilliant lights, laughter, and music sweet and pure poured out of the opening. Astron saw long banquet tables groaning under piles of glistening fruit and heavy flagons coolly sparkling with a patina of dew. Scores of lithe dancers pirouetted in complex patterns. Laughing jugglers kept dozens of small objects whirling above their heads.

"Nimbia, Nimbia," dozens of joyful voices called out. "Our hillsovereign returns."

"She has triumphed at last."

"Finvarwin has been pleased. Look, he gives her three changelings as prize for her great worth."

173

"Alert the scribes and the tellers. There will be work for all."

Astron saw a throne of polished stone being pushed into a position of prominence on a dais bathed with colored lights. Two long lines of what looked like pages formed on either side. Small girls began strewing delicate flower petals from the base outward onto the grass of the clearing. Stout-cheeked pipers stuck long-stemmed pipes into bowls filled with nearly solid gels. With straining lungs, they forced upward bubbles of air that burst and sprayed all those about to their laughing delight. Fragrant odors tickled Astron's nostrils and beckoned him forward.

Nimbia said nothing. With a grim smile, she walked on the path laid for her and beckoned Astron and the others to follow. Accepting a cape richly embroidered and encrusted with jewels, she mounted the steps and sat on her throne. Nimbia looked about the gaily decorated surroundings and Astron saw her face sadden. She breathed out a deep sigh.

"I do not return in triumph," she said simply. "And those that accompany me are responsible that I return at all."

The music stopped as did the clank of flagon and flatware from those who prepared the feast. Smiles fell from the faces of those nearest. Eyes lowered. Many of the faces looked away. For a long moment, the silence filled the hilltop; even the creak of boots and rustle of tunics against one another was stilled.

Then, from the periphery of the hillock, a single piper began playing a slow, sad melody. Others caught the tone and added to it. One of the females close to Nimbia choked on a small sob. Tears began to glisten on the faces of a dozen more. In barely an instant, the infectious joy transformed into a chilling sadness.

Nimbia nodded in apparent acceptance of the changing mood. She motioned over the heads of those nearest and Astron felt the ground begin to vibrate as it had when they approached. He saw the narrow band of pale blue sky start to shrink into nothingness. Like a great

174

piston sinking into a cylinder, the surface on which he stood descended into the earth. In an instant, the hilltop again rested firmly on the ground.

The bright lights reflected by the jeweled panels and mirrors shone with undiminished intensity. Even though Nimbia had retreated underground, the area around her throne remained far brighter than the daylight outside. As the descent halted, Astron saw dimly lit passageways radiating in all directions. Great bins lined the hallways, like the walls of Phoebe's cabin. From some spilled the powders and woods that Astron recognized as essential for the summoning of great djinns. Others bulged with strange prickly spheroids, covered with sharp barbs or intricate lattices of thorns. In the distance were rows of doors and dark cross corridors radiating farther into the earth. The extent of the queen's underhill could not easily be judged.

Two of the pages, taller than the rest, pushed each other timidly from the crowd that had gathered about the throne. Each wore a tunic embroidered with the same designs as those on Nimbia's cape. Their copper daggers were sheathed on belts inlaid with gold.

"Might not what you have wrought survive despite Finvarwin's judgment?" the first one asked.

"My creation will live on unaided for a lifetime or more." Nimbia nodded her head. "Such strength am I sure that it possesses. But without the thoughts of others, it will not expand to be more than what it is now. Eventually, it will grow sluggish and decay."

Nimbia paused and looked over the heads of the assembly. She closed her eyes and seemed to absorb the mood of the piping which now swelled to a persistent resonance that could not be ignored. Tears appeared from fluttering eyelids. She slumped into the folds of her cape.

"The penalty is a severe one." She opened her eyes again at last. "Servitude to Prydwin for us all—this underhill to become one of his, rather than our own. We will be toiling to carry his baskets of pollens, blowing on the pipes as long as he commands, plucking the blossoms

175

that he decrees, whether they are part of our harmonies or not."

"You should not have attempted it without a mate," the second page said. "All of us regard your craft to be of the greatest quality, as strong as your own great beauty. But forgive me, my queen, even so, the challenge was far too great."

Nimbia looked for a long time at the second page before speaking.

"You knew of the risk as well as any other," she said softly. "You and every other page underhill. Almost any would have sufficed, provided that he had the strength of heart."

"But it could not be me." The page stepped back suddenly. He waved his arm about those who clustered around the queen. "Perhaps someone else," he muttered, "someone more worthy. Your beauty is too great. One such as I would never have a chance."

"A single page," Nimbia repeated, "and yet not one came forward. Not one chose to accompany his queen, despite what decorum demanded. I do not understand. Can the prize be of so little value?"

"A prize has greater value the less it is shared." A third voice, deeper than the first two, sounded from the rear. Astron saw a male slightly more heavy-set than the rest push his way forward, the lines of a frown etched into his forehead. Dark black ringlets of hair curled above deep-set blue eyes. He appeared slightly older than the other pages, and Astron noticed that several of the females followed him with keen interest.

"This is not the time and place to air old accusations, Lothal." Nimbia stirred slightly on her throne. "They are no less true now than they were when the two of us—"

"The rages have cooled, my sovereign." Lothal bowed deeply with an almost jeering smile on his face. "I do not come forth pressing a suit that you have more than adequately demonstrated I can never win. I speak merely as another loyal and concerned subject for the benefit of us all."

176

Astron saw Nimbia stiffen, but the queen said nothing. She motioned for Lothal to continue.

The courtier bowed a second time and then stood facing Nimbia with his hands on his hips. "Your wit is a sharp one. Despite everything else, I will always have admiration for that. Perhaps, from what you see happening again and again, you can finally deduce a basic truth for your conduct." He paused and turned to face the others, extending his arms slowly in great arcs.

"The queen can have anyone here she chooses." He looked at several of the females who wore bands about their waists with the same markings as those of a nearby male. "Even ones already bound can hardly resist the great persuasion of her beauty—we all know that in our hearts."

Lothal whirled abruptly and again faced Nimbia. "Any one she chooses, that is, so long as her choice is for one only." His cheeks flushed suddenly. Veins stood out in his neck. "I did not submit to share with another; and by all that lives of its own volition, neither will any other here. Amend your ways, Nimbia. Change the greed for more than one; that is all you deserve, despite the loveliness you possess. Amend your ways, and then a champion will come forward to share the tasks of creation with his lady."

"I was faithful to you from the first day to the last," Nimbia said softly. "It was your jealousies and no more, Lothal, that churned in your heart. You saw evil where there was none. Nothing I could have done would have convinced you otherwise." Nimbia threw up her hands. "And we could not create, so long as your own inner being was so troubled."

"If you were not queen, I would not let such assertions go unchallenged," Lothal shot back. "You try to use the power of your station to gain what even your beauty cannot grasp."

"Challenge whatever you will." Nimbia shook her head and pulled the edges of her cape in tightened fists, with knuckles showing white. "I give you leave as I have given you leave each time before. Try to find any proof that I was ever other than loving. You cannot, because none was ever there. Come, Lothal, I would forget the pain and accept you even now, if it would spark the creation that would save our underhill."

Nimbia looked at Lothal expectantly but his jaw was firmly set. He would speak no more.

Nimbia sighed. "We waste the time of all those that have assembled here," she said finally. "And there is little time that is left." She waved her arm at the banquet rooms beyond. "Feast, my people. Make merry while you can. Prydwin's pipers will come for us all soon enough."

The mournful melody of the pipers abruptly stopped. There was a moment's pause and then they began again, this time with the lively air that Astron had first heard when he arrived. Tentatively, two of the younger females began to dance. With a sudden enthusiasm, three of the pages mimicked their steps. Nimbia began clapping her hands. A smile reappeared on her face. In what seemed like an instant, the mood transformed into the gaiety it had been before.

"I do not understand." Phoebe raised her voice above the music. "What has happened to her? The moods of the woman on the throne change faster than the purest quicksilver."

"My previous sojourns were brief," Astron said. "I witnessed the ring of djinns for the first time just as you did."

"The mysteries of the realm can wait for later," Kestrel said. "More important is the reason why we came. If this Nimbia thinks we are her savior, then ask her for a boon before she forgets. What does she know of the things we seek?"

Astron hesitated. Nimbia had saved him from the sentrymen of Prydwin—far more so than he had her. And the passions shown by the fey evidently were quite similar to those of men. He would like to have listened quietly for much longer.

"Excuse me, Queen Nimbia," he said, "but I have a request—knowledge in exchange for the small service

178

we have performed in your behalf. If perhaps you know the location of harebell pollen or how to gain audience with a sage among you who knows the riddle of the ultimate precept..."

Nimbia stopped in mid-clap. She turned and regarded Astron for a moment with an amused smile. Then she broke into a gale of laughter, clasping her sides and poking her elbows at whomever was the closest.

"Yes, harebell pollen," she said. "That is all it would take. Who needs the logical precision of the male to temper the leaps of intuition if harebell pollen could be tossed through the ring? Even Prydwin's greatest triumphs—the realm of the chronoids, the realm of the reticulates—both could be challenged in a single judging. Yes, harebell pollen indeed."

Nimbia tried to say more but she clasped her sides again, unable to speak. Astron looked from side to side for explanation, but saw only other mirthful faces. His nose wrinkled. He turned back to face Kestrel with a shrug.

Nimbia suddenly stopped laughing. She tapped Astron on the shoulder. He saw that her face was completely sober.

"It is the way of the fey," she explained. "We cannot sip life in only half measures, but must drink deeply from the cup of emotions. It is no less than the first dictum— reality must mirror passion. How else can we create with a vividness that will live of its own volition?"

Astron started to reply but Nimbia shook her head. "For now, no more words," she said. "Do not disturb the joyousness of the feast. I owe my people no less." She reached out and gently touched his arm. "Even though you are no more than a demon, I wish that you would abide with me for a while. Abide with me, since your saving of a queen might not yet be complete."

## CHAPTER FOURTEEN

# *Bubbles of Reality*

ASTRON blew out all the candles except for the one on the far end of the oaken table. The remaining light was feeble, but he had had more than enough time to get familiar with the placing of even the tiniest obstacles in the small circular room. Fifteen marks Kestrel had gouged into the doorframe, one for each arising from his sleep. For the entire duration, Astron had been confined to the one room.

Despite the urgency, he had achieved no new progress toward his goal. The growing frustration made his stembrain continuously active. A feeling of constant uneasiness ached just below his consciousness. He could not still the rumbling, no matter how hard he tried. With each passing tick of time, the chances of the survival of his prince and hence his own shrunk all the more. Something had to be done soon, no matter how interesting the other distractions.

They were not prisoners exactly, but Nimbia's sentrymen made clear with the force of their thoughts that wandering around underhill was highly discouraged. After the queen had dismissed them, they had not seen her again. Apparently Astron and his companions were left to their own devices until she saw fit to call them back to her presence.

Astron directed his concentration at what he had constructed. The idle time had not been a total waste, since there was much he had learned. The oaken table with the candle was straight on three sides, while the fourth was curved to meet the contour of the stone wall to which it was pressed. Square cells would have been much more efficient, Astron knew. Using stone instead of wood certainly must stress the mechanism that raised and lowered the hilltop, but he gathered that such practicalities were not the concern of the fey.

Next to the candle, hung from a cantilevered scaffolding made of twigs and branches, was a watersack from one of the large vines that grew aboveground. Astron had carefully pierced and drained the bladder and then refilled it with lamp oil obtained from another resinous herb. With bits of copper wire hooked into the surrounding leaves, the spherical globe was elongated and flattened, distorting it into a thin vertical disk.

At the other end of the table, the book of thaumaturgy that Astron had obtained from the archimage stood upright in a scaffolding similar to the first. The candle flame flickered through the orb of oil and cast a diffuse glow of light on the upright parchment, illustrating an image quite similar to the one Astron had constructed on the bench.

Astron studied the illustration for a moment more and then the arcane symbols written beneath it. The abstractions had been difficult to grasp at first, but the examples had helped a great deal. He turned to the bag of oil and moved it to a mark he had calculated before, roughly midway between the candle and book.

The diffuse halo of light on the parchment coalesced into a much sharper dot. Astron grunted in satisfaction. He cupped his hand in front of his lens so that only its very center received the candleglow and watched the focus on the book decrease to a single point of whiteness.

Astron moved the position of the book toward the candle and then adjusted the lens to regain the proper focus. He measured the distances from page to oilbag and oilbag to candle and checked the results with the predictions of the formula. After a half-dozen trials, he blew out the remaining light and sat in the darkness, contemplating what he had learned.

The ones who call themselves masters in the realm of men treated knowledge in strange ways, he thought. The basic principles of bending rays of light had no intrinsic connection to thaumaturgy or any other of the crafts known to mortals. But because these laws were used by practitioners of the magical arts, they were shrouded in secret like the rest. One went to a thaumaturge for telescopes or heating lenses, even though a glassblower could construct what was needed just as well without any recourse to the art, if he knew a few simple formulas. Unlike Prince Elezar's riddles, which extracted a price but once, knowledge in the realm of men was hoarded and reused again and again, demanding a fee each and every time.

Astron's reverie was broken by a pounding on the door. "The hillsovereign commands your presence," a voice on the other side said.

Astron scrambled out of his repose, opened the door, and burst into the hall. Perhaps at last he could continue the search for the answer to Gaspar's riddle.

He was joined shortly in the narrow curving hallway by Kestrel and Phoebe. While Astron had pondered the mysteries of thaumaturgy, they had spent much time together learning the fundamentals of the language of the fey. And the demon could not help noticing how much stronger the attraction between the two of them had become.

He had no chance to comment on the fact, however. In a short moment they were ushered into the presence of Nimbia in the central throne room. Nimbia wore a gown of iridescent pink that billowed and filled the high chair on which she sat. On either side, two pages stood at solemn attention, their copper spear points perfectly straight and aimed at the sculptured ceiling overhead. The openness that was present when Astron had first arrived had been replaced by substantial-looking panels that blocked everything behind from view. Footfalls echoed from the unadorned walls. Somewhere in the background, pipers still trilled melancholy airs.

"I apologize for my lack of attention," Nimbia said as they entered, "but the emotion had to run its course.

182

Nothing has changed, of course, but at least now I can be a more proper hostess."

"How do you seek?" Astron ignored the courtesy. He quickly reviewed the questions that he had decided to ask at the first opportunity. "I deduce from what I have seen that you command the ring of djinns to bridge between realms that you have never seen before. How do you know they are there? Would not the action be one of discovery, rather than creation?"

A weak smile appeared on Nimbia's face. "I see our control of your kind is not something you ponder lightly," she said.

"I appreciate the extent of your power," Astron answered. "The youngest hatchlings are taught to avoid the lure of the fey." He wrinkled his nose. "But even the mightiest djinn cannot respond to an order poorly formed. He cannot pass through the barrier to another realm unless you explicitly direct him there. If he knows it not and neither do you, there is no way an opening can be formed."

"But we do know the realms where the ring is commanded," Nimbia said. "We know them because they are formed by our thought. We do not discover other realms, demon; they are created by the fey exactly as you have heard us say."

Astron opened his mouth to speak again, then slammed it shut as the significance of what Nimbia had said began to sink into his stembrain. She spoke casually, as if what she said was of no great matter, but the words brought forth images as staggering as those in Palodad's lair.

"You create realms," he said slowly, trying to fight off the stunned numbness that began to tingle through his limbs. "You are the ones responsible for the realm of daemon, the realm of men, and all the others."

"No, no, not the demons," Nimbia said. "As you well know, your realm spans the space between all the others. It must have existed far before the oldest memories of our own. Somehow it is different from the rest.

"And as for the realm of men, none of my brethren

183

would admit to such an act—conceiving something so misformed. Perhaps ages ago, before our art reached its present level of perfection, it was accomplished—or maybe it was the other way around, we are all the product of the fancies of men. Otherwise still, both could be the discarded first attempts to achieve perfection by yet some other beings. If that is so, it explains why so many of the realms are similar."

"What do you mean?" Astron persisted. "What realms—"

"Of the ones you saw on the slopes of the glen," Nimbia said, "I was the author of the last. I conceived the waves of black and the forces that gave them motive power. It was my thoughts that strained against the compressive forces that push against all the realms, trying to crush them to nothingness."

"I am sorry," Astron said. "You speak too quickly. I do not understand."

Nimbia's smile broadened slightly beneath her sad eyes. She gestured to one of the sentrymen standing in a doorway at the rear of the hall. "Pipes and cooling gels," she commanded. "I must explain what to the fey is common knowledge and second nature."

Astron watched as three pages shortly appeared, each one carrying a bowl of a steaming and viscous liquid. Behind them came three more, these bearing tripods and long metal pipes under their arms. The bowls were set erect in the stands and each of the trio handed a horn.

"You saw the pipers display this art when we returned from the judging," Nimbia said. "It is a festive symbolism of what we accomplish with our thought." She pointed in Phoebe's direction. "Let the female start. The brew before her is the most fluid."

Phoebe handled the horn tentatively but Nimbia waved her on. "Insert the pipe and blow," she said. "Show the power of creativity."

Phoebe thrust the flared end of the horn into the clear broth and took a deep breath. She exhaled forcefully and Astron saw a riot of tiny bubbles cascade to the surface and burst.

"Secondly the man," Nimbia said.

Kestrel frowned but positioned the long pipe into the liquid. He tentatively puffed into the horn and then strengthened his efforts. Astron saw agitation in the broth but little else. Kestrel's frown tightened. He inhaled deeply and pressed his lips about the mouthpiece of the horn. With bulging cheeks and eyes, he forced his breath through the long passageway into the brew.

Astron saw the surface ripple and then a single tiny bubble float gently upward. Kestrel lowered the pipe from his mouth, breathing deeply from the effort.

"And now the demon," Nimbia said. "Show who is the mightier of breath."

Astron stepped forward reluctantly and placed his hands on the pipe. He had no great need for moving large quantities of air in and out of his body and doubted that his strength matched that of a man. Nevertheless, he blew as hard as he could into the resistance.

For a long moment he strained and nothing happened. He concentrated on constricting his chest as far as he could. He clamped his elbows to his sides and strained with the muscles in his back. Then, just as he was preparing to abandon the effort, he felt a sudden lessening of resistance. He looked into the broth to see the beginning of a bubble emerge from the bell of the horn. With a hatchlinglike delight, he pointed at what he had done but halted in mid-gesture as the fluid collapsed the emerging bulge back into the pipe.

Nimbia nodded. "Imagine each realm as a bubble in a great sea," she said, "resisting the surrounding pressure by outward forces of its own. If the powers of expansion are insufficient, the bubble collapses into nothingness; but so long as they are strong enough, the realm survives.

"And what is the nature of this outward-directed power? Nothing less than the belief that the realm does indeed exist. If I can formulate a consistent system that has enough clarity in my mind, a rift occurs in the great sea; a tiny bubble forms that pushes back the oppressive forces and exists where there was nothing before.

"The effort required is a staggering one, far far greater than what you experienced with the gels. It is not everyone that can do it. But to the extent that I give my creation a compelling richness, others will also become enamored of its beauty. They, too, will think of it often, adding to the forces that keep it alive. So long as we ponder its being, the crush of destruction can be withstood."

Astron wrinkled his nose. For a long moment he pondered what he had heard. "It sounds like the balloons in the realm of men," he said at last. He propped the mouthpiece end of the horn carefully on the floor while he watched the bell end rise slowly from the clinging viscosity in the bowl. "Are you the only ones with such a power?"

"Beings in other realms can perform these creations as well," Nimbia said. "Why, even humans with their fancies and tales for the sagas have probably created universes, even though they know not what they have done. Their passions can sometimes be as great as our own. The recording of these ideas on parchment is an analogue to what we do with our song tellers—spreading knowledge of the creation, so that others can experience the wonder and aid in its existence."

Nimbia's eyes took on a faraway look. "As for the ability of the fey, it is the nature of our very own realm —the dictums of magic that are part of it, the storm of our emotion; these are the things that make us perhaps the most proficient."

"When the tales are put away and men read them no longer?" Phoebe looked up from where she was stirring the thinnest of the three fluids with the end of her horn. She spoke in a halting voice, the unfamiliar words of a new language setting heavy on her lips.

"If the creation has by that time not achieved a sufficient vitality of its own, if it has flaws and inconsistencies like a poorly constructed watch, it will eventually run down and be compressed back into the nothingness of the sea—just as you saw with the attempt of the demon." Nimbia paused and her eyes widened. "But if the construction has been a sufficiently skilled one, with sentient beings of its own that believe in themselves, in their own existence, then the realm remains. Those inside provide the outward pressure that keeps the crushing forces of the all-enveloping sea at bay—a true creation of great art.

"That is what we strive for. It is the ultimate goal to which any fey can aspire—to create a new realm equal to our own, one that exists in and of itself, with all the thought being provided from inside, rather than the continued attention of those who first brought it into life.

"You saw the vitality of my creation when viewed through the circle of djinns. It lived, lived of its own volition! There should have been no way for Finvarwin to judge it inferior to empty motions of Prydwin's—despite the fact that what I did was accomplished without a mate."

"If you think the outcome of your efforts not to be fairly determined," Astron said, "then why do you try? Surely, with all that you command, there are other amusements that would serve as well."

Nimbia shook her head slowly. "There is nothing to compare to the joy of creation," she said. "The sense of accomplishment of bringing into being an existence out of the void. To be denied that pleasure is the greatest penalty that the high king can exact."

She waved her arm about the throne room. "The melancholy is not only my own. Even though only a king or queen is able to force a realm to spring from the void, everyone who serves contributes their thoughts to make it grow. They all savor the feeling of accomplishment, the thrill and wonder when the realm takes on a sense of being of its own, the pride when other underhills view what they have wrought."

Nimbia shook her head a second time. Fresh tears glistened in the corners of her eyes. "It is the duty of a hillsovereign to provide the basis, so that all can share. Her own sadness is all the greater because she must bear the responsibility of so many in addition to her own."

"Duty," Astron said. "Is not that from the subject to

the prince? You seem to state that it is the other—"

"The other realms have witnessed this melancholy, although they do not understand." Nimbia ran on, apparently not hearing the interruption. "In times past, other underhills unable or forbidden to create on their own have been reduced to merely watching. But just to observe realms who owe none of their existence to your craft makes the restrictions all the more heartpiercing. Usually we remain underground, so as to block out even the hint of pipes from others who are more fortunate."

"Then you do look into the realm of men," Kestrel said. "It could be that our tales are not by mere luck the same after all."

"My own underhill has not viewed the affairs of humans," Nimbia said, "but that does not preclude the actions of many others. And as you probably have surmised, the ring of djinns can be seen through from either side. No doubt if you have legends of strange beings, piping music, and forced gaiety appearing out of the mists and then vanishing again, it is because of the fey."

Nimbia stopped speaking. She dabbed at one tear on her cheek and stared off into the distance, apparently consumed by her own innermost thoughts.

"We asked before about the ultimate precept," Astron said after a moment. "Could it be that it too plays a part in the construction of these creations?"

Nimbia looked back down at Astron. She slowly shook her head. "Of such I have not heard," she said. "Our realm is governed by seven dictums of magic, like all the rest. The last two are those of dichotomy and ubiquity as you well know. They are the basis for the communication with the mighty djinns of your kind."

"Then perhaps one of the others," Astron said.

Nimbia rubbed her cheek dry and flicked back a golden curl over her shoulder. She shrugged again and began reciting, as if she were a broodmother instructing her latest clutch. "Of the first I have already spoken—reality follows from passion. Our temperaments are not placid, like those of the skyskirr. Instead, they are the fuel that fires our imaginations when we attempt to wrest a new universe from the void.

"The second as simply stated—strength comes from the lattice—guides our thoughts as we try to create. It is easier to conceive of a realm with dictums of magic close to our own, rather than more exotic ones about whose existence we can only guess.

"The third is a warning—weakness comes from contradiction. As I have already explained, a realm will eventually wind down and stop, because the postulates that we use in its beginning do not mesh into a harmonious whole.

"Of the fourth, even you have probably heard enough —two is greater than one and one. Somehow, when we are paired as loving mates, the creations are more fertile, more exotic, more likely to live.

"The fifth is stated—reap what you sow. It is the pollens we toss into the rings that somehow unlock the thoughts deepest within us, that give rise to our most exciting thoughts. Each type has its own—"

"Wait. Pollen did you say?" Astron interrupted.

"Yes," Nimbia said. "We do not know for sure exactly how they play a role in the process, but none of the fey attempts to create or embellish without a large supply on hand." She motioned to one of the sentrymen standing in the entryway. He retrieved a small chest that he brought forward and placed at Nimbia's feet.

Nimbia opened the arched lid. She gingerly reached in to withdraw a prickly sphere like the one Astron had seen Vastowen toss into the ring. It was far larger than the others, however, as big as a small melon. Nimbia held it delicately with extended thumbs and forefingers.

Astron looked at the globe carefully and understood Nimbia's cautious touch. The entire surface of the orb was covered with clusters of tiny barbs. Smaller hairlike shafts radiated in all directions from each of the prickly pylons and, in a blurry haze, these were anchorage for tinier projections still. Beyond the craft of the finest weaver in his own realm, the structure of sharp piercing

189

points iterated into infinitesimals, far smaller than the eye could see.

"We toss pollens through the ring of djinns to seed our thoughts in the void," Nimbia said. "Our success seems greater the more massive they are. To create something of value before Prydwin comes, I would need to use the largest of all, but in all of my underhill I have only this one."

"Are they hard to find?" Phoebe asked. "Could a human wizard help in their retrieval?"

"The flowers that produce them abound in a glen not too far away. The problem is not in harvesting them but harvesting them now. At present, the glen is alive with the hum of its guardians, and no one dares enter until they have gone on their way. After so many did not return, wisely did Finvarwin issue the prohibition—"

"We seek a pollen as part of our quest," Astron said. "This one that you desire, what is its name?"

"This would be called harebell in the realm of men." Nimbia nodded at the sphere in front of her. "That is why your question on our arrival struck such a chord. Of course, of all that I could wish, it would be the best. But of all that there are, it is the one I cannot obtain."

"Harebell pollen—and you can create," Kestrel said excitedly. "Create for Finvarwin so that you can get answers as a boon—answers that Astron seeks." His face broke into a broad grin. "Wipe the tears, Nimbia," he said. "I have a deal for you."

## CHAPTER FIFTEEN

# *Harebell Pollen*

ASTRON adjusted the straps that ran across his chest. He had gotten quite used to the tunic and leggings of men, but now the rucksack was a totally new sensation. He looked out between the columns of the raised hilltop and saw Kestrel urging him to hurry. Beside the human stood six of Nimbia's sentrymen, each carrying a long copper-tipped spear in addition to the dagger at his side. Their faces were rigid with tension; none showed Kestrel's enthusiasm to be under way.

Astron took a step forward and then hesitated. The opening in the wall to the left led to the throne room. He poked his head through the doorway and saw that Nimbia was alone, still sitting on her throne where they had left her when the planning was complete.

Despite the short length of his training, Kestrel had been most glib. Whatever dangers lurked in the harebell glen, he had said, they well might not affect human or demon at all. With a modest escort to protect against a chance encounter with Prydwin's forces, he and Astron would fetch the pollen and share with Nimbia what they obtained.

Then, with boosted confidence from the pollen's potency, Nimbia could create something that Finvarwin certainly would approve. They would not wait for the next judging or to see if they could fend off Prydwin's attack, but go directly to the high king for a special presentation. Phoebe could even help in the control of the ring of djinns. At the very least, Finvarwin's previous judgment would be reversed and Nimbia's underhill regain its independent status.

With Finvarwin's answer to the riddle and the harebell pollen as payment for Palodad, the old demon would
get Elezar restored to power and he in turn would explain to Alodar the innocence of Phoebe and Kestrel.
With a little luck everyone would achieve exactly what
was desired.

When Kestrel had finished, Astron saw Nimbia's
spirits begin to lift. Now, a few hours later, as he prepared to leave, the sadness had totally vanished from her
eyes; she stared off into space, presumably thinking of
her new creation.

Astron scraped his pack along the doorjamb and Nimbia turned at the distraction. She smiled and beckoned
him to enter.

"Any more questions, inquisitive one?" she asked as
Astron drew closer.

Astron looked at the perfectly sculpted face and
graceful limbs. Another unanswered puzzle leaped into
his mind. "You spoke of the great melancholy that comes
when those of your kind cannot create," he said softly. "I
have seen your tears and I believe. But before we came,
before Finvarwin's judgment, what then was the corresponding joy?"

Astron shrugged and folded his fingertips to his chest.
"We shared thoughts in the forest," he said. "There I
glimpsed a sadness even deeper than that which is lifting
now."

For a long moment Nimbia did not reply. She sighed
and beckoned Astron to sit on the steps leading to her
chair. She gathered her jeweled cape about her as he
squirmed to get comfortable with the pack pulling on his
back.

"Yes, indeed it is a conundrum." Her voice took on a
hardened tone. "As you say, I am no less than a queen of
underhill. My life should be like the foolish tales that
men record in their sagas, with scores of smitten pages
vying with one another to do my bidding and any hinted
wish their fondest desire. Eventually, from all the rest I
would pick the bravest, the kindest, the one most fair.

192

Together we would spend our lives in a blissful happiness, about which others can only dream.

"It is not so, demon." Nimbia shook her head. "There are no hovering suitors trying to outdo one another to gain my favor. Most of the males in this underhill seem completely dumbfounded in my presence; their self-esteem seems to melt with my smile. Hardly any dare believe that they would succeed against what must be many others and so they do not try.

"And the few that do hold their own value in high regard, the ones that, in desperation, I have run to, offering to subject my will to theirs—without exception, they have proven to love themselves far more than me. To one of them, I have been no more than an object, a trophy to prove yet again his own great worth."

Nimbia paused and sighed. "Even if I were able to accept that part of it, despite how much I might try, the liaisons have never been pleasant. Underneath the bragging of conquest, my mates have been consumed with insane jealousies, irrational fears that they cannot forever hold me as their own, and that I will tire and shame them in front of another.

"It is a fantasy, demon. I do not fully understand why, but for one such as I there is no such thing as living happily ever after."

Nimbia looked at Astron with eyes once again filling with sorrow. He felt a strange stirring. The queen had shared with him some of her innermost thoughts and feelings and done so unbidden. There was no question of the domination and submission of wizardry of which he was familiar. She had trusted and given of herself freely. He knew something of another thinking being in a way that he had never experienced before.

A sense of compassion for Nimbia's plight bubbled up within him—and more importantly, an urge to show that he was worthy, that he understood, and that her trust was well-placed, with a friend rather than a stranger.

"I—I was born without wings," he heard himself blurt without thinking. "Unlike my clutch brethren, neither could I soar through the realm nor weave more than the

193

simplest of matter. I have become a cataloguer, an observer of the bizarre in other universes, and a value to my prince."

Astron lowered his voice to a whisper and continued. "But I know of what you speak, of pains deep in the stembrain that no matter of higher logic can ever completely cover. I am only a shadow of a demon, Nimbia, only a small part of what it is my birthright to be. I look at the mighty wings of the splendorous djinns as they send the air into pulsing eddies with their strokes and a rage at the unfairness of it all burns deep inside. I lower my membranes and cover my ears from the power of the great explosions that my brethren can ignite at will, and a melancholy perhaps as deep as yours stirs from its deep burial."

Astron opened his mouth to say more but the words escaped him. What was he doing? His mind recoiled in numbness. The thoughts that he struggled so hard to keep buried were whirling unabated. And he had done no less than articulate them to one who was not even in the domain of his prince. He rose on one knee to withdraw but his limbs rapidly began to stiffen.

"Forgive me," he mumbled thickly. "Those words, those thoughts, they were not meant for another. I, I have—"

Nimbia reached out and placed her hand lightly on Astron's shoulder. "Thank you," she said, seeming to ignore completely his sudden discomfort. "That is exactly what I needed. You serve your hillsovereign better than many of my own kind."

Astron managed to shake his head, straining against the tightening tendons. Then he caught Kestrel entering the throne room and felt a sudden relief at the human's presence.

"Yes, I am finally coming," Astron said. Awkwardly he rose to his feet and adjusted the pack on his back. "A final word with the queen to learn more of the dangers."

Kestrel shrugged and motioned over his shoulder. "Walk with the rest of us now or catch up later," he said.

Kestrel left the throne room as rapidly as he had come. Astron scrambled to follow. Another confusion had piled on top of the rest. He had not spoken to Nimbia of dangers. For the first time in his life, just like a human, he had told an untruth.

The trek to the glen of harebells proceeded uneventfully. The constant twilight did not waver. No one else was seen on the grassy trails. Shortly after Kestrel and the fey arose from their second sleep, the party began climbing a final hillock crested with giant ragwort and broad-leaved thyme. Astron inhaled deeply the aromatics which hung heavy in the air.

Behind them, the lush green carpet spread as far as the eye could see, eventually vanishing into the softness of fog and mist. Like blemishes on smooth skin, clumps of mushroom, golden cowslips, and foxglove scattered across the low-lying grasses indicated the presence of springy marshes with ground far wetter than the rest.

"What is it?" Astron heard Kestrel growl ahead of him. "We have come too far to begin slacking the pace now."

He looked up the trail and saw that the fey had stopped and Kestrel had almost closed the distance between them. Kestrel scowled and flexed his back, pulling at the straps of the rucksack he bore. Apparently the adjustment did not help; in irritation, he slipped out of the burden and let it fall heavily to the ground.

"The shrill vibrations are worse than I have ever known them before," the first of the fey said as Astron caught up with the rest.

"What vibrations?" Kestrel shook his head. "I do not hear a thing." He flexed his back again. "All I know is that we have been pushing hard for two days and the end is in sight. Now is not the time to have second thoughts."

"The irritation is part of the effect," another of the fey said. "Perhaps the sounds are too high for your ears, but they are there, nonetheless. You feel them, even if you cannot hear."

Astron strained to catch some sense of what the others were talking about, but he heard nothing. Although demon sight was keen, their hearing was inferior to that of many other beings. Nor did he feel any of Kestrel's irritation or the growing agitation of the fey.

"The risk is too great." The first shook his head. "Better to bear the burdens of Prydwin's pollensacks than not to exist at all. Your words may have been smooth enough for the queen, but she does not risk the dangers of the glen herself."

He flung off his pack and grabbed at the arm of the second. For a moment the two hesitated and then, after wide-eyed glances back up the hill, they bolted in the other direction, gathering speed as they ran. The panic was contagious. The remaining four did not even bother to lighten their loads. Fighting each other for the center of the trail, they sprinted off after the others.

Kestrel watched the fey depart and kicked at his own rucksack. Astron shrugged but said nothing. He stepped past and continued up the slope. For a long while, Kestrel stood with hands on hips scowling. Then he gathered up his equipment and scrambled to catch up with the demon. In a moment they were peering out from under the cover of a ragwort leaf into the glen of the harebells.

The hill sloped downward from the ridge under a cover of thick-leaved grasses, just as it had on the other side. But midway down the slope, a wall of skyward-pointing leaves poked out of a heavy mist and blocked the view. From what looked like a thick forest of upraised green swords, fragile stalks rose even higher, almost to the crests of the surrounding hills. Impossibly slender, the ropelike shoots wavered in gentle rhythms, as if trying by an act of delicate balance to keep from crashing to the ground. And on the end of each, looping over and hanging as a massive weight, was a deep-bowled blossom that swung back and forth. All of the flora of the realm possessed massive proportions, but the harebells seemed among the largest of all. A man or demon could easily hide within a single flower, if he climbed that high.

After a moment's observation, Kestrel stirred and started down the hillside, but Astron grabbed his arm and held him back. The demon pointed at a hint of blurry motion above the mist and then at a second and a third. One of the harebells rattled with energy. Brilliant orange-and-black stripes emerged from the petals and then hovered still.

"Bees!" Kestrel exclaimed as the recognition came to him. "Giant bees the size of the flowers." He put his hands over his ears. "And the noise—it is their wings. They buzz so fast that one can barely hear."

Astron looked at the large insect before it darted away. Knowing what to look for, he spotted several more flitting through the flowers. Large, multifaceted eyes, like great blackened shields, rode above a mouth siphon bristling with golden hairs. The wings were a blur about the bright abdomen, to which were attached legs folded in an intricate maze. From the rear protruded the sharp tip of the stinger, glistening with venom. Astron shook his head. Judging from the size, the poison would be totally unnecessary. The thrust of the lance would bore right through the chest as surely as a shaft of steel.

"If it were not for the tales of no one returning, we could risk it," Kestrel said. "Just walk out and pick a stalk that none of the bees seems interested in. Perhaps we could even shake some of the pollen to the ground."

Astron did not immediately respond. Quickly he ran over in his mind what he had learned of bees in the realm of men. "Smoke," he said after a moment. "Perhaps the ones that venture close can be subdued, if we surround ourselves with sufficient soot and ash."

"There is little here that will burn." Kestrel shook the leaf overhead to release a shower of water. "Nothing about is sufficiently dry."

"There is one thing," Astron said. He reached into his pack and pulled out the single grain of harebell pollen he had brought with him to ensure positive identification. Delicately, he placed it on the ground just beyond the cover of the ragwort, frowning in distaste at the many prickly barbs that pierced his fingertips.

He withdrew one of the oil bladders he had used when studying thaumaturgy and stretched it into a crude lens with his thumbs and forefingers. "I had wanted to try the experiment when we got above ground, anyway," he explained as he adjusted the focus. "Even with diffuse light, the energy might be converged enough if the material is sufficiently combus—"

The harebell pollen grain suddenly began to smoulder. A ringlet of dense black smoke bubbled from the surface and rose into the air. Kestrel coughed. Astron put down the lens. He saw the surface of the pollen glow into incandescence around the origin of the fire and the circle slowly begin to spread outward in a growing ring. The smoke thickened and cascaded from the pollen in billowing waves, far in excess of what one would expect from such a small amount of flame. Like a black fog, it began rolling down the hillside toward the harebells.

"Smoke subdues bees in the realm of men." Astron motioned Kestrel to follow him as he stepped forward from under cover. He stopped and picked up the smouldering grain. "Let us move quickly before it burns itself out."

Kestrel watched Astron proceed halfway down the slope and then raced to catch up. Together they reached the slender stalks of the harebell without alarming any of the bees which buzzed overhead.

"You stay here and keep the fire going," Kestrel said when they reached the base of the nearest flower. "I will climb up and shake loose what I can."

Astron nodded and watched Kestrel wrap himself around the ropelike stem that soared into the air. The demon placed the pollen grain at the base of the plant. With both hands, he fanned the dense smoke sluggishly upward, enveloping Kestrel as he slowly rose.

Kestrel reached the bowed apex of the harebell without incident. Then, letting his feet hang free, he descended hand over hand onto the bowl of the flower itself. Astron watched him tentatively test the strength of an individual petal and then pause, apparently trying to figure out the best way to get inside.

Two of the bees swooped in Astron's direction; but at the last moment, they both turned aside and buzzed off toward different flowers. Evidently the smoke was not something that they voluntarily wanted to encounter. Astron kept fanning the heavy billows outward and upward, watching warily for any signs of agitation among the darting insects.

He looked up to see Kestrel dangling in midair, one hand holding the tip of a bluish petal and the other reaching for the knobby stamen that protruded from the center of the bowl. In an instant, Kestrel vanished inside the bloom. Then a moment later, a shower of pollen grains just like the one that was burning began to cascade downward to where Astron stood.

Astron stopped his fanning and removed his pack from his back. Scampering about like a small child, he harvested the grains and stuffed them into the empty pouch. He gathered a dozen grains and then three or four more until the pack was filled. He brushed his hands with satisfaction. Nimbia would be well pleased with what they had done.

When the flap was secured and the pack returned to his back, he glanced at the burning pollen grain and saw the color of the smoke lighten into soft grays. The burning ring of fire started to sputter. Only a tiny disk remained of what once had been a sizable volume. He looked upward to call Kestrel down and his stembrain suddenly jolted in spasm by what he saw.

The bright abdomen of one of the bees protruded from the flower into which Kestrel had vanished. A second was buzzing angrily around the stem, apparently awaiting his turn. Astron reached back to untie the pack, but then he saw the wings of the first bee flutter to life in agitation. Its stinger began to extend and the entire body contort inward toward the blossom.

Astron shook his head savagely to rid himself of his stiffness. He bent forward and blew on the smouldering pollen grain, bringing the flames back to life. A wave of smoke billowed out over the ground and covered his feet in inky blackness.

Astron started to fan the coiling tendrils skyward; then thought better of it. They would be too diffuse at the height of the blossom. He grabbed the grain gingerly in one hand and cupped its prickly surface carefully against his tunic. Savagely pushing aside yet another wish for wings, he grabbed the stalk and awkwardly began to climb.

Astron heard a high-pitched whine for the first time as he struggled upward, evidently caused by the confines of the harebell petals against the insect's wings. In agonizing slowness, he proceeded, occasionally catching glimpses of Kestrel's dark silhouette through the translucent blues of the petals. The human's body was pushed up into a tight ball at the very base of the flower, trying to avoid the larger blob maneuvering itself deeper into the bowl.

Finally, Astron reached the height of the drooping calyx of the harebell. All he could see of the flower's interior was blotted by the carpet of coarse orange-and-black hairs on the back of the bee. He wrapped his legs as securely as he could about the swinging stem and stretched out his hand containing the burning pollen grain.

Only a small curved disk remained of what once was a sizable sphere. He blew down the length of his arm but the flame responded only sluggishly. A few wisps of black rose into the bowl of the flower. Astron exhaled vigorously, pushing as much life as he could into the remains of the smoke. The twitching of the bee as it twisted itself deeper into the harebell slowed but did not stop altogether.

Astron looked at the remains of the pollen grain and the progress of the bee. Something more desperate would be needed if Kestrel was to be saved. Almost without thinking, he discarded the last dying embers and coiled himself up into a ball on the wavering stem. Then kicking as best he could, he hurled himself across the distance to the dangling flower, grabbing the hairs on the bee's back with both his hands.

With a noise like ripping paper, the bee's claws tore

through the petals as the added weight pulled it downward. In an instant, the insect was dragged free; with Astron clinging to its back it hurled toward the ground.

Once free of the confines of the blossom, the huge wings exploded into a blur of action. Stinging blasts of cold air raced across Astron's body as the insect tried to right itself. The bee lurched to the right and Astron felt a stab of pain in his shoulder as he struggled to maintain a grip. With a flip that hurled Astron up over the insect's back, the bee wobbled into a horizontal position. But the ground came rushing up too fast. With a jarring thud, they crashed into the ground.

Astron felt the air rush from his lungs as he slammed into the bristly back. Stunned, he rolled to the side and fell to the ground. The bee tried to rise on its legs, but only uncoordinated spasms shook its body. Its wings fluttered out of synchronization, blowing up a scatter of dewdrops among the wide blades of grass that covered the slope.

Astron looked quickly about, trying to clear his vision. He saw motion near the base of the stem and guessed that Kestrel was scrambling to safety. A pungent odor began to fill his nostrils; he saw the stinger of the bee at his side fully extended and glistening with a foul-smelling oil. In awkward steps on three legs, the insect was gradually turning its abdomen about to where Astron swayed as he tried to regain his composure. His head still rang from the contact and, against his will, he fell to one knee.

"Come on," Kestrel shouted behind him. "Somehow they can communicate. Look, the others are coming to the aid of the one you brought down."

Astron felt a firm grip under his arm and rose reluctantly to his feet. He followed Kestrel's tug and began to place one foot in front of another. Almost mindlessly, he picked up speed and began running up the slope. The ringing in his head grew more intense and almost painful. He placed his hands over his ears, trying to concentrate on keeping up with the human as he ran.

Almost without knowing, they reached the ragwort

201

and burst over the hill crest. Astron's vision began to clear; the high buzz in his ears started to fade away. In a few moments, they had raced down onto the wet flatlands and were heading back to Nimbia's underhill.

"You did it again, Astron," Kestrel said after they had caught their breaths. "You saved me when you had no real cause. First Phoebe and then you. I'm starting to expect it. It's almost enough to restore my faith in human nat—"

Kestrel paused, looked at Astron's demonic features carefully, and then laughed. "Well, maybe that would be going just a bit too far," he said.

CHAPTER SIXTEEN

## Nimbia's Challenge

ASTRON and Kestrel retraced their journey across the hills and glens as rapidly as they could. Without the fey to guide them and no directional aids in the sky, their progress was slowed. More than once, they wandered away from the faint trails and were set right only by Astron's keen eye and memory for detail. It was only after Kestrel had risen from his fifth sleep that they estimated that Nimbia's underhill was drawing near.

The last lush green hill beckoned them forward. Sparse groupings of blooming foxglove and withered cowslip past its prime dotted the hillocks. A carpet of ferns crowded close onto the muddy trail that squished in wetness with each step.

"So you knew nothing of thaumaturgy before possessing the archimage's book," Kestrel said as he paused for breath where the slope steepened. "Burning lenses and alchemical balloons. You are well on the way to becoming a master of many arts yourself."

Astron shook his head. "No, as I have tried to explain, nothing I have done involves any magical skill. I have learned only of adjuncts that can be used independent of the crafts—by you as well as any other."

"This journey has given me no more knowledge of the magical arts." Kestrel shook his head. "Indeed, if it were not for Phoebe's safety, I would not even be here." He shielded his eyes from the diffuse glare, trying to catch sight of something familiar. "Come," he said, "we have wasted too much time already."

"It is because I am a cataloguer," Astron continued as they resumed their march. "Unlike my brethren, I look beyond the facts as they are presented to the deductions that logically follow."

Despite his rush, Kestrel laughed. "If I were to judge, looking beyond what is apparent is perhaps where your faculties need mostly to be sharpened."

"What do you mean?" Astron wrinkled his nose. "As you have said, I was the one who calculated that balloons of lead could fly, that—"

"And the one who did not understand how a group of wizards would react when presented the opportunity for monetary gain." Kestrel held up his hand to stop the protest. "Nor even how to entrap the imps which you say you have known for eras.

"There is more to thought than a logical progression from one truth to another, Astron. Sometimes there is value as well in postulating alternatives, in letting ideas flow free."

Astron's puzzlement deepened. "I do not understand. How can such lack of discipline help me in my quest? Our course is clear; we merely have to follow the path to its end."

Kestrel rubbed the back of his neck and frowned. He looked up to the hilltop. For a long moment they trudged in silence.

"Well, for example, consider the matter of this Gaspar of yours," Kestrel resumed after they had climbed thrice the height of a man.

"He is not my prince," Astron said. "He would find

my existence not pleasing. In a tick of time, I would be given to the lowest of his djinns for sport. I serve Elezar, who finds pleasure in riddle and delicate weavings, rather than explosion and chaos."

"Exactly so." Kestrel panted. "From what little you have told me, Gaspar is a demon most unlikely to compose a riddle that would baffle your prince. Even if he could, it would not be his style. Think of it, Astron. Why has Gaspar acted as he has? From where has he obtained the plan to baffle your prince? There are inconsistencies here that cry for explanation." Kestrel shrugged and then put on a fresh burst of speed.

"That is what you should be thinking of," he said, "the deeper meaning of the riddles, not the relative weight of air and lead."

Astron adjusted his pack and hurried to keep pace. "Then what is the answer?" he asked. "Tell me what secrets this other way of thinking reveals. Do you mean to imply that Gaspar is under the control of a wizard, just as Elezar has succumbed to the archimage—that there is a being in some realm with a will great enough to subdue a prince of the lightning djinns?"

Kestrel stopped a second time at the crest of the last hill, while Astron struggled to catch up. "I do not know enough of your realm," the human said. "Perhaps there is no substance to my conjecture and everything is proceeding as it has been presented. But, as I have suggested, let your thoughts roam free. Perhaps, when you least expect it, an insight will come."

Astron wrinkled his nose. "It is hard to see the utility of such speculation," he said. "Although if that is the process by which you found a way to put imps in a bottle—"

The scene which stretched before them suddenly reached Astron's consciousness. He looked once at Kestrel and they both began to race down the slope. At the nadir of the glen, Nimbia's hillock stood elevated on the slender pillars as it had on their first arrival. But this time the underhill was ominously quiet and empty.

In silence, they ran onto the heavy stone flooring that

had been raised from below the ground. Obviously no one was about. Many of the interior walls and partitions had been removed and carted away. The dais of the throne room was bare. Empty sky showed through, where before had hung a delicate tapestry of vines. Two empty vats tipped on their sides were all that remained of the store of pollens and seeds. Several flutes and horns were scattered in a litter of leaves and copper swords on the stone floor. Here and there, spatters of blood mingled with the remains of other debris.

Kestrel and Astron raced about the empty corridors and then descended into the passageways below ground. They found almost everything ransacked there as well. They entered Astron's cubicle and saw that only the book of thaumaturgy remained, tossed into a corner, pages down. Evidently its strange script was of no interest to whoever had come. Astron turned to leave but Kestrel ran forward to the book. He flipped it over and pointed excitedly to the inside of the front cover. There in a precise script Phoebe had left a final message.

"Pipers of Prydwin have been seen in the glen," Astron read aloud. "Nimbia fears that he plans to come just before the next judging and claim the bondage that is his due. Even without the pollen, she must create for Finvarwin. It is one last desperate chance, even though Prydwin will certainly be there. I will accompany her and aid with my wizardry as best I can."

Kestrel quickly counted on his fingertips and looked at the notches carved in the doorjamb. "It is already the time of the next judging," he growled. "To the glen with the stream. If Phoebe and Nimbia escaped before the arrival of Prydwin's sentrymen that is where they will be."

Astron tapped the bulging pack on his back. "But without the pollen there is little chance they will succeed."

"Exactly," Kestrel shouted as he sprinted back up the stairs. "Somehow we must break through the ring that guards the glen and get them the help they need."

Astron felt his stembrain stir. Pulling Nimbia out of

the ring with total surprise was one thing, but breaking through to Finvarwin's rock long enough to use the hare-bell pollen properly was quite another. A shuddering spasm squeezed the breath from Astron's chest. He remembered all too well the crushing power of the combined wizardry of the pipers. He had expected one of Kestrel's clever deceptions as the means to allow Nimbia to compete again, not an insane dash that the humans enjoyed so much.

Astron watched Kestrel bound up the steps three at a time. Obviously the thoughts of Phoebe in peril had been too much for the human. He had surrendered to the panic of his stembrain, rather than think through what must be done. Grimly, Astron forced calm onto his own churnings. He would have to use the best of his reason to convince Kestrel to formulate a plan.

Astron laid a hand on Kestrel's shoulder to restrain him as they peered out from the cover of the ragwort. The temptation to wrestle with the human's will flitted through his mind, but he put the thought aside. There was no time for that. He would have to hope that the logic on which they had agreed would work instead.

"Look at them down there," Kestrel whispered desperately. "They are all alone, with not a single piper to guard them. At worst, Nimbia will become a slave to Prydwin; who knows what will happen to Phoebe."

"Yes, look at them," Astron answered. "Phoebe is cloaked. No one questions that she might not be one of their own kind." He touched the reassurance of the hood he had scavenged from the debris of Nimbia's underhill. "I can pass through the ring with the same pretense. Your presence will only sound an alarm."

"You are a demon and know nothing of this sort of thing," Kestrel growled. "If it were not for the fact that your command of the language is better, I would be the one wearing the cape."

"It is what we have agreed," Astron said quietly. "Propose another plan if you have one better."

Astron saw the muscles in Kestrel's face contort with

indecision. After a long moment, he sighed and slumped to the ground. "Go ahead," he whispered. "Just remember to answer any challenges the way I have indicated, quickly and with confidence—as if it is totally bizarre that there should be any suspicion."

Astron nodded and began to rise, but Kestrel caught him by the arm. "And none of those fool questions of your own. There is much at stake here, not a petty exercise in collecting data for one of your catalogues."

Astron pushed away a sudden rush of irritation. "Cataloguing is by no means petty," he muttered. "No other djinn under Elezar's command—"

He slammed his mouth shut. Kestrel was right. There were more important things to attend to now. He looked down toward the bottom of the glen, from under the cover of the ragworts. Finvarwin stood adjacent to his rock. Next to him, a circle of djinns arched into the sky as they had upon Astron's arrival. Prydwin stood in front of the flaming ring, partially blocking a view into another realm.

Within the fiery window, Astron saw what looked like two armies engaged in hand-to-hand combat, breaking limbs and spattering blood with intense dedication. The warriors on each side were thin-framed and delicate, like the fey. Their blows struck and parried in an almost stylistic dance, creating complex visual patterns that grew and decayed as the battle progressed. From the very center of the conflict, precisely straight paths of ashen white radiated out in many directions on a plane of gray and continued into the vanishing distance. Astron shook his head; he had never seen or heard the likes of such a place before.

A little farther to the right, he recognized Phoebe, despite the cloak; and next to her, similarly disguised, must be Nimbia, nervously pacing while she waited. As before, copper-daggered sentrymen ringed the slopes of the glen, adding the force of their wills to the control of the djinns who strained to bridge the gap between the realm of the fey and those that lay beyond.

Astron grimaced and concentrated for the last time to

push the tuggings of his stembrain far beneath his conscious thoughts. He adjusted his hood to cover as much of his face as possible and stepped out onto the grassy slopes.

He walked slowly down the hillside directly toward one of the sentrymen, looking past him toward the bottom of the glen.

"Halt," the guard said when Astron was close enough for him to hear the swish of his cape. "Prydwin defends his creations against a challenger from a far underhill. He displays no less than his realm of reticulates. There is to be no interference until the judging is done."

"I bring pollen that is plentiful in that far underhill for my queen," Astron said. "She is expecting my presence and I must pass."

A strange thrill ran through Astron as he said the words. They were filled with untruth and tasted strange on his lips. Yet he noticed that the sentryman did not immediately reach for his arms. Instead he rubbed his chin in indecision and looked closer at what had interrupted his concentration.

"Lower your hood so that I see that you indeed are not from a local glen," the sentryman said. "King Prydwin did not capture Queen Nimbia and all of her followers when he seized what had been granted to him in the last judging."

Astron's stembrain rumbled. He felt sharp impulses rip through his legs, compelling him to step backward. He clenched his fists and willed his thoughts into control. "I am disfigured," he said quietly. "A dagger such as yours severed an ear from my head and left a great scar. I wear this hood to cover my shame. Surely you can let me pass so that no one will see."

The sentryman hesitated. Astron stepped boldly forward. "In any event, I am within your ring," he said as he glided past. "You will have opportunity to challenge me again after the judging is done. For now, I must obey my queen, who bids me come forth."

The sentryman frowned, but made no attempt to follow. Through squinting eyes, he watched Astron slowly march down the slope. Astron forced air into his constricted lungs. The strange thrill blossomed into delicious triumph. He ran his tongue over his teeth, trying to savor every aspect of the feeling.

He had succeeded in getting past the guard, but not with a display of strength, as would one of his clutch brothers, or even with the knowledge of the cataloguer. He had woven an appearance of reality and it had been accepted.

He looked at Prydwin standing near the circle of djinns as he approached and then at Nimbia and Phoebe pacing nearby. Astron reached over his shoulder and grabbed the topmost of the prickly pollen grains from his rucksack. "The seeds for your planting, my queen," he said. "May your thoughts grow and prosper."

Nimbia's eyes widened in surprise and then she smiled. She said nothing, but pointed to the ground at her feet where Astron was to dump his burden. Astron removed the pack from his back and glanced again at the opening into Prydwin's realm. He saw the dancelike battle continue with an almost glacial slowness. A few spans away, the hunched figure of Finvarwin squinted at the motions with what looked like unwavering concentration.

"You see the vitality of the combat, my high king," Prydwin said. "It intensifies rather than diminishes."

"Enough," Finvarwin rumbled. "Let us see the offering of the cloaked ones who come from far away."

"Yes." Prydwin waved the demon ring to opaqueness. He stared at Nimbia's cloaked form and smiled. "I too have curiosity about this new creation—indeed, the creation and creator both."

Nimbia tugged at the corner of her hood and turned away. While everyone watched, she took a position in front of the ring. After a moment, she gestured that she was ready. Astron saw her drop to the ground, coiling into a tight ball and pulling her arms around her knees. Without speaking, she began rocking herself back and forth. For more than a hundred heart beats, nothing happened. Then a tiny spark of painfully brilliant red burst into being in the precise middle of the ring.

Nimbia screamed as if in pain and then forced a hearty laugh from deep within her chest. The amplitude of her rocking increased as more peals rang from her lips. She tossed back her head and the hood fell away to reveal her golden curls.

Astron felt a twinge in his stembrain. There could be no doubt about who she was. He saw two of Prydwin's sentrymen snap to alertness and step forward with daggers drawn. But their hillsovereign waved them to be still. With the broad smile still on his face, he struck an exaggerated pose of complete ease.

Nimbia's agitation increased. With a violent tug, she flung aside the cape and rose to her feet. Her laughter turned to tears. With violent sobs that racked her body, she raised her arms toward the ring, imploring the grayness to dissolve away.

She had known that the disguise would not long be effective, Astron realized in a flash. Her identity could not be hidden when so much passion was required for what she must do. There had not been time to create before the judging. It had to be done while all the others watched. And yet, she had come, rather than slink away to safety in the brush when her underhill was attacked. It was her duty, she had said, her duty to those over whom she was the queen. Astron shook his head. Such a thought would be completely foreign to the prince to whom he owed his fealty.

The pinpoint of light expanded sluggishly into a small disk, pushing against the gray void. The circumference seemed to tremble in a series of spasmodic expansions and contractions, oscillating in a complex rhythm, but slowly growing in diameter. When the disk had become the size of a small melon, Nimbia nodded to Astron, pointing at the pollen at his feet and then the disk.

Astron grabbed one of the harebell grains and lofted it at the vibrating circle. The aim was good, and it struck near the center, but bounced back at his feet. Of course, he thought quickly, transporting solid matter between the realms was a hard task for even the strongest of djinns.

It was the reason why Elezar had sent him to the realm of men in the first place.

He motioned to Phoebe to pick up the pollen and try where he had failed. Phoebe frowned in confusion at first, but then understood what must be done. Her lob struck the disk near the edge, but apparently close enough to what Nimbia desired, because the circle exploded into a blaze of color, expanding to banish all of the gray.

"An empty palette," Prydwin called to Finvarwin. "There is nothing there. As soon as Nimbia releases the pressure of her thoughts, the creation will collapse back into the void."

"Nimbia, here?" Finvarwin turned his attention for an instant away from the ring.

Nimbia ignored the taunt and directed Phoebe to continue tossing the pollen into the ring. The wizard hurled another grain and then, with increasing speed, began throwing more.

Astron watched the orbs as they sailed through the ring and seemed to strike the disk of red. Each seemed to transform as it flew. The prickly spines grew and bent at right angles, forming transparent squares of yellow; the bulbous central body wasted away so that only the boxes remained. Like checkerboards with some of the cells cut away, each pollen grain deposited a haphazard pattern of connected squares in the new realm, some with only two or three components, others with dozens or more.

Then, after the last grain thrown had been transformed, there was a sudden pulse of light. The plane of red shifted to a brilliant blue. But more importantly, Astron noticed, the patterns of squares had all simultaneously transformed as well. Some had vanished; new ones had appeared. The background pulsed a second time, shifting back to red and then again oscillating to blue. With each shift, the patterns of boxes transformed— some dying entirely, others growing in grotesque and complex ways, seemingly spawning children that evolved on their own.

Astron watched fascinated as the patterns unfolded. He concentrated on the simple ones that cycled through a series of repeating shapes and then suddenly saw the law that governed the behavior. He looked at Nimbia in admiration, struck by the clean simplicity of what she had done. Each square lived or died in the next cycle, depending on the number of its neighbors. With two, it remained from one oscillation to the next; otherwise it vanished. New squares were born according to a similar rule.

The elegance of the creation swept through him. He felt a great longing to plant a seed grouping of cells himself and see what would happen and to watch the pattern live and die. It was exactly the type of thing that would satisfy the cravings of the fey. Nimbia had created a most unique realm with a vital life force all its own. Surely Finvarwin would see the merit of what she had done.

Astron looked back at Nimbia and saw her collapse into a heap. "I call this the realm of the conways," she panted in almost total exhaustion. "It is a universe based upon—"

"I apologize for the wasting of your time with meaningless competition," Prydwin interrupted. "This is no better, Nimbia, than your offering the last time you were called forth."

"It is worse." Finvarwin squinted into the ring of djinns. "I see nothing but the dull repetition of red and blue. A well-defined realm, it is true, but one that bores after the briefest of inspections."

"But it is indeed my best!" Nimbia tried to regain her feet, but could not find the strength. "Look at what is there, Finvarwin. How can you so lightly dismiss what I have done?"

"Nimbia." Prydwin smiled. "Surely, even with the cloak, you must have known I would suspect—an unknown hillsovereign who mumbles to the high king only the minimum necessary to be granted a turn to present, an unknown hillsovereign indeed!"

Prydwin turned to Finvarwin. "You have already

212

granted me the boon of Nimbia's underhill, venerated one," he said. "What additional might I expect now that I have won the wager doubled?" He turned and called back up the hill. "Sentrymen, seize them. This time she will not escape."

Astron looked at Finvarwin but saw that the old one was unmoved. He swayed slightly on unsteady limbs but otherwise did nothing to explain his decision.

"No!" Nimbia cried out. "A second punishment will only add injustice to the first. It is not the fault of those who have dwelt in my underhill that these creations have failed to find your favor, Finvarwin." Slowly she extended her arms trembling from exhaustion, offering her wrists for bondage. "If any payment is to be made, it is the duty of their queen and no other."

"What, this is Nimbia?" Finvarwin said. "The hooded queen and she are one and the same?"

Astron watched Finvarwin's squint deepen as Nimbia struggled to stand. The hunched figure reminded him somewhat of Palodad, physically infirm yet continuing as he had for perhaps eons before. Age should have brought increased wisdom and the ability to judge better what his senses presented to—

Astron stopped in midthought. The explanation burst upon him. "He cannot see!" he shouted to Nimbia. "He can no longer discern detail—only large movements and general shapes. Finvarwin has judged your creations inferior because he never noticed the structures of what was really there."

Astron's thoughts raced. Just as in his experiments, sharpness of vision in a living being was a matter of lenses and bending light. He remembered the book of thaumaturgy and the many interesting diagrams it contained. Dropping to the ground, he began pawing rapidly through the contents of his pack, looking for what might give Nimbia one last chance.

With a surprising nimbleness, he fashioned some bits of copper wire into two small circles, connected them with an arc of metal and then attached longer straight segments on either side. He grabbed at one of the large

213

flat leaves near the stream bank and tore it into two disks that fit over the rings of copper, hoping the oozing sap would hold them firm. With a last segment of wire he punched a tiny hole in the center of each of the green disks.

"Here, try these." He raced up to Nimbia's side, extending his construction forward for Finvarwin. "Place them astride your nose and over your ears. The scene will be dim but a pinhole works as well as the finest correcting lens. I have tested the effect in Nimbia's underhill and seen how sharp the focus can be."

Astron's hood flew backward as he ran, but he was too excited to care. Finvarwin must see Nimbia's creation as it was meant to be viewed.

"The demon," Prydwin shouted suddenly in recognition. "The one who kept Nimbia from me, as was my due at the last competition. Challenge him, pipers, make him submit to our collective will."

Astron grimaced. The memory of his last ordeal sprang frightfully into his mind. And within their circle, there would be no way he successfully could resist.

"Like this." Astron demonstrated with the glasses and then thrust them into Finvarwin's hand. He started to say more, but felt a sudden compelling jolt. Staggering under crushing pressure, he sagged to his knees.

Through glazed eyes, he watched Finvarwin, with agonizing slowness, bring the strange object to his face. Astron pushed forward a resistance against the mental onslaught; but deep in his stembrain, he knew he would fail. His thoughts became sluggish, compressing in ways that were distasteful and bizarre. He saw the sentrymen racing closer, and among them Kestrel pounded down the hill with the rest.

"This is most amazing!" Finvarwin exclaimed. "There is more to your creation, Nimbia, than I first suspected. Yes, look at it—most clever, far more elegant that what Prydwin has offered to be compared."

"What is the ultimate precept?" Astron skrieked. "What law is supreme over all the rest? How does one start a fire in the realm of daemon? The prize for winning—the answers I must know."

"No, I am the winner." Prydwin swiped at Finvarwin's glasses, knocking them to the ground. "Do not be misled. It is some sort of demon trickery." He looked quickly about the glen. "Yes, there are four altogether. Get them all, the one still hooded and the other sprinting down the hill. Get them all while I reestablish contact with my realm of reticulates. Look again as you have before, my high king, and you will see."

Astron struggled to think what he should do, but he felt his being compressed into nothingness, all the sharp corners of his essence being smoothed away. With a dull thud, his head sagged to the wet earth. In a strange detachment, he noticed Kestrel being shoved to earth near his rucksack and Phoebe thrown beside it.

"Be careful, Prydwin," Astron dimly heard Finvarwin say. "Even a hillsovereign must abide by the decisions of the high king."

"I will accept no punishment for the likes of this," Prydwin growled.

"First, a competition that has been fairly won deserves its just reward," Finvarwin continued, "and then we will see what additional judgments are appropriate besides."

The high king paused briefly and cleared his throat. "Realities are no more than bubbles," he said. "That is the most profound truth that I know. If there is an ultimate precept, then somehow that knowledge must be a component part."

Astron tried to pull meaning from Finvarwin's statement but he could not. All he could do was focus on Prydwin's strident voice.

"There shall be no reversals of opinion, I say. If I cannot have Nimbia, then neither shall she have me. Quickly, sentrymen, I command you—all of them through the flame."

Phoebe's scream blotted out what Finvarwin said next. The last thing that Astron remembered was a sensation of being lifted and then being hurled through the air.

# PART FOUR

# *The Two Realms Of Symmetry*

## CHAPTER SEVENTEEN

## *Rotator's Move*

KESTREL shook his head, trying to force his thoughts to order. The disorientation was not as great as the first time he had travelled between realms, but it was there, nonetheless. He felt Astron's pack slide from his grip and crunch into a sea of sand that surrounded him as far as he could see. Vaguely, he remembered grabbing at the pollen sack as he was hoisted from the ground by Prydwin's sentrymen and bodily tossed at the ring of djinns. When he hit the plane of the vertical circle, he had felt a tremendous deceleration, like a ball of cotton hurled into a vat of thick molasses. The pack was almost wrenched from his grasp, but somehow he had held on and burst through to the scene that lay beyond.

He sat at what looked like the edge of a desert oasis. Astron lay crumpled at his side apparently unconscious. By Kestrel's feet was a placid circle of clear water with a diameter about twice the height of a man. He felt the rough bark of a tree at his back and saw five more arranged around the periphery at the vertices of a perfect hexagon. Phoebe wallowed to alertness in front of the tree directly opposite his own, trying to get her bearings. Next to the wizard, Nimbia slumped in a disarray of tunic, leggings, and cape.

A path of crushed white stones radiated away from each of the trees into the distance, across a featureless gray plane, vanishing in an indistinct horizon that blurred the separation of ground and air. A gentle breeze bathed the left side of his face and, just as in the realm of the fey, he could see no sun, only a diffuse light that seemed to come from all directions.

Kestrel cursed himself for being so impetuous. But then what else could he have done? When Prydwin called his sentrymen down to Finvarwin's rock, there had been no option but to bolt from cover to offer what aid he could. Phoebe had been in danger, and he could not just idly stand by.

But there had been too many. Like a sack of flour, he had been hurled through the circle of djinns into the realm of Prydwin's creation. Dazed from the jarring impact, he had watched helplessly as the others followed. Before any of them could stir, the portal back to the realm of the fey clouded and then closed.

Kestrel started to rise in order to see farther from the oasis, but felt a great weight that resisted his motion pressing downward on his back and legs. He increased his effort and managed to stand, although his body twitched from side to side from the buffet of small unseen forces.

"Stop," Phoebe cried from across the pool. "Stop whatever you are doing. Somehow you are pulling me upward. I cannot move freely on my own."

Kestrel looked again at Phoebe and saw her more or less erect but hunched forward and grasping toward the ground with empty hands. He felt his own fingers suddenly start to wiggle. Then, when Phoebe flung her arm backward to clutch at the tree behind her, his own body followed in an almost perfect imitation. Kestrel frowned and released the tension in his legs. He collapsed to the ground and saw that Phoebe did the same in unison.

"Somehow we are bound together," he said in amazement. "There is great resistance when our motions do not imitate one another. What kind of strangeness is this?" He glanced quickly to his side. "Astron, wake up! Explain what is going on."

Kestrel saw the demon stir slightly and, out of the corner of his eye, Nimbia move as well.

"It is the realm of reticulates," Kestrel heard Nimbia say in an exhausted voice. "Prydwin considers it one of his two masterpieces, despite the eternal strife and pain." She drew in a deep breath. "The effort to create is most exhausting. Give me a moment to regain my strength, and I will explain more."

Astron coughed and raised his head. Kestrel saw his nose wrinkle in puzzlement and then his dark eyes dart about the gray landscape. "Symmetries," he muttered, "like the hexagon of trees and the four of us at opposing vertices."

"Yes," Nimbia said. "This realm abounds in things that look the same under reflections, rotations, and other complex rearrangements. That is the way it was constructed. Actions that build symmetry are reinforced; those that break them are strongly retarded."

"Most interesting," Astron said. "I even have difficulty holding my mouth shut when I listen to you speak."

"You saw the battle before Prydwin shifted the view to this isolated node." Nimbia's voice rather than increasing in strength grew still more faint. "This realm is one of violence; we must be away."

"But the reason for our quest," Astron said. "It has not yet been completed."

Kestrel looked again at the unfamiliar desolation and felt a sense of strangeness and dread far more intense than what he had first experienced in the realm of the fey. "Let us heed Nimbia's words and begone before we encounter something we cannot handle."

"I have no answer to the riddle," Astron persisted. Struggling against Nimbia's resistance, he pulled himself to a sitting position. "As far as I can tell, the words of the high king about reality and bubbles have little to do with a flame in the realm of daemon. How can they save my prince from Gaspar's attacks?"

"Then tell it to the other, the one you call Palodad," Kestrel said. He pointed at the rucksack at this side. Phoebe's arm jerked in response. "Perhaps the one who reckons can analyze some hidden meaning, once you have paid him with the pollen."

"Palodad." Astron shuddered. He stopped speaking as membranes flicked over his eyes. "I had hoped to

221

seek out my prince directly," he said after a moment, "but your logic is correct. It is to the decrepit one that we must turn for aid and succor. Yes, Palodad first and then, with what he will hopefully add to the answer, search for the hiding place of my prince."

He looked across the oasis at Phoebe and Nimbia. "A fire, wizards," he said. "Break down the barrier between the realms and contact the one that we must."

"I do not have the strength." Nimbia rocked back and forth like a rag doll. "Certainly not the firmness of will that is needed. Let the human female try. She has been most eager to prove her worth."

Despite the difficulty in moving, Phoebe managed to smile. Fumbling with the pockets in her cape, she retrieved several matches but they tumbled out of her grasp onto the ground. She bent forward to pick them up but clutched only empty sand several handspans from where they fell.

For a moment Phoebe bent over awkwardly, deciding what to do next. "There is much resistance," she growled as she wrenched her head upward. "With what little kindling I have in my cape it is not such a small task as one might believe."

"It is the force of the symmetries," Nimbia said. "If you were broken free you could act alone."

Kestrel saw the demon look about the hexagon of trees and his nose wrinkle in thought.

"Yes, I believe it is the fact that we four are paired at opposite vertices," Astron said after a moment. "Kestrel, if you can move to another while Phoebe remains where she is, then the symmetry will be broken. All of us should then be free to act independently."

Kestrel quickly rose and turned toward the tree on his left but Phoebe's gasp of breath stopped him short. He looked in her direction and saw her body wrenched to the side, preparing to pace to the next vertex around the periphery just the same as he.

"No, not so fast," Astron said. "Relax your muscles and let Phoebe get situated first, perhaps with her arms

222

wrapped about the tree. Nimbia can help her resist and then you can move away."

Kestrel breathed out slowly. He did not quite understand what Astron had in mind, but clearly they had to try something other than what first sprang to mind. As he let the tension out of his limbs, he felt insistent tugs that turned him back toward the tree. He let the forces wash over him and, without resisting, stepped up to the coarse bark. His arms rose from his sides and extended about the trunk. With a tight grip, his hands clasped together on the other side. Across the pond, he saw that Phoebe was also hugging her tree in the same relative position as he.

Then Astron rose and approached the trunk from the opposite direction. The demon's arms widened into a semicircle. On the other side of the oasis, Kestrel saw Nimbia extend her arms around Phoebe's tree and grasp her hands together behind the wizard's back. At the last possible moment, however, Astron brought his hands sharply downward. Rather then intertwining behind Kestrel, the demon's fingers dug into the bark at his sides.

"Now," Astron said. "Gently release your grip and step away. With Nimbia's help, Phoebe might be able to resist following."

Kestrel grunted in understanding and began to uncoil his fingers from one another. He felt the same strong resistance to his efforts and heard Phoebe gasp in exasperation as her hands also became unjoined. Kestrel stepped backward and saw Phoebe arch in response, her feet moving from the base of the tree while Nimbia struggled to hold her firm.

Kestrel took another step and then, more quickly, another. He felt as if he were walking upstream in a swift current. But each step was easier than the one before and finally, midway between the trees, the force vanished altogether; in complete freedom he turned and walked to the next vertex of the hexagon.

Kestrel saw Phoebe slide to the ground, oozing out of Nimbia's grip. Tentatively, the wizard waved her arm and then shook her entire body. The smile returned to her face for an instant, and then she sobered into a serious expression. Busily, she retrieved her scattered matches. Reaching into her cape, she brought forth some small twigs and parchment and built them into a small papered cone at her feet. She returned to the tree which Nimbia still clasped and ripped several sheets of loose bark away from the trunk.

Pulling her robe about her, Phoebe kneeled by her assemblage of materials and struck a match against one of the scraps of wood. The head of the match skittered against the rough surface but did not light. Phoebe cursed softly and tried with a second matchstick, this time bearing down harder and paying strict attention to what she was about.

Halfway through her swing, however, the match broke in two. Frowning, she gathered five of the sticks together in a tight grouping and tried again. Even from where Kestrel stood, he could see the force of her stroke. The grate of the yellow-tipped heads growled far out into the featureless expanse of the desert.

But again no sparks resulted from the swipe. Phoebe's scowl deepened. Moving quickly, she clasped the matches with both hands and ground the cluster a second time against the surface of the bark. Again nothing happened and she began stroking repeatedly, each time more intensely than before, hardly pausing between swipes and ignoring the splinters of matchwood that spewed away from where she worked. In an instant, they were all destroyed, with not even the tiniest glow to show for her effort.

Phoebe looked over at Kestrel, crestfallen. She kicked at her mound of kindling and sent it flying. "The wizards of my council," she said sourly. "They were right after all. When it came time to do my part, even make the simplest of flames, I choked like a doxy from the sagas." She reached for her cape and flung it to the ground. "Even with the mantle of the master, I must turn to another to get the simplest job done."

"My apologies but I am still too weak." Nimbia shook

her head. "The struggle at the tree took away whatever remaining reserves that I had." She looked slowly out into the desert, scanning the horizon. "It is your powers that we must use, wizard. Get us away before it is too late."

Kestrel looked up into the tree under which he stood and spied a cluster of pear-shaped fruits. "Perhaps we are proceeding a bit too hastily," he said. "We have just been through a great deal. Let us eat first. Then one of you can try again."

To Kestrel's surprise, Phoebe shook her head violently and then sagged to the ground. For a long moment, she stared at the splinters in her hand and did not try to speak. "I have failed us all," she said after the longest while, "failed us all and precisely when it was needed most. Evidently, my words in the chamber of the archimage were no more than bluster. I failed in my cabin with the anvilwood and now a second time here."

"It is not so serious, Phoebe, just the strangeness of this realm. With a bit of food—"

"Do you not understand?" Phoebe's voice strained with a hollow sharpness. She waved at the refuse strewn about her. "I cannot start a fire here, Kestrel. I know. I can feel it. Perhaps it is within the ability of one truly worthy of the logo, but I cannot, regardless of the kindling."

"Then later, after we have all had a chance to rest."

"You are not listening," Phoebe exploded. Frustration and anger shot from her eyes. She clasped her fists tightly and beat them against her arms. "It is not a matter of demon control," she said. "I did not even get that far. It is just as pompous Maspanar and the others chided. Experimentation with tiny imps in the confines of one's own cabin is one thing. The measure of a true wizard is quite another—that which is accomplished when the consequences of failure are more than the loss of a fee.

"Not a spark. Not even a single spark. It is not merely a matter of new surroundings. It goes far deeper than that. I can feel the inhibition. I am no wizard, not in this place, not anywhere in all of the realms." She stopped suddenly, then looked across the oasis at Kestrel. "I am sorry, sorry that I made you come."

Kestrel looked at Phoebe and saw her self-esteem begin to melt from her expression as he watched. It was her only real reason for the quest, he thought. She had wanted to prove herself the equal of the others above all else. He glanced at the litter of matchwood and shook his head. She alone would know the limits of her prowess. If she could not start a fire, what she said must be true. And now, despite the unknowns they were yet to face, even if he could protect her physically, what could he do to mend the way she suddenly had come to feel about herself?

Phoebe looked at Kestrel sadly. "There is more than my shame, Kestrel," she said. She lowered her eyes and sloped her shoulders, sighing deeply. "Without a flame, we cannot get passage to any other realm—to that of men, of the skyskirr, or even back to the fey. Unless Nimbia can be aroused, we are marooned here—marooned forever."

Kestrel pressed his hand against his stomach. Enough time had passed that he could be reasonably sure of no ill-effects from the fruit. Climbing the tree and tossing what he had picked across the oasis had been easy enough, although Nimbia ate little and seemed to doze in a deep lethargy when she was done.

Kestrel grimaced. The fruit had been sweet and tangy, but helped his mood little, if at all. He looked at Phoebe and frowned. Despite his most careful words, she refused to be consoled. In an almost mindless obsession, she had assembled specimens of every different type of material she could find in her proximity, blades of grass, a handful of sand, tree bark and fronds, even the skins of the fruit they had eaten. But using one of the water lenses from Astron's pack to focus the diffuse light, she had succeeded no better than with her first attempt. There was no hint of flame, not even the tiniest wisp of smoke.

And now, rather than lifting Phoebe's spirits, he felt the crushing reality of her words growing with each passing moment. The featureless plane that expanded to the

226

horizon in all directions made the feeling of entrapment all the more intense. Perhaps there were great cities and enchanting delights just out of eyesight, but Kestrel thought it unlikely. The glimpse he had of this realm while still with the fey looked very much the same as what he saw now. Except for the presence of the fighting warriors, he recalled seeing only the same bleached straight-line paths radiating from a central point into the vast desert that was totally lacking in detail.

Kestrel kicked at the shiny metal protruding from the sand at his feet. He had not noticed at first, but at least three of the trees had some artifacts that appeared to have been hastily buried near their roots. The one where he sat was a filigree of wrought iron that terminated in a menacingly sharp point. No amount of simple tugging would free the ornate shaft from the ground. In front of where Nimbia dozed was what looked like the edge of a brass disk of substantial diameter, at least twice the height of a man. From the vacant node to Kestrel's left protruded a thin curved strip of steel that slowly oscillated in the gentle breeze.

But such things were properly only of interest to the demon, Kestrel thought. There were more important things about which to be concerned. He counted the fruit remaining in the branches of the trees and then the clear water of the pool. How long before they had eaten all that was here? he wondered. And if not great cities, would there be other oases like this one just beyond the horizon?

Kestrel stood to get a better view of a fruit cluster partially hidden by a branch. Suddenly he felt his left foot drag to the side and his entire body twist to follow. Phoebe gasped. He saw her reach suddenly to fling her arms around her tree, her legs sailing out nearly horizontal. In a flurry of sand and snapping capes, both Nimbia and Astron were tossed into heaps. Like tumbleweeds, they began to bounce out into the desert along one of the whitened paths.

"I surmise it is another symmetry," Astron shouted

backward as he tried to regain his balance. "Something acting on everyone and pulling us away."

Kestrel tried to turn and snatch the tree now at his back, but he was too late. The unseen force intensified. He was slammed earthward as if struck by a giant. He scrambled to his knees, but immediately was cast back into the ground a few feet farther from the pond. Kestrel spit out sand and clawed with his fingers, but he could tell that his efforts would be to no avail. He felt his body begin to drag across the coarse surface. The sand grated against his bare skin and then started to sting as his speed increased.

Faster and faster he flailed over the ground until even the wind whistled with his passage. A cloud of dust boiled up about him, forcing him to shut his eyes to keep out the bouncing grains of sand. The stinging on his forearms intensified from a mild irritation to a blistering pain. Kestrel raised his hands and arched his back to reduce his contact with the abrasive that surely would grind through his skin. With a gut-straining gasp, he managed to pull one leg forward under his chest and then savagely kick downward. He bounded from the desert floor and, in response to the reduction in friction, felt a rapid acceleration.

Kestrel fell back down earthward in a flat trajectory and then, like a stone hurled across a pond, skipped back into the air. This time his path straightened out parallel to the surface and he skimmed along in a straight line. As if he were a bead on an invisible wire, he hurled across the vast nothingness.

Kestrel cautiously opened one eye. When he saw that the cloud of dust had fallen away, he looked about. Phoebe and the others were also airborne on courses parallel to his own, all streaking across the plane above one of the white paths that had radiated from their oasis. He called out to Phoebe, but the whistle of the wind carried away his voice. He waved once and felt relieved when she shook her hand in reply.

Kestrel strained to look over his shoulder and saw that the oasis was already a mere speck in the distance.

As he watched, it disappeared into a haze. He turned back to squint in the direction they were travelling and detected a similar blur of detail on the horizon up ahead.

Kestrel watched the features sharpen as he approached. He recognized the tall trees and the white lines of other paths converging from different directions. He scanned their lengths as far as he could see, expecting the same emptiness on them all. But on the one that ran out across the plane to the right he noticed a hint of motion. Others were also coming to this oasis—warriors like the ones he had seen fighting within the ring of djinns.

As the two groups merged, Kestrel saw the shine of armor. He heard the clink of hard metal, even over the whistling wind. He fingered the pommel of the copper dagger from the realm of the fey, but took little comfort from it. The odds would be greater than five to one, even if Astron and the two women brandished arms as well.

Far more rapidly than Kestrel could think of what to do, he arrived at the new oasis. As abruptly as the forces had torn him from the other, they died away. He tumbled in a heap and offered only token resistance to the waning push that rolled him into the trunk of the nearest tree.

The warriors came to an abrupt halt at approximately the same time. With the precision of dismounting horse riders, they steadied themselves and remained erect. Kestrel grabbed his dagger, fearing the worst; but the warriors, after a brief inspection, paid him and the others little attention. With a few bellowed grunts that Kestrel thought he could almost understand, they quickly dispersed to each of the six trees that ringed the small pond in their center.

In an instant Kestrel was surrounded by a half-dozen tall and lean men with chalky complexions, only a few shades different from the paths that seemed to run from oasis to oasis. The first two began immediately to set up a small table from spars and hinged planks they carried on their backs, while a third uncoiled thick parchments crisscrossed with brilliant red and blue inks.

One of the men spoke and Astron immediately answered. Again Kestrel could make out most of what was being said.

"Since all of this is Prydwin's creation it is no wonder that we can converse," Astron explained. "It is merely a small change from the normal speech in the realm of the fey." The demon shrugged. "It is perhaps a detail on which Prydwin did not spend much effort."

"Your presence contributes to our freedom of movement," one of the warriors repeated, "and for that you have value. Though your appearance is different from either rotator or reflective, I do not suspect you of being chronoids, since your hands are empty of the foul artifacts they transport into our realm against the protocols."

"Share in our celebration of victory," another said. "The reflectives never suspected the richness of our symmetry until it was thrust upon them—no less than fourteen, and now they have been expulsed from every one. They did not have a chance for an exchange of bodies, not a one."

"From which did you come?" a third asked. "One of the lesser triangles of the central pentagram, or perhaps an octagonal node from the hypersphere of the great triad?"

Kestrel opened his mouth to speak but Astron was quicker. "What is the map?" the demon asked. "The lines in red and the nodes in blue with the crossed-out annotations—what do they mean?"

"It is the rendering of the great polytope, all that there is," answered the first. "See, already we make the changes that mark the victory." The warrior stopped and jabbed rapidly at the parchment. "It is all in accordance with the second protocol—all moves are simultaneous. We have occupied nodes here and here and then those over on the other side. They form the vertices of a figure with more than thirty edges. The reflectives were too concerned about this minor symmetry of three adjacent nodes here to notice what we had done.

"Look at the pattern closely, see how all thirty-seven form a beautiful pattern that is invariant if it is rotated through the small angle drawn over there." The warrior's face widened in a satisfied grin. "As the first protocol states—the greater the symmetry the greater the power. In perfect synchronization, those of us occupying the first node of the set began the journey to the second; those at the second unto the third. The reflectives who occupied part of the pattern were totally unprepared and the pressure to preserve symmetry was too much to resist. They were dragged from their fortifications into other nodes where yet more of us waited. We have won possession of more than a dozen."

Kestrel looked at the map where two of the warriors were busy erasing some sort of symbol by some of the nodes and replacing it with another. He glanced at Astron in confusion, but then relaxed when he saw that the demon had not wrinkled his nose.

"This map then is a reproduction of all that we see." Astron waved his arm outward toward the desert. "These oases are the nodes and the lattice lines the paths between them."

"It is a record of all the realm," added one of the warriors.

"And the symbol you are erasing—the nodes that are marked with it are under the control of the ones you call the reflectives." Astron stopped and studied the parchment for a moment. "You hold your territory most unlike the fashion of the realm of men," he said. "Look at how interspersed you are. How can you possibly say who has the greater advantage?"

"It is not a matter of adjacency, but of symmetry. Look at the beauty of the nodes that we possess. Of very high order are the subgroups that describe our lands."

"And that symmetry gives us power, power to strike at a dozen vertices as one, power to use the innate forces of the realm to aid us rather than fight against it in furthering of our aims."

"But why fight at all?" Astron asked. "What motivates you against these you call the reflectives?"

"Their symmetries are most foul," the first of the warriors spat. "They are invariant under reflection whereas ours remain the same when subjected to rotations instead. And as the fifth protocol states—victory is total, only one of two will be left. It is the duty of every rotator to resist reflectives wherever we can, to strive to eliminate them until none are left to poison the beauty of the true symmetries that we will build when they are gone."

"I don't understand any of this," Kestrel said. "It must be some sort of threadbare dream—scattered oases in a vast desert linked by geometrical designs, warriors engaged in mathematically obtuse campaigns. What of women and the crops that supplement these few fruits? Who weaves the clothes you wear on your backs and from where do the woolens come?"

"Most of your words make no sense whatsoever," the first warrior said. "Our lives are to fight the reflectives until either we receive mortal wounds or have totally won. The fruit of the trees provide us subsistence; our armor protects us from blows. Of these other things we have no need."

"But replacements," Kestrel persisted. "What happens when some of your number are indeed struck down?"

"Replacement?" the warrior echoed. "I do not comprehend. We fight the reflectives until one of us is victor. If some of my comrades fall, we recompute the symmetries for the numbers remaining, so that we have freedom of movement about the subnodes, as you see we have done here. There are no replacements. There never have been since the beginning of time."

Kestrel looked quickly about the oasis and noted that the warriors were deployed in what appeared to be a random fashion only at first glance. Closer examination revealed that the subgroups by each tree were different in many distinct ways from all the rest. Each had a different number, and the heights and weights were well distributed as well. The camp tasks they had undertaken were all unique and the identical weapons were stacked only where other differences outnumbered the similarities.

232

Kestrel glanced at Phoebe's almost vacant stare and Nimbia's listless shell hunched next to her. He looked back out onto the featureless desert. All that he could see was no more than the creation of one of the fey, he realized. It all had come into existence only by the force of thought—just like a scribe transcribing flights of fancy for the sagas, leaving out all nonessential detail. One could not really expect any more.

And they were marooned! The words boomed through his mind. Marooned in a universe in which all life apparently had to offer were the few simple rules of a game.

<br>

CHAPTER EIGHTEEN

## Artifacts of the Chronoids

KESTREL looked across the new oasis at Phoebe and forced his face into a smile. He had lost track of the number of nodes to which they had been transported, but it would do her spirits no good to show how low his own had sunk. Far better it would be as well if they could share the same subnode, but the rotators, with their rigorously balanced deployments, insisted that they be kept apart.

Nimbia on occasion seemed a little more alert, but most of the time she still dozed in her stupor at the base of the tree to the right of Phoebe's. Although Astron was at Kestrel's side, the demon again was occupied with learning about some obscure detail of the realm. Kestrel was alone with his thoughts.

More than he feared, the life of a rotator was one of almost complete ritual. In a rigid sequence they would plan, eat, sleep, and then, simultaneously with everyone else in the realm, rush over the sands to a new node that

233

looked almost exactly the same as the one they had left behind. Then, if the new node were unoccupied and there were no battle, the cycle would begin again. Plan, eat, sleep, move—they were merely playing pieces on a complex board, jockeying for position without ceasing.

Kestrel looked at the six fruit-bearing trees that ringed the small pond of water and then out over the featureless desert, trying to channel his thought in a more productive direction. He kicked at the sand at his feet, barely missing another shaft of ornately carved metal.

"Abel, what are these things?" he called out to the commander of the warriors. "Half of the oases we have visited seem to have them protruding from the ground."

One of the warriors looked up from where he had been conversing quietly with two others over the small portable table covered with the maps of the nodes. His complexion was slate gray like the rest, but streaks of black ran through his hair. His eyes were steady and unblinking in a face not creased by either smile or frown.

"They are the devices of the chronoids," Abel said with disgust in his voice, "the machines of beings of another realm—another realm just the same as yours. In our haste, we do not bury them as we might. They are a violation of the protocols."

"Another realm." Astron looked up from the scroll he had been studying intently. "We are not the only visitors you have seen?"

"Indeed not," Abel said. "Ever since the reflectives seized the origin, the visits have been most frequent. The chronoids look much as we do and they engage in some great struggle not so very different from our own. But their weapons are not similar in the least and they are difficult for us to understand."

"What kind of weapons?" Kestrel said, suddenly interested. "Something that would give you an advantage if you had them instead? Do they by chance involve the use of fire?"

"We would not use the devices of the chronoids." Abel pursed his lips. "The reflectives do so only at great

234

peril, since they work so imperfectly in a realm different from which they were intended." The commander stopped and looked at Kestrel intently. "More importantly, they are not part of the tradition that stretches back to the memories of our creation. Only the reflectives would think of trying something so base to gain advantage."

"But where are—"

"Perhaps it is worth the effort to show you one of the foul things," Abel said. "Then you might better understand." He gestured to one of the other gray warriors. The second began to protest but Abel's stare cut short the words. The warrior spat at the ground at his feet and then began digging into the sand. Shortly he retrieved an oblong box of metal and brought it forward for the others to see.

"Why, it looks like a clock," Astron exclaimed as the object drew closer. "A device for measuring the passage of time. See the three ornate bands of metal pivoted at the center of the circular face with symbols about the rim."

"These devices do much more than merely count the swings of a pendulum," Abel said. "Just as our realm is governed by the symmetries of space, so is that of the chronoids ruled by the symmetries of time. With these clocks, as you call them, they manipulate the order of events in strange ways."

"Here, in the realm of the reticulates, the devices behave in manners even more bizarre. The manipulations of time are somehow transformed to ones of space instead. In battles where the reflectives possess them, I have seen entire moves undone against our wills, even though we held the advantage—whole squads of men exchanged with those of our enemy so that we were outnumbered, rather than the other way around."

"How did this clock come to be here?" Kestrel asked.

"Somehow the reflectives have found a way to communicate between the realms, exchanging men with the chronoids for weapons that aid their own cause. Recently the reflectives seem to have increased the frequency of their contacts. The artifacts are more and more abundant. Ten thousand moves ago, we would find them only at one node in a score; now we see them at virtually half."

"And the rotators choose not to use those clocks?" Astron asked.

"They disturb the protocols." Abel again puckered his lips. "Their very presence somehow has changed the third and fourth laws so that they no longer operate as they should. And in our realm, strange things happen with them that even the chronoids never intended. Who knows when they will affect the first, second, and fifth laws?"

Abel looked out over the sands and shuddered. "Besides the forced transport of bodies to other nodes, I have heard of things happening inside as well." He paused and seemed to chew on his tongue. "I cannot totally explain, but the transformations of the clocks in the realm of reticulates can change more than just the physical. No, despite any possible advantage, we prefer to bury what we find in the sands."

One of the warriors from another of the subnodes called to Abel. The commander abruptly turned away without another word and resumed his duties. The abruptness of the rotator did not bother Kestrel. He had come to realize that there was little need for courtesy in a realm such as this. But the information he had learned had been most interesting. Perhaps there was something in what Abel had said that would help them in their plight. Kestrel looked at Astron, trying to draw out the significance of what he had heard, but the demon was again fully occupied by the parchment in his lap.

Kestrel saw a flash of color at another of the subnodes and immediately his attention was drawn away. Something was happening that he had not seen before. A giant sling had been strung between two of the trees. While he watched, a roll of brilliant red cloth was launched in a high arc into the sky. Like a streaking comet, the material unfolded into an eye-catching arch that could be seen far over the horizon. After it had plummeted back to the ground, several of the warriors raced out onto the desert to retrieve the cloth and roll it back up into a coil.

Kestrel saw four of the warriors at one of the sub-nodes scanning the horizon, three looking out along paths that ran to adjacent nodes, and two others at angles in between. Almost as soon as the signal bolt was retrieved, Kestrel noticed a flash of motion down the line of sight that was farthest to the left. Another banner of red soared up into the sky in answer to the signal.

Then in a clockwise direction from the first, just barely above the horizon and far more distant, four more banners answered as well. All eyes turned to the right-most path, the last of the six, but the sky remained calm; there was no arch of color sailing into the sky.

A sudden babble of excitement erupted from the rota-tors. Even though they had not yet eaten, shield straps were tightened and a dozen or more began practicing stylized jumps and feints with their swords.

"What is happening?" Kestrel asked Astron.

The demon stopped tracing his finger across a copy of the node network and listened to the rush of voices that Kestrel could not quite follow.

"The prospect for battle is high." Astron looked up from the map. "Imagine that this node is one vertex of a hexagon, just like one of the fruit trees around the oasis. The rotators also occupy the one on the left and then, on the far side of the center, three more as well." The demon pointed down the path to the right. "A contingent of reflectives just vacated this node before we arrived; they must be one adjacent move away, most probably at the last node of the six."

"So the warriors here arm for a fight against an enemy they have not even seen," Kestrel said. "The node on the right may be occupied by twice as many—or they might run before the battle can be engaged."

"That is not the way it is done in the realm of reticu-lates," Astron said. "After some study, I think I under-stand better how the moves are made." The demon stabbed at the map. "The rotators occupy five of the six vertices of a hexagon; simultaneously they will all move to the node at the very center of them all. The forces of symmetry will be enormous; the reflectives at the sixth node will be drawn in as well. They will be unable to resist. And with the warriors from five nodes against those of one, the outcome of the battle should be quite favorable."

Kestrel studied the parchment on Astron's lap with the cryptic squiggles, trying to make sense of what the demon was saying.

"Besides," Astron continued, "it is a good move for us as well. It is in the right direction."

"What do you mean?" Kestrel brought his attention back to the demon.

"It places us one vertex closer to the origin," the demon said. "Look, I have been studying these maps and identified this one point as the center of all the others. All the symmetries pivot about it. Just like the center of the hexagon to which we will be moving, there is one vertex that is the origin of the entire realm."

Kestrel shook his head. He still did not understand.

"The origin is least bound by the forces of symmetries," Astron continued. "There is no other node which must have the same activities in order for things to balance. There the unusual is more likely to occur. It is the one node where we have some hope—some hope of performing wizardry and building a fire."

Kestrel felt his spirits lift. "Yes," he exclaimed, "you just might be right. How else could the reflectives communicate with the chronoids if not through the flame. And Abel said that since they have captured the origin, the contacts have become more intense." He looked at Astron's map with far keener interest.

"After the battle, we will press on to this origin?" Kestrel asked.

"Not necessarily. If the reflectives do not see such moves as part of their overall plan, they will travel elsewhere, and it will be difficult for us to resist being carried along."

"Then they will need a little convincing." Kestrel

238

smiled and rubbed his hands together. His thoughts began to jump as he looked back to Abel with calculating eyes.

"What about a trap?" he asked. "Now that I think of it, this move to the center of the hexagon seems very obvious. Suppose it is part of some greater symmetry that is being planned by the reflectives."

"I had not thought of that," Astron exclaimed. The demon looked at Kestrel and wrinkled his nose. "Another example of the kind of thinking you were talking about as we returned from the glen of the harebell, I suppose. But yes, if I can understand the strategy of the move with such little exposure, how subtle indeed can it be? Why would the reflectives move to the node that completes the hexagon, rather than choose another oasis that does not impress symmetry so strongly upon them?"

Kestrel did not bother to hear the rest of what Astron said. He sprang to his feet and walked to the subnode that was occupied by the commander. Fortunately the rotators had so carefully distributed everyone about the oasis that the resistance of maintaining symmetry could almost totally be ignored.

"Commander," he said, "how cunning have the reflectives proven to be in the past?"

Abel looked up from the map he was studying and pursed his lips. "The reflectives do not act with cunning. If they did, I would grant them a small token of respect. Instead, they employ any methods to enforce advantage —poisoning oases just as they leave or imitating our signal flares with messages of deception."

"And you?" Kestrel smiled. "The rotators do not engage in such tactics when the alternative would be a defeat?"

"Certainly not." Abel glowered. "It is the fundamental difference between the two of us. We wish to rid this realm of the reflectives, it is true; but for the rotators, the end does not justify all means."

Kestrel looked to the horizon and rubbed his chin. "Suppose I can provide you a method that will result in substantial advantage," he said, "something that might tip the struggle permanently in your favor."

"I do not know the customs of your realm," Abel said. "What you judge to be of no consequence might be totally out of concert with what we rotators believe."

"It is more a a matter of cunning than the poisoning of wells," Kestrel said.

"Speak and I shall judge," Abel said. "If what you say has merit, then I will pledge my token to your command and all of those who can be communicated with by sky-ribbon as well."

Kestrel looked into the cold gray eyes and hesitated. Among men, he had seen such an expression only in the most steadfast of wizards. "I do not seek your command," he said quickly. "I propose only to offer advice. If it is accepted, then the results will be compensation enough for those who travel with me."

"I command or I do not," Abel said. "If your plan is accepted, then you carry the burden of responsibility of our lives. That has been the way of the rotators since the beginning of time."

Kestrel looked around the oasis uncomfortably. Enough of the stone-gray warriors at other subnodes had overheard the conversation that they were looking at him intently. His goal was to get Phoebe away from another realm as well. He glanced out over the sands and felt a return of the feeling that had pulled at him until just moments before. There was no other choice. He would have to see through Astron's idea and work out the consequences later.

"I think that rather than moving to the center of the hexagon that we now occupy," Kestrel said at last, "we should strike for the origin of the realm by another route. The present maneuver is too obvious; it is most likely a trap. What do you say to surrendering responsibility if such were my first command?"

"Your scheme is one of correct moves and nothing more?" Abel asked. "No special weapons or tricks outside the custom?"

"No, none of that," Kestrel said. "But that is not the point."

"That is the point entirely," Abel said. "A scheme with honor is all that I ask. Sketch for me on the map the moves you propose. If they show greater merit than the plan for the moment, then we are yours to lead."

Kestrel stared back at the cold unblinking eyes and frowned. He looked for some hint of reservation in Abel's expression, some indication that the gray warrior was merely agreeing until he revealed more of what he had in mind. But the face was void of veiled tension. The commander appeared quite willing to hand everything over to Kestrel, provided that it aided in the cause of the rotators. The gray warrior took his words totally at face value and trusted him in what he said.

Kestrel's sense of discomfort grew. This was totally unlike his dealings in the realm of men. There, he always sought to find the hidden failings, the weakness that he exploited to consummate the deal. And when he was done, his conscience was not bothered; an honest man would not have been tempted by what he had to offer in the first place; in the end, just desserts were served. But this time he had no real reason, other than his own, to move in the direction of the origin. It was an out-and-out swindle, with lives at stake, besides.

"No, forget it," Kestrel said. "Your plan is perhaps best after all. Proceed to seize the center node of the hexagon. The demon says that it moves us closer to the origin as well."

"Your words cannot be so easily put aside," Abel said. "The origin has been a matter of some concern since it was seized by the reflectives some three hundred moves ago." The warrior touched the sword pommel at his side. "If you indeed have a scheme of merit, you must tell us your plan so that we can judge."

Kestrel hesitated, but Abel did not waver. With a slow deliberateness, the warrior began to withdraw his sword. Kestrel glanced at Astron waiting expectantly and over at Phoebe staring vacantly into space. He quickly pointed at the map.

"It is merely a conjecture," he said, trying to buy time with his words. "See, here is the node at the center of

241

the hexagon. And here are the five vertices occupied by your own men. The sixth here you suspect to be possessed by the reflectives, and by converging simultaneously you hope to draw them in with you."

"That is apparent to all," Abel growled. "What is your plan that has superior merit?" Several other warriors stopped whatever they were doing and drew closer to hear Kestrel's words.

"Apparent to all—as you state, that is exactly what I wish to emphasize," Kestrel said. His eyes raced over the map for an idea. "But what about—what about the ring of vertices that surround even these six, the ones that lie even farther from the center of the hexagon? Yes, that is it. When you perform your maneuver, all six of the corners of the hexagon will be vacated; if the reflectives possess all of the nodes further out, they can move in to this one and the other five totally unchallenged. You will be surrounded and outnumbered at least two to one. The reflectives might sacrifice one unit the size of yours, but the rotators will eventually lose five in return."

A murmur of surprise erupted from the warriors who were listening. Quickly they passed on what had been said to the others. Kestrel was not quite sure where his thoughts were taking him, but at least Abel's sword arm had relaxed.

"A sacrifice of one to gain five." Abel looked at the map and back to Kestrel with respect. "I would not have thought of it, nor would any other of our side. It would be just like the reflectives, though; shedding some of their own blood, so long as it produced a greater gain." He paused and puckered his lips. "Your logic has great force. What, then, is the alternative?"

"It is only conjecture," Kestrel repeated, "a thought experiment about what might be the reflectives' intent. I have no proof that it is so."

"But as you said, the convergence to the center of the hexagon is so obvious. It is rare that the reflectives would let themselves be maneuvered into such a state.

242

After all, they have been struggling for as long as we. Tell us the rest and then you can lead."

Kestrel frowned. Moving away from the center of the hexagon rather than toward it probably would be no worse than what Abel had originally planned. Perhaps the next node in fact would be totally unoccupied and no harm would be done. And they, in fact, would be closer to the origin. He pointed out over the horizon.

"There," he said. "We should move to that node and the other five units should move outward as well. If we encounter any of the reflectives, then the ratio will be no worse than one to one."

Abel squinted out over the desert and then nodded. He turned back to Kestrel and unclasped his sword belt. "The plan has merit," he said. "Assume the command. We will do as you say."

Kestrel looked one final time into Abel's unwavering eyes. He waited for some tiny twinge or movement, but saw none. "Signal the others," he said in a resigned voice. It was not exactly what he had had in mind. "Inform them of the plan so that there is no loss of life through misunderstanding. I will do as you say." Reluctantly he took the offered belt and put it around his waist. If felt far heavier than it should.

CHAPTER NINETEEN

## Spatial Transformations

KESTREL watched impatiently as the last of the fruit was squeezed into the bowl. It was too tart to be drunk undiluted, as he knew from his first experimentation, but the elaborate method of mixing by the rotators seemed to serve no real purpose. He looked out over the unchanging desert and shrugged. They could do nothing, of course, until the time of the next move. Perhaps the purpose of the empty rituals was no more than to keep everyone occupied.

Kestrel saw Abel carefully decant oasis water into the bowl on top of the thick juice. The liquid ran down the side without mixing and formed a crystal-clear layer on top of the opaque orange sludge on which it rode. Besides the former commander, two other warriors flailed at the wrung-out pap on large flat stones, pressing it into a thin layer of sticky paste. Before the next move, the gentle breezes would have dried the pulp into a fine orange powder that was carefully packed away against the contingency of arriving at a node with nothing fresh to eat.

When the last of the water had been added, Abel opened a spout near the bottom of the bowl and let the juice slowly flow out to fill a large spoon. Then, with a practiced deftness, the rotator stopped the flow, raised the spoon back over the top edge of the bowl, plunged it into the water layer, and stirred it vigorously about. The juice sprayed into a shower of the fine droplets that quickly added a hint of orange to the transparent crispness of the water, but somehow did not disturb the darker opaqueness that rested beneath.

Using the same spoon with a hinged cover over the top, Abel next extracted some of the water and plunged it into the denser juice. He manipulated a lever that released the spoon's contents and again swirled it about, slightly lightening the deep color in the process.

Kestrel yawned, partially from the tension of waiting, but also because he had seen the ritual more than a dozen times. Abel returned the spoon to the spout near the bottom of the bowl, collected some of the lower liquid, and mixed it with the top. Again he extracted some of the result and swirled it with the bottom. With each transfer the water became more and more cloudy, the juice more and more fluid and transparent, and the horizontal line marking the boundary between the two harder and harder to detect.

Finally, after perhaps a score of transfers, the boundary line began to buckle and writhe. Fingers of liquid

244

started to intertwine and merge. In an indefinable instant, the two liquids coalesced into one with no distinction between them. Abel grunted in satisfaction, and the warriors began lining up with their cups and gourds.

Soon everyone had their fill of juice and wind-dried bread. In a rigorous sequence, the warriors began nodding off to sleep, assuming a variety of positions, some leaning against the trees, while others curled up into tight little balls near the roots.

Kestrel watched the eyes of the last one close and then smiled across the pond at Phoebe. Now that he was commander, he should at least be able to move about as he decided, especially since Abel now dozed with the rest. He had to try again to break Phoebe out of the depression that seemed to grow with each passing moment. And, he admitted as well, the softness of her touch was something that he was beginning to miss more and more.

Kestrel glanced at Astron and saw the demon stirring the contents of one of the flour tins with his little finger. The demon wrinkled his nose as a tiny cyclone of tiny orange particles swirled up into the air. Two subnodes around the oasis from Kestrel, Nimbia sat and stretched. Finally she looked as if she were recovering from her effort of creation. It appeared that neither of them would need his attention.

With a grin of anticipation, Kestrel started to walk toward Phoebe's subnode, but then halted. Abel always seemed to sense when the next move was about to begin, he thought suddenly. The commander would shout the call to order and begin assembling the warriors in flying formation with just precisely sufficient time to start moving when the tug of the second protocol hit the oasis.

Kestrel slapped the pommel of the heavy sword. It would not do if everyone staggered awake in disarray while he was in mid-dalliance with Phoebe, despite her need for cheering. He scowled at the direction his thoughts were taking him. Such concerns were madness. What difference did it make what Abel and the others judged of his actions? They were no more than creatures of imagination. He had no real allegiance to them. They were merely the means to the end of achieving deliverance.

He ran his fingers over the smooth grooves which spiraled up the hilt of the sword. It was heavy, true, but even in the short time he had worn it, despite the undercurrent of the entrapment, there was a degree of excitement as well—something he had not felt since before he first met Evelyn. All the warriors now nodded to him with that subtle hint of respect that only Abel had received before. He was now more than just another body that broke the symmetry of the node; he was the commander in whom they trusted the course of the next move.

Kestrel looked out over the desert and sighed. His emotions began to churn in a sudden tumble. Creatures of imagination or not, they deserved better than he. There was no deceit in Abel's eyes or in any of the others' that followed him—only trust in the one who wore the sword.

Kestrel stepped back to the tree and folded his arms across his chest as he had seen Abel do at least a dozen times before. Slowly he began counting in his head, ticking off the featureless time as best he was able. After twenty thousand counts, he decided, then I will sound the alert.

Kestrel bobbed and weaved in the whistling wind. The time to the next move had passed quickly enough, and he had got the troop off in fairly decent order. Strong eddies created by the rucksack on his back rocked him about. Unlike the rotators, he was unable to keep a completely smooth trajectory over the expanse of sand. But the grace of his motion was not Kestrel's primary concern. Far sooner than he wished, the distance to the next oasis, the one that Astron said put them a step closer to the origin, was melting away.

As he squinted into the haze, he saw the tops of the ring of trees appear over the horizon and then the lower trunks. He held his breath, hoping that his wish for an unoccupied oasis would be realized, but soon he saw it was not to be. Shadowy forms of many men loomed into detail. If they were rotators, surely Abel and the others would have known. He saw the glint of arms and, at the edge of the water, a towering construction of dull metal that emitted loud clicks radiating out across the sands.

"Is there any particular formation that you use when approaching a hostile oasis?" Kestrel called out to Abel on his left. He patted the thick copper blade at his side, but received little reassurance from it. It looked as if they would be slightly outnumbered and had little hope for surprise.

"It depends on how they are deployed about the subnodes," Abel called back. "If they are evenly distributed, the force of symmetry will deposit us in a similar fashion. If they have most of their men at one of the trees, then the fewest of ours will have to face them. The bulk of our own will land at a subnode across the oasis from them."

"What is the machine by the water?" Kestrel asked.

"Something exchanged with the chronoids, you can be sure," Abel said. "I have seen nothing of that size in any of the moves that I can remember. Be on your guard; the dance of combat might be tricky the first time you engage."

Kestrel started to say more, but thought better of it. Concentrating on exactly where he would land and whom he immediately would be facing was far better than idle chatter. He glanced at Phoebe, sailing along behind him and slightly to the right. He did not like the possibility of her being separated and sent off to another of the subnodes, but there was nothing he could do about it. Astron and Nimbia would have to take care of themselves as best they could.

As they drew even closer, the details of the oasis began to crispen in the hazy sky. A lookout on top of one of the trees shouted an alarm. With a flurry of activity, the warriors at ground level started adjusting their weapons. From the distance, they looked no different from the rotators, having pale gray complexions, leather vests, leggings and boots, and blades of orange-copper at their waists.

Kestrel saw two of the reflectives run to the machine and begin straining against a large key thrust into one of its sides. From their angle of flight, Kestrel's group could see around the corner of the plate of metal into the unshielded innards of the device. Giant cogwheels with the height of a man meshed with teeth the size of interleaved fists. A

247

loosely coiled escapement banged against a long ratchet that ran the full length of the cage. Axles squeaked and gears whirled as the key brought the mechanism to life.

Kestrel did not have time to observe more. With a final whoosh, he swerved to the right as he approached. His teeth clanged with the contact with the ground. For a moment, his vision blurred from the shock.

Kestrel shook his head and reached for his blade, finding a sudden resistance to the motion of his arm. He looked quickly about and saw one of Abel's lieutenants at his side and two of the reflectives facing him an arm's length away.

He strained again for his blade, but the resistance was greater than before. One of the reflectives laughed, and the other eyed him with a satisfied grin. Kestrel looked again at the lieutenant, then back to the reflectives. With the skill of a synchronized ballet, the two warriors facing them reached in unison for their swords, and the rotator copied their motion, flowing with it, rather than trying to resist. Kestrel pushed toward the scabbard a final time, but to no avail. He had not noticed it before, but of all those who fought, he was the only one who was right-handed.

With an awkward thrust he twisted his left arm down his side, fumbling to draw his sword and pushing away the thought of the hopelessness of what he was doing. To his surprise, it did not fall from his grip as he pulled it free, but soared to a guard position in front of his body, just like the others.

The warriors yelled and swung viciously downward. Kestrel felt his arm follow through with the rest. With a grating shriek the blades slipped past one another and crashed point-first into the ground. Then as one, all four of the combatants lifted the swords and lunged forward, turning bodies to the side to avoid the duplicated thrusts by their opponents.

The motions were not totally precise copies, however. Straining as best he could, Kestrel was able to twist his blade horizontal as he drew it back. Trembling from the resistance, he turned a cutting edge slightly to the side and sliced into the leather vest of the reflective as the warrior drew back.

Kestrel darted a glance to the lieutenant and saw a trickle of blood on his right arm. Quickly he understood how the battle was waged. The forces of symmetry compelled all of the lunges to be nearly the same. The strikes were aimed to be near-misses, rather than vital thrusts. And then the extra straining effort or slightly longer reach would do the real damage while avoiding a similar wound in return. Kestrel grimaced. He gripped the pommel more tightly, but the strangeness did not go away. If anyone would be at a disadvantage, it would be he.

The four closed again, this time with backhand swipes across the body that stopped just short of the neck. Kestrel strained to push his blade forward while tipping his own head to the side. He felt his arm quiver but proceed no further, while his opponent shook his own blade back and forth in tiny arcs, trying to break it free to strike a finger-width more.

Kestrel took a deep breath and gritted his teeth. Tightening the muscles the length of his arm and twisting his torso, he slowly increased the pressure, realizing that, if all four pushed too hard simultaneously, they would all suffer the same. He saw his blade cover half the distance to the bulging artery of the reflective and then sucked in his breath as a prickly line of pain caressed his own skin. Almost instinctively, he halted his plunge and reversed direction, but the pressure did not release. The grin on his opponent's face broadened. He was trapped immobile and could not move.

Suddenly the huge clockworks at the water's edge sounded in a deep resonant gong. Kestrel heard a cry of surprise. Out of the corner of his eye, he saw a flurry of motion at the next subnode in line. The clock struck a second time. In a blur, his sword spun from his hand high into the air. Simultaneously he felt the pressure release from his neck.

Kestrel craned his head upward to see his sword and three others arch in a complex swirl and then fall back toward the earth. Spinning with precision, the pommel of one fell back into his grip, just as the first had left it. With a scrape of skin, the pressure returned to the side of his neck. The four swords had been interchanged.

The clock sounded again, and the lieutenant choked out a startled cry. Kestrel saw his thin face contort in puzzlement and then dissolve into one of the reflective's grins. Other cries sounded from all around the node, and then Kestrel felt the pressure on his neck suddenly release. He looked into the face of the warrior across from him and blinked at the sudden change. The smile was gone and the round cheeks somehow thinned into the gaunt expression of the lieutenant. At the edge of his vision, he saw the two remaining warriors in unison disengage from one another and turn to strike Kestrel and the one he now faced from the side.

Kestrel fumbled to turn and meet the new threat. Somehow, his adversary had been switched. The one who faced him fought on the same side. It was just as Abel had tried to explain. The striking of the clock mixed up things spatially in strange ways—even the inner beings between the rotators and reflectives were being transformed!

Kestrel struggled to rotate clockwise. But as he did, the warrior who faced him strained to move in the opposite direction. For what seemed like an eternity, they fought against one another, while the two reflectives smoothly pirouetted and prepared to strike.

On the third gong of the clock, Kestrel heard more cries from around the oasis. First one and then two other rotators suddenly were catapulted into the air. Their bodies were wrenched into unnatural trajectories and hurled toward the horizon with breathtaking force. Almost instantly, reflectives sailed into view and landed in the spots vacated by their foes. At several of the subnodes, the ratio of fighters was shifted to a definite disadvantage for the rotators. Through the tumult of battle, Kestrel saw Astron near the clock key, standing frozen with a blade woodenly in front, not able to fend off thrusts that were being aimed at the demon from both left and right.

The clock sounded again. This time Kestrel recognized Phoebe's shriek intermingled with the rest. He looked skyward and saw her and three reflectives from her subnode rise into the air and then vanish like the rest. Kestrel pushed against the lieutenant straining in the reflective's body and looked hastily back at the sword now being drawn back to strike at his midsection. For an instant, he hesitated, uncertain whether to stop the resistance or to assist the lieutenant's efforts instead, whirling back clockwise, hoping to rotate completely and meet the attack after a full circle.

Before Kestrel could decide, he heard the clock strike a note deeper than before. A sudden blur of nausea welled up within him. The scene before his eyes shimmered and then turned to a blurry gray. He felt a wrenching disorientation and then a sudden rush of heat as if he had a great fever. His body seemed suddenly strange and he staggered and almost fell; the resistance to his motion had been suddenly changed.

The blur dissolved. Kestrel blinked at what he saw. No longer was he at a subnode with three other warriors but near the clock itself. Reflectives on either side were drawing their swords, arms back across their bodies, preparing for deep thrusts toward his chest. He held his own sword pointed directly out in front, unable to move to one side or the other. He saw a net of tiny scales on the back of his hand and running up his forearm into his sleeve. Somehow he was conscious of a stubble of minute bristly hairs in the web of his fingers and between his toes.

Kestrel looked back across the node and saw what looked like his image still locked in synchrony with the lieutenant trying to ward off the attack coming from the side.

It could not be possible! Kestrel tried to deny the thought, but the feeling of all of his senses could not be denied.

"Astron," he called across the sand. "Somehow we have been transposed like the others. Do not fight the lieutenant. Turn clockwise with him and swing totally about."

But he need not have bothered. With the final gong of the clock, Kestrel saw his body vault up into the air and

251

then streak away like the ones before. Grimly he forced his attention back to how he was going to ward off the two reflectives with a sword that was frozen in position in his alien left hand.

## CHAPTER TWENTY

## *Demonlust*

ASTRON cautiously felt the sand under the strange fingertips. First there had been the blurring and transformation so unlike a journey between the realms. And then the flight away from the fighting to this deserted node. He must still his stembrain before he could think further.

Astron tried to flip down his membranes and then frowned in annoyance when they would not come. He shut his eyes and tried to ignore the unsatisfying blackness. Mentally, he reached for the panic that should be upwelling and concentrated on making it still.

His eyes blinked open. He looked about, surprised. There was no panic, no rumble of the base of his skull. He felt an internal discomfort from the flight and jarring landing, and his heart seemed to throb for no apparent reason, but otherwise he was in complete control of his thoughts.

Astron looked about puzzled. He saw Phoebe stagger to standing at the subnode to the left but noticed no other occupants of the oasis. Dimly, he remembered a reflective passing him halfway in his flight, going the other way. He released the sword he still held in his left hand and absently watched it fall at his side. His nose wrinkled as he saw small curly hairs on the back of his hand and arm, providing a wiry cover to a pale, smooth skin.

Kestrel, he thought. What had the human shouted about the transpositions that the reflectives were effecting with the huge clock of the chronoids? He held both arms up and then touched the smoothness of his forehead. He ran a finger over the more or less even row of teeth in his mouth and, reaching to his back, felt no knobs where the degenerate wing stubs should have been.

He breathed deeply and marveled at the feeling of the air coursing in and out of his lungs. A growl sounded in his stomach and a pleasant longing teased at his mind. Unbidden images of meat sizzling on a spit and the smell of fresh bread flitted, real and compelling.

"Oh, Kestrel, thank the random factors that you are here," Phoebe shouted as she ran to his subnode. "The blood and fighting with all that overpowering restraint was far worse than the alchemist's foundry. We are lucky to have survived."

He was not Kestrel, Astron thought. Words of denial started to form in his throat but his tongue felt strange and he only managed a cough instead.

"What is it?" Phoebe asked as she held wide her arms and stepped forward, beckoning.

Astron motioned for her to stop and took a cautious step backward.

"What is it?" Phoebe repeated. "Tell me everything is all right. I can stand no more chaos and surprise."

Astron looked at the tension etched deeply in Phoebe's face. The events had been unsettling, perhaps more so to a human than to one of his own kind. Whatever was decided upon to do next, he would certainly need her aid. And he knew from struggles through the flame in eons past how fragile was the will to survive. It was perhaps best to explain all that had happened at a better time. He wrinkled his nose and then slowly began to speak. The tenor of the first words startled him, but he held all the tiny muscles that were alive in his face rigidly taut.

"Do not be concerned." He measured his words carefully. "For the moment, we are safe. Take a minute to bring your stembr—your feelings under control and then we can proceed."

"But we are separated from the others. What are we to do?"

"To the origin," Astron said quickly. His thoughts

253

seemed to rush forward without the benefit of deliberation. "There is no change in our intent. There you will summon a demon to get us home."

Phoebe pulled a folded map from a pocket in her gown and began to open it, but then shrugged. "It is kind that you still show faith in my ability, Kestrel," she said softly with eyes lowered, "but in truth, the reality of my abilities has become clearer with each passing moment. Reaching the origin may be all well and good; but without Nimbia fully recovered, there is little point for such a journey." She looked out over the sands back in the direction from which they had come. "And how can we proceed the way we want when these forces of symmetry flip us from node to node? Without Astron, how do we stand a chance? He seemed to have a knack for figuring out these mathematical things."

"Yes, the devil," Astron said grimly. He shook his head to keep his thoughts straight. "Once a djinn is under your command, you can task him to soar over this desert until he finds the others. But if the demon were here, the first thing he would do is—" Astron stopped and for the first time looked critically about the oasis.

It was very much like all the rest, a quiet circular pool of water surrounded by six trees at the vertices of a hexagon. Strewn all about, however, was the debris left by the reflectives who had occupied it before the battle and the transformations. At the adjacent subnode on the left stood a pile of branches hacked from the treetops to make soft beds. Denuded branches and an axe were tossed in a heap nearby. At the next subnode around the periphery was one of the devices of the chronoids in obvious disrepair. Stacks of gears, springs, and ticking escapements were scattered about a nearly empty framework. Directly across the pond, three or four thick leather vests stood in a heap next to a pile of eyelets, buckles, and sewing thongs. Two nicked and rusting swords rested against the tree behind. A ring of stones outlined the cooking pit at the subnode adjacent to the armory and the remains of parchment maps gently stirred at the fifth. Just like the rotators, the reflectives carefully organized their camps so as to maximize their freedom from the compelling forces of symmetry.

"From the looks of things this node served as a camp for perhaps a dozen," Phoebe said.

"And yet when the battle began, evidently it was occupied only by two," Astron replied. "Otherwise now you and I would not be the only occupants." He waved his arm out over the bleached sands. "The rest must have dispersed to yet other nodes and then converged back to where the rotators attacked. Perhaps it had something to do with the working of the devices of the chronoids."

He looked over the disarray a second time. "One thing is for sure. There is more than enough here to break up the symmetries between the subnodes for the two of us. We can move about with comparative ease."

Astron's voice trailed off. The glimmer of an idea popped into his mind. Slowly he paced off the two longest and straightest tree branches and dragged them around the periphery to the dismantled device of the chronoids. There he rummaged through the stacks of debris until he found six gear wheels of approximately the same size.

"What are you doing?" Phoebe called out.

Astron ignored the question. "Go across to the armory and start cutting the vests into leather strips. We will concern ourselves about your abilities later. For now, let us get this thing built before some part of my mind is able to convince me otherwise."

Astron unbuckled the harness from his chest with a deep sigh. His muscles ached. What had been the pleasant longing in his stomach had turned into an insistent discomfort. He looked over his shoulder in the dimming daylight and saw Phoebe unfastening the half-dozen belts that held her to the long wooden frame. She had not complained during the entire trek, and surely the strains on her body must have been the same as his.

"Go and gather some fruits." He waved at the node that was before them. "I will pull the engine the rest of the way."

Astron looked at the deserted node and then back at the horizon the way they had came. The node that he

255

and Phoebe had been transported to was well out of sight. Even though a good portion of the time had been consumed in constructing the bizarre apparatus that fettered them, they still had managed to walk from one node to another. After a rest, they might be able to manage two moves, rather than one.

Astron ducked under the branch on his left and smiled at his handiwork. The felled tree branches had been bound by leather straps to form the irregular framework of a long box. If stood on end, it would tower three times the height of a mundane djinn. At front and rear, a row of gears from the device of the chronoids formed a framework for the smaller branches jammed between their teeth. Like giant rolling pins, they spread the weight across the sand and allowed Phoebe and him to push the contraption along the bleached path from one node to the next. Sometimes, with a burst of energy, they were able to sprint forward against their harnesses and then raise their feet and coast for a few moments before friction brought them to a halt.

Far more important than the practicalities, however, were the other additions to the craft. Five more gear wheels of odd sizes were hung along the sides at haphazard positions. Here and there, small clusters of greenery sprouted at odd angles. The rusted swords all pointed skyward from three of the four top corners and the cooking pots swung from the cross struts. Even though it gave them some difficulty in steering, the harnesses which bound them to the frame were offset from one another. Astron was near the center of the very front while Phoebe was halfway to the rear and nearly touching the left side.

At first Phoebe had protested adding all the extra weight and the number of belts that she had to wrap around her waist. But when the first tug of the symmetries had come and passed over them with barely a ripple she understood the intent. They were not two single individuals but coupled together as one. Their engine was in all probability unlike anything else in the realm. Totally unique, there was no increase in symmetry in moving it to a particular node or switching it with anything else. They could move between nodes as they chose without constraints or regard to the actions of others.

"There is ripe fruit enough that we can provision for several moves," Phoebe said as she returned to the engine. She untied several of the canisters still gently swinging from the frame and beckoned Astron to the subnode where she had laid out a cloth.

Astron finished pulling the engine to the water's edge and then sat down across from the meal that Phoebe had prepared. With a dedicated savagery that surprised himself, he began to gobble down the slices almost as fast as Phoebe could prepare them, hardly bothering to sprinkle on the flours from the canisters that balanced the meal. Only dimly was he aware of the cool pleasure of the juices that dripped over his hands or the tartness that tingled in his mouth.

When he was finally done, he leaned backward with a feeling of contentment totally unlike anything he had experienced before. He shook his head in wonder. The sensations were quite pleasurable ones, but such a weakness it must be for humans. Without food and drink, their thoughts would soon be driven to distraction; they would abandon all reason, just as if their minds were seized by the most powerful of stembrains. And unlike his own kind, there would be no hope for remaining in control.

Astron looked at Phoebe through half-closed eyes. There was much risk in this quest for his prince and yet much reward as well. He had learned things that no other cataloguer could have even suspected. Even Palodad probably had no notion of the concept of hunger or of how it truly tugged at one's will.

Phoebe smiled back at Astron and swept the remains of their meal aside. Deftly, she closed the distance between them and put her hand up to touch Astron's cheek. "I wonder about the others, Kestrel," she said, "but there is some advantage for the events as they have happened. For the first time in a very long while, we are alone."

Phoebe slid her hand behind Astron's neck and put

her lips to his. Astron choked in a moment of confusion but words would not come. He found his arms reaching around Phoebe and pulling her even closer to him. As he did, he felt a strange new feeling course through his body. He sucked in his breath at the intensity of it.

He was keenly aware of the softness of her back under the palms of his hands, even though her jerkin was in between. The press of her body tightened everywhere it touched. Without thinking, he maneuvered so that the pleasure of it would be greater. Astron felt his pulse quicken and his breath grow more shallow.

Desire swirled through his thoughts until only the tiniest ember of rationality remained. This was not like the duty for the broodmothers in any way at all. No cataloguer had dreamed of its potency, of that he was quite sure.

"You know that it does not matter," Phoebe said softly. "It does not matter what happens, Kestrel, just so long as we are together."

Kestrel. The name jarred to a halt in Astron's mind and did not go away. It was Kestrel that Phoebe was giving herself to, and not a wingless demon who could not weave. It should be the woodcutter's pleasure and not his.

Astron looked into Phoebe's expectant eyes in confusion. It would be Kestrel's body, nonetheless. Her sensations would be the same. And he would catalogue yet another experience of humankind. It was his duty to his prince. Astron licked his lips. The yearning was crisp and sharp, like the most brilliant sodium flame. Perhaps if it was not the first time, if he were more jaded to the senses of men, it would feel different, but he was feeling the rush of emotion now and must decide what to do.

"It is a compelling pleasure," Astron heard himself mumble. "In the realm of men, pleasure is regarded as a great good."

"The pleasure is because it is you," Phoebe whispered.

How much of what he was feeling was merely the construction of the bodies of men? Astron wondered. How much was some part of Kestrel that still lurked around the edges of his thoughts? What happened exactly when two awarenesses were switched, anyway? Was Kestrel, in the body of a demon, experiencing the same temptations with Nimbia? Did the woodcutter still remember his human emotions and seek to gratify them as best he could?

A sudden wash of reluctance cascaded over his desire. Kestrel and Nimbia—it would not be right. She did not deserve to be deceived in the way that the woodcutter exploited his own kind. And if she did consent, it would be because she thought it was Astron the demon, not a weak-bodied human slave given to hunger, thirst, sleep, and who knew what other tugs and emotions.

"What is the matter?" Phoebe said. "You feel so stiff, so uncertain."

Astron pulled Phoebe tight one final time and sighed. "It is not right," he said. "Now is not the time." With an ache in his loins, he then awkwardly disengaged and gently pushed her away.

"Then when?"

"After we have reached the origin. After everything has been restored to the way it should be."

Phoebe cocked her head to the side but gradually her smile returned. "All right," she said. "Perhaps the burden of our escape rests a little more firmly on your shoulders than I realized. I should be carrying more of the load, rather than be the weepy prize of the sagas. There will be time enough when we are safe."

She turned and groped for her cape. "After our rest, let me take the front position in the engine. You will need your wits, if we encounter a node that is not vacant."

Astron heard the sound of a blown kiss and then silence. He looked out into the desert and let his feelings slowly dissolve away. Getting to the origin was of the utmost urgency, he thought, but no more important than reversing the transformation between Kestrel and himself.

The next moves passed quickly. Phoebe made no further reference to the events of their first rest. As they made steady progress toward their goal, her spirits soared in proportion. Getting more accustomed to the sand engine,

259

they were able to increase the number of nodes traversed in a single move from two to three. As with the first, each one they visited had been unoccupied; evidently the reflectives had all moved elsewhere in their struggle with the rotators. But as they drew closer to the origin, Astron knew, they must finally encounter a challenge and have an explanation that would be believed.

Toward the end of the sixth move, as they tugged to reach a node only three away from the origin, Astron saw what he had been dreading throughout the trek. The silhouettes of warriors reaching for fresh fruit stood out from the outline of the treetops. Voices mingled with the methodical ticking of rectangular shapes scattered around the oasis. A lookout sounded an alarm and a half-dozen swords were drawn in expectation of their arrival.

Astron felt his discomfort grow. Despite Kestrel's explanations, the concept of deception was still unsettling. He would have to sound convincing, using facial muscles he could barely control. And with no experience, he could not judge the inherent credibility of the tale. He knew it was totally false; why would not the others deduce the same? He felt the sweetness of the air course in and out of his lungs, and a slight taste of apprehension not unlike the stirring of the stembrain began to awaken within him.

"We bring greetings from the chronoids," Astron shouted as the engine grew close. "An example of our most powerful of devices for you to observe. If the offered price is high enough, you will be able to remove the rotators from scores of nodes."

Astron felt his chest tighten while he waited for a response. Involuntarily, his eyes darted from side to side, searching for which way to veer, if they charged, even though Kestrel had told him that one looked straightforward and smiled.

"I am Jankol, squad leader for the reflectives." One of the warriors stepped forward from the rest. He was rail-thin, with narrow eyes that pinched together in the middle of his face. "Despite the words of the doomsayers, more devices of our allies we can certainly put to good use—especially since the increase in vigor of the rotator attacks."

Jankol paused and puckered his lips. "The signal bolts cannot be wrong, yet it is still hard to believe. First, they captured a node, although substantially outnumbered. Then, with an almost obsessive passion they have massed, not scores, but hundreds to take more nodes from us still. The rumor is that they follow a new leader, but it is hard to see how that could make much of a difference."

Jankol paused a second time, looking up and down the engine that Astron and Phoebe had constructed. "A device that looks more primitive than any we previously have seen, to be sure," he said after a moment. "How can it have such power, if it is from an earlier time?"

Astron let out his breath. It was just as the human had said! The basic premise was accepted unchallenged. Now if he could only invent quickly enough to fill in the details. With a final surge, he pushed the engine into their midst and called for Phoebe to halt. While his mind raced for an answer, he slowly unbuckled the leather straps of his harness.

"This engine has the power of immunity to the forces of symmetry," he said after a moment. "How else could we travel from node to node, totally unaffected by the moves of your struggle with the rotators?"

"Immunity?" Jankol said. "How can that help? The other devices you have given intensify the force, rather than decrease it. Why, with some we can even force exchanges of body or mind." He waved his hand at the pond. "That is what we amass here—in preparation for the great battle to blunt the drive of the rotators."

Astron looked quickly around the node. The equipment of the reflectives was configured in much the same way as the first that Phoebe and he had encountered alone. This one was fully occupied with over a score of warriors, however, and not one, but three timepieces were sitting at the edge of the pond.

"Over forty nodes can you clear with what we have brought," Astron said. "Does it really matter how? The important point is the price. What have you given in exchange for the devices you have collected here?"

Jankol's lips puckered for a moment and he rubbed his chin. "Why, the price is the same for each one. It was fixed by the first. You would know that from your past, if you come afterward." He stopped and looked for a long time at the lashed-together engine. "You must be from a more primitive time indeed, but then how could the first have been the beginning of all the rest."

Astron felt the tug of muscles that were not there, but his nose wrinkled slightly, even with the human equipment. He did not understand what Jankol was saying and no one had as yet sheathed his sword. A false step would be disastrous. "Yes, a more primitive time," he said slowly. "Perhaps you had better tell us what has happened since."

Jankol shrugged. "As you know, your realm is a series of nodes, just as ours. But rather than being laid out in space, somehow they are points in time. The forces of symmetry compel each one to repeat the events that have occurred on the one downstream. The first node to establish contact explained that periodically others would follow; the transaction would be the same.

"But if you are from an earlier time and this is the first contact, what we call the first would have known of it. It would be in their history, unless—"

Jankol trailed off and his eyes took on a faraway look. "Unless the inhabitants of your node are far more successful than any that have preceded you. It would portend that your power is great indeed. Yes, yes, we will trade for your engine, the same as we have given for the rest. If it can do as you say, we will not have to consult with the other nodes. Six volunteers who will transfer to your realm and join in your own struggles."

"Six?" Astron asked cautiously. Kestrel had taught to say little while uncertain and ask questions whenever possible. There was less risk of exposure that way.

"Why yes, six," Jankol said. "As I have stated. It was the agreement of the first node with which we made contact."

"This device is more powerful," Astron said.

"Perhaps in your own realm," the leader replied. "But

262

as with the others, I expect it will work imperfectly here. After all, you build them to force the swapping of future and past in your own domain, and, when transported here, the effects are somehow warped. It is as if there were some additional outside interference that makes them behave in ways totally unexpected. There is no guarantee that it will provide any greater advantage over what we already have."

The logic in Astron's mind whirled. Kestrel probably would conclude that Jankol was pressing to close a deal. That would indicate that the transfer of six between the realms was too cheap a price. For something that could indeed influence scores of nodes, he could get more. But then this was exactly the situation that the woodcutter tried to maneuver into. Perhaps the inhabitants of the realm of reticulates were not so very different from men, after all.

"What I really desire is transport to the origin," Astron said, "but I suppose that the price for that is too dear. I understand that the rotators are the ones who occupy it and it would cost you much to seize it."

"The rotators in possession of the origin? That was some time ago and—" Jankol stopped and rubbed his chin. "Such a trip would be costly indeed," he said after a moment, "much more than the device you bring, despite its claim. There is no way we could exchange six and transport you there as well."

"The device is all that I have," Astron said. "Take us to the origin and for that I will explain its many virtues so that you can use it as well. Then I am sure you will agree to exchanging a dozen rather than six."

Jankol puckered his lips. "An explanation after the journey but before the exchange," he repeated. His eyes darted quickly to the other reflectives, as if in warning, and no one spoke. "Once we are in possession of the power, then, in good faith, we will decide what the additional payment will be. Yes, yes, I think the reflectives can agree to that. Of our good faith you can be assured."

Astron felt some of the tension dissolve, but not all. He

wished he could be more sure, but it seemed to follow the pattern that Kestrel had explained. Now if he could only get Phoebe's flame started before the reflectives discovered that their duplicity was the lesser of the two.

## CHAPTER TWENTY-ONE

## Coalescence of Space and Time

ASTRON had waited anxiously while the reflectives signalled from one node to the next that they were coming. Jankol could not quite believe that he could travel with Astron and Phoebe in their engine without worrying about the forces of symmetry. The time to the next move had been half spent before they finally were on their way, pushing the engine in the sand with Jankol and two of his lieutenants harnessed in the very rear.

Astron had hoped that, with the additional muscle, their rate of speed would improve, but the warriors were unused to much walking and the pace was hardly more than he and Phoebe had managed alone.

"Kestrel, I still do not understand the point of the rush," Astron heard Phoebe gasp beside him as they approached the node one away from the origin. "As I have said, without Nimbia or the services of some other wizard, it is futile to press as hard as we have done. And even if we get to where you seek, Jankol and the others will—will expect what you have promised."

"We will face the events one at a time." Astron glanced to the side between breaths. "Do not waste your energy with idle words. Concentrate only on our objective."

Astron heard the confidence in his voice as if someone else were speaking. His demon's mind knew the truth of what Phoebe said, but somehow his body would not admit it. Instead it seemed totally caught up in pushing onward toward his goal. His mouth was dry. His muscles ached from the strain. Irritating pains occasionally shot from his shoulder where the leather had begun to dig into the soft, unscaled skin. Even the weight of the rucksack containing the harebell pollen had become a heavy burden. Yet there was no other choice but to continue. To stop would be to surrender to the despair of the stembrain or whatever humans had in its place. To be marooned forever was a very long time for a demon.

"The chronoid with the long hair is correct." Jankol suddenly stopped pushing against his harness. "The next move is about to take place. We can rest here comfortably until it is over and then resume travel when we are refreshed."

"What about the rotators?" Astron said. "Had we not better circle around this oasis and continue?"

"But we are indeed fortunate," Jankol said. "Our own brethren now occupy this one and—perhaps several more as well. There is no reason why we will not be welcome."

Astron started to reply when he heard a deep vibrant gong from the direction of the oasis. He felt a tingling in his feet. The ground started to vibrate at a frequency just below his hearing. His nose wrinkled. A flick of motion from the oasis caught his eye. The trees had begun to oscillate. In slow unison, they swayed from side to side. Then the water from the pond sloshed outward to bathe the roots on one side. A great wave of sand, like a ripple in a blanket, seemed to race toward him with breath-catching speed.

The tremor passed under Astron with a mild shifting of his support. He felt his thoughts turn sluggish and difficult to understand. He heard the reflectives call out to the oasis, but their voices had become twisted, sputtering sounds that he barely recognized.

Then, just as suddenly as it had begun, the tremor in the ground stopped. The distant rumbling died away. Astron's head cleared and he was able to think.

"We should not wait until the origin," Jankol said. "My comrades at the oasis say that they prepare for a massive attack. If we are to use your device, it will be here and now. Evidently the rotators press too force-fully; we must employ everything that we can."

Astron's nose wrinkled. He tried to capture the subtle flavor of his disorientation, but with each passing heart beat it faded farther and farther away. He looked back at the oasis and the large clock that was ticking at the water's edge. He saw the warriors there testing the sharpness of their swords, some of them still stretching and arching their backs. Despite the striking clock and trembling ground, they had just barely aroused from their sleep.

Rotarians and reflectives—the two sides were not so very different, he thought. Without prior knowledge, he would be hard put to tell them apart. Images of the ritu-alistic regimen swept into his mind—plan, eat, sleep, and move; scanning parchment maps of the polytopes, mixing water and pulpy juice, carefully planning non-symmetric sleeping positions around the oasis—

Astron stopped short and looked at the clock striker as it cocked for another stroke. The vision of the swirling juice and water stuck in his thoughts. "Perhaps it is not so wise," he said quickly to Jankol. "All of the inter-change with the realm of the chronoids—what happens when you have shifted so much that there is little to tell their universe from yours?"

"We have a bargain." Jankol ignored the question. "Your device is to aid along with all the rest."

Astron started to say more when the gong sounded a second time. Again he saw the treetops start to sway back and forth. The water in the pond spewed from its banks in a foamy spray. A wave of sand much higher than before pulsed away from its creation.

"Brace yourself!" Astron yelled as he was suddenly thrown from his feet. With a wrenching groan, the long beams of the engine snapped their leather bindings and he tumbled to the ground. Gears ripped from their lash-ings; tins of flour dropped to the sands, exploding their contents in sprays of deep orange. As if he had been struck by lightning from the realm of men, Astron heard a painful clap of thunder that filled the air and reverber-ated into a distant rumble that left him dazed. The sky seemed to shimmer for a moment with thin lines of iridescence arching from horizon to horizon.

Astron breathed the sweet taste of air deeply and shook his head from side to side. As the sky began to return to its former steady brightness, he saw Jankol and his lieutenants, completely unfettered, trying to lash the engine back to the way it had been.

"No, no more use of devices of the chronoids." Astron's tongue felt heavy in his mouth. "Stop them all. Wait until we understand better what the consequences truly are."

Jankol stopped his mending. He puckered his lips and looked at Astron through squinted eyes. "What you say is most strange. On one hand, you speak of the virtues of a device from another realm; on the other you entreat instead that such engines not be used. It is a behavior somewhat inconsistent for one truly from beyond the flame."

Astron felt a sudden stab of panic. "No, there is no inconsistency," he answered quickly. "You see it is merely a matter of, a matter of—" He tried to look Jankol squarely in the eye but when the words would not come, he turned his face aside. Scowling, he wished for Kestrel's quickness of thought.

Jankol waited a moment more, then drew his sword. He motioned for his lieutenants to fall in line beside him. "I should have trusted my first instincts," he said. "What is the truth, strange one? Tell me why you and the long hair look so different from the rest we have seen."

Astron looked quickly to his side at Phoebe slowly regaining her footing. Awkwardly he drew Kestrel's heavy sword and pointed it at the three who advanced at him with synchronized steps. He felt his chest tighten and the air come in short gulps.

But before Jankol and the others could engage, Astron saw one of the lieutenants falter and then fall out of step. The eyes of the reflective widened and he waved his sword arm in an exaggerated flourish off to the side. Jankol stopped uncertainly and then squinted all the more in Astron's direction. "Your device still seems to disrupt the symmetries," he said. "We cannot engage you as one. It feels so very uncertain which are the correct steps to take." He darted his eyes back to the oasis and then at a large blur moving in quickly over the horizon.

"First the battle." He waved his own sword in Astron's direction. "After the victory, I will return with others, dozens if need be, so that we will overwhelm you despite the tricks that you play."

Without another word, he motioned his lieutenants to follow and ran with great effort through the loose sand in the direction of the pond.

For a moment, Astron watched them go. He glanced at what appeared to be a hurling mass of men drawing closer to the oasis and made up his mind. "They will be back shortly," he said to Phoebe. "And even if they are not, I think we can little afford to wait for another stroke of the chime. You must act now. Perform your craft as never before."

"What do you mean?" Phoebe frowned. "I have told you more than once—"

"Forget what has happened." Astron reached out and shook her by the shoulders. "It is a characteristic of the realm. No one could have started a fire at the spot where we first arrived, not even the archimage himself. But now we are much closer to the center than we were before, perhaps close enough that the violation of symmetry caused by the flame will be small enough that it can be overcome. The origin itself would be better, but we cannot afford to wait."

He paused and then reached out and squeezed Phoebe's hand. The thrill of the previous move suddenly surged anew, but he managed to push it aside. "You are a wizard," he said. "A wizard as much as any other—but only if you practice your art."

"The words of symmetry have no bearing, Kestrel." Phoebe shook her head. "I can feel the failure even before I begin." She slumped her shoulders and began to sag back to the ground. "There is no point to endure the frustration, no matter whatever else might come. I can imagine the laughs of my council as clearly as if they were here."

Astron felt a sudden surge of anger and frustration

well up within him. He almost choked over the intensity of the emotion. "I do not care about your council," he yelled. "Put them from your mind." He gulped air and rushed on. "I have heard tales of the encounters with the great wizards, far more than you might guess. I know the characteristics of the ones who were successful, the ones who controlled the mightiest djinns. They did not care about the opinions of others. The practice of their craft was not for fame or good-standing with those who would be their peers.

"It was for themselves they struggled, Phoebe. The measure of success was against goals that were known by themselves alone. The reward was increased self-esteem—acceptance of their own true worth, not the fickle opinion of the lesser ones around them whom they did not choose to control. Think! Why do you want to be a wizard? So that you can be regarded as an equal—or know deep within yourself that you are unique and comparable to none?"

The oasis clock struck a third time. The sky began to shimmer as it had before and the iridescent lines stood out in a much bolder relief. Astron thought he could see faint images of gearworks at the nodes where they intersected and, with them, shadowy figures of men winding huge springs. Another wave of sand rushed at them from the oasis. This time he was more prepared and he pushed Phoebe to the ground before the wrenching jerk ripped away their footing.

As the wave passed, Astron felt a sudden blur of nausea. The trees of the oasis distorted in a blurring rush, as if one were somehow racing by them at a breakneck speed. The broken frame of the engine creaked and groaned where it had fallen. With lifelike spasms, the cracked beams and snapped leather thongs reached for one another, as if they were trying to mend. Some of the spewed flour arched upward from where it had struck the sands and cascaded back into canisters just before their lids suddenly snapped shut. Astron felt another wave of disorientation. His thoughts slowed and then started off slowly in a direction that he did not understand. They bounced around his head like fragments from a language not quite his own. He could only sit stunned and wait for the feeling to pass.

Eventually, the firmness of the sands returned. Astron started to say more to Phoebe, but saw that already she was preparing to start a fire. Clutching a match tightly in her fist, with a sweeping stroke she ran it along the length of one of the rough-barked branches at her side.

The matchhead grated with the contact and then glowed red from the friction of passage but did not light.

"Better than before." Astron shouted encouragement before she could speak. "Better than before. You must try again."

Phoebe grunted in reply. She grabbed three matches tightly together and with deliberate strength ground them against the wood. The heads sparked dully and then almost unexpectedly burst into a feebly smoky flame.

For an instant Phoebe's eyes widened in disbelief. Then she shook her head. "Some kindling—here in the pouch." She motioned with her free hand. "Make a loose pile of it, Kestrel, before the matches burn out."

Astron grabbed at the small pouch and pulled out dry needles and bits of string. He smoothed a depression in the sand and quickly constructed a fragile dome of small struts and spars. Shielding the delicate flicker of fire with her hand, Phoebe bent the matches to the kindling. She caught her breath waiting for the fire to grow.

Tendrils of smoke enveloped the needles and bits of bark. For a brief instant a small speck of tar began to glow red. But then the weak fire faltered and started to die. Helplessly, she watched each little tongue of flame grow dimmer and, in a final puff of smoke, wink out.

Phoebe fumbled for more matches. "The last three." She held out her hand. "And I see no way that they can be any better than the rest." She sighed and looked at Astron with tears forming in her eyes.

"No, wait," Astron said. "Keep your composure. It is just a matter of the kindling. We need something that more easily absorbs the heat of the matches, something with a large surface area for a given volume." Desperately he looked about trying to seize upon an idea. He heard the sound of clashing swords at the oasis and, somehow above it, the ticking of the clock. The results of each gong had been more violent than the one before. Perhaps they could not withstand the next. They had only moments left before something must be done.

Astron closed his eyes and wrenched at his memories as a cataloguer. Fires, flames, the barrier between the realms—there must be something that he had learned that could be used. What was the purpose of all of his knowledge if not—

Astron stopped with a sudden thought. He lunged at the clutter at Phoebe's feet and pawed through the debris from the engine. "Strike the last three matches," he yelled. "Just as you did before. You are indeed the wizard; without you we cannot succeed."

Phoebe hesitated but then turned back to the twisted branch. She struck the matches a first time. When they did not light, she tried again. Astron turned his eyes away, not having time to watch as she struggled. Groping in the sand he found a flour tin with weak walls and with a quick thrust jabbed a hole in the side near the bottom with the tip of his sword. He felt a sudden slice of pain in his soft hands where he had gripped the blade for control. The sudden wetness was sticky but he pushed the discomfort out of his mind. With a wrench he flung off the top of the tin, sending it sailing away.

Out of the corner of his eye, Astron saw Phoebe returning with the barely flaming matches as before. He twisted his head to the ground and placed his mouth around the indentation he had made in the tin. His shoulder felt the rumble of the ground and he had to use both hands to steady the small container in front of his face.

"Here," he shouted, "as soon as you see the spray."

Astron filled his lungs and blew into the small hole. At first the packed flour on the inside resisted the pressure. Most of his breath spilled back out onto his face; only a small portion blasted into the tin and bubbled toward the upper rim. A fine mist of flour danced from the surface into the air.

"Now," Astron gasped. "Apply the fire when I blow again."

Astron expanded his chest and exhaled even harder, sending a visible white spray skyward in a tiny geyser. Phoebe pushed forward the matches and then dropped them in the tin in surprise. An orange-red flame with tongues the length of a forearm suddenly sprang into life.

"Bring over the branches and some of the wreckage of the engine," Astron gasped between breaths. "Spark, kindling, and fuel—they are all essential for any blaze. Unless we supply the third, the fire will go out as soon as I stop." He resumed blowing into the tin, each puff sending the flames higher into the air.

Phoebe nodded and quickly twisted one of the jutting branches of the frame over the spot where Astron lay. The bright tendrils from the burning flour powder bathed the lower contour of the log and then arched around it to flicker higher in the sky. Almost instantly the peeling bark caught fire and a scant moment later began burning on its own.

Astron ceased blowing and tried to stop the rapid breathing so that he could speak again. The human body had disadvantages that appeared at the most awkward of times.

"Be careful, even in your haste," he gasped. "The first mind that you contact might be too pow—"

"Camonel." Phoebe's voice boomed out with a sudden vibrancy. From her cape she sprinkled into the fire some powder that looked the same as what Alodar had used in his keep. "I demand the presence and service of Camonel, the one who carries." She darted a quick glance at Astron and smiled. "Oh, Kestrel," she said. "You had faith in me when even my own will faltered. Perhaps I am in some way unique, as each true wizard must be, not the equal of any other but—"

"Careful!" Astron repeated. "You do not know—"

There was a sudden rush of sulphur-tinted air. The great brown djinn that had carried Astron and the others to the realm of the fey stepped from the fire. "The one who reckons instructs that I do not resist," the massive demon said. "Tell me what you wish and I will obey."

"Another of your kind and an inhabitant of the realm of the fey," Phoebe said. "Quickly take us to them wherever they may be."

The djinn bowed. With one powerful swoop of its long arms he coiled Astron and Phoebe to his chest. A single beat of his wings soared them into the air. But before Astron had time to think, the oasis clock struck a fourth time. Straining to look over his shoulder, he saw the sky shimmer into a painful brightness. The network of iridescence intensified and did not fade. Massive clockworks propelled from the glowing nodes and raced earthward. Halfway to the ground, the machineries passed startled rotators and reflectives hurling skyward in return.

Astron felt another wave of disorientation stronger than before. Although he could not be sure, it seemed that even Camonel faltered, loosening his grip and fluttering to the ground.

"It all runs together in confusion," he heard the djinn mutter as he struck with a slight jolt. "Many nodes fused into one. I need not search them out for all that you seek are now here."

Astron felt the wings pull back. With dizzy steps he staggered from the larger demon's embrace. He saw that he was at the edge of a single expansive oasis surrounded by dozens of trees, rather than just six. At most of the subnodes, hundreds of warriors flailed away at each other in a massive mêlée, every one of them locked in step.

Astron quickly scanned the nearer subnodes and jerked to a halt. Three over from the nearest, he recognized his own body backed against a trunk with a bloody sword waving threateningly at a cluster of reflectives who attacked from the water's edge. Beside him were Abel and a score of rotators, each one trying to mimic their leader's stance. More than a dozen bodies were strewn from the gently sloshing surface of the central pond to the feet of those who defended against the overwhelming odds.

"Forget about their squabbles," Phoebe called from the protective cover of Camonel's wings. "Astron, Nimbia. I succeeded after all. After two failures I have succeeded when it was needed. Finally I have been able to summon a djinn and command him to carry us home."

Astron saw his own body jerk in recognition of the voice. The sword dipped in apparent salute but then returned to parry the thrust aimed at his side.

"Not now," Astron heard his own voice say. "It is too soon. They have trusted me without question. A dozen nodes we have won. Until the last, I cannot let them down."

"But something more has happened," another voice yelled. "Look about you, demon. The chances are too slim."

Astron turned to his right. There, at a virtually deserted subnode, he saw Nimbia holding a swordpoint to the throat of a reflective on the ground and waving with her free hand across the pond to Kestrel. Her tunic was in tatters, one sleeve torn free and the frontpiece ripped deeply across her chest.

Astron started to call out, but the words choked in his throat. Through Kestrel's eyes, she looked exactly as he had remembered her, but somehow it was not quite the same. Her body possessed a new sensuousness, a compelling beacon of desire that blotted out the urgency of he moment. It was just the same as with Phoebe, he thought in sudden confusion—the same as with the human, except that the exposure and the danger made the feeling much more intense.

Astron looked to either side of Nimbia's subnode to see if any reflectives were attempting to attack it. With leaping bounds, he began racing to where Nimbia stood, waving Kestrel's sword above his head.

"Kestrel, what are you doing?" Phoebe shouted behind him. "Help cut a path for Astron. He is the one that needs your help."

Astron shook his head and looked back as he ran to the subnode occupied by Abel and the others. Kestrel, laboring in his slight demon's body, would need aid soon indeed. He returned his attention to Nimbia as he approached and saw her eyes widen in confusion. Only at the last moment was he able to force himself to stop. He sucked in his breath and struggled to regain control. Worse than a stembrain, he thought grimly. It is this human body with its strange desires.

He stared at Nimbia intently and slowly let out his breath. The questioning look remained on her face but she did not retreat. No, there was something more than just the impulsive lust. Astron tried to sort through his thoughts. Something was greater than the mere animal passions of the realm of men. What was it that compelled him? In his own body how then would he feel?

The ground shook with an audible rumble. Astron looked at the edge of the pond and saw dozens of clocks all ticking in synchrony and preparing to strike. He jerked his attention back to what had been their original plan. "Phoebe, the djinn," he yelled. "Instruct him to contact Palodad as he did before."

"I am already with you." Camonel's deep voice boomed out behind Astron. "I speak with the voice of Palodad, the one who reckons, the one who is awaiting what has been promised him."

Astron turned. "We did not find the answer to the riddle," he called out. "High king Finvarwin said words that do not seem to relate."

"Did you secure the harebell pollen? Have you obtained what I have asked?"

"Yes, more than a half-dozen grains." Astron felt the rucksack still on the back of Kestrel's body. "But—"

"Describe them to me."

Astron looked at the clocks' strikers reach back to their maximum extent. "There is no time," he said. "Something must—"

"What, time did you say, there is no time?" Camonel flung back his head and his laughter boomed out over the oasis. "Here there will be time eternal. Do you not see what is happening? Before there were two separate realms. Soon there will be but one. The laws have mixed so that there is nothing to distinguish one universe from another. Like two bubbles pressed together, the surface between them has dissolved away. They distort and strain, but inevitably merge into one. The single realm

275

that results will obey the symmetries of both space and time. With the next stroke of the gongs, these beings that call themselves rotators and reflectives will have their game continue forever, circling about a single oasis in pursuit of one another and playing the same move over and over and over. Yes, a beautiful symmetry that—"

"Tiny barbs and upon them smaller filaments still," Astron interrupted. "The surface of the pollen has a structure finer than that possible from the most skilled weaver. I have had no chance to study them further. But then, how can it matter? Although you might be satisfied, it does not help to answer—"

"Oh, but indeed it does." Camonel clasped his sides to control his laughter. His eyes defocused and took on a faraway look. "Barbs and filaments, you say. Yes, exactly what my calculations predicted. It is but a small reason why I am known as the one who reckons. That is why I sent you. Even without the answer, I had hoped that the pollen would still provide a piece to the puzzle."

"Then Prince Elezar," Astron said. "How does he fare?"

"Gaspar has found his dark node and driven him from it. The spark of life shines no longer in most of his followers. He is adrift, virtually alone, somewhere in the darkness of the realm, awaiting his end. I must have the pollen and the cataloguer quickly. It is the last hope that Gaspar will not be victorious in the end.

"But enough. Now, human, before the strike of the last gong that locks this realm into an eternity of repetition, clasp the pollen tightly and enfold yourself in the arms of my agent."

"There are four of us altogether," Astron said.

"No, just you and the cataloguer," the voice rumbling from Camonel said. "Of the others there is no need."

Camonel stepped forward, stretching his wings out to full span. Astron looked at Nimbia and then at Kestrel still slashing with a sword a half-dozen subnodes away. "Come." The djinn's voice boomed with authority. "Come, bring the pollen to Palodad's domain, and then we will speak of riddles and the precepts that lie beyond all others. The pollen and the cataloguer—both are essential. For no less will I continue to aid in your cause."

"No!" Phoebe's voice sounded above the demon's own. "You have stated that you have submitted. It is my commands that you must obey."

Camonel hesitated. Slowly he turned back to the wizard. "But there was no true struggle," he said slowly. "It was only because Palodad had instructed—"

"I command you to take us away," Phoebe said. "Away from here to safety for the four of us who do not belong."

"Not even a mighty djinn can find his way when the reality about him changes as he flies," Camonel said. "If we hesitate too long, I cannot be sure of even finding the lair of the one who reckons."

The clocks struck in synchrony with an ear-shattering peal. The ground began to weave and buckle, making it difficult for Astron to keep his balance. Off in the distance, he saw the sand rise in a huge wave that climbed halfway into the zenith. The sky above blinked in a kaleidoscope of rapidly changing colors.

"Away," Phoebe shouted. "To the first flame that you can find. I care not where."

Camonel grunted. "Dominance or submission," he muttered. "There can be no in between." Astron saw the mighty djinn pull Phoebe to him with one hand and then swoop to retrieve Nimbia with the other. Cradling them in his stout upper arms, he plucked Kestrel from the surrounding mêlée and then returned for Astron and the rucksack.

As the wings folded shut about him, Astron heard screams of dismay and pain, and then Abel's strong voice shouted above the rest. "We have broken the protocols and new ones come in their place. Look about you, reflectives, and see what you have done. Unwittingly, you have invoked the strongest, the ultimate of them all—coalescence follows from similarity. We are merged with the universe of the chronoids and now we are truly doomed."

With a crash of grinding reorientation the wave of sand hit the oasis. A chant of eat, sleep, cycle, eat, sleep, cycle began to ring in Astron's ears. He felt a wave of nausea far stronger than any that had gone before. Everything went blurry, and he seemed to be tumbling head over heel. The sweetness of the air suddenly lost its pleasure. His aches and pains dissolved away. In resignation, he succumbed to the protection of what was again his stembrain, only dimly aware of the closeness of Nimbia at his side.

# PART FIVE

## The Realm of the Aleators

## Chapter Twenty-Two

# *A Little Bit of Luck*

KESTREL looked at his outstretched hands and saw that they were his own. Evidently the last transformation in the realm of reticulates had restored him and Astron to their proper bodies. He shook his head to clear it of the last of the strange feelings. He had felt a robustness that had coursed through his veins with a pounding vigor. His basic needs for air, food, and sleep had been inherently satisfied and had not troubled his thoughts, even on the lowest level. The immortality of a demon's body he could well believe.

But to be facing an existence that stretched out forever with so little control over one's own thoughts! Kestrel frowned at the horror of it. It had been a constant struggle to keep from raising his sword stiffly over his head and plunging to certain death against any of a dozen reflective attacks. Eventually he would have succumbed. It was just too great an effort to remain on guard all the time—on guard against yourself and what your own thoughts might cause to happen.

Kestrel started to sit up and then hesitated as he became more aware of a gently rocking motion that pushed him from side to side. Looking about cautiously he saw that he was lying at the bottom of a concave wooden hull. Curved spars arched upward from under a keelboard under his back to gunwales well above his head. The last dying embers of a fire hissed in a smoky soup of bilgewater and soot. Below his feet he could see Phoebe's crumpled form and, beyond her, what probably were Nimbia and Astron stirring as well.

Kestrel looked skyward and groaned. The canopy

281

was pale blue and lit by a small reddish sun, far smaller than what he was used to in the realm of men. Again they were somewhere else from where they wanted to be. For a moment, he lay on the rough wooden planking, trying to put his thoughts together. The strain of the last few moves had taken its toll on his mind, as well as on Astron's poorly equipped body. Having to think consciously of every thrust and parry, rather than rely on instincts learned over many years of getting out of scrapes, was as exhausting as heavy labor.

Kestrel sighed. Yes, the effort had been exhausting, but somehow rewarding as well. If not for the gong of the clocks on the final move, the rotarians he led might have captured the node, despite the odds. They had depended on him and he had been true to their trust. He had risen to what was his duty and discharged it well. If not for the clocks, then who knew what could have happened? Perhaps there might be some way to go back, despite what the djinn had said, after Phoebe was safely home—go back and rescue those that had put their lives in his hands without questioning that he would respond in return.

"It is worse than the desert," Kestrel heard Phoebe say as she rose and came to his side. Her depressing lethargy seemed to have vanished. Even with the unsure footing of the small boat, there was confidence in her tread. "Look, Kestrel, there is nothing in sight. In the realm of reticulates, we arrived at an oasis where we could eat and drink." She looked at him intently and smiled. "It is worse than the desert and I do not care."

Kestrel looked out over the gunwale and blinked at what he saw. They were at sea with no sight of land on the horizon. Kestrel whirled to look in other directions, but there was little difference. The only feature was a thin line in the distance, separating ocean from sky.

He glanced down the length of the long boat, but, except for Nimbia and Astron, he saw that the hull was bare. They had no sails, oars, food, or water. Near his feet, the last ember of the dying fire cooled to a soggy gray. Evidently they did have at least one leak.

Kestrel put his arm around Phoebe and attempted a

brave smile. She smiled back and drew closer. "At least, this part is better than the last few moves," she said. "You hardly touched me when we were separated from the others."

Kestrel started to explain what had happened, but thought better of it. There would be time enough for that later, after they had reached safety. "How big a fire do you need to summon the djinn again?" he asked, waving at the charred splints at his feet. "Evidently in this place a blaze in a small wooden boat is not something totally bizarre."

"No, do not struggle with a demon now." Astron suddenly shook his head from where he was trying to stand near the stern. "Something is not right about the summoning. There is too much risk."

"What do you mean?" Phoebe said. "I have brought forth Camonel before and I can do it again. Do not worry, Astron. I have my full confidence now. Kestrel had faith in me and that was enough."

"I do not question the power in your craft," Astron said. "It is the words of the djinn that give me the suspicion. You have taught me, Kestrel, to look beyond the words to the meaning behind." The demon paused and wrinkled his nose. "How do we know that it was truly Palodad speaking through the mouth of Camonel? The one who reckons is a recluse, more concerned with the flipping of the imps in his own domain than delving into the working of other realms. He wants the harebell pollen grains as part of a bargain, it is true, but the insistence that I must accompany their delivery seems out of place."

"I do not know the workings of your kind." Kestrel shook his head. "So I cannot speak to how well your conjecture hits the mark. But if not this Palodad, then who else would speak through the flame?"

"Gaspar," Astron said. "He is the one who stands to lose, if we are successful in our quest. Without the pollen, we cannot expect any more of Palodad's aid. He is the one who is tracking down all those with allegiance to the prince he wishes to destroy—the one who would want my return far more than any other.

"And even though Phoebe controlled Camonel to ef-

283

fect our rescue, the djinn is free to act in matters that she does not explicitly proscribe."

"From what you have told me of Gaspar," Kestrel said, rising to stand, "it is unlikely he would have the skill for such complex charades. Indeed, you even said that his posing of the riddle was a surprise to your prince." Kestrel tugged at his chin and looked out over the featureless sea. "There is also the matter of the outside influence in the realm of reticulates. Given the confining nature of the protocols, what would start the barter with the chronoids in the first place? Why would even the reflectives continue when the unpredictable results from using the engines began to interfere with their plans? Who was responsible for the torrent of exchanges at the end? It is as if there were someone else behind all of this, someone far wiser than Gaspar manipulating him as well as other things."

"Prydwin!" Nimbia sat up, suddenly alert. "It all fits together when you think of it. It is his creations that have been coalesced. Although I can think of no reason why he would wish it so, because he knows the details of their creation, no one could cause the merging any better than he. Who else would be concerned about what happens to harebell pollen, if not one of the fey? Suppose that the prince of the lightning djinns did not have a free will of his own, but was under the domination of my kinsman?"

"Yes, Prydwin," Astron said. "You may very well be right. Most of my kind have little concern for the workings of other realms. Except for cataloguers such as myself, they dwell instead on instant gratifications that forestall the great monotony. Far more plausible is a being from somewhere else manipulating events for his own personal gain."

"Then what is our plan?" Phoebe asked. "Unless I can control a demon, we are marooned here as surely as we were before."

"Do not misunderstand," Astron said. "Despite appearances, we have made progress on our quest. First we learned that it was the realm of the fey in which we must look. There we successfully acquired the pollen grains that Palodad desires."

"And in the realms of symmetry," Nimbia cut in, "we heard Palodad say that their physical design somehow was important to the answer of the riddle."

"Only if indeed it was Palodad," Astron said. "Of that we cannot be certain." He shook his head. "No, it is the one who reckons whom we must contact directly to be safe," he said. "No intermediary agent will do."

"Then tell me of his mental signatures," Phoebe said. "When we relight the fire, he is the one I will seek."

Kestrel saw Astron's membranes flick down over his eyes and his nose wrinkle to the side.

"It is not quite that simple," the demon said after a moment. "I doubt I could accurately describe the character of Palodad's will. He is old, old even by the standards of my kind and his thoughts—" Astron trailed off and shook his head. "Mankind would probably call him mad," he continued, "and I am not so sure that I do not agree."

Kestrel saw Astron clench his fist and suppress a slight shudder. "No, I must be the agent, as we have agreed before. But in light of our suspicions, I must return unaided—return and seek out Palodad directly, rather than rely on the intermediary of any of my kind."

"Would it not be better to take the pollen with you when you go?" Kestrel reached behind his back and patted his pack. "With nothing to offer, what would be the motivation for Palodad to aid us any further?"

"I cannot carry the harebell pollen through the flame, Kestrel," Astron said, "at least not in my—my present state. Remember the reason that Elezar directed me to your realm was to secure the aid of mankind to perform the cartage. Even the most powerful of djinns has difficulty with objects that do not possess minds of their own."

"Then clasp me somehow to you," Kestrel said. He looked at Phoebe and smiled. "I have already experienced three realms other than my own in aiding in the adventures of a wizard. One more can hardly make any difference."

"I am not a mighty djinn." Astron shook his head. "Although I require the flame of anvilwood and not simple pine or fir to pass between the realms, skills in weaving or transportation I have none. We must somehow find the tree most similar in this realm so that I can return alone."

Kestrel thought for a moment and then looked at Astron intently. "How can you be sure?" he asked. "With so many fetters of logic about your stembrain, how can you be sure?"

"Fetters? What do you mean?"

"And how can you know the inner thoughts of a demon." Phoebe laughed. "Even the best of wizards can only guess."

Kestrel started to answer, but then shrugged. A crooked smile came to his face. "It does not really matter," he said with a wave of his arm. "I doubt we will be able to find the proper wood surrounded by—"

Kestrel stopped and stared out over his outflung hand. Between the bobs of the waves, he thought he caught sight of a mast and sail just at the horizon. Impulsively, he began to wave his arms. "Look," he shouted. "Look to port. It is a ship, a large ship, sailing our way —what luck, what incredible luck indeed."

His feelings flipped with a suddenness that made him giddy. He pulled Phoebe close and gave her a hug. "I have sampled enough of what you are like, demon." He laughed. "Sampled enough from a fresh perspective that I have seen parts that even you are unaware of. But first let us attend to our safety in one realm before we take on the challenges of another."

"Over there on the starboard." Nimbia suddenly pointed. "There is one—no, two more, in addition to the first."

Kestrel took his eyes from the ship to port gradually drawing closer. There seemed little doubt that they had been seen. He looked to starboard and shook his head in amazement. Near the stern was another tall mast, and directly abeam was a third. There was such a thing as luck, but this was incredible. How could they have been placed in the precise center of a circle of ships in a totally featureless sea?

Kestrel looked at Phoebe, but she did not seem to care about the coincidence. She was jumping up and down as much as he. The boat rocked with each leap, and Nimbia stumbled as she tried to maintain her balance. Astron reached out and grabbed her awkwardly by the shoulder. Kestrel saw the demon's nose suddenly wrinkle with the contact. The eye membranes flicked into place, and he quickly withdrew. Nimbia smiled and reached out in return, grabbing Astron's retreating hand.

Astron held his arm out stiffly like a stick figure drawn by a child. Nimbia steadied herself and closed the distance between them.

"The retriever of harebell pollen, the swordsman leader of the rotators, and even the gentleman-in-waiting for a queen of the fey," she said. "One has difficulty remembering that you are a merely a djinn from beyond the flame."

The crook in Astron's nose sharpened. "I am a demon, you know full well," he said slowly. "But the power of my brood brethren is not mine to command. I am but a cataloguer, serving as best I can."

"And to whom is it that this service is rendered?"

"Why, to my prince, of course," Astron said. He paused and looked away from Nimbia's gaze. "And, of course, to the success of the quest of Kestrel, Phoebe, and—and Nimbia as well."

"And when the quest is over?"

"I have not thought of it," Astron said. "It is not the nature of demonkind to think of what lies beyond the present. It leads to brooding on the inevitability of the jaded senses and the ultimate despair of the great monotony."

"But as I have observed, you are no common demon," Nimbia said. "And for me, the end of the quest poses the greatest uncertainty for us four. The two humans will no doubt return to their own kind." She waved her arm in Kestrel's direction. "And you, if you so choose, will flitter back to some depressingly plain patch of mud in the void of your realm. But what of Nimbia, a queen of the fey? There is no place to which to return. Ever so much worse than before, there is no one with whom to share. Who will serve me with distinction in a manner of which I could be proud?"

Astron wrenched his hand free of Nimbia's grip. "Your

words prick at my stembrain," he said. "It is difficult to maintain rational control." For a long moment he stood silent; then his membranes cleared and the muscles in his face relaxed. He looked at Nimbia and spoke softly. "Do not be deceived," he said. "I am no weaver of matter; no wings of great lift sprout from my back. I am only a cataloguer whose power derives from the few facts that no other has learned. There is no special destiny for one such as I."

"In the realm of the fey and, I suspect in others as well, one is measured by his deeds, rather than his inherent potentials, whatever they might be. I remember tasting your inner doubts when you rescued me from Prydwin's sentrymen, demon. And I have seen you lead hundreds of rotators with clumsy hands and little regard for your own safety as well." Nimbia reached out and touched Astron gently on the cheek. "There is much more that you can learn, cataloguer," she said, "much more you can learn of yourself."

"Avast, you in the dory," a deep voice suddenly boomed across the waves. "Reduce your efflux so that the others will sail away."

Kestrel turned his attention from Astron and Nimbia and looked over at the ship approaching from portside. It was nearer than the others, and details of its superstructure could now be discerned. A single short mast stood in the middle of a deck that was both wide and long. A lateen sail billowed in a stiffening breeze that had not been there before the arrival of the vessel it propelled. The broad bow and even broader beam were wider than those of any barge that Kestrel had ever seen. It seemed hard to believe that the small area of cloth presented to the wind could be adequate for a hull easily the length of two score men.

Even more remarkable, Kestrel thought with a start, was the fact that he understood perfectly the words that had been spoken. Except for a slight accent, they sounded like the speech of an Arcadian from across the sea in the realm of men. This, then, was not another creation of Prydwin; but if not, how amazing that the language turned out as it did.

"Reduce your efflux," the voice repeated. "You have impressed me as much as you will. I regard you as wealthy. To spill more luck to the winds will up my assessment not a quantum more."

Kestrel looked up at the deck, puzzled. He saw a rotund man wrapped in pinkish silks and a purple sash pulled tight into an overflowing girth. Bushy black hair, as dark as night, tumbled out of a small turban down the sides of his face into a curly beard. The deep-set eyes squinted cruelly into the reddish sun. The smile wrinkles looked shallow and seldom used.

Three or four others dressed like the first huddled about their leader, each one holding high a small cage of gold that contained some small white-furred rodent contentedly munching away on greens. The neck of each man was bowed under the weight of at least a score of chains. On every chain hung small trinkets; some were mere gauze bags tied with ribbon, others intricately veined leaves pressed flat on slabs of slate.

"Why, you carry no plenuma," the black-headed one continued as the two vessels drew quite close, "no plenum chambers at all." He reached for a monocle of colored glass hanging from a chain about his own neck and quickly cocked it into his eye. "By the rush of entropy, it is in spontaneous discharge from all four of you—spontaneous discharge, as if you had been building pressure for a lifetime and using none of it until now."

He waved over his shoulder to the center of the ship. "All right, I withdraw my words. I am most certainly impressed, more certainly than I have ever been before." He paused and intertwined his fingers across his expansive girth, rocking back and forth silently as if enjoying a secret joke. "But mark you," he said after a moment, "I am not so awed as to forgo absorbing the flux for myself. And if you do not have plenum chambers, let us find out how good are your wards against the sucking chambers of Jelilac, the most fortunate."

A man much smaller than Jelilac suddenly vaulted over the gunwale of the larger ship and, with hardly a glance to see where he was going, landed firmly in the

289

dory between Phoebe and Nimbia. He carried what looked like a bowl of soapy water in one hand and a large pipe in the other. Without spilling a drop or hesitating to catch his balance, he adroitly settled into a squatting position and submerged the pipe into the bowl.

Kestrel noticed that he had as many chains about his neck as the rest, perhaps even more. All along the arms and legs of his silken tunic were embroidered tiny leaves of clover, and each of his fingers was wrapped in bows of red ribbon.

"Luck begets luck." The newcomer noticed Kestrel's stare. "It is the third tenet." Then, without further comment, he began to blow on his pipe, causing a bubble to form in its bowl. His first few puffs on the pipe seemed easy, and the glassy surface expanded with rapid jumps. But when the bubble had reached the size of a fist, Kestrel noticed that the veins in the pipeman's neck began to stand out and his cheeks redden from the effort to force air down the stem of the pipe. It reminded him of the sport of the fey, but it was somehow different, and he suspected the effort served a practical utility.

As Kestrel watched, the surface of the bubble began to darken and take on what looked like a tough, leathery texture, far less elastic than any balloon. By the time the pipeman had finished, he had created a sphere perhaps the size of a person's head with a dark opalescent surface that light just barely shone through.

The piper dropped his grip on the pipestem. With a grunt, he removed the bubble from where it still adhered to the bowl. Then he quickly stretched out his arms and touched the orb to the hem of Phoebe's cape. There was a sudden spark of light that jumped from the draping material into the interior of the sphere. For an instant Kestrel saw what looked like a churning maelstrom of dense red smoke within the confines of the globe; but as the light vanished, the image faded away.

Phoebe immediately stumbled. Kestrel reached out just in time to break her fall on the hard planking of the small boat. "Just exactly what do you think you are doing," he shouted angrily at the piper. "What is that thing, anyway?"

The piper looked at Phoebe's sprawled form on the deck and then hefted the sphere at his side. "I suppose it does seem a bit uncivil," he said. "Certainly for this exchange, you deserve at least the most basic of talismans in return." He reached into his pocket with his free hand and offered Phoebe a necklace like one of the many he wore about his neck. What looked like the preserved foot of a small animal dangled from the lower end.

"Only good for simple accidents, I admit," he said. "But then Jelilac covets each dram. It is the way of all who wish to live more than the briefest of moments in the realm of the aleators."

Kestrel grimaced. Understanding the language was almost too good to have happened. Without it, perhaps things would have proceeded more slowly and given him time to size up better the situation they were in. He reached out to grab the offered talisman but the piper easily whisked it out of his reach. With a deft and fluid motion, he flung it over Phoebe's head, where it settled in a perfect position about her neck. "For the lady," the piper said. "And watch your manners, or Milligan might decide that you end up with nothing at all."

Kestrel reached out a second time for the piper's leg, but the little man was too swift. As Kestrel's hand closed on air, Milligan had touched the globe to Nimbia's tunic, and a brilliant arc jumped to it as before. Nimbia teetered, but Astron was slightly quicker than Kestrel had been. Not hesitating to avoid contact, he steadied the queen so that she did not fall.

"Hmmm," Milligan said. "Perhaps it would be better to give this one a chance at food and drink. If you concentrated on subsistence alone and depended on the others for protection, you might get enough to share." Again he reached into his pocket and withdrew another pendant necklace, this one an ebony lump of wood carved in intricate whirls.

Kestrel lunged out at Milligan from behind, but the little man quickly turned and held the sphere chest high to absorb the force of the rush. The spark that jumped from Kestrel's outstretched hand sent a stab of pain up his arm.

He felt a sudden tugging sensation all over his body and then a rushing away of some essence that he could not quite identify. A wave of discomfort swept over his senses; in a weakened stupor, he sagged to the bottom of the dory.

With clouded vision, Kestrel watched the sparks dance from Astron's body as it had the others. Only dimly was he aware of a leather thong that pierced a small heavy stone being placed over his slumping head. Offering only the most feeble of protests, he let himself be hoisted by a crane up to the deck of the larger ship. He clutched his hands to a growling stomach, suddenly quite aware that he had not eaten for what seemed like a very long time.

"Your contributions have mellowed Jelilac's temper," Kestrel heard Milligan say some hours later. He shook his head and willed himself to focus on the little man standing before him. He felt a second talisman being hung about his neck and then a third. Looking to both sides, he saw Phoebe and the others rousing as well. They had been piled in a tumble about the single mast of the sloop.

"Ordinarily, with ones so destitute as you, the only choices he would offer would be trials with long odds indeed," Milligan continued. "But the idiocy of such a great concentration and not even the slightest of wards has him most amused. As it is, he needs to refine a rather mundane procedure before landfall at the casino. Surely at least one of you four will survive."

Kestrel staggered to his feet and looked about quickly. Except for the helmsman and Milligan, none of the crew were above deck. The dory in which they had arrived was battened to the port gunwale and a long ladder lay at its side. The glassy calm sea looked the same, although the other ships were no longer visible. Off the port bow in the distance was a sliver of brown above the horizon that indicated the first signs of land.

"We are travellers from afar," Kestrel said, "and understand little of what you speak." He ran his tongue across the dry roof of his mouth. "But decency anywhere would demand that you offer at least some food and drink."

"Offer subsistence, offer it freely from one to another."

Milligan threw back his head and laughed. He waved his arm in a wide, flat circle out to the horizon. "Do your eyes not see the vast expanse of waste — salt water everywhere and only tiny pinpoints of land. There is no food to offer to another. Even one such as I has had occasions of hunger, despite all that I carry about my neck."

Kestrel started to respond, but the doorway leading below deck suddenly slammed open, and two seamen appeared, carrying a long table between them. "Ah, spinpins," Milligan said. "Jelilac is feeling mellow indeed. He must think that crown is certain to be his."

Kestrel looked more closely at the table as it was positioned crosswise on the deck just in front of the mast where he stood. On one end was a simple maze, a box of wooden partitions divided into compartments, each the height of a hand. Doorways were cut in many of the walls connecting the confinements together; some were empty, but in most were standing geometric arrays of tiny bowling pins. A single doorway pierced the perimeter. Near it lay an intricately carved spintop and a pile of string.

A third seaman appeared from below deck, carrying a small vertical frame on which, near the top, was hung a blade of shining metal. At the bottom were two sheets of wood paneling between which the sharp edge apparently dropped. The panels were plain and unadorned, except for a hole about the size of a finger that had been drilled through them both. The seaman positioned the apparatus near the spintop and clamped it to the table. He ran a string from a hinged release mechanism for the blade and tied it about one of the pins standing in the maze.

"The principle is quite simple," Milligan said as he moved to the ladder at the side of the dory. Struggling with its long length for a moment, he thrust it into a vertical position and twisted its orientation with a flip, so that the topmost rung fell against the mast.

"Even the simplest child knows that one's luck decreases by walking under a ladder," Milligan said. "The effect can be reversed only by quickly retracing one's steps the other way."

"We have such a tale from whence we come," Kestrel

293

said. "But it is the nonsense of ancient crones, nothing more."

Milligan frowned and was silent for a long moment. "Minions of the crazed Byron," he muttered while he clutched at the talismans about his neck. "Minions of Byron, and not one, but four." His eyes narrowed and he looked at Kestrel keenly. "No, that cannot be. You are attempting some sort of a deception to free yourselves from your plight. No fatalists could have accumulated such auras as yours. You struggle for the crown, just as does Jelilac and the rest."

Kestrel frowned in turn. Very little of what Milligan was saying made any sense. He looked down at Astron as the demon stirred and struggled to sit. Kestrel wished that he were fully alert. Some of his deductive observations would be quite useful about now.

"Anyway, the reversal raises an interesting question," Milligan continued. "It is one that Jelilac stumbled on to, the kind of insight that makes him a true contender to be archon over us all. The throne has been vacant since Sigmund's luck suddenly turned sour. Soon we will all assemble to judge which aleator now possesses the greatest power." Milligan looked down at his chest and stroked three of his talismans. "Although, under the right circumstances, who is to say what will happen in the casino where the die is cast? Yes, who is to say which is the most deserving, the most faithful to the tenets of our creed?"

For a moment, Milligan stopped speaking, his eyes burning with secret thoughts. Kestrel looked back over the bow at the land steadily growing on the horizon. He eyed the two battens that held the dory and scanned the deck for signs of any other useful gear. With so few crewmen on deck, the right circumstances were the ones he was interested in as well. He began to think more clearly. Perhaps it was best to keep Milligan engaged in conversation until the others were fully alert. Then they just might manage an escape from whatever Jelilac had in store for them.

Kestrel glanced at the ladder and then back at the table. The construction for both was rather crude and unvarnished. He could see that more than one type of wood was used in each. On the other hand, perhaps such a risk was not even necessary. A fire on deck could serve just as well. That was a possibility worth exploring before attempting the longer odds of an escape.

"What do you have carved of anvilwood?" He smiled innocently. "I am a collector and most interested in any small figurines that you have to show."

Milligan broke out of his reverie. "Anvilwood?" He laughed. "There is none here on Jelilac's barge, to be sure. You must indeed be from an islet far away. Every aleator who has stopped sucking his thumb is taught to avoid such a luck drainer whenever he chances upon it." He stopped and laughed again. "It would just be the perversity of luck that such as you would be desirous of finding some. Throughout the realm, prisoners convicted of the worst crimes are sent to uproot the trees when they are discovered and hack the branches to bits. For others, the risks in touching are just too great. The only piece that I know of is at the casino for the trials to be archon. And even that Jelilac and the others will strive to destroy, if given half the chance."

Kestrel frowned. They would have to get away after all—and then, from the sound of it, journey to one very special place. He looked up at the ladder. Perhaps it could serve another use. They would need oars, even if they managed to drop the dory over the side. He glanced back at Milligan. The little man seemed to enjoy talking. For the moment it probably was best to keep him occupied.

Kestrel fingered the three talismans hanging about his neck. "This one looks something like a match stick." He held it out to Milligan. "Where we come from, it is a mark of great honor, since only a few we call wizards have the capability to build a flame. I suppose that here such skill is also a great rarity. No one such as yourself could hope to accomplish such a feat."

Milligan cocked his head to one side. "If it were not for the aura you possessed, I would agree with Jelilac and judge you most insane," he said. "Of course I can light a fire. Why, so could any child. It is not a question of ease, but one of law. On all corners of the great sea, a flame is prohibited under penalty of death."

Kestrel frowned, but Milligan continued. "The second tenet states that the entropy of luck always increases. There is no way it can be avoided. Each transfer from one to another, even each use that dilutes it back to the ether—all such transferals reduce its potency. The last thing that anyone would want is a flame that completely disorders its fine crystalline structure and renders it useless.

"Why, even an archon could become a pauper, if he approached too close to a fire. Without his luck to guard him, all of his great displays of state on the islands would be washed away by the next giant wave that sweeps across our sea. Even if he possessed the strange book of figures that Myra is reputed to have found, his ships would start to wander aimlessly, missing all of their ports. In the time of a single sigh, he would find that he had come to possess nothing, neither food for his next meal nor even clothing to ward off the chill. And each and every one who but an instant before stooped in the deepest of bows would shun his misfortune, casting him aside and letting him wander to his death, unheralded and alone.

"No, the object of us all is to find ways to increase our luck, to concentrate it into tighter and tighter confines that enhance its potency. It is the only way to survive, to move ahead, and to strive for the mantle of the archon. The fatalists cannot be right. Things should not be left to the will of the cosmos. Outcomes are determined by men with luck; he who has the greatest will certainly emerge the winner."

"I would think that skill or wit would somehow be important as well," Kestrel said. Cautiously, he placed one hand on the ladder and looked at the rungs. Perhaps, if the sidebeams were ripped apart they would serve well enough. He smiled inwardly and looked at Astron. It was something the demon probably would have thought of, and yet it came to him first.

"In the dim past, skill and wit did determine the outcome of many events," Milligan answered. "We contested by might of arms and clever strategies of state. But then, as our legends record it, wise archon Williard with overwhelming odds was defeated by a force a tenth his size when his horse stepped into the only squirrel hole on the field of battle. An errant arrow hit his second in command in the throat, and, without a leader, the army stumbled into a mire.

"Luck triumphed over all else; and from that day to this, everyone who strives for power concentrates on increasing his own luck and dissipating that of others. Skill and talent mean little to one who can select a marked token from a bowl of thousands with but a single thrust of his hand."

"Then what need do you have of this experimentation?" Kestrel asked. He placed his hand firmly on each of the ladder's sidebeams and strained outward while smiling in Milligan's direction. "If starting a fire is of no use, then whatever else of value can we be to you?"

"The means for accumulating and dissipating luck are not written in stone monuments for all to see," Milligan said. "It is only by centuries of trial and error that the methods that we use have come to light. Doubtless many more efficient techniques yet remain to be discovered." He waved his hand in a wide circle. "Luck is all about us, albeit at very low pressure. Certain actions seem to compress it into smaller volumes and increase its potency to alter events.

"As I have said, when one walks under a ladder, a portion of whatever one possesses leaks out into the ether. Immediately reversing direction prevents the loss before it can transpire." Milligan paused and ran his tongue over his lips. "But what if one circled back and walked under the ladder again in the second direction, the one that prevented the loss. Perhaps then the vector of transaction would remained fixed in a positive direction, each circuit under the ladder increasing one's luck, rather than dissipating it away.

"That then is the test. The first of you, I care not which, will walk once under the ladder and then spin the top through the maze. He will be what we call the control. The second will walk once and then immediately reverse before taking the test. The third, after reversing direction, will continue around the mast and back under the over-hang a dozen times more. The last will not reverse directions at all but rotate the dozen times in the same sense as the first."

"What will the spinning top prove?" Kestrel asked while he slid his arms up the ladder to feel another rung.

"It is a test of luck, to be sure," Milligan said. "The spinning top caroms through the compartments in a manner that no one can predict, scattering pins at random. The count of how many are felled is the measure we wish to monitor. If all the pins are toppled before the one attached to the blade, then the game is stopped and you are lucky indeed."

"And if the blade topples," Kestrel said. "What does that prove?"

"The finger you place in the hole will be severed, a most unlucky outcome," Milligan said. He looked quickly back at the maze on the table and then smiled at Kestrel. "The beauty of it is that you all have ten. We will be able to run some forty trials before we are done."

Kestrel decided he had heard enough. It did not matter if the others were fully alert or not. With or without oars, they must be away. "Astron," he yelled, "unlash the dory. Get it back over the side." With a grunt he twisted the ladder from its resting place and crashed it downward on the middle of the table, hoping that the force of the blow would break it apart.

The ladder bounced harmlessly off of the horizontal surface, however, the bottom end kicking up painfully into Kestrel's thigh. He staggered a single step and then sagged to one knee, his leg refusing to give him support. As he fell, he pushed at Phoebe, propelling her forward toward the gunwale where the dory was lashed. He rolled over on his back, expecting to see Milligan spring at him with some weapon, but he saw instead the little man feverishly fingering the brightest talisman which hung from his neck.

"Jelilac, Jelilac," Milligan screamed. "They are followers of Byron. Despite the great auras they once possessed, they follow Byron, to be sure."

Kestrel rose to kneeling and grabbed Nimbia about the

shoulder. Crawling with one hand on the deck, he urged her in the direction he had pushed Phoebe. Looking forward, he saw Astron fumbling with the mooring knots, apparently not making any progress in getting them untied.

Two seamen cautiously came forward, their fingers outflexed and reaching for the thongs of leather about Nimbia's neck. Kestrel staggered erect and pointed wildly into the sky. "Look," he shouted. "Not one shooting star, but two. Not to witness it is a great misfortune."

He held his breath for an instant, but the two sailors were totally unaccustomed to such a blatant deception. As one, they turned and began searching the clouds. Kestrel limped forward a single step. As he felt his leg again give way, he staggered against the nearest of the seamen. A ring on the sailor's hand scratched his cheek as he fell. Concentrating as hard as he could, he managed to grab hold of the loops and chains about his neck and pull the man to the ground.

Kestrel gathered up as many talismans in his hands as he could manage. With a back-wrenching yank, he snapped them from the seaman's neck. The sailor screamed. With an almost animal fury, he began clawing at Kestrel's arms to get them back.

Kestrel flung them in the direction of the dory; although several went over the gunwale, two landed at Astron's feet. Almost immediately the knot on the last fetter unraveled. The demon quickly reached down and grasped the bow in the cradle of his arms and hoisted it up over the low railing. Phoebe and Nimbia reached the stern and lifted it up as well. In an instant, the small boat splashed down onto the waves.

Kestrel crawled forward to the gunwale, blocking out the seaman who scrambled on the deck with him to retrieve the two talismans that remained. Kestrel reached to scoop them up a second time but grimaced as sharp splinters from the deck dug into his palm.

Astron bent down, grasped the talismans tightly in one hand, and then grabbed Kestrel by the arm with the other. Kestrel reached out for Phoebe and Nimbia. Without thinking further, they jumped together over the side.

The salt water stung Kestrel's cheek when he hit, but he paid it no heed. Lashing out blindly, he felt the side of the dory and grasped for a hold. Through sea-spattered hair, he saw Milligan leaning over the rail, cupping his hands to his mouth.

"There is little enough gain in what you have stolen," he yelled. "Basic enhancers and navigator's fetishes are all. They are organic and soon will decay. About enough to see you safely to the island in the distance and survive a wave or two, but little more. And there, if you stay out of the clutches of doubting Myra and her arcane devices, you will learn well enough the difficulty of finding food and drink with what little auras you now possess."

Milligan looked back over his shoulder and laughed. "Followers of Byron," he said. "With the spintop, at least one of you might have had a chance."

Kestrel saw the distance between the dory and the sloop begin to widen. From somewhere, a fresh breeze had begun to blow them apart. He tried to hoist himself a little higher to see the direction they should begin to paddle. Despite the aches and pains, he felt the cold of the sea and the renewed gnawing of his hunger. Basic enhancers and navigator's fetishes, he thought. Even if they were lucky, would so little be enough?

CHAPTER TWENTY-THREE

## *The Darling of Destiny*

ASTRON stirred with discomfort. He watched Kestrel clutch the tripstring firmly in his grasp, preparing for the moment that he would jerk away the twig that propped the splintered beam from the sandy beach. The small quail was just partway into the trap. It would be the dozenth try, and Astron doubted it would be any more successful than the rest.

He looked at Phoebe and Nimbia, huddled motionlessly near the wreckage of the dory. The heavy wave that had dashed them against the beach had destroyed their only means to travel elsewhere with any speed. The small, reddish sun was almost to the crest of the hill spine that hid the interior of the island. A heavy copse of trees covered the entire slope. Only the sandy beach that curved out of sight in both directions was devoid of the thick vegetation. Perhaps in the interior, they would find bigger game or even someone more sympathetic to their plight. But nightfall was coming too soon. For the moment, they had to hope for a single meal and find what cover they could in the wreckage of the boat.

Astron twisted his shoulders, ignoring Kestrel's sharp glance to be still. He wished he could be more sure of the path they were taking, seeking out anvilwood rather than letting Phoebe summon Camonel to their aid. But which was truly the lesser risk he could not decide. The uncertainty stirred his stembrain, forcing him to tighten his control.

He looked again at Nimbia, trying to recapture the pounding emotion that had gripped him when it was Kestrel's body he had possessed. It was not the same now, of course, but the experience had touched his rational centers as well. He remembered their closeness when hiding from Prydwin's pursuit, the piercing inner sadness that she exposed to him more than any other, the strength of duty she felt to her hill dwellers that was stronger than that of any prince. Even in abstraction, sharing more of her thoughts would bring a great pleasure, perhaps as keen as the discovery of new facts from beyond the flame. What would it be like, he wondered, if their relationship went deeper than that of a broodmother and sire?

Astron stopped the direction of his thoughts short and wrinkled his nose. He shook his head in the manner of men. She was no less than a queen and regarded him in quite a different light. At no time, he recalled, had she even bothered to call him by name. She spoke with kind-

301

ness and praise, but always as she would to a servant, one perhaps to be her single loyal retainer when the quest was finally done.

If only it were finally done, he thought ruefully. He had been away from Elezar far longer than he had intended. Could there still be any hope that his prince was alive? And with Gaspar triumphant, his own grisly fate would only be a matter of time. Somehow, he must get the harebell pollen back to Palodad and trust that whatever he had learned would provide a sufficient clue to solve the riddle. Without that, then anything else did not really matter.

Astron pushed away the reverie. He turned his attention back to the immediacy of their problems. He watched the quail take another timid step under the overhang of the beam. Its tiny head twitched from side to side, looking for predators. Then, in two quick thrusts of its bill, it poked at the seeds that Nimbia had gathered along the beach. Kestrel yanked on the string unraveled from Phoebe's cape and wrenched the twig free. The beam seemed to hover for a moment in midair and then crashed to the ground, shearing away a few feathers from the quail as it ran clear.

Kestrel pounded his fist into his hand. "So close," he spat. "I should have waited a second more until the bird was more centered under the beam."

"Such is not our luck," Astron said. "And if the words of that Milligan are true, never will it be. It was only the lifetimes of unspent luck that we brought with us upon entry to the realm that ensured our rescue from the sea and a language that you and Phoebe understand as well as I. But Jelilac and Milligan evidently have drained all of that away. The ordinary trapping skills from the realm of men will do us little good here. We must approach the cause of our problem, rather than deal with its symptoms."

"That is easy enough for you to say," Phoebe growled irritably. "You do not need food and water as do the rest of us."

"I am well aware of the metabolic needs of men," Astron said. He waved his arm toward the treeline in the distance. "Despite the peril, we must leave the sterile surroundings of this beach."

"Or perhaps we should all clutch these talismans and hope that a gamefowl walks out of the forest and lies down at our feet," Phoebe said.

"That is the essence of the solution," Astron agreed. "In this realm, we must strive to increase our luck and raise it to the point that the improbable happens as a matter of course. Then whatever we need will immediately follow."

"Yes, Astron is right." Nimbia pulled at the chains about her neck. "We have only survived as well as we have because of whatever minimal protection these necklaces provide."

"And how does one go about effecting this increase?" Kestrel said. "We have no masts or ladders here, and even Milligan was unsure of what would be the result."

"That is only one way," Astron said. "Surely the aleators have many other means. We must approach them again, only this time much better prepared."

"I do not care for the likes of Jelilac." Phoebe shook her head. "Perhaps others will be the same. We must instead act on our own. Despite your misgivings, Astron, contacting Camonel is our best chance."

Before Astron could reply, he heard a deep sighing noise from the direction of the water. He looked seaward and saw the foaming crestline of waves begin a rapid retreat, exposing the slope of land far beneath the extent of the lowest tide. Astron looked farther out over the ocean. Although he could not be sure, the line between the water and the sky seemed much higher than he had remembered it before.

"What is it?" Kestrel asked.

"A wall of moving water," Astron said. "Just as Milligan hinted—a tidal wave, some among your realm call it. Quickly, there is little time. Run for higher ground and climb into the trees." He raced over to where Nimbia sat and pulled her to her feet. Spinning her about, he shoved her in the direction of the slope rising from the beach.

Kestrel pounded his fist into his hands. "What rotten

luck," he growled. In apparent frustration, he reached up to pull the talismans from his neck, but then thought better of it. He lifted Phoebe from the ground. In imitation of Astron and Nimbia, they began running hillward on a slightly different path.

Astron and Nimbia sprinted up over the sandy ground into the darkness of the forest without speaking. Nimbia paused a moment at the base of the first climbable tree she found, but Astron motioned her onward. Stumbling into darkness, they picked their way farther into the dense canopy. Behind him, Astron could hear a muted roar drawing closer. Kestrel and Phoebe were nowhere to be seen.

Finally Astron stopped and pointed at a low-hanging branch. Together he and Nimbia scrambled up from limb to limb into the foliage. Despite his scales, rough branches scraped against his hands and snagged his leggings, but he did not pause to pick at the splinters. His head poked through to sunlight as he pulled himself to a slender, swaying branch that barely held his weight. Looking seaward, he saw the huge wave crest and topple over upon itself. With a booming crash, a wall of foaming water pounded onto the beach and began racing uphill.

The sandy slope was covered in an instant. Like popping embers in a fire, the trunks of the closest trees snapped from the impact and then were buried under the waterline. The dense grove of timber slowed the rush, but still it roared up the hillside. Astron flicked down his membranes, hoping that the fury of the onrush would be spent before it reached them. He saw row after row of treetops disappear beneath the churning sea and huge trunks bobbing up behind, completely stripped of foliage. The cool sea-green muted into muddy browns, and a web of debris formed on the once clear surface of the water.

The wave front surged closer, slowing as it came. Midway up the slope, the breathtaking speed seemed to be blunted. Then the wave top crashed, to rise no more. But still the water level climbed higher in a relentless swell. Astron saw the first tendrils snake about the base of the tree in which he had climbed and then the water level rise above the ground. Swiftly, the lower branches were submerged. Astron tested what remained of the trunk above his head but he already knew he could climb no more.

He looked across to Nimbia, hanging awkwardly on the branch across from his own. Before he could speak, the cold water reached his feet and then surged over his head. With an irresistible pull, he was yanked from his perch and then struck in the side by an uprooted trunk. Astron thrust his hands into the thick and deeply grooved bark and grabbed hold of the log as it passed. He scrambled around the side and thrust his head into the air, just in time to see Nimbia floating past. Releasing part of his grip, he grabbed and pulled her to the trunk. Dimly, he was aware of passing over a crest and then tipping downward to cascade into an interior valley below.

The next few moments were a blur of splashing spray and jarring caroms off of the trees on the downslope side. Somehow, Astron and Nimbia managed to hang on to the trunk that bore them and at the same time avoid being caught between it and the other trees into which it crashed.

They reached the bottom of the small valley and then hurled partway up the other side. The water slowed gradually to a halt. With a slow ponderous motion, it reversed direction and began to move back down toward the valley floor. But its momentum was nearly spent. The trunk moved sluggishly with the flow. With one final bone-jarring jolt, it crashed to the ground, letting the burbling water race ahead.

Astron held on to his grip for a few moments more, listening to the hiss and gurgle receding into silence. Slowly he dismounted and slid his feet to the ground. In a moment, Nimbia joined him, her face blanked in a daze. Oblivious to their deliverance, she looked at the wet clothing that sagged about the curve of her body.

"If you had the power of weaving, you could dry these instantly," Nimbia said. She fussed a moment at her tunic, still not mended from the battles in the realm of reticulates. "But since you do not, demon, turn your head while I disrobe."

Mixing with the dizziness of their ride, Astron felt a

subtle stirring in his stembrain, a tantalizing feeling from before, which he could not quite recognize. They should immediately begin searching for Kestrel and Phoebe, but something else tugged at him.

Astron started to answer, then halted. A flicker of movement up the interior slope above the high-water mark had caught his eye. Almost thankful for the distraction, he touched Nimbia's shoulder and pointed at what he saw. A small tendril of smoke struggled skyward from the foliage.

"Perhaps another aleator," he whispered. "One evidently with luck to burn. Keep on your clothing. This time we will be more forewarned."

Astron led Nimbia up the hillside. The ground became far more rocky and the canopy of trees gave way to scrubbier underbrush and finally an open clearing. Astron strode forward boldly, mustering as much dignity as he could in his soggy clothing. He saw a single figure sitting on a rock beside a small fire, over which was roasting some sort of pig. A horse was hobbled nearby. Next to it, a large pack was propped against a small tent of bright blue.

Upon the noise of their approach, the man looked up slowly from his contemplation, but no expression of surprise crossed his face. Cold blue eyes stared out under a head of golden blond hair, cut shoulder length and straight, with no curl. The face held the smoothness of youth, unwrinkled and without trouble—almost that of a child just aroused from sleep. Broad shoulders, heavily muscled, flexed under a thin, sleeveless shirt that sparkled with an iridescence in the last rays of sunlight filtering into the clearing. The throat of the shirt was thrown open; not a single talisman dangled about the sinewy neck.

"Whom do you seek?" A measured voice cut across the distance, each word unhurried and more of a command than a question.

"Did you not hear the crash of the wave?" Astron walked forward, motioning Nimbia to follow. "I would expect to find anyone who was able to hear its warning cautiously returning to ground from the safety of a high tree, rather than calmly fixing a meal."

"The wave would have reached Byron or it would not." The man shrugged. "There is no need to prepare for what is meant to be."

Astron hesitated a moment and searched about wildly for one of the spheres that Milligan had used to capture his and the others' luck. He saw no signs of one and took another step forward. After his experience with the reflectives, it seemed far easier than before. "You are one of exceedingly good fortune," he said. "I have heard that even the smallest fire dissipates what one has accumulated back into the ether."

Byron looked at Astron sharply. "Are you here to tempt me?" he said. "To test and see if I am worthy?" He stopped and darted his eyes to Nimbia as she approached. Astron watched Byron's nostrils flare and his hands suddenly coil into fists. The warrior's eyes ran slowly over her body and torn tunic. The beat of his pulse stood out strongly on his neck.

"You tempt me, indeed." Byron's voice rumbled quietly. "What is it that you would have me do?"

Astron scowled in annoyance. He recognized the reaction and understood it far better than before. Stepping in front of Nimbia, he threw wide his arms, shielding her as much as he was able.

"We might have something of great benefit," he said quickly. "It all depends on what you can offer as a fair payment in exchange."

"If it is luck of which you speak, then there is no basis for a barter," Byron said. "I have none to offer, nor do I seek any for what I must do."

Astron stirred uncomfortably. "What exactly is it that, ah, that you must do?" he asked.

"Why, travel to the grand casino to contest for the crown with all the others," Byron said. He slapped the long broadsword at his side. "But not in the same manner. If I succeed, it will be because fate wills it, not because of twists of luck."

Astron's interest immediately heightened—the grand casino, exactly where he wanted to go. Only with a firm resolution did he stop himself from looking back at Nimbia with a smile. "We have experienced firsthand what happens without luck," he said carefully. "Just to survive takes more than a little amount."

"Only because some of the aleators have so distorted it," Byron spat. "They lead the realm to destruction with their tinkering, they work with fluids better left alone. Look," he said, apparently warming to the subject. "The first tenet says that luck is a gas, a perfect one that flows from high pressure to low. Without interference, it distributes itself evenly throughout the realm, favoring no one over another. The forces of fate are free to operate, to work the destinies that are intended for us all.

"But what happens when it is compressed, scooped up from everywhere into a small number of concentrations under the control of only a few? There is less left in the ambience. Without participating in the forbidden rituals, everyone else is stripped of what is his due share. To step from a hut becomes a great adventure; to fill one's stomach is a hunt of great exhaustion. Even the elements are perturbed into extremes. For the fortunate, the air is always clear and balmy. In compensation, gentle rains and waves are compressed into great disasters that prey on those who do not have the protection of the proper talismans.

"With the great accumulations come great new strains and forces," Byron went on, "distortions in the very fabric of what must happen to us all. Those who have accumulated luck must dispense some modicums to their followers, constructing all sorts of charms like those useless husks that drape about your necks. They war not with merit, but depend entirely on those who can force chance outcomes to go their way."

Byron stopped and set his lips in a grim line. "But I will stop them all," he said defiantly. "It is my calling, and to it I will be true."

"You say you have no great accumulation of luck of your own," Astron said. "How do you hope to accomplish your goal?"

"Soon my followers will return and report what they

have seen in the bay on the far coast. There Myra has dropped anchor with both her ships. We will attack on the morrow, and one of them will become mine. With it, we will cross the great sea.

"I will stride into the grand casino and win, although luck I have none. Luck favors the believer, states the fourth tenet; it is fickle and hence runs in streaks, professes the fifth. Great manipulations for enhancement and devices for reversing good to ill are built upon the two of them, but neither shall I use."

"But if you have no advantage and they—"

"I am destiny's darling," Byron thundered. "The great sagas of our past have finally been incarnated in me. I am untouched by wind or wave. I am the one to weave together the last threads of the tapestry of our fate into one final design."

Byron stopped and looked into the growing darkness. "It is true that how I will triumph is hidden. Even I do not know the means. My journey to the grand casino may be but a testing, a proof that I am worthy of being the instrument of fate. But in the moment of crisis, in the final spin of the wheel, my power will be revealed and I will be victorious, as from the beginning of time it is written that I would."

A sudden shout from up the hill cut off Astron's reply. He looked to the crest to see a line of torches in a staggered line.

"I am here," Byron called back. "I am here and the way is safe. There are no concentrations of luck with which you must contend."

With excited voices and the sound of crunching underbrush, the group on the crest began to pour down the hillside. Although the way was fairly clear and the torches gave sufficient light, Astron saw the two dozen men, women, and children pick their way carefully, holding on to one another for additional security and giving the fallen snags and large bushes a wide berth.

In the very center of the group, carefully supported on both sides, was one far older than the rest. Wisps of long white hair streamed from around a crown splotched with spatters of red and veins of purple. The eyes were nearly closed and a trickle of spittle ran from the corner of the face that sagged. Bare stick-thin arms flapped idly with the jostle of each step. The feet shuffled after one another, as if actuated by the mechanism of a child's toy.

"Centuron." Byron nodded in response to Astron's gaze. "His fame among the aleators is almost as great as—well, almost as great as mine. For over one hundred cycles of the sun, he has survived without benefit of the magical arts to shape his luck. He is the living proof that my cause is right and that I will succeed."

Astron watched the procession draw closer, noting their gaunt and sallow faces. Except for the excitement of meeting, they showed animation only slightly greater than Centuron's. With stooped shoulders and panting breath, they converged on Byron's camp, some looking with hungry eyes at the roast pig.

One separated herself from the rest. Dirt streaked her face and her hair was in tangles. Suitably cleaned, the woman would be a beauty, Astron thought, but the rigors of the trek had made her barely distinguishable from the men.

"We must move on quickly," she said. "The minions of Myra have found two others adrift in the wake of the last wave. We overheard them talk of two more whom they wanted as well. Soon there will be search parties throughout the hills."

"Kestrel and Phoebe," Astron shouted. "Were they injured?"

"They seemed to walk well enough with no assistance from their guards." The woman shrugged. "But, of course, such a condition is only temporary if Myra has experiments to run. I would guess she would use them in the games at the grand casino, if not before."

"Then we must get to that beach and—" Astron began, but Byron put up his hand to stop.

"What else, Sylvan, what else do you bring?" he said.

The woman nodded. Slowly she pulled a pack from

her back and dumped its contents at Byron's feet, a dozen ears of a black-kerneled corn, three large apples, and a scattering of small seeds.

"We saved as much as we could for your great contest, Byron, but the little ones need more than an equal share."

Byron waved at Astron and Nimbia. "It is well that you have procured what you did, Sylvan. There are two more, and I have not yet decided if they should be fed as well."

"Wait," Astron said. "By all means let the little ones eat. I for one have no need."

"No, I have spoken," Byron suddenly thundered. "I am the chosen one and my commands must be obeyed. The sacrifice of all others is of no importance. Their destiny is only to ensure that I succeed."

"We do not question." Sylvan lowered her head and stepped backward. "Even old Centuron has taken less than we might otherwise offer."

"Ah, if you do not know exactly what power you will have," Astron said, "what convinces you that you indeed are this darling of destiny?"

Byron's eyes blazed. "You are sent by the fates to tempt me!" he said. "You wish to test how firm is my resolve." He looked again at Nimbia and drew his lips into a grim line. "Very well. I will show to the overseers of our fate the extent of my mettle. You shall accompany me and yet both remain untouched." His stare locked on Nimbia and he ran his tongue over his lips. "Yes, untouched," he said, "until it is properly time."

Astron's stembrain suddenly bubbled with a fiery vexation. "Do not be overly concerned." He turned and spoke to Nimbia in the language of the fey. "Despite my size, I will serve you still. You merely need—"

Astron stopped as he noticed Nimbia's smile. She let the top of her tunic sag in disarray. "It sounds as if he invites us to join him," she said. "Accept, accept in the name of a queen of the fey."

311

## CHAPTER TWENTY-FOUR

# *Mark of the Manipulator*

KESTREL wiped the moisture from his brow and held his breath. He looked at the rope-suspended blade that slowly oscillated back and forth over Phoebe's outstretched body on the cabin deck. She was bound hand and foot, spread-eagled between four pegs anchored in the polished planking. Only by pressing herself firmly against the horizontal could she just barely avoid the swipe of the sharp edge against her neck.

Kestrel could hope for random outcomes no longer; the next click of the levers must pull the rope upward rather than let out any more slack. Desperately, he looked at the tinted windows sternward through which filtered the last rays of the setting sun and then at the sloping cabin walls, searching for some other way out of danger than the one of chance he was offered. The clutter of spinpins, glassy spheres, and instruments of small tortures he recognized from Jelilac's sloop, but nothing that would be of aid could he see.

The aleator named Myra sat in the corner behind a small table and tracked his darting eyes with a cold stare. Grabbing her chin between thumb and forefingers, she slowly brought her fingertips together, gathering up the loose flesh. Kestrel heard a raspy scrape from the contact, like that of a man testing a half-day growth of beard. A loose-fitting tunic did little to hide the angular bones underneath, and patches of splotched skin shone through beneath thin white hair pulled straight back and tied in a knot.

Myra's two ships lay at anchor side by side, far closer than the mooring one would expect in the realm of men. But with each wave that shifted them about, the two craft always avoided colliding at the last instant. The massive vessels seemed to be ably manned by very small crews, although the hold of the other ship, Kestrel had noticed when he was hustled aboard, was full of hammocks, men-at-arms, and others fettered with heavy chains.

"Just one more toss of the ball into the hoops," Myra said. "Just one more, and I will be satisfied that your words carry no true meaning. Your talk of powerful wards that shield your wealth is too implausible, too—" Myra stopped and shuddered. "No, I will not doubt," she said. "I will prepare for the games at the grand casino with the rest. Luck is the true basis of our existence. Without that, what is the purpose?"

Kestrel squeezed the rubber ball in his hand. The array of small circular openings in the slanted panel across the cabin seemed to blur in the dimming light. The gentle rocking motion of the barge did not help matters much; but even without the added complication, he knew he could not ensure that the sphere fell into one of the hoops that he wished.

Kestrel glanced at Phoebe, trying to smile encouragement, although he felt little inside. They had been apprehended after the passing of the tidal wave almost as easily as they had by Jelilac on their arrival in the realm. This time, however, since they had no real luck to be siphoned away, the glassine spheres did not become charged with the oily, amber smoke.

Kestrel reached back and touched the lumpiness of his rucksack and felt the presence of the pollen. There was no telling if the grains still had any value after the soaking, but without Astron, he had decided it probably was best to maneuver things so that Phoebe could summon Camonel. Somehow, he had to convince Myra that she could not get at his vast store of hidden luck and her only recourse was to destroy it with fire.

He glanced into her rheumy eyes and scowled. The aleator had proven to be quite stubborn. Just like Jelilac, she had insisted on subjecting them to a test that quantified the extent of their fortune.

"One more mishap will not prove what you wish." He

313

waved at the complicated apparatus at his side. "I have done as you instructed more than half a dozen times and my skill with the tossing ball has not changed in any noticeable way. My wealth is shielded. Not even the slightest efflux leaks from the wards."

"No one with true wealth keeps it all hidden." Myra shook her head. "At least some is contained in simple talismans to ward off the trivial misfortunes of the ambience. Why, the tosses of anyone with even a minimum of luck would find the hoops connected to the lever that raises the blade. By now it should be swinging just beneath the beams. The fact that, instead, you have sent it up and down in an almost random fashion indicates that the power of your wards is only a fantasy. You are paupers and nothing more."

She hesitated a moment and then motioned to the guards at her side. "Just in case there is an element of truth in what he says, subject him one more time to the linkage of reversal. Then have him make the final pitch."

Kestrel felt his chest tighten. One more trip of the wrong lever would prove fatal to Phoebe. Grimly, he searched through his mind for something that would give him an opening, some hidden crevice in Myra's character that he could exploit. Kestrel's thoughts tumbled while he watched the complicated mechanical linkages at his side shuffle together a thick deck of cards. He felt mild shocks from copper wires wrapped around his ankles while he watched, but by now they were no more than an annoying irritant. When the mixing stopped, he reached forward without prompting and selected one from the deck, just as he had done many times before.

He flipped the bit of stiff parchment faceup on the table and reached for the second, not even bothering to notice the ornately decorated woman with cold dark eyes staring back. "The whole deck is probably nothing other than the black queen," he grumbled. "The fact that I draw ten or so of them in a row proves little."

"Of course they are all the same," Myra said. "How else can one's luck be convinced that it is of the wrong sign? It is fickle as the fifth tenet states, and once it is flipped, it will bring nothing but misfortune. If, by some chance, you do possess some wealth and I cannot have it contributing in a positive fashion to my own, then it will serve instead as a weapon against the others when we game in the grand casino."

Kestrel took a deep breath. He had to gamble on what little knowledge he had. "The book with figures," he said slowly, "the one that Milligan says you possess. It sounds to me to be no more than a navigator's almanac. Is it why he calls you Myra the doubting?"

Kestrel noticed a sudden flicker in Myra's cheeks. Her eyes widened almost imperceptibly, but then returned to their piercing stare. He waited expectantly. The signs were not much, but perhaps indeed he had chanced upon something he could twist to advantage.

"Could you be so bold," Myra said after a moment, "actually to follow the instructions as they are written, without knowing the consequences?" She waved her arms about the cabin. "None of my minions would dare attempt it, despite the apparent advantage."

Myra stroked her chin and then shrugged. "Jelilac has a great store of luck for use in the games, perhaps the greatest of all. I would rather husband each dram of mine and not waste any on getting from here to the casino, wherever that might be."

"You do not know?" Kestrel said. "A navigation almanac would be most basic on such a sea as this."

"Perhaps in dimmest memory, there were such things," Myra said. "But to use them would be counter to the basic tenets of any aleator. We sail where the winds take us, and, if we truly believe, it will be where we desire. Our luck provides. To use a calculation, no matter how reliable it might be, is a statement of distrust."

Myra leaned forward until her face was a hand span from Kestrel's own. "Luck favors the believer," she said, "just as the fourth tenet states. If you sincerely trust in it, you will weather your trials unscathed; if you doubt, then it gives the fifth tenet a chance to wreak its havoc.

"The book and the device labeled as a sextant which accompanies it," Myra continued in a hushed voice,

315

"they must come from someone beyond the farthest extent of our realm—from someone whose wish is to do us harm, to make us doubt in our very foundations and in our reasons for existing at all."

Myra drew back and squinted at Kestrel. "No, it would do great ill for me or one of my minions to perform the calculations that would point us where we wish to go. I have often wondered if it were good luck or ill in the first place that led me to find it in the smoking ashes of a lightning-struck fire."

She reached out and tapped a long slender finger against Kestrel's chest. "But one so foolhardy as to spout of invincible wards, to him there surely could be no harm. He would not fear the misfortune that might result from following the ritual or from the weight upon his thoughts about what he has done."

Kestrel looked back into Myra's eyes, unblinking. He weighed the risks and decided that the chance was worth it. It might not be more than simple sightings, and he would be done. With just the right words, it would free Phoebe and give her a chance at Camonel as well.

"Of course, as I understand the third tenet—luck begets luck—" he said, "the ritual might not be one of misfortune, but would enhance whatever one possesses at the outset instead." He shrugged and smiled. "And since both of ours are still intact, the increase might be most significant—significant enough that even the chances of Myra the doubter will become slim in the grand casino. Yes, by all means release the woman and we will do it. I believe, I believe deeply in our triumphant success."

Myra frowned and rubbed at her chin. "Your speech is glib," she said. "Most glib for one so close to disaster. Perhaps there is some truth in what you speak after all."

Her eyes lost their focus, and for a long moment she looked past Kestrel out onto the sea. "Jelilac," she muttered. "It is he that I fear the most. Against him, I must marshal every resource. It would be folly not to take advantage of what my luck has offered."

She looked back at Kestrel and smiled. "There is also the second tenet," she said. "The entropy of luck always increases. Your wards might be a marvel of which I know not, but no matter how cleverly constructed, I doubt that they could withstand the heat of a flame."

Kestrel steeled himself from smiling in return. He forced a look of apprehension onto his face. "Just a moment." He licked his lips quickly. "We have excellent shields, it is true, but I said nothing about being so foolish as to subject them to a fire."

Myra's smile broadened. "Ah, the composure does seem to waver a bit," she said. "Perhaps you were right. Nothing in this room would provide a sufficient test."

"You know as well as I what happens when fire is applied to any container, no matter how clever its construction." Kestrel put protest into his voice. He waved his arm about the room. "Never mind what I said. You can do with us what you will with any of your devices; but like everyone else, we shun the flame." Kestrel stopped and lowered his eyes. "Please," he said softly. "We have struggled too long to build up what we have. Anything but a fire."

"Thus it shall be." Myra slapped her side. "Yes, this will be far more rewarding than any of the simple tests that the likes of Jelilac would try." She looked over her shoulder and yelled out onto the deck. "Bring the kindling and the spark. We shall set them out on a raft where the logs can be the fuel. After he has performed the ritual as the tome instructs, whatever luck they accrue will be burned entirely away."

"But—" Kestrel began.

"Silence," Myra commanded. She motioned to a sailor in the hatchway and he came forward, clutching a large leather-bound book like a servant with a tray. Balancing on its upper surface was a sextant of gleaming metal.

Kestrel forced his eyes to open wide and then slumped his shoulders. Hanging his head, he stepped aside while two more sailors pulled the swinging blade out of the way and untied Phoebe. He squeezed her hand as a signal for silence as she rose to her feet. They could be safely away, he thought. With just a little more luck— He stopped the race of his thoughts. Holding his breath, he managed to offer a token resistance to the arms that propelled him out of the cabin as the final piece of convincing.

As Kestrel watched with what he hoped was a defeated expression on his face, the entire crew seemed to come alive with a blur of activity. A small raft was lowered over the side, tethered to a long rope, and pushed by poles away from the hull. Matches and kindling were assembled and an archer was ferried across from the second of Myra's ships.

While he and Phoebe were guided by knifepoint to a small boat, the archer began donning a thick, padded vest and hood. In silence, the two of them were rowed out to the raft and unceremoniously pushed onto its rocking deck. Kestrel saw the archer place his hands in thick gloves with which he could barely grasp his bow. Bulky shields were placed behind his back. At arm's length, he gingerly struck a spark that caught some curly shavings on fire. The archer dipped a tar-soaked arrowtip into the blaze, involuntarily flinching backward as it burst into a smoky flame. Aiming awkwardly, he nocked the shaft and pointed it at the small raft.

Kestrel turned to Phoebe and smiled. "I hope that this idea is a better one than tossing the ball into the hoops," he said.

Kestrel put down the book and arched his back. Most of an hour had passed. He looked at the archer still straining at attention on Myra's barge and felt a grim satisfaction at his discomfort. It had, of course, been too much to expect that he could read as well as understand the language of the realm, especially since their initial luck had all been siphoned away by Milligan. A little more time would be a reasonable enough amount for study, he judged, and then he would go through the motions of sighting.

"When I am done and shout back the heading," he said to Phoebe, "they will undoubtedly give the instruction to fire the shaft. Let it start the raft burning and then use some of the powder you obtained from the archimage to summon Camonel to our aid."

"What about the sextant and book?" Phoebe said. "If

they are from beyond this realm, might not they reveal some clue about Astron's riddle as well?"

"The sextant is of some arcane design, but I think I have figured out how to use it in a convincing fashion." Kestrel shook his head. "Except for a few unusual features, the book appears much as one would expect, page after page of tables." He shrugged and again shook his head. "If Astron were here, he might make something more of the instructions, but the significance I cannot tell."

Kestrel rapidly thumbed through the bulk of the volume, grunting as the pages fell through his fingers. "It must have been constructed by more than one scribe, and certainly they did not talk to each other. See, the style changes with the entries for every few days. Initially there are four columns on each leaf, with what I guess from the accompanying logos to be the position of the sun on the upper half and the brighter stars beneath. Next, it changes to data in rows, if the headings are to be believed, and after that the solar elevations are completely separated from the rest. On and on it goes, with fancy scrollwork and then harsh starkness, changing the format every fortnight or so."

He set down the tome and laughed despite himself. "It certainly was designed to be well used. The entries run on and on for what must be hundreds and hundreds of years. I doubt that anyone would really care, unless it was passed on from one generation to the next. Surely what is here will last Myra and her crew before a twentieth is spent."

Kestrel shrugged and hefted the sextant. "But enough of that. Prepare to toss your powders into the fire." He looked in the direction of the setting sun and found the brightest of the evening stars. The slosh of the waves against the raft was definitely greater than against the massive sides of the barge. Only with difficulty was he able to keep what he looked at in the center of view.

Kestrel grunted at the heaviness of the sextant, swinging it slowly to the second sighting. The screws felt awkward to his touch and wobbled in their shafts as he tried to adjust a cursor. He ran his hand over the blistered skin of iron that framed a cloudy lens. The craftsmanship was quite primitive, but he supposed it did not really matter. The heading he would shout back to Myra's barges would be the first that popped into his mind. It would depend solely upon her luck if it were accurate or not.

When he had completed the last sighting Kestrel thumbed through the book as if he were searching for corresponding entries. Phoebe tensed at his side with her hand in the pocket of her cape, ready to toss out the powder. After a moment, he stood up on the rocking platform and cupped his hands to his mouth. "A third of a circle away from the direction of the setting sun," he shouted. "The calculations have been made and there is no doubt about—"

Before he could finish, the archer released his bow. The arrow sliced through the gathering gloom of night and hit the raft squarely on the side closest to Myra's ships. Kestrel bent over and fanned the flames, no longer caring about what the aleators thought of his actions. He looked at Phoebe and saw her face flushed with confidence. With clenched fists, she waved her arms upward, seeming to add energy to the flame. The sparkling powder danced from her hand and fell squarely into the blaze.

Kestrel felt his own tension grow. Soon it really would be over. Without the rush of combining realms Camonel could head directly to wherever they wished. He could find Astron and Nimbia and send the small demon back to his own realm. Then with Palodad— Kestrel stopped. He had not fully thought through the reason they wanted to find the anvilwood and send Astron home alone in the first place. Suppose he was right and Camonel was under the control of some wizard; perhaps even Prydwin was manipulating things beyond his own realm. Kestrel touched the sextant at his side and frowned. Manipulations in another realm—a navigator's almanac and sextant served exactly the same end.

Kestrel reached out and touched Phoebe's shoulder, even though he knew he should not. "Wait a moment," he said. "Perhaps it would be better if it were some other demon that you—"

Kestrel's words were cut short. With a hiss of foul-tasting air, the massive djinn stepped from the flame and stood as a sinister, dark silhouette against the last rays of the sun.

"I, Camonel, submit to your will because my prince Palodad instructs it," the demon said. "There is no need for a struggle of wills. Speak your command and it will be mine to perform."

"Never mind about princes and allegiances in the realm of daemon," Kestrel said before Phoebe could speak. Her eyes darted to him, but he rushed on, ignoring her puzzlement. "It is your mastery which we wish to know. Yes, not princes but masters. Is the wizard here the one who dominates your will totally so that you must do all that she asks, or is there another who instructs you instead to say the words that prevent any true struggle from taking place?"

Sparkles of blue began to dance about Camonel's teeth in the twilight. In the faint glow, Kestrel saw the demon's scowl grow into one of true menace. For a long moment, the djinn was silent. Then his rumbling voice again came forth.

"Where is Astron, the one who walks? It is not only the pollen. He is needed as well."

"Your master—who is it truly?" Phoebe asked suddenly, apparently catching the drift of Kestrel's thought. "Now that I think of it, each time was too easy. I was too flushed in victory to examine closely how I felt. You merely said that I was yours to dominate, but never was there a true test."

"Prince Palodad instructs that I serve and—"

"Not him," Phoebe interrupted. "Not another demon —your master. What is his name?"

Kestrel sucked in his breath. He looked up at the glowing yellow eyes of the djinn and felt a cold numbness creeping down his spine. If Camonel was not under Phoebe's control, what would happen then?

Again Camonel was silent for a long moment. His face distorted in indecision. Finally he answered in a staccato popping of sparks that shot from his teeth and lips. "I am to do whatever I am asked by you, provided that it does not conflict with what I otherwise have been told."

321

"Then the need for Astron to accompany the pollen, Palodad's words that the grains held some clue to the answer—"

"Of that I cannot say." Camonel shook his head.

Kestrel grabbed the sextant, just as a large wave sloshed into the raft and tumbled Phoebe into his side. "Is your master the manipulator?" He waved the instrument in front of Camonel's chest. "Is it he that brought about the collapsing of the two realms of symmetry? Did he leave the sextant here so that those like Myra would doubt, so that there would be damage here in addition to the rest?"

"Yes," Camonel said. "To speak of the manipulations themselves I am not bound. But this is only one realm of the many that swim in the void. What is your command? There is much yet to be done."

"And Gaspar," Kestrel continued. "Is your master behind his riddle as well?"

"Gaspar is a demon of little brain," Camonel said. "Even though he is a prince, he could never—"

"Take us back to the realm of men," Phoebe said. "Then return and find Astron and Nimbia as—"

A sudden wave bigger than any before raced under the raft. Kestrel tipped forward, just barely managing to grab Phoebe before she fell. The water lapped over the edge of the logs and spilled into the fire. In a flash of smoke, the flame was instantly doused and Camonel was gone.

Kestrel tried staggering back to his feet, but the agitation of the sea increased. Stunned by what had happened, he looked out in the growing blackness toward Myra's ship and heard the aleator calling out over the bulwark.

"The first is spent but it has done its job. See the increased agitation of the surf. A great wave is coming and their luck does not ward it away. Pull them back aboard and we will slip offshore a league or so until the disturbance passes. Then on the morrow we will set sail as the glib one has directed. Keep them in bondage. If I can think of no new amusement during our journey, then certainly they can serve as shields on the floor of the casino."

Almost in a daze, Kestrel pulled Phoebe to him and held her tight. He looked at the last wisps of smoke from the doused fire and cursed his luck, what little there was of it. Now they would have to travel to the casino. There would be no chance that Myra would be persuaded to light a fire again. Yes, to the casino and hope that Astron would somehow be there as well. He kicked the sextant overboard and then gave the almanac a shove—devices of the manipulator, the one behind the merging realms and the riddle as well. There might indeed be something of significance to them, he thought, but it would take someone like Astron to discover what it was. Now, until they dropped anchor, he had to focus all his attention on keeping Myra's thoughts away from more testing with her swinging blade.

## CHAPTER TWENTY-FIVE

## Broken Talismans

ASTRON peered out from the cover of the brush at the line of the crest. Leaves of deep green scattered tiny droplets of dew as he pushed them aside. Behind him, buzzing insects filled the interior slopes of the island with a blur of sound. No one had yet stirred from either of Myra's ships lying at anchor in the bay below. But in only a few moments more, Byron's force sneaking down the hillside would inevitably be discovered.

From the look of the anxious faces of those who had followed the tall swordsman, not everyone was as convinced as he about their rôle in his destiny. Armed only with blade and shield, they would be no match for aleators with necks ringed by talismans. But surely at least some would survive long enough, Astron thought. Long enough to bolt and flee back up the slope along the wide path that ran by his hiding place. And just as surely, some of Myra's aleators would follow.

Astron tightened his grip on the rope of twisted vines

that ran from his hand down onto the wide path past the bush. There was every chance that it would break or even come untied from the base of the tree across the way, but he could think of nothing better to try.

He glanced at Nimbia, kneeling at his side, a sword of steel dangling from her hip. "The words you had me say to Byron about my prowess in battle felt most uncomfortable," he said. "I am a cataloguer, not a hewer of men."

"I saw how you led the reticulates at more than a single node," Nimbia answered. "Do not be concerned about the discomfort, demon, though the modesty is becoming."

Astron wrinkled his nose. He should have felt pleasure in Nimbia's words, but he did not. Somehow the aid he offered to Byron increased her stature, rather than his own.

"Nevertheless," he growled, "too much time has been wasted in my translation of fluffs of conversation back and forth. It is better spent in observation of the realm, collecting facts that later can be used to advantage."

Nimbia smiled. "I do not consider the exchange of information a waste," she said. "You are serving me well. Without the facility of your tongue, I would know nothing of Byron beyond grunts and stares." She stopped and lowered her eyes. "And just as important, he would know as little of me."

Astron felt his annoyance grow. He did not care for the way that Byron stared at her when she was distracted elsewhere. When in Byron's presence, she behaved like a human female from the sagas. Her interest in the aleator went beyond the needs of their riddle-quest or even wresting some anvilwood from the grand casino. More than once she had laughed when he translated Byron's words and shook her head at the chastisement he suggested as a reply.

"Byron has made clear more than once that his destiny is his primary focus." Astron pulled tentatively on the rope. "Everything else is of little concern."

"A secondary position would not be so bad." Nimbia

shrugged. "I have not fared nearly so well in the realm of the fey." She flipped golden curls over her shoulder. "He is comely enough so that no one would whisper when we are seen together. Among his own, he commands a station of respect, one that fittingly links with a hillsovereign."

Nimbia stopped and looked Astron in the eye. "Besides, when all is done and you return to your own realm, what then is to happen to me?"

The wrinkle in Astron's nose deepened, but Nimbia did not seem to notice as she rushed on.

"I can tell that he is interested," she said. "Constantly he devours me with his eyes. His boldness is far better than the hesitant glances and turned-away faces that were the features of most when I was the one who held sway. Yes, he has great interest; and yet, at the same time, he shows measured restraint. Unlike the others who become victims of their own lust and interpret each gentle hesitation as a stunning rebuke or a sure indication that there is someone else, he is game for the chase."

"You have special qualities as well." Astron stumbled. "Your creations were as much for your minions as yourself. No prince have I seen display such concern. You would have earned your diadem, even if it were not given by default. And a wizard besides—only ones of that ilk can a djinn ever truly respect. You shielded me in the tree when—"

"Enough." Nimbia laughed. She reached out and touched Astron on the cheek. "You need not sing of my virtues, demon. Your place in my retinue is secure. It is rather *I* that should list the praises so that you are encouraged to even greater glories for your queen."

Astron started to reply, but then quickly snapped shut his mouth. He halted the idle flexing of his grip about the rope and froze dead still. Without moving, he looked at Nimbia expectantly.

Nimbia's face clouded in puzzlement. "Demon?" she said. "What is the matter? Did something happen in that stembrain of yours?"

"I am waiting," Astron said simply. "Waiting to hear the list."

Nimbia threw back her head and laughed. Her voice tinkled like a shower of golden brandels tossed against a shield. "Very well," she said after a moment. "You deserve no less."

Nimbia eyed Astron critically and then touched her index finger to the palm of her other hand. "First, there is the keenness of mind," she said. "In no other of your realm have I observed such an ability for deduction."

"Palodad and other princes that rule—" Astron blurted out, suddenly uncomfortable, as he had been before. But Nimbia put her finger to his lips for silence and then placed another beside the first.

"Secondly, there is the dedication to your quest," she said. "Despite the hindrances and dangers, you pursue the goal with an unrelenting intensity. Surely I have seen it matched in none of the mighty djinns with their easily distracted flitter of thought. And, now that I think of it, none in the realm of the fey would have persisted as long as have you."

Astron felt the beginning of a smile appear on his face, despite the discomfort. Other delicious feelings began to stir underneath. He wanted again to protest the sweep of her hyperbole, but thought better of it as Nimbia retracted her hand and began to say even more.

"Last, and perhaps most important, demon," she said, "is the comfort that you bring when we are together. I do not have to worry about somehow breaking through an impenetrable shyness or warding off a self-image that never can be satisfied. I do not have to remember that I am a woman and you are a man."

The seductive sweetness bubbling up inside Astron suddenly turned sour. Somehow Nimbia's words of praise were no longer a delight. Despite his best efforts to keep a placid composure, he felt his eye membranes quiver and his stembrain stir from its slumber with discontent.

Astron shook his head in the manner of men. Why did all of her words now affect him so? Was there a residual effect from his transposition into Kestrel's body that he somehow still retained?

Before he could begin to sort out any of the confusion of his thoughts, he saw the first of Byron's men appear on the crest. The aleator had thrown sword and shield away and was running as fast as he could. Astron scowled and pushed the feelings away. They would have to be examined later. First there was the matter of the darling of destiny and passage to the grand casino.

Three more of Byron's minions crested the hill in full rout and then six after that. Immediately behind the last, tall, well-fed swordsmen with purple surcoats over close-knit mail came racing close behind.

Astron looked out across the trail as the first of Byron's men staggered past and then back to Nimbia to see if she was ready. The rest of Byron's followers sprinted down the path into the interior of the island with the first of Myra's aleators on their heels. Astron saw a half-dozen talismans dancing about the necks of those in the foreground. Gritting his teeth, he let them pass. A score of swordsmen sped by, shouting and laughing as they ran; then behind them came a half-dozen stragglers more, not so richly endowed as the rest.

Astron waited until the last three were just beginning to rush past the hidden rope. Then he jerked it tight and held it as firmly as he was able. The first aleator unexpectedly leaped over a small boulder jutting in the way and hurled clear of the trip rope, evidently not even noticing its presence. The other two, however, were caught just above their ankles and pitched forward onto the ground. Both landed gracefully on glove-protected hands; but more importantly, just as Astron had hoped, the talismans about their necks hurled free to land a few body lengths beyond.

"Now," Astron shouted, "now, Nimbia, while we have a chance."

Nimbia sprang out onto the trail, her sword pointing the way. The two sprawled warriors rose to their feet; then their eyes widened in terror as she moved between them and their charms. Instantly they returned to their knees

327

with hands spread wide, indicating surrender. One looked longingly at what lay a few feet away and began to sob.

Astron ran out behind Nimbia and scooped up the treasures. He flung them over his head and then turned after the third warrior who had stopped to see what was happening behind. Astron waved his sword with one hand while pointing at his own chest with the other. "Not one standard issue but two," he said. "You do not have a chance."

The third warrior froze. He unbuckled his sword and let it fall. Sagging on one knee, he bowed to the ground. Astron did not hesitate. He ran forward and, despite the small rocks that seemed to get in his way, pulled the third set of talismans away from their wearer.

"Over there." He pointed his sword back to Nimbia. "Do exactly as she says."

Astron saw the man-at-arms nod in submission. Without waiting to ensure that he fully complied, Astron began running down the trail as fast as he could manage not to stumble. So far, everything was proceeding as he had hoped. The aleators were so conditioned to depending on luck in everything they did that, without their charms, they felt completely helpless. When confronted with an opponent better endowed, they gave up rather than attempt a fight.

Astron bounded down the trail, catching up with two more warriors who ran behind the rest. He tripped over a bared root in the trail and barely kept from falling. Circling his sword over his head, he froze his face in a beserker's stare, yelling an incoherent challenge. Over a dozen talismans now bounced from his chest as he ran, and the men-at-arms' eyes immediately focused on their dance.

Just as the others before, the two warriors immediately assumed postures of surrender, letting Astron snatch their charms with a clumsy swipe before they guessed his intent. More aleators looked backward, and a shout of warning coursed through their midst. The pursuit of Byron's followers slowed and then completely halted.

Byron's warriors sensed the slacking of pursuit and

halted their own flight. With a rallying cheer, they turned and began to strike at the aleators who were looking over their shoulders at what was attacking their rear.

Astron yelled as fiendishly as he could and slashed blindly left and right. Aleators on both sides stepped backward, tumbling over one another and off the trail into the brush to get out of the way. One of Myra's captains in the vanguard caught sight of Astron's weight of treasure. He looked down at his own chest, barely ducked a swipe at the side of his head; then with a shudder, he bolted from the trail into the brush. Two more followed his lead, then a half-dozen more on the other side of the trail. In barely an instant, only five men-at-arms remained, all facedownward, offering their swords in surrender.

Astron pulled to a halt, barely believing what had happened. More than a score of well-armed warriors had been routed by a single foolhardy rush. Shaking his head, he grabbed the talismans that remained and added them to the rest. With stooping shoulders, he walked slowly back up the hill to see how Nimbia was faring in her stint at guard duty. For a moment he felt a rush of elation. He had performed as well as could have been expected of even a mighty djinn. But then, just as quickly, he put the thought aside. He was still a long way from securing any anvilwood. There was yet the rescue of Kestrel and Phoebe to be managed. The lightning djinns that pursued might discover them at any time. And Byron? If he had survived the rush down the slope, what more could be expected from the one who seemed to covet Nimbia more and more with each passing moment.

Astron scowled at the frustration born of the inactivity. His stembrain was becoming increasingly difficult to control. He looked about the evening campfire erected just down the seaward slope from the crest of the hill and shook his head. Byron sat on the other side of the dying flame, talking quietly with two of his lieutenants and one of the captured warriors, as if the day had been the same as any other. The bloodstained rags which bound the tall warrior's leg looked blotched with black in the dimness of evening. Felled by the first man he met, Byron had been left behind when his ranks broke and began retreating up the hill.

Then, when Astron and the others returned in triumph, the aleators that remained in Myra's ships all transferred onto a single barge and sailed away, leaving the other vessel behind. Evidently, she had reasoned that she was confronting a force much more powerful than her own and did not wish to suffer the same defeat. With the next dawn, Byron had said, his own band would follow the same course and be led by her luck directly to the grand casino.

Astron ran his hand over the skin of his neck. Reluctantly, after the abandoned ship and the prisoners had been secured, he had given up the talismans to be destroyed. His arguments about the men-at-arms who had run into the forest possibly returning were ignored. The luck had to be dissipated back into the ether. Byron had insisted. To do less would not be true to his quest.

Astron looked over at Nimbia on the far side of the clearing. At least for the moment, she was occupied with other thoughts than tending to the tall warrior. Instead, the queen was watching with interest the preparations of Sylvan and Centuron for the breaking of the charms.

Astron rose and stretched, trying to remove some of the tension that froze the muscles of his back into tight knots. He supposed he should investigate the dissipation process as well. There might be something to be learned that could be used later. Besides, it probably was the last chance to talk to the hillsovereign without Byron being in the vicinity. Tomorrow they would be confined together in the barge for the final journey across the sea; then once in the grand casino, from what little Astron had gleaned, there would be little time for anything other than struggling for survival.

As Astron approached, Nimbia was peering over Sylvan's shoulder and gesturing, while the aleator slowly stirred the contents of a small cauldron over a sputtering flame. Nearby a second fire was roaring fiercely as it consumed branches of dry pinewood that Byron's fol-

330

lowers had faithfully carried with them from the beginning of their trek.

"I think I understand what you ask," Sylvan said, "but a more intense flame makes the film too fragile. The only purpose of the heat here is to thin the liquid to the proper consistency."

"It looks like the sap of what we call the soapbark tree in the realm of fey," Nimbia said to Astron as he drew near. "Here the aleators tap the trunk and let it drip into waiting buckets."

"The same is done for syrups in the realm of men," Astron answered as he fell into the mode of automatically translating.

"This is for a greater purpose than delighting the tongue," Sylvan said. "Without its protection, the risk of contamination is far too great."

"I thought that fires destroyed the concentration of luck," Astron said. "If you must ruin the talismans, why not just toss them under the stewpot while it heats?"

"The heat would crack the shell that resists the great pressure of the gas, it is true," Sylvan said, "but when it rushes out in a burst, there is no way to tell which way it will surge. It might all lodge in a nearby tree or worse yet, in one of us who attends the fire. No, the luck must be released slowly in a way that we can control."

"Then you coat the talismans in this paste?" Astron asked.

"Watch and you will see." Sylvan shook her head. She motioned for Centuron to come forward, and the old man lumbered up, holding one of the talismans at arm's length, as if it had a foul odor.

Sylvan dipped a circle of wire into a cauldron and then drew it back. Astron saw that it emerged with a thin film of the soapbark sap stretched across its interior. She blew gently on the film, deforming it from a plane into a bulging hemisphere. Centuron continued forward until the dangling talisman met the shiny surface and then passed through it to the other side. Sylvan exhaled one more strong burst of air and a glassy bubble separated from the ring, completely enveloping the talisman.

331

"Now we can apply the heat." Sylvan looked back at Nimbia. She took the leather thong from Centuron's grasp and slowly moved the talisman with the encompassing bubble over toward the second fire. The bubble bounced slightly, but remained suspended, not touching the charm at all but somehow remaining hanging from the point where it was pierced by the thong.

Sylvan held the talisman bubble over the fire so that it was warmed by the rising heat, but the flames did not touch. Two or three others of Byron's followers gathered around Sylvan as she adjusted the height of the bubble, all silently waiting for what would happen.

For several hundred heart beats Astron detected no change. The fire crackled and wisps of smoke rose into the air, enveloping the bubble in a sooty haze as it floated skyward. Then, just as his interest began to sag, he noted a slight change of color on the surface of the brightly painted wood inside the glassy sphere. The yellows and reds began to fade. The blues paled into gray; the whites started to blister. In a moment, the polished surface turned to a dull, ashen indistinctness. The charm seemed to start vibrating, although Astron could not hear a hum. The sharp outlines of the intricate carving blurred. With a sharp crack like the breaking of an egg, a jagged rip appeared down one side from top to bottom.

Astron saw a sparkling iridescence suddenly shoot from the fissure and dissipate itself against the interior curve of the bubble. Like the spout of a tiny geyser seeded with reflective glitter, the essence of the talisman rushed out of its confinement and began to fill up the sphere. Sylvan waited a long while more until the exhaust from the charm had slowed to a barely discernible trickle. A slight opaqueness filled the bubble, where before it had been perfectly transparent and clear.

"Now for the controlled outgassing," Sylvan said, motioning to Centuron, who was already making his way forward with a circle of twine about one hand and a needle in the other.

"Popping the bubble would serve no better than cracking the talisman unprotected," Sylvan said. "But the strength of the soapbark film is high. It allows us to proceed with much more care." She took the circle of twine from Centuron with her free hand between extended thumb and forefinger. Very gently, she placed the ring against the surface of the bubble and quickly withdrew.

Astron saw that the band of twine did not penetrate the surface but, instead, floated on its glassy slickness, pulled into a tiny, perfect circle.

"It is the surface tension in the liquid," Astron said. "The same force that holds the bubble together in a sphere against the gasses inside deforms the string into a ring."

Sylvan ignored the comment. She carefully turned so that the floating circle was aimed away from the rest of the camp and outward toward the open sea. Reaching from the side, she quickly stabbed the needle into the small ring of film trapped by the twine.

Astron expected the bubble to pop with an explosive spray of what was contained inside, but it did not. Instead, only the small ring of film within the circle vanished, leaving the bulk of the bubble intact. Wisps of the glittering gas oozed through the opening out into the air in a gentle flow.

Astron watched, fascinated, as the bubble slowly contracted. Totally unlike a fragile sphere of film and rather like a balloon made of a cow's bladder in the realm of men, the orb grew smaller in a stately manner. As more and more of the glittering gas vented to the outside, the surface tension contracted the bubble into a tinier and tinier volume. Finally the radius became so small that the film touched the ragged edge of the rip in the talisman. With a tiny pop, the bubble flashed into nonexistence.

"Most interesting," Astron said. "I suspect that such a procedure would work with the soaps in the realms of men and the fey as well."

"But to no great practical use," Nimbia said. "There the laws are different. It would serve only to amuse the young."

"Perhaps," Astron said, wrinkling his nose.

Back near the main campfire, Byron suddenly threw

back his head and laughed at something his lieutenant had said. Nimbia quickly looked his way and then flushed as she noticed everyone watching what she had done.

"It is too bad," Centuron rumbled. He waved at the two fires as Sylvan stirred the small cauldron. "Some luck can be undone." He looked at Nimbia and shook his head. "Yes, the dabblings of men can be unmade but that which is bestowed by fate at birth is a burden forever."

"What do you mean?" Nimbia asked after Astron translated. She glanced at Sylvan and hesitated. "Are you the one until now the most in his favor? I am sorry, but if nothing yet has been decided, then surely there is no harm—"

Nimbia's words trailed off. Sylvan looked down at the cauldron and began stirring more vigorously without answering. The queen looked back to Centuron, eyeing the old man carefully. "What is your wish in the matter?" she said. "Is Sylvan here a personal favorite? If not, certainly the words of one so venerated will carry a great weight, if there is to be a decision."

The old aleator coughed and stood a little straighter. He closed one eye and studied Nimbia a long time before answering. "Can you not imagine how heavy the burden of time hangs over my head?" he croaked. "Do you not wonder what it is which drives me to rise on each new morrow, rather than curl up into nonexistence, disturbing as few as I can?"

"What does that have to do with—"

Centuron raised his hand and swept trembling fingers in a wide arc. "All of this that we see, all of the realm that lies beyond I have sampled more than once in my prime. And if Byron is cut to ribbons as soon as he enters the floor of the grand casino, there will be no more mysteries of which I long to taste."

Centuron coughed again. Astron noticed that an intense gleam came into his eye.

"But suppose he is not," the old aleator continued. "That is the chance of it that makes it all worthwhile. If somehow, without manipulating the tenets of luck, the pompous one manages to survive to the final struggles, then there is where I want to be—at the very center of the realm, when all those who have cast their lot with the vagaries of chance begin to doubt the foundation of their existence.

"Yes, I know of the futility; even Byron only guesses at it. Years ago, messengers through the flame revealed to me the workings of a distant master's plan. When the walls become dim and icy fingers of the void start to clutch at each and every heart, when I finally lie down to die, then it will all be worthwhile, knowing that I do not cease to exist alone.

"So you see, your question does not require an answer, unfortunate maid. With either outcome, your wish will be denied. Either the sands will run with Byron's blood or—"

"Do not mind his prattle," Sylvan cut in. "I suspect that it depresses him that you are so unlucky and there is nothing that he can do."

Nimbia frowned. "Without luck, yes, I understand that," she said. "It is what happened when we first arrived—but unlucky? What do you mean?"

Sylvan looked back down at the cauldron for a moment and then directly at Nimbia. "Why, your beauty, of course. How unfortunate to be saddled with such a burden."

Nimbia's frown grew deeper. She reached up and straightened a loose strand of hair. "I know that I am fair," she said. "It is what gives me an advantage when it comes to Byron's affections, I do confess, but—"

"Think, woman," Sylvan said. "Byron cannot be the only one. The souls of how many men have been warped by the closeness of your presence so that their inner worths were hidden? Whom do you know that has acted so that you could judge him as he truly is?" She glanced at Byron. "What you do is tempt him from his destiny; and if you succeed, then whom else will he blame?" Sylvan paused and shook her head. "No, I do not rue the fact that you have him smitten. I pity you instead."

CHAPTER TWENTY-SIX

## *The Grand Casino*

KESTREL steadied himself against the gentle roll of the ship in the quickening breeze. He shielded his eyes from the emerging sun on his starboard and squinted at the smudge directly ahead of the bowsprit. The air was hazy with the remains of a clearing fog, but already he could see what must be the tall thin towers that marked the corners of the casino. Myra might not have deduced that it was her luck that brought them to the proper destination, rather than his guess at the course, but they were there, nevertheless.

They had been beset by calm for most of the first day at sea. At the dawn of the second, a lookout had spied a mast on the sternward horizon. The crew had buzzed with the speculation that they were being followed by the savages who had decimated the entire company of men-at-arms. Little that Myra had said changed the growing apprehensiveness of their disposition.

Kestrel had listened closely to the description of the one who had led the charge down to the beach and almost succeeded in boarding before they were safely away. He dared not hope too much, but perhaps there was the slimmest of chances that somehow it was Astron who followed their every move through the swirling fog and occasional gusting winds, though the description did not sound right.

Phoebe came to Kestrel's side and reached up to massage the tense muscles in his neck. He felt tight and drawn out, like an archer's bowstring before its release. For the two full days at sea he had just barely managed to convince Myra to direct her experiments elsewhere and save him and the wizard for the contest in the casino.

"It is not your burden," Phoebe said softly. "Myra

336

would have toyed with the others, regardless of what you said. Your words were not responsible. They did no more than shield me from certain harm."

Kestrel shook his head. Each time that Myra had been dissuaded, she merely turned instead to another of the unfortunate ones who were prisoners below deck. Cries of pain and pleas for a quick death echoed through his mind. A terrible weight bore down on his shoulders.

"But for what?" Kestrel said. "I have done no more than postpone the inevitable. Myra has made it quite clear that our purpose on the casino floor is to be human shields against the weapons directed at her by the other competing aleators." He grasped Phoebe's hands in his. "I am sorry," he said, "sorry that my wit has not been as strong as it needs to be."

Kestrel looked back at the cabin in the stern. He released Phoebe's hands and felt his fists clench tight. He remembered Milligan's theft of his luck without even a hint of warning and the small value Jelilac placed on their lives.

This quest had become one of mounting obligations, he thought. First, his pledge to Phoebe, then the debt he owed to rescue the rotarians who trusted him as leader, and now, if somehow he could manage it, Jelilac, Milligan, Myra, and the others like them should be made to pay for all they must have done.

Kestrel turned to look back at the shore. Drawing Phoebe close, he watched the towers of the casino become more crisp and clear. He sucked in a chestful of air slowly, then spilled it back into the salty spray. Brave words, he thought ruefully, not what one might expect from a scheming woodcutter—especially not from one who could calculate quite well the chances of surviving without luck in a casino filled with talisman-wearing aleators. He shook his head as he flexed his fingers about the sword pommel that was not there, trying to fan the flame of his conviction so that it masked the growing fear.

Kestrel pushed the bizarre thoughts away. Grimly he stood, silently watching and waiting for what would happen next. In a little more than what he judged to be an hour, Myra's ship cast anchor in a crowded harbor. Her followers and prisoners came ashore into a surging mass of aspiring aleators and their own retainers. Everyone in the realm, Myra had said, would be there—if not a possessor of enough wealth to compete, then certainly to watch to see who the next archon would be.

In the confusion of mingling bodies, one might expect someone to break for freedom, but those without talismans knew better than to try. With faces heavy with resignation, they shuffled into position as their masters directed. Kestrel kept Phoebe close, his eyes darting all about, looking for a sign of Astron or a chance to communicate through the flame.

Except for the casino itself, the island was bare of structure, low and sandy with no plants taller than bushy shrubs. The building was shaped like a huge hexagon with high walls that Myra had said enclosed a many-tiered stadium. From each vertex of the polygon, the towers soared even farther into the sky. At the apex of each, attendants stood ready near the signal beacons that would flash the results of the competition across the sea to those whose luck prevented them from arriving in time. The walls were thick, covered by many layers of fading paint that had withstood countless years of high surf and spray. Portions of old murals peeked out from behind the peeling layers of those placed on top. Faded scenes of previous victories; cornucopia brimming with talismans and devices of chance blended into the mute drabness that surrounded them.

Midway in the face of each of the casino walls, high doors thrice the height of a man stood open. Into each slowly snaked the retainers of the aleators, climbing into the high seats to cheer their lords onward.

"You two shall be in the vanguard of my contingent." Myra pointed in the direction of Kestrel and Phoebe as other aleators jostled past. "For each contender, a full dozen is allowed on the floor, but it is folly to have every minion's neck heavy with capsules of great fortune. A single reversal could spell the end of serious contention. I think it is better for at least four to be luckless as newborn babes. Let the machines of Jelilac and the others do their

338

worst. It will not be talismans of true power that feel the slings of their wrath."

Myra waited until all the aleators at the nearest door had entered. Then, with a majestic swirl of a cape she had donned for the ceremony, she walked slowly into the casino. Immediately inside the outer shell, Kestrel saw the stairways leading up into the stands on either side. Pressed against the high ceiling, globes of bioluminescent fungi bathed everything in an eerie soft light. Directly ahead, a tunnel ran onto the floor of the casino itself. The ground underfoot was bare earth, almost muddy from the humid air.

Myra motioned her followers, except for the chosen twelve, to take the stairs to the left and ascend to the highest seats, as far removed as possible from the rest of the spectators. When the last had begun to climb, she nodded to Kestrel and Phoebe to begin their entrance.

Kestrel clutched empty air at his side with a feeling of futility. He felt his pulse begin to race. On Jelilac's sloop, he had managed to escape, but here in the casino there would be too many. He started to speak when a sudden crashing boom exploded outward from the casino floor and echoed down the tunnel walls.

"Minefields," Myra grunted without losing a stride. "Evidently one of the contestants did not enter sufficiently prepared."

Another explosion ripped down the passageway. Then a third came, this one mingled with cries of pain and a roar from the crowd. Kestrel moved forward as slowly as he could with the tip of a sword planted squarely in the small of his back. He stepped in front of Phoebe just as he reached the tunnel entrance and looked out into the bright light of the contesting field, squinting to see what was happening.

From the other entrances were emerging more contingents, each with a dozen retainers surrounding a richly dressed aleator shouting commands. Nearer the center of the casino floor, still other groups surrounded their leaders, but in most cases their number had been reduced from the original dozen. Only six still protected a corpulent, well-dressed lord in their midst, and one of those limped, with his left arm hanging useless at his side. Their goal evidently was the same as the rest of the contenders, to reach one of the shallow pits dug into the ground and surrounded by chalky white boulders and low barriers of tumbled logs.

The group proceeded cautiously and then, with no apparent reason, veered sharply to the left. With a flash of angry yellow, another boom ricocheted through the stadium. Kestrel saw the retainer on the far right suddenly hurled up in the air, his body bent like a handful of broken twigs.

"Come," Myra said as she arrived at the entrance. "We will show them that my luck is sufficient to find a path to a fortress without fear or hesitation." She prodded one of her talisman-protected men-at-arms forward, and he began pacing rapidly out onto the casino floor. "Follow his footsteps, follow them exactly," Myra commanded. "Match him step for step, if you wish to survive until you are needed later."

Kestrel hesitated while he watched the man-at-arms suddenly veer sharply to the left and then just as quickly resume his course toward the protective barricades. He felt the sharp prodding in his back and sucked in his breath. Stepping out into the warrior's footprints, he reached behind to pull Phoebe's hand. He took two tentative steps and then half a dozen more, matching the zigzag path of his predecessor as best he could. Moving with increasing haste so that he would not lose the trail, he pulled Phoebe after him, only dimly aware of Myra and her other followers snaking behind.

A sudden crack sharper than the boom of the mines suddenly pierced through the din on Kestrel's right. He felt a sudden rip of pain in his hand and looked down to see a streak of blood, as if he had been neatly nicked by a blade. He looked up to see the nearest boulder of the barricade just ahead. Instinctively he snapped Phoebe forward and tumbled her over the rock, just as a second pop sounded behind him. As he jumped for cover, what sounded like a shower of pebbles skittered against the thick granite behind.

"A grenade," Myra muttered behind him as she was helped over the rock by two of her retainers. She stopped and coughed, trying to blow the dust from her lungs. "Shrapnel will find the unlucky. About that there can be no doubt."

Elsewhere in the casino, the other contesting groups were also seeking what shelter they could. Those who arrived the latest were beginning to erect makeshift barriers of shields and protruding lances on open ground as far removed from the other contingents as possible. More grenades began to soar through the air, lofted from one group to the one closest. The dull boom of the mines was replaced by the staccato pop of many tiny projectiles.

One of the less protected groups sallied from their cover and raced with swords drawn at the adversaries on their left. Kestrel expected to see a protracted and grim struggle like the carefully choreographed dances of the reticulates, but instead, in a brief mêlée, the encounter was over. Half of the attackers stumbled and fell when they engaged their opponents; the rest were dispatched by the first lucky swings of carelessly aimed swords. Kestrel shifted his focus and saw another brief flurry erupt on the opposite side of the casino floor and, far to the right, yet two more.

"The ones whose wishes exceed their stores of wealth," Myra said at Kestrel's side. "They mimic the contest of old when strength of arm and cleverness of siegecraft determined the victor. Soon they will all be gone, and those of true potential will struggle as it should be done."

Fulfilling her prophecy instantly, a strong voice suddenly rang through the din. "A challenge, a challenge of true virtue to masqueraders on our left."

Immediately the crowd fell silent and all the hostilities ceased on the casino floor. Kestrel craned around to see Milligan standing on the top of a small boulder near one of the tunnels with a megaphone to his mouth. Evidently Jelilac's had been one of the last contingents to arrive.

"We do the great practice of our art disservice by such crude measures," Milligan continued. "Avoiding mines and the shrapnel of grenades takes a measure of luck, to be sure, but it in no way answers which of us has the greatest power and hence the authority to rule." Milligan paused and circled to address the stands at his back. "Remember our heritage," he said. "This very edifice is enshrined with the name of the grand casino—not the arena, not the stadium, but the casino where all is ruled by chance. The events to be decided here are to be based upon the pristine twisting of gaseous luck, not the slashing of bloodied blades."

The crowd roared in approval, but Milligan motioned them back to silence. "Yes, luck is to be the mechanism of decision—luck, pure and unsullied with irrelevant skill."

He pointed at his side to a large glass bowl with two transparent tubes snaking out of the top and filled with tiny white spheres. "Of all those who have assembled to struggle here Jelilac is the most mighty, the one with the greatest hoard of fortune. He issues a challenge to one and all. The first to have three numbers discharged will be the victor. The vanquished will cease their struggles and submit all talismans to aid in the greater cause." Milligan paused and then shut his eyes. Extending his arm, he pointed out across the casino floor and spun about three times, quickly pirouetting to a sudden halt.

"You!" He laughed as he sighted down the length of his arm toward a small fortification across the floor. "You shall be the first to test that Jelilac's luck is the most potent of all."

Kestrel turned to watch a young aleator rise from cover and shake his head. "No, that is not my plan," he protested. "My only hope is to win against others similarly endowed and capture what luck they have remaining after the battle. Only by that means would I have the chance to face the likes of Jelilac in the end."

The crowd roared in disapproval. For a long while, the high walls of the casino echoed with their lust for the confrontation. Kestrel squeezed Phoebe's hand and tried to settle into a comfortable position. At least for the moment, everyone was distracted and no grenades were hurling their way.

He watched Milligan and two other retainers set up a large wooden frame and then drape it with tapestries embroidered in intricate designs. A long hose was connected to one of the tubes protruding from the glass bowl and run back behind the panels where Kestrel could not see. In an instant, the tiny spheres began to dance in the confines of the bowl, like a boiling liquid just about to erupt. In the distance, Kestrel saw that each ball was inscribed with a few strokes of precise lettering in black ink.

"Your numbers," Milligan shouted over the fading din of the crowd. "Everyone here demands it. Remember the fourth tenet—luck favors the believer. If you have doubts and hesitate, then surely you will fail."

The aleator across the casino floor looked wildly out into the stands and then slumped his shoulders. He grasped at the handful of talismans about his neck and tightly clenched shut his eyes "Seven, nineteen, and thirty-seven," he shouted after a moment. "And by the third tenet, may these charms beget all the fortune that I will need."

Milligan laughed and marked the selected numbers on a huge slate handed to him from within the canvas framework. "Nine, forty-two, and forty-three," he called out without apparent thought and added them in a line below the first. "Now we shall contest in the manner in which it has always been intended."

Milligan removed a cover from the second tube emerging from the bowl, and the crowd again fell silent. No one moved while the white spheres churned and frothed. After a short while, one of the balls bounced into the conical orifice that fed the exit and popped out into Milligan's waiting hand. "Forty-two." He laughed as he held up the orb and waved it over his head. "Forty-two on the very first ball, even though over two hundred spin about."

Before Milligan had finished speaking, a second sphere followed the first. Another of Jelilac's retainers dashed out from the cover of the framing and caught it as it arched into the air. "And forty-three." Milligan laughed again. "I can see the marking clearly from here." He looked across the casino floor and shook his head.

"You may as well make ready. It appears that the wealth you wager against Jelilac is meager indeed."

Milligan turned his attention back to the glass bowl just in time to receive the third ball emerging from the tube. "The third is nine," he said. "Yes, after the first two so suddenly, there could be no doubt."

Most of the crowd broke into enthusiastic cheering, although Kestrel saw one small grouping high in the stands sit silently with faces pulled to their chests. Milligan waved both arms over his head to keep up the volume of sound as he tripped across the casino floor to the aleator who had been defeated. With a theatrical flourish, he accepted an armload of talismans and carried them back to Jelilac's framework.

"Who is next?" he shouted. "Who is next to challenge? Jelilac is ready to battle with one and all."

Kestrel looked at Myra out of the corner of his eye. He saw the old woman slowly shaking her head. "Not yet," she muttered. "Each contest dissipates a little of Jelilac's wealth back into the ether. And there is always the chance that he will not be able to beat them all. I will wait until the last, when my own opportunity is the best."

Kestrel scanned the casino floor and saw the wave of a banner from another of the fortifications. A new cheer went up from the crowd. "Five, thirty-nine, and fifty-two," a voice heavy with resignation sounded in the distance. "I may as well be next. It seems that at the last moment, my luck turned fickle. This fortification is made of anvilwood, not simple fir or pine like the rest."

The cheer reverberating in the stands suddenly stopped. Milligan nearly doubled over with his laughter. "Barrier logs made of anvilwood," he said. "The custodians of the casino have prepared for this contest better than most." He waved back at the glass bowl and the churning balls. "One, two, and three," he said. "Let us proceed quickly so we can get on to the next."

Anvilwood, Kestrel thought quickly, the very reason for coming to the casino in the first place! He touched the rucksack still hanging on his back. Again he scanned the rising stadium seats and the array of contestants on

344

the casino floor. "Astron, where are you?" he muttered.

He glanced down at Phoebe and shook his head. With a sigh, he settled beside her and watched the dance of tiny, white balls. With all the contingents on the casino floor, it would take some while to get to Myra. Maybe by then the demon would appear—or failing that he could figure out how to get a flame lit for Phoebe on his own.

The roar of the crowd was deafening. Of all the contingents that had swarmed onto the casino floor so many hours before, only Myra and Jelilac remained. Kestrel felt the tension grow in Myra's retainers. With each new challenger, they had hoped that Jelilac's luck would turn, but it held steady and true. Some of the opponents had taken more effort to defeat than the others. For one, over seventy spheres of no consequence popped free of the miniature maelstrom before Jelilac received his third victory. Another actually had one of his selections and for a moment trailed only two to one. But in the end, Milligan's master emerged triumphant over all, collecting the largesse of talismans and adding them to his store.

"And now Myra." Milligan pointed at the one fortification still occupied in the center of the floor. "What are your guesses, old crone? The hour grows late. We have been at this for the better part of a day."

Myra grasped the talismans about her neck and hesitated. She squinted at the bouncing spheres while the bowl was being reloaded and then around the vast interior of the casino, as if looking for a sign. "We both have warriors and shields still unspent," she called out in a hoarse voice. "It has made no sense to bring the fated twelve, if they are not to be used."

"You talk as if you had a great store of wealth, Myra," Milligan shot back. "As great as Jelilac's own. But the ruse will not shake his beliefs. Having the dozen slash at one another is only a distraction. Eventually it will come down to the spheres." He paused and waved. "If you wish to increase the stakes, then it will be done. All talismans forfeited by the loser as before—but in addition, the retainers are to be given to the victor to do with what he will."

Kestrel felt Phoebe tighten against him, but he did not know what to do. Myra or Jelilac—which one emerged the winner did not really matter; in either case, their fate was the same.

Myra scowled. She quickly counted the talismans about her neck and then looked around the now nearly deserted casino floor. She rubbed her chin and shook herself with a great sigh. Grabbing the largest stone hanging on her chest, she stared back at Milligan. For a long moment she did not waver. Then a hint of a smile formed on her lips.

"Done," she said. "Only instead of three balls let us make it two."

Two of her retainers bolted to their feet but Myra motioned them to be still. "Why not?" she muttered. "You have seen what has happened to all the rest. This way our chance is the greatest, slim though it might be."

Milligan frowned. "But only two numbers increases the variability of the outcome even more," he said. "A truly lucky stroke could win, despite where lies the preponderance of wealth."

"Precisely." Myra cackled. "Luck favors the believer and I will take what is my best chance." She stopped suddenly and then reached into the paraphernalia her retainers had lugged out onto the floor. Kestrel watched with surprise as she extracted the navigator's almanac and opened it to a random page. He had thought it at the bottom of the sea; apparently it hadn't quite gone overboard from the raft.

"Eight and twelve," Myra called out after she had stabbed her finger down onto the parchment. "If I cannot win by simple luck, then calculations shall help me instead."

She held up the volume with both hands over her head and turned slowly around so that everyone could see. The shouts of the crowd suddenly fell silent, as if their tongues had been sliced by a blade. For a long moment, no one stirred. Then a troubled murmur arose from the far end of the casino and flowed around the tiers.

"Calculations," Milligan said after a moment. "It is not our way—worse even than the slash of sword and clang of shield."

"Eight and twelve," Myra said. "Perhaps now even Jelilac is beginning to have some doubts?"

"Never!" Kestrel heard Jelilac's voice boom out from the protection of the canvas framing. "The old woman is desperate. I choose ninety-three and one hundred forty-two. Let the mixing begin."

For a moment, Milligan did not move. Kestrel saw his shoulders twitch before he motioned for the air to begin pumping into the bowl. Almost instantly, a ball popped out the second tubing and everyone waited in hushed anticipation to see what it would be. "Thirty-four." Milligan set it aside. "I admit that you will not be as easy as any of the rest, Myra, but even with calculations, Jelilac will prevail."

Myra said nothing but stared back with unblinking eyes. Kestrel could see the stringy muscles in her arms draw into tense bands. He had to try something. Anything was better than just waiting to see which would be the victor.

"Yes, thirty-four," he shouted suddenly. The prattle of numbers he had used many times before when posing as a magician came easily to his mind. "Eight and twelve— eight and twelve are twenty and thirty-four minus twenty is fourteen, which is just two numbers from twelve. Two numbers, two—two is precisely the total to be chosen— as the calculations said they would be."

Milligan frowned but said nothing. He reached for the next ball. "Ninety—" he began, but Kestrel cut him off.

"Yes, in the nineties," he said. "Eight times twelve is ninety-six. The numbers emerged according to plan."

Another ball bounced up to the exit orifice, but before it could start its journey it suddenly fell backward into the rest. The whirl of random motion died away. In an instant, all the spheres were lying quietly in the bottom of the bowl.

Jelilac emerged from the confines of his shelter. With

347

a waddling gait he walked out to stand at Milligan's side.

"I have stopped the blower," Jelilac said as he glanced quickly at Myra's tally on the board. "If you truly believe in the power of your calculation, I have another proposition to offer instead."

Myra tossed back her head and laughed, the tension suddenly gone. She glanced once at Kestrel and smiled. "You said that I would not cause doubt, Milligan," she wheezed, "but your master's words speak otherwise. Do not mind this old book. It does not really matter. It served to pull a lucky number from the air. It means no more than that."

"I am willing to up the stakes still further," Jelilac said, "and give you better odds."

"You heard what my minion said," Myra answered. "The flow of luck is in my direction. There is no incentive for me to change."

"If we employ instead the giant spinner, I will give you nine portions out of ten of the field," Jelilac said. "And in addition to the twelve, I propose that we become part of the prize pools ourselves."

"No, not the spinner," Milligan said. "It is not proper. We have agreed not to succumb to the temptation that was offered. Let us continue with the dancing spheres. Surely you will prevail."

Myra squinted. "Nine out of ten," she said, "and your body to probe with my pinchers as I see fit." She slapped the almanac at her side. "Why not?" she cackled. "Your luck is potent, but it cannot be that much greater than mine."

Jelilac grimaced and motioned back to his retainers. "I will be archon." He answered the question forming on their lips. "If we do not duel with the same tools, then how can we be sure?"

Milligan opened his mouth to protest, but Jelilac's stare turned him aside. He stood silent while two of the master aleator's retainers emerged from behind the tapestries carrying a large wooden frame into which a hundred pegs had been pounded in the outline of a great circle. With his head shaking, Milligan propped the panel upright. He offered no more aid as the helpers affixed a stout shaft onto an axle that protruded through the center of the frame. Kestrel saw that a flap of stiff leather was affixed to one end of the shaft and protruded just far enough to touch the circle of pegs.

"You may start the spinner into motion, Myra," Jelilac said with tension in his voice. "Then before it has completed its third spin, I will call out the ten numbers that I select as my own."

Myra stepped from the fortifications. With a flourish of her cape, she walked across the casino floor, avoiding the mines that remained. When she reached the frame, she bowed slightly toward each of the six sides of the casino. Then, with an elaborate gesture, she grasped the opposite end of the spinner from the one that held the leather flap. The few remaining murmurs of the crowd vanished in anticipation.

"A moment." Jelilac held out his hand. "Please do not begin until I am ready." Moving as quickly as he could, he joggled back into the cover of his canvas-draped box. For a moment, there was silence. Myra scowled, but waited, a smile of anticipation growing on her face.

Kestrel twisted uncomfortably. He had changed the contest slightly, but not enough to make any real difference. After one spin of the wheel, what hope did he and Phoebe have? If only there were some way to get a fire started before—

"I smell smoke." Phoebe suddenly sat up out of her slump at Kestrel's side. "There behind the tapestries, I am sure of it. Jelilac is starting a fire."

There was a sudden whoosh of wind that billowed from behind the tapestries, straining them against the hooks that held them to the frame. Kestrel felt a sudden rush of heat and then the odor of rotten carrion, like that he had detected before.

"Camonel," he said. "Phoebe, can it be? It smells just like Camonel." He shook his head, confused. "But Milligan said that the aleators avoided fire at all costs because of the second tenet."

Phoebe's answer was cut off by Jelilac's booming

command. "Now," he shouted. "Perform your best calculation, Myra, because no matter what the method, I am the one who will win."

Myra gave the bar a mighty wrench to send it whirling about. Just as she did, a burst of yellow flame shot upward above the tapestries for everyone to see. In a sudden panic, Jelilac's retainers exploded out of the box, rushing onto the casino floor. Two immediately stepped onto mines, and startled cries mingled with a spray of hurling limbs. The spectators in the stands astride the tunnel behind Jelilac's framework screamed in panic. Those in the rows nearest began climbing into the tiers above, trampling on those not fast enough to get out of their way.

"Mark." Camonel's deep voice rumbled above the din. The djinn pushed aside the canvas and stepped next to the rotating spinner. "It passed vertical, master, just as I spoke."

"Jelilac, what is this?" Myra backed away from the demon that towered over her. "I saw this monster on the raft. You deal with the manipulator far more than have I."

"You stoop to using calculation. Then do not be surprised if it is employed by others." Jelilac followed the djinn into the open. A dark curl of smoke indicated that the fire that summoned Camonel still smouldered inside. "I will be archon, woman," he said. "Soon it all will be decided."

"Mark," Camonel shouted again. "I have timed the initial rate of rotation, master. You have said that that would be enough."

Kestrel grabbed Phoebe by the arm, lifting her up to standing. They had another chance to bind Camonel to her will, and this time there would be no water to douse the flame inadvertently. He started to leap over the barrier and run to the demon, but then hesitated. He glanced at the craters and twisted bodies between his fortification and Jelilac's canvas box. Scowling, he pulled her back down to safety.

"There is too much risk of the mines," he said. "Phoebe, you must try to control him from here."

"It is too far." Phoebe shook her head. "I have already attempted the binding of his will, but the control of his master is too strong."

"Eighty-three through ninety-two," Camonel boomed for all to hear. "One tenth of the numbers but that is the region in which the spinner will finally reside. My master has calculated it and there can be no doubt."

"Calculation," someone shouted in the stands. "Not calculation! No!"

"Calculation," another echoed with a groan. "In the final battle, luck is pitted against calculation and skill."

Kestrel saw a wave of agitation radiate out from those nearest Jelilac's box. The aleators in the stands were mere spectators no longer. Even those scrambling to safety slowed and turned back to watch. On the side of the casino farthest away from the action, a low murmur tinged with despair began to build and grow.

"But if luck loses to some other method, then what is the purpose, what is the meaning?" Myra shrieked above all the rest.

The moaning of the crowd increased. Kestrel saw an entire section clasp hands and begin swaying back and forth to the cadence of a chant: "Calculation, calculation and skill."

Kestrel felt a twinge in his stomach. The ground under his feet suddenly felt less firm. He glanced up at one of the large windows in the far wall and saw that apparently the fog had begun to move back onshore. A subtle vibration began tickling the soles of his feet and migrating up his legs into his spine. Obviously, the use of something other than luck in the confrontation of Jelilac and Myra was deeply disturbing to all those who watched. And somehow the mood was contagious, affecting everything about them as well.

"Something is happening." Kestrel drew Phoebe close. Something, something—the thought suddenly hit him— something like two realms of symmetry starting to merge.

"Yes," Phoebe said. "I feel it, too. Only this time, there is no other realm of which the aleators speak." She glanced wildly at the dimming rays of the sun, filtering through the colored glass. She pressed herself into Kestrel's side. "And if not merging, what transformation could it possibly be?"

Kestrel looked helplessly at the distance to the fire behind the tapestries and the mighty djinn standing arms akimbo in front, watching the spinner slowing to rest. He felt the heel of his boot begin to sink into an oozy soup. Except for the burning tapestries, the high corners of the casino seemed to start fading away. Things were converging too fast. He would have to chance getting Phoebe closer to the demon, no matter what the risk.

Kestrel took in a deep breath and prepared to vault over the barrier. Perhaps if he ran ahead, she would see where it was safe to follow. But before he could move, a new voice sounded from a tunnel behind him.

"Stop," it said. "The contest has not yet run its course. There is the entry of one more who destiny decrees will win. Yes, it is I, Byron, who has come as it has been preordained."

## CHAPTER TWENTY-SEVEN

## *The Will to Believe*

ASTRON looked out over the nearly deserted casino floor. Only two contingents remained of what initially must have been many. He saw the djinn Camonel standing next to a spinner that was gradually slowing to a stop. Behind him, Jelilac was motioning the sluggish beam onward so that it would come to rest just to the left of the vertical.

Astron saw smoke curling above the canvas tapestries from the fire that had brought forth the demon and, not far away, what looked like anvilwood in another of the low barricades. Near the center of the floor, the second group of aleators stood transfixed, all watching the final sweep of the spinner. Astron's membranes flicked down over his eyes. In their midst, there could be no mistake; there was Kestrel with the pollen-filled knapsack still on his back.

Astron looked out at the scatter of small craters and mangled bodies and hesitated. Kestrel would use some clever tactic, he thought, rather than rushing pell-mell into certain danger. His stembrain strained to be free, but, despite the urgency, he had to think and plan.

Byron started out onto the casino floor. Astron tugged at his arm. "Why challenge two groups when, if you wait a moment, you will have to contend only with the victor?" the demon said. "Fate will determine which of them it is to be."

Byron grunted. He relaxed the tension in his sword arm. The blade slowly arched earthward and buried its tip into the soft ground. The aleators in the stands saw that the tall warrior had stopped his challenge and turned their attention back to the slowing spinner.

"Ninety-one," Camonel called out as it barely slid past one peg and then stopped as it touched another. "Ninety-one, just as it has been predicted."

The murmur of the crowd grew in intensity. Only a few shouted accolades pierced the indistinct rumble that coursed from tier to tier.

"Your talismans, Myra." Jelilac beamed in triumph. The aleator paid no attention to the waves of sound mounting behind him. "You were the most likely to offer serious competition. With your defeat, no other can seriously offer a challenge now."

"But you used calculation." Milligan suddenly shook off his restraint. "It is not right. Not by such a means should you become the archon."

"The most trusted advisor is a position coveted by many." Jelilac frowned in Milligan's direction. "Do not protest too much, or I will have to select another." He motioned to the retainers that remained, directing them to fan out and receive the spoils of their victory.

Astron saw Myra slump into a heap. She squinted at the spinner, resting clearly in the region that Camonel had predicted, and shook her head. "Nine chances out of ten," she muttered. "It was worth the chance." She glanced at

Jelilac's smile and then turned away. "I will offer no resistance to the removal of my charms," she said, suddenly sounding far more ancient than she looked. "Remember, I am but an old woman." She waved her arm back to the central barricade. "Come, my followers, come. Do not resist. It would be ungracious to prolong my harm."

Astron saw Kestrel and Phoebe join the procession winding its way across the casino floor to Jelilac's canvas frame. The demon looked quickly at Byron, but the warrior had not yet lifted up his sword. Moving the pollen closer to the fire could only help, but it was not yet time to act.

"No! I cannot let it happen." Milligan suddenly sprang away from the rest. He drew a short dagger from his belt and waved it over his head. "It is luck that shall triumph in the end; it must be the stronger. It must. It must."

Jelilac's frown deepened. He motioned to two of his retainers, and they drew their swords. Cautiously, they began to close in on Milligan from both sides.

A great roar of approval suddenly ripped through the stands as Milligan deftly dogged the attack. He drew his own blade and slashed at one as he passed, streaking the tunic sleeve with red. Ducking his head, he just barely missed a tumbling grenade which exploded harmlessly behind.

Short strokes of the dagger somehow darted through hastily erected guards, and two more of Jelilac's followers sagged to the ground. Jelilac's eyes widened. He quickly stepped backward and looked at the massive djinn standing by the motionless spinner.

"Help me!" he cried as he clutched at his chest. "My talismans are many, but now that I have experienced the power of your master's predictions and been close to the flame, I no longer feel so confident that they—"

Jelilac's voice trailed off. He looked in disbelief down at his stomach and then clutched his hands over a gaping wound. His face turned ashen white. With eyes staring into nothingness, he slid to the ground.

For a moment, Milligan stood silent, staring at what he had done. Then, as the realization dawned, like the doll of a thaumaturge, he jerked back into life.

"I am the victor, the archon." He danced back with his bloody blade. "As our creators must have intended —luck favors the believer."

The roar of the crowd intensified. Some started leaping up and down, shaking the tiers in violent oscillations. Milligan smiled and waved his dagger over his head with one hand while fondling the talismans about his neck with the other.

"No." Camonel's impassive expression suddenly distorted into one of malice. His voice was heard even above the chanting spectators. "Luck is not to be the victor. My master does not wish it so." With a speed surprising for his size, the djinn batted at Jelilac's framework, tumbling it aside. He reached backward and extracted a burning branch of pinewood from the still smouldering fire.

"I am a weaver of matter," he growled as he waved it menacingly in front of Milligan's face. "Here, in a realm other than my own, it is easy." Deep furrows etched into the djinn's forehead. He studied the dance of flame for a moment, and then the log seemed to burst asunder. Five globes of what looked like white-hot magma arched from his hand and landed in a pentagon around where Milligan stood.

"My master has calculated, and five will be enough," the djinn boomed out so that everyone could hear. "The heat is intense, and eventually each and every charm he carries about his neck will crack. The one you call Milligan will succumb to calculation, just as have all the rest."

Camonel tossed back his head and laughed. "Let the fogs of nothingness come forward," he yelled. "Let them come forward and dissolve all that there is. Then there will be one less. Where once there was a realm, there will be only the nothingness of the void." He stepped back suddenly into the flame. The fire roared with a burst of yellow brightness. Then he was gone.

The yells of aleators in the stands stopped just as suddenly as they had begun. The low murmur of unrest and disbelief from before instantly returned. Like a pendulum gathering energy with each swing, their emotions rocked back and forth, each time more violently than before.

355

Milligan tried to dance between two of the glowing globes of fire on the ground, but backed up and hesitated when the outermost of his talismans began to blister. Astron saw beads of sweat pop out on his forehead above eyes starting to fill with helpless panic. He bent forward and blew tentatively on the fiercely glowing globes of light, then shook his head when he saw that they were perturbed not at all. He raised his hands expectantly, as if calling for the intervention of unseen gods. For a long moment, he did not move. Then, in an almost perfect imitation of Myra, he slumped into the center of the pentagon that surrounded him. One by one he began removing his talismans and tossing them at the flames.

"Then the newcomer," Astron heard someone in the stands nearby shout. "The one on the sidelines yet to be heard. He is the chance, the final chance that luck will triumph after all."

Somehow the spectators all heard and understood. Again they stopped their keening. As one, they held their breaths.

"Luck has nothing to do with my presence here," Byron called back. "It is the decree of preordained fate. I carry no talismans, and I do not need their aid in my fight."

Shrieks of despair exploded from the crowd. Their emotions swung back to despair far deeper than before. Whole blocks of spectators suddenly rose from where they sat. With eyes suddenly brimming with tears, they began to embrace those next to them with heart-wracking sobs. Astron felt the ground tremble as it had done in the realm of the reticulates and felt the caress of a chilling wind across his cheek. It was as if a dam had finally broken. There was no hope left that would stem the outrushing tide.

"It is just as I was foretold such a long time ago," Centuron called out behind Astron in flushed excitement. "And by the fates, Byron is not even needed. The self-doubt has started even before he appeared. I have survived long enough, long enough to see it happen. Even if he does not triumph, the end will be the same."

The keening of the crowd rose to an ear-piercing crescendo. Moans of anguish became more frequent, and loud sobbing mingled with the rest. Astron wrinkled his nose. The ground under his feet definitely felt less firm than when he had first entered. The pillars and arches that held aloft the roof of the casino were somehow less distinct than before. Only a deep black painted the high window where the sun had been.

A growing uneasiness coursed up Astron's legs and into his chest. The phenomena were intereseting, but he could not force himself to consider dispassionately exactly what was taking place. He felt his stembrain writhe within the confines of his control with far greater power, straining to be free. He looked about the casino floor. All of the aleators there had fallen to their knees. With eyes focusing on nothing, they rocked back and forth and keened with the rest. Only Kestrel and Phoebe were still alert, looking apprehensively all about. Astron had waited long enough. Now was the time.

Astron looked at the beckoning anvilwood and then turned back to Centuron. "The mines of which you spoke as we entered," he said. "What is their danger? Quickly, I must know."

Centuron squinted at Astron and then threw back his head. The laughter tumbled from his lips in gasping wheezes. For several moments, he shook in spasms, unable to regain control. Astron clenched his fist in frustration, eyeing again the distance to the anvilwood, Camonel's smouldering fire, and Kestrel and the pollen, unable to decide which was to be the first objective.

"Byron and the others." Centuron ignored the question when he finally could speak. "They are all one and the same, driving down the one path to mutual destruction. Each in his own way has surrendered his free will to the ether and has given up any stake in determining events by his own volition. And with each such submission, on a level far below their conscious thought, the self-doubt has increased and the reason for existence has become less firm. We indeed are the mere puppets of some other creator, a bubble of life breathed into being by gods that have walked away."

357

"Demon," Nimbia said suddenly. "I do not like what I see. The fey can create realms out of their thoughts, but that is not what sustains them, once they are born. Only so long as the occupants believe in their own existence does what they inhabit continue to resist the pressures that push against them from the outside. All the aleators here—look at them. They slump and—"

Centuron interrupted Nimbia's words with another peal of laughter. "We are all gathered here, almost all of the occupants of our realm. We now face what we have hidden in our hearts and refused to believe. There is no purpose to existence. The triumph of predestination over luck proves it. It is the end of the universe and everyone that it contains."

"There are thousands here." Astron shook his head. "One spin of the wheel and a few words cannot affect everyone so."

"Despite your great misfortune, you are not one of us," Centuron said. "You cannot know the importance of what has transpired."

"I wish to continue living," Nimbia said fiercely as she placed her hands around Byron's arm. "Surely others do as well."

Centuron waved at the casino walls a final time. "Observe the dissolution of the fabric of existence," he said. "You and your companion are too few to keep alive an entire universe when it no longer has the will to live."

Byron looked down at Nimbia and then glanced at the fuzzy haze seeming to blur the spectators on the wall farthest away. He licked his lips and patted Nimbia's hand on his arm. "Perhaps Centuron is right," he said in a husky voice. "Perhaps afterward there will not be enough time."

Byron released the grip on his blade. He wiped the back of his hand against his lips and looked with glowing eyes at Nimbia. "There is nothing more I can do about the others." He waved back toward the center of the casino floor. "But now, at least I can succumb to the joys of my temptation." He spread his hands wide and, with a slow deliberate motion, reached to draw Nimbia to him.

"Wait, wait a moment, Byron." Nimbia hesitated and

358

then smiled. "I know you do not fully understand my words, but this is not what I had in mind." She waved her arm around the casino. "First we must do something about the will of the people. If you truly are a leader, then rally their beliefs to save us all." Her smile brightened. "Do your duty. Then you will deserve the reward."

Astron's stembrain boiled. He gritted his teeth, pulling it back under control. He looked at Nimbia's smile and then back at Byron, baring the fangs that were no longer there.

"No," Astron said. "The hillsovereign is not yours to do with what you will. As she states, her favor is to be for the most deserving—and not because of what emotions she excites, but the qualities she has inside. She is not yours, Byron; she is—she is mine!"

Not fully realizing what he was doing, Astron fumbled for the sword at his side. He glanced around the casino and saw the closing fog obscuring the farthest stands. The sound of the keening faded into softness and then vanished altogether. The ground underneath his feet felt like a thin sheet of linen loosely stretched over a tub of water. The wetness of the swirling fog began to glisten on his cheeks, as if he were exposed to a gentle rain.

"Do not be overly alarmed, demon," Nimbia said quickly. "I am sure that Byron has sufficient nobility to be different from the—"

She stopped as she saw the gleam in Byron's eye intensify. He spread his arms in a wide circle. Nimbia took a step backward and then halted as her foot touched the edge of the stadium wall. She looked back helplessly, her eyes growing wide with fear.

"It is your fate to be so unlucky," Byron said. "Such beauty was meant to be consumed."

"Underneath it all, I am a person like anyone else," Nimbia said, pain and disappointment putting a bitter edge to her voice. "Judge me for that and nothing else. That is all I ask."

"The allure is too great." Byron shook his head. "There is no one who can resist, no one who can look past the exterior with dispassion to see if there is any other value inside."

"Somewhere there must be at least one." Nimbia put out her hands to ward off his approach. She looked about frantically and then stopped when she saw Astron rushing to her.

"Dem—Astron!" she shouted. "Astron, help me. He is like all the rest. Only you are different. Please, quickly do something. There is so little time."

"The mines! What are they?" Astron yelled at Centuron as he stepped in Byron's way. "Tell me so that I may act."

"We do not know where any are buried." Centuron waved his arm. "But it does not matter. They will dissolve with the rest. Far better that—"

"Buried," Astron interrupted. "Did you say buried?"

"Why, yes—"

"That explains the blotchy appearance of the casino floor," Astron said. "With my membranes down I see far into the red, even into what is called heat in the realm of men. And turned earth is colder than that which has been in contact with the air."

He broke off and reached behind to grab Nimbia's outstretched hand. Ducking to the right, he avoided the swat of Byron's arm and started running out onto the casino floor, pulling her behind. He jogged to the right of a seemingly different-textured plot of ground and then sharply veered back to the left. Behind him, he heard Nimbia stumbling after and Byron's heavy tread in pursuit.

Astron cut to the side and felt his heel rip into the softening earth. Like a folded blanket, the ground wrinkled under the thrust. His foot dug deep into the earth and then, with a sudden lack of resistance, seemed to poke through into a chilling nothingness underneath. Frantically, he reached down and jerked his leg free, watching an inky blackness curl upward out of the hole.

From the corner of his eye, he saw that Byron had retrieved his sword and was waving it wildly over his head. "I am too swift for you," the demon called out suddenly as a glimmer of an idea darted into his mind. "And until you catch and overcome me, you will not have the hillsovereign."

Byron ran up to where Astron pulled at his leg. He

moved one step in Nimbia's direction and then hesitated. "Guard your backside," Astron said, waving his own blade as convincingly as he could.

Byron turned and looked down at Astron. The look of lust on his face distorted into one of battle rage. He gripped his sword with both hands and raised it high in the air. With an ear-piercing yell, he brought it down in a vertical swipe directly over Astron's head. The demon waited until the last possible moment and then jerked aside, just missing the slash.

Byron's sword dug deeply into the softening ground, burying itself almost to the hilt. Immediately, the warrior tightened his grip on the pommel and strained to extract his weapon. As Astron had hoped, the blade trembled, but did not bulge. He scrambled to his feet and again took Nimbia's hand. "I have decided," he said. "To Kestrel and Phoebe. It will be a moment before Byron is a menace again."

Together they zigzagged their way to the remains of Jelilac's contingent. The swirling fog had penetrated almost to the first few rows of seats. Astron could no longer be sure that any of the aleators in the stands were still there.

"The pollen," he shouted, pointing at Kestrel's rucksack as he dashed up upon them.

"The anvilwood," Kestrel answered as he motioned to the abandoned fortification to the right of where Camonel had stood.

"And the flame." Phoebe pointed at the remains of Camonel's fire. She looked at the crumpled tapestries lying nearby. "There is wizard's work to be done."

"Wait a moment," Kestrel said to Astron as the demon dropped Nimbia's hand and started to head for the anvilwood. "I have learned some things that might be important in the quest. Whoever merged the realms of symmetry planted the seeds of calculation in this universe as well. Look, there is the evidence of the navigator's almanac."

Astron skidded to a halt. "A book, did you say? That is most interesting and might indeed provide a clue."

"Not now," Phoebe shouted.

"I have tried to analyze the facts just as you would and extract the most important," Kestrel yelled at Astron's back when the demon resumed running to the other fortification. "Of all of the features of the almanac, it seems to be most strange that it lasts for centuries, and yet, every few days, the format is completely different."

Astron started to wrinkle his nose, but he realized he did not have the time. Reaching the anvilwood barrier, he began hewing with the sword as if it were an axe, sending splinters flying. He managed to dislodge two large logs. Abandoning his blade, he lifted them in the circle of his arms. Staggering with the load, he weaved his way back to the fire which Phoebe had fanned into a respectable blaze, despite the growing wetness of the air.

The tiers of the casino had become completely hidden in the dense black fog, and only hints of the massive support pillars were outlined where the high ceiling should be. The illuminating spheres of fungi had been reduced to dull glows. Only the fire pushed back the darkness of the encroaching gloom. It looked as if they were on an island in a fogbound sea.

Astron tossed the logs onto the fire and prepared to step into it himself, but then hesitated. "There is insufficient time." He shook his head. "You all will be gone before I can return."

"Then transport us to another realm," Phoebe said. "Like a mighty djinn, you must somehow carry us through."

"There certainly is no time for that, even if I were able," Astron said. "Piercing through one barrier to the realm of daemon is hard enough, let alone two."

"You must think of something, Astron." Nimbia touched his arm. "Look! At the very edge of the mists, I see Byron wrenching free his blade."

Astron looked at the inviting lick of the flame. The color and smell beckoned him with an almost irresistible allure. He could easily step into the warm, enfolding embrace and vanish from the peril. He watched the shrinking horizon of visibility and felt his stembrain stir in panic.

He reached out and felt the softness of Nimbia's hand still on his arm. Memories of the passion he had felt in Kestrel's body returned with a surprising sharpness. He

362

looked into her eyes and saw the confidence in his abilities that she seemed to radiate back to him.

"I will try as would my clutch brethren," he said softly as he walked into the flame. "The arc will be small, so you will have to squeeze as much as you can."

"Where will you take us?" Nimbia asked.

"If I am successful, just into the realm of daemon," Astron said. "To the darkness of my own den. Perhaps none will be waiting for us there."

He paused and studied the expression on her face. "It will be quite strange, but perhaps, after what you all have experienced, not so bizarre that you cannot act. We must get the pollen to Palodad. Remember, without that, eventually we will still fail."

Astron turned away his face and pulled his thoughts within himself, trying to shut out totally the collapse rushing inward. Groping mentally, he felt the fabric of resistance between the two realms and probed it for the flaw, the subtle discontinuity created by the burning of the anvilwood that would create the opening back to his home.

For how long he searched Astron could not tell, but finally he found it, a slight thinning in the essence of resistance that could be pierced by the strength of will. Astron concentrated on the familiar comforts of his own den—the ruggedness of the rocklike walls and the shelves that protruded from them, displaying the artifacts he had collected from the other realms. He envisioned with satisfaction the three volumes standing in a row between the shell and rock crystal that he used as bookends in the manner of men.

Astron strained against the resistance, pushing it inward, thinning it further, making it more transparent so that he could see and smell what he desired. There was a small pop and then a sudden ripping. He felt himself being drawn away, shrinking into the flame and tumbling into the comforts of his own lair.

For a moment, Astron let the feeling build within him, seeking to slip away and vanish from the dangers all about. His toes slid through the flame and dangled into the ceiling of his lair. Then his ankles followed.

Astron stopped his slide with a start. This time it had

to be different. He could not luxuriate in the narcotic sweetness of coming home. He stilled himself and stopped his transition. Instead, he concentrated on building an arc in the flame such as he had seen the mighty djinns form in the realm of the fey.

The ripping of the barrier halted, barely big enough for him alone to slip through and little else. He arched his back and placed his hands down into the fire, knotting his muscles and straining against the suddenly increased resistance. He felt the fire of the anvilwood climb up on his legs and arms and eventually meet in the small of his back. Sharp tendrils of pain accompanied their journey, somehow racing along the fibers of his being, reaching even into his fingers and toes and screaming with hurt.

Astron's jaws tightened and his vision blurred. "Quickly," he croaked. "I do not know how long I can maintain an opening this large."

"But I can hardly see anything." Kestrel peered into the arch beneath Astron's body. "It is a wall of flames and in its very center a dark disk hardly big enough for a child."

"It will have to do," Astron persisted. "First Nimbia and Phoebe, and then you can follow."

Phoebe gathered her cape about her and ducked her head between outstretched arms like a diver preparing to leap from a high cliff. She aimed her fingertips at the dark disk and slowly began to work herself through the opening.

Astron gasped as her head slipped through and he felt the widening bulge of her body. The pain intensified into an agonizing torrent. Only dimly was he aware of her passage and that of Nimbia who followed. He tried to focus on how close the swirling fogs had closed on them; but in the blur of his vision, he could not tell.

Kestrel came last, and Astron could no longer remain silent. He howled as the searing pain seemed to rip him asunder. Flashes of reds and yellow washed over him. Wave after pulsing wave dug deeply into his torso, seeking out every atom of his existence and wrenching it about.

"I cannot get through," Astron heard Kestrel call out. "It is the rucksack. The opening is too small to let it pass."

"Then take it off and try the grains one by one," Astron

heard himself answer. He ground his teeth and gasped to make his tongue do as it was commanded. He felt his last reserves of strength begin to wane. The nearest corner of his stembrain was dangerously close to breaking free.

"Kestrel," he choked hoarsely. "If, by some chance, I am unable to follow, you must act with my kind just as you have done with the imps in your own realm. Convince whatever demon passes by my lair to transport you to Palodad." He sucked in his breath in a spasm. "But do not let Phoebe wrestle with the old prince. Just get the pollen to him so that, in the end, Nimbia can be safe."

"One grain will just have to be enou—" Kestrel's answer was drowned by an increased roaring in Astron's ears. Dimly, he was aware of the prickly barbs of a pollen grain being passed through the barrier to waiting hands on the other side and then Kestrel's all too massive bulk straining to follow.

Astron felt his muscles begin to tremble and his consciousness falter. He could resist no more. The barrier closed with a sudden pop and he collapsed onto the flame, the last remnants of his tunic and leggings vanishing in smoke.

"Where have you hidden her?" He looked up to see Byron standing above him with the sword aimed at his eyes. "Quickly, tell me. There appears to be so little time."

Astron's thoughts bounced about his head. He could not control their direction. He tried to push his chest from the smouldering ashes, but his arms trembled and he collapsed back to the earth. Pools of wetness lapped at the flame. Directly in front, he saw three or four of the giant pollen grains begin to shake and bob as rivulets of water wound their way through the dense thicket of radiating spines. Beyond Byron's boots, all he could see were the dim glows of Camonel's fire spheres and, presumably, the shadow of Milligan still slumped in his confinement.

"Talk, I say," Byron persisted. "Tell me in which direction she has run."

Astron looked up at Byron through glazed eyes, but did not speak. The chaos continued to build in his mind. Lead balloons, pollen grains, ultimate precepts, bubbles

365

of reality, symmetries, talismans, almanacs, lightning djinns, the archimage, Nimbia—they all boiled and churned, linking together in strange patterns that the ordinary discipline of his mind would not allow.

Byron scowled and pushed the tip of the sword to Astron's nose, but the demon did not move. The warrior pressed against the guard, bringing forth a drop of ichor and then abruptly pulled the blade away. "An aleator until the end I see," he growled. He looked at the sputtering remains of the anvilwood fire and quickly spun on his feet. "Let us see how loose your tongue becomes when faced with what you believe to be your bane."

Astron saw Byron move out into the dimness and thrust savagely with the sword. He returned in an instant with one of the fire spheres affixed to the tip of his blade. Despite the drenching wetness that seemed to drip from the heavy air, it still managed to sputter and glow. Byron studied the dance of flame for a moment and then thrust it at the nearest of pollen grains at his feet, plunging the two globes together into the soggy ground.

As Camonel's sphere submerged into the water, the fire sputtered out. But just as it did, the pollen grain touching it burst into a white-hot blaze of its own, suddenly glowing with a piercing intensity far more fierce even than what had ignited it.

Astron watched the burning harebell pollen float in the pool of water and burn at the same time, sending up a bubbling cloud of steam to add to the inky fog. He looked at another of the grains directly in front of his face and almost abstractly admired the beauty of the branching net of spines that bristled almost into nothingness.

"Of course." His mouth suddenly seemed to move of its own volition. "It is the same principle as the flour in the realm of reticulates. The tips of the barbs are so sharp and fine that they are perfect for the beginning of a flame. The pollen burned in the realm of the fey; even here in water, it can sustain a blaze."

Astron tried to shake his head free of the ricocheting thoughts, but the undisciplined stembrain would not be reconfined. He saw Byron free his sword from the fire sphere and stab instead at the burning pollen grain. With cruel menace in his face, the warrior brought it forward toward Astron's unprotected eyes.

"And the more difficult the environment, apparently the more intense the fire," Astron babbled on. "The grain smoked and smouldered in the realm of the fey. Here, even water cannot stop the rage of its blaze. In a realm in which it is truly diff—"

Astron stopped. Despite his fatigue he bolted up to sitting. With a savage wrench, he forced back his stembrain, trying to regain control of his mind.

"It does no good to back away." Byron pressed forward with the burning orb. "A few more steps and you will dissolve into nothingness, as have most of the rest."

"I have solved the riddle!" Astron yelled, ignoring Byron's threat. "It is as Palodad suspected all along, but probably did not dare voice for fear that he might be wrong. The evidence we have here is proof enough. How do you start a fire in the realm of daemon? Why, with harebell pollen, of course. It is the kindling where nothing else will do. Harebell pollen, harebell pollen! It was with us all along. The quest truly is over. The ultimate precept—I have discovered the answer at last."

Byron watched Astron's apparent disregard for the burning globe and hesitated. "The ultimate precept," he said, puzzled. "Old Centuron used to speak of such a thing. Destruction is preordained, he would say. Destruction is preordained—either the sphere of existence is pierced from the outside or the will to believe decays from within."

"No, all of that speculation does not matter." Astron pushed aside Byron's blade. "The wise men of the realms guessed, but they did not know. 'Reality is a bubble,' Finvarwin said. 'Like the pipers blowing into the bowl of quickening gel, it is created by thought.' 'Coalescence follows from similarity,' Abel shouted when his realm was merged with another. Just as the juice and water were mixed for his warriors, two bubbles can be melted into one. And indeed, if the will to believe decays from within, the bubble will col—"

"Luck will be archon." A voice sounded behind Byron. The warrior spun just in time to see Milligan stagger forward out of the gloom with his dagger still in his hand. "With one vertex of the pentagon removed," the aleator said, "I was no longer confined. Luck will be archon, even if I am the only one left who believes."

Milligan began to lunge at Byron, but the ground under his feet gave way and he suddenly sank up to his waist. "The cold! My legs!" he shouted. "It feels as if they are no longer there." An expression of deep shock began to spread over his face as he sagged. With a desperate stab, he reached out with his dagger and swiped at Byron's calf. The warrior staggered to one knee and swung his sword, forcing the burning pollen grain toward Milligan's head.

"If I shall not succeed, then neither will any other," he cried as he smashed the blazing sphere against Milligan's cheek. He grunted as the other aleator's blade struck home again, this time in the warrior's chest.

"It is my destiny." Byron coughed up a spatter of blood. "My destiny just as Centuron said."

Byron's final swipe caught Milligan squarely on the jaw. With a cry of pain cut short, flesh and hair were suddenly consumed in a sickening belch of smoke. For an instant, blood spurted like a fountain from the top of Milligan's neck. Then the small aleator slumped forward to bleed over Byron's more massive form.

Astron hesitated. He watched the black mists sweep even closer. The remaining fire spheres could no longer be seen. In addition to the whirl of thoughts he could barely control, he felt the pounding panic of his stembrain increase. His limbs stiffened and he could not move. He must get the anvilwood burning again quickly—but he could not.

Despite himself, Astron wrinkled his nose. Besides the solution to the riddle, something else was bothering him. What else was it that Centuron had said about an ultimate precept? How could knowing about harebell pollen be such a powerful secret? Like mismatched elements of a magician's ritual, everything did not fit into a harmonious whole.

Astron gritted his teeth and tried to calm the rush in his mind. Wisps of fog coursed about him and he felt a prickling on his skin, as if it carried strong acids to dissolve him away. He looked at the bodies of Byron and Milligan, beginning to fade into the blackness.

He must remain in control, he thought as he struggled with the forces inside himself. He had to marshal discipline as never before. To succumb now would certainly ensure defeat. He had his duty to his prince; he must—

No, the passion thundered in his head. If only for his prince, then indeed he need not struggle more. With a stembrain running amok, to dissolve here in the realm of the aleators was as good a fate as any. But it was no longer only for his prince. The quest was for Nimbia as well.

She had called him by name, he recalled with sudden clarity—not "demon" but "Astron." "Astron, help me," she had said. It was a recognition that he served her not as subject but as equal. Yes, she was the one for whom he would continue the struggle. It was for Nimbia—Nimbia, queen of the fey.

Astron took a deep breath in the manner of men. The thought of pleasure not yet tasted flowed through his mind, bringing a small measure of calm. Yes, for Nimbia. For Nimbia and—and for himself being with her as well.

Straining against the stiffness in his limbs, Astron reached down and picked up Byron's sword. With jerky spasms, he touched the pollen grain to the remains of the anvilwood. Despite being half buried in the ooze, the logs again sputtered to life. Just as the last rush of blackness reached him, Astron struggled to merge with the flames.

PART SIX

# The Ultimate Precept

CHAPTER TWENTY-EIGHT

# War of the Realms

"I do not like it." Kestrel frowned as Phoebe pulled away from the embrace. "What little strength we have grows weaker the more separated we become."

"The devil is hardly bigger than Astron." Phoebe waved at the demon struggling to grasp Nimbia securely around the waist. "It is clear that, at most, he can carry only two." She put a finger to the woodcutter's lips. "We only lose time by churning again through what has already been decided. Nimbia and I are to take the harebell pollen to the one called Palodad. If any sort of problem develops, it certainly makes more sense to have available the skills of two wizards, rather than one. You are to stay until Astron appears, and then he will somehow figure out a way for you to follow."

Kestrel scowled at the demon standing in the wash of light that flooded outward from the open doorway. The devil beat his leathery wings, pulling Nimbia a hand span away from the brief landing that ringed the hollow stone. Sprays of hair from the ears and nose formed long stiletto shadows that fell across a pockmarked face. The lower jaw merged into loose, hanging flesh that hung from the neck like a bulging sack.

Kestrel had found the devil cowering under the lowest shelf in what must be Astron's lair shortly after he recovered his senses from the transition. Only with difficulty was he able to interrupt a frightened babble of abject submission to explain the task that must be performed. The women's insistence had been surprising; now, in troubled resignation, Kestrel watched Phoebe surrender to the folds of the demon's free arm. In a heart beat, both were gone into the deep blackness that seemed to permeate most of the realm.

Kestrel turned his attention back to the curving walls of Astron's lair. He touched the rough surface and felt the stone seem to warp and flex. Thinner than paper, he thought. It was remarkable that it was able to hold a shape with his weight pressing on a membrane of similar material that divided the hollow sphere horizontally in half.

Only the single circular opening to the outside broke the blank expanse of the walls. All available space was covered, either with shelves or pierced with hooks from which hung lamps, flower petals, spoons, key rings, thimbles, scissors, squares of printed cloth, and a lock of hair.

A single cushion sat on the rough flooring next to a pipe, a pile of small bones, and a pen and bottle of ink. The low-hanging lamp nearby illuminated a scrap of parchment on which a carefully drawn line of script had been abruptly halted in midstroke.

Kestrel stepped around the cushion and headed for the dim outline of a spiral staircase disappearing into a circular opening near the far wall. He should have explored thoroughly before Phoebe's departure, but the presence of the devil was too great of an opportunity to waste. The bottom half of the lair was probably like the top and, once Astron appeared, it would not really matter what—

A sudden wheeze of pain filled the confines of the chamber and stopped Kestrel in midstride. He looked quickly about the collection of artifacts and grabbed a long, two-pronged fork. It would be of little use in the realm of daemon, he thought ruefully, but he could find nothing more potent.

A second wheeze followed the first, and then a rustle of movement from down below. Kestrel retreated a step, gripping the fork warily. He saw the deep glow of yellow eyes emerge, and then a figure loomed into the light.

A ragged robe of deep sea-green with one sleeve torn entirely away hung over a slender body that limped with each step. A wide and angry scar ran from brow to chin on an otherwise delicate face. The remains of an upturned nose sat atop once slender lips, now swollen and red.

"I am Elezar, the one who is golden," Kestrel heard a voice rasp with difficulty between each dragging step. "I knew that my cataloguer would return, as was his duty to his prince, but I fear it is most likely far too late."

Kestrel raised the fork cautiously and held it in front of his chest. His eyes darted quickly about the confines of the lair, trying to locate just exactly where he had materialized and hence where Astron was also likely to appear.

"You speak in the tongue of men," Kestrel said softly. "I understand even though I am not the one you seek."

"I heard your petty debate and the final resolution." Elezar sagged to the cushion. "Since the outcome was the proper one, I did not interfere. Getting the harebell pollen to the one who reckons is all that is important now, despite the risk that Gaspar's minions might see the transit. It is the last hope. If it fails, then I am resigned to what will follow." Elezar waved at the fork. The edge of a smile tugged at his lips. "Put away the weapon," he said. "I do not have the strength to harm you, mortal. If you strive for the same goals as my cataloguer, then it is not my intent to do you harm."

Kestrel eyed the prince, but could read nothing in the damaged face. "We had heard that Gaspar even drove you from your hidden node," he said, "and pursued you into the very blackness of your realm."

"Gaspar does not have the wit to know where to look," Elezar spat. "To find me in the well-lighted lair of the vanished cataloguer, after he once had determined it abandoned, is entirely beyond his ken."

Kestrel could not bring himself to relax. Astron should have appeared by now. Without the demon's aid, who knew what Phoebe and Nimbia were getting themselves into? And a prince of demons, even if sorely wounded, would be more than a match for a man with no skills in wizardry.

"Then what now?" he said cautiously. "What is the will of the prince?"

"We will wait," Elezar said. "Wait and see if Palodad has sufficient time to unlock the secret to the riddle."

Kestrel did not reply. He lowered himself to the stone floor, but kept the fork at his side. Imitating the impassive resignation of the prince, he steeled himself into inaction.

Time dragged slowly by. For what seemed like eons, Elezar did not move. Occasionally a soft wheeze escaped from his lips. With each one, the glow in his eyes dimmed even further.

Finally Kestrel could be still no longer. He stirred uncomfortably from where he had slumped against the wall. The inward sloping curve pressed against the base of his head and gave no support to his back. He glanced at Elezar, sitting in regal quiet on the cushion, and scowled.

With each passing moment, his agitation had grown, but he did not know what to do about it. Hours must have passed since the prince lapsed into silence, and even though Astron had said that the flow of time was not quite the same between different realms, surely he would have appeared by now. He glanced again at Elezar's crumpled form. Even if wounded, he thought, could a prince be persuaded to carry a single man to the lair of—

"Gaspar, Gaspar, the prince of lightning djinns has observed my passage!" A sudden shriek cut into Kestrel's thoughts. He looked up to see the devil that had transported Phoebe and Nimbia twitching with spasms on the landing just outside the entrance to the lair.

"Grab control of your stembrain, or I will do it for you." Elezar suddenly sprang to life. "Speak with coherence. I, your prince, demand it."

"He observed my passage to Palodad's lair, and upon my return, forced upon me where you were. I, I am—"

"Silence," Elezar thundered. "The risk was worth taking. If you have failed, there is no point now in lamenting what might have been. Into the sky with you, assemble all that remain from their hiding places, and draw them here." The prince looked about Astron's artifacts and smiled. "Yes, here at the den of a mere cataloguer. For a final battle it is most fitting."

"If Gaspar has defeated you before, what hope do you have now?" Kestrel sprang to his feet. He felt his apprehension tighten like an alchemist's vice. Everything was crashing down, just as Astron had feared from the first. Even Elezar seemed resigned to his fate, and Kestrel and his friends were in the middle of it, with little hope of escape.

"Do not give up," Kestrel said. "Get help from the other princes."

"More than half have thrown their lot in with Gaspar," Elezar said. "The rest cautiously await the outcome before they declare. No, none in the realm of daemon dare light their domains to aid the one who is golden."

Elezar stopped speaking and, for a long moment, seemed to look past Kestrel into the stone wall behind. "At least it will not be surrender to the great monotony. The few weavings of energy I have saved for the last will give Gaspar as much pain as he plans to inflict upon me."

"If not your own kind, then from the other realms," Kestrel said quickly. His thoughts spun. He would have to come up with a plan as he had never before. "From the archimage, the fey, the skyskirr, and the reticulates as well."

Elezar's eyes narrowed. He eyed Kestrel speculatively. "The denizens of other realms regard my kind either with fear or loathing. What would make them want to enter into a struggle not their own?"

"Let me handle that," Kestrel said. "First the archimage, and then we can appeal to the others. Contact any wizard in the realm of men and state that you have news of the woodcutter and female wizard. I heard Alodar ask to be informed, just as we vanished into the universe of the fey."

Elezar was silent for a moment. "Your words disturb my stembrain," he said. "I was prepared to meet Gaspar even on his own terms if there proved to be insufficient time to unravel the riddle. Now you give me one more tendril of matter to grasp. Even for a prince, there comes a moment when he must finally put aside the last of foolish hopes."

Kestrel waited without daring to speak again. Heart beats of time throbbed away. But finally a cloud seemed to lift from Elezar's face. The fading spark in his eyes glowed with a new life and he nodded.

"Tell each that you contact that they must first attempt to bridge through the flame," the prince commanded the devil just as he was about to leave. "Get the message of the woodcutter to the archimage so that he in turn will try to contact me here."

The devil shuddered a final time. Then with a trembling beat of his wings, he fluttered away. Kestrel saw pinpoints of light in the distance behind him assembling into a precise row and Elezar followed his gaze.

"Each one is a lightning djinn," the prince said. "They are forming a barrier between me and Palodad's lair. Soon they will move forward to attack us here. Your tongue must not only be glib but quick as well."

"The risk is a great one." Kestrel heard Alodar's words come from Elezar's lips. The contact had been established far quicker than he had hoped, but, as he glanced out the entrance of the lair, he wondered if even what he proposed would make any great difference. The pinpoints of light had intensified to eye-stabbing glows. Their number had increased until it looked as if a continuous arc streaked across the black sky. With each passing moment, it grew thicker and longer, arcing outward to surround Astron's lair so that there would be no escape.

"But if it is not taken," Kestrel shot back, "then the loss is certain." Somehow the archimage was able to hear because of his contact with Elezar's mind. It was as if the two were together in the confines of the hollow stone, rather than an indescribable distance apart.

"When you agreed to help send Phoebe and me through the flames before," Kestrel continued, "it was because of what would happen to the realm of men if Elezar should fall. Nothing has changed to alter the validity of your decision."

"I still am not totally sure of the truth of your words," Alodar said. "And if I and the wizards of other realms come forward and fail, there will be no defenses left to be sure."

"Would you rather wait and take on Gaspar's might one by one?" Kestrel said. "Which strategy offers you the better chance to turn aside the threat?"

For a moment, there was silence. Elezar sat on the cushion, unblinking, with his hands folded into the lap of his tattered robe. "Your arguments are most persuasive," the demon mouthed Alodar's words at last. "They ring true despite whatever other doubts I might have."

Kestrel felt a slight prickle of amazement mingle with the urgency that bubbled within him. He was using no deception at all. He did not have sufficient composure to think through all the twists and turns that would be necessary for one such as the archimage. And yet it was working. He was speaking the truth and Alodar was taking him at his word.

"But perhaps most telling is the fact that you are there," Alodar said. "There and willing to take the risks along with the rest. It is the mark of a hero, rather than one looking out only for himself."

Kestrel's thoughts jerked to the side. "No, not a hero," he said. "Not me. I am not concerned about helping to save the baseness of other men. It is only for myself, only for—"

Kestrel stopped and slammed shut his mouth. Only for Phoebe, he thought—and for the reticulate warriors, for Nimbia's underhill, and even for any of the unlucky aleators who still survived—any who had to endure the tortures of their fellows who did not care.

The injustices that had befallen him were not unique; they extended through seven realms as well. And they would continue to do so until someone came forward and took the cause of many as his own, until someone like the archimage felt the duty to look beyond himself and to strive against the Prydwins, Jelilacs, and Gaspars to save the worthy and unworthy alike.

The feeling of amazement grew. Was what he had been striving for on this quest really anything less? He could not turn aside now, regardless of what escape he suddenly was offered. If that was what constituted being a hero, then perhaps it was not such a foolish rôle after all.

"Yes, I think that we will need someone to coordinate all of the contingents," Kestrel heard himself say. "Someone with experience in all the realms on which we will call for aid. I am ready to serve. Even though it might be hopeless, I will carry out what clearly is my duty and that of no one else."

"Then it is decided," Alodar said. "Send what demons through the flame that you can, Elezar. I will have the wizards ready to be ferried back for your aid."

"Next the fey," Kestrel said to Elezar as Alodar's presence faded. "And then the reticulates and perhaps the skyskirr as well."

A hint of annoyance at being ordered about washed across Elezar's twisted face, but Kestrel hardly noticed. Despite the growing terror outside, he felt far better about himself than he had in a long, long time.

"Nimbia, Nimbia are you safe?" Astron shouted as he squeezed through the vanishing opening between the realms. He felt the chill of nothingness on his legs and barely managed to pull them through with a loud pop just in time. What had been the realm of aleators was completely vanished, collapsed into nonexistence by the pressure of the void.

Astron sagged to the familiar stone flooring of his lair in a heap. The struggle against Byron had been most draining and his body cried out to rest. But his stembrain still bubbled in agitation. He knew he could not stop, not until he was sure Nimbia was safe and his alone. Immediately, he must carry the harebell pollen to—

Astron stopped. His lair was empty. They had gone on ahead without him. He rose to his feet, looking about wildly for some clue, and spotted the pen and ink next to the pile of fishbones where he had left them in what seemed like long ago. Hastily, he scooped the scrap of parchment from the ground and read the script that had been added to his own.

Almost in disbelief, Astron looked out of the open portal to his lair and saw the glowing sky that confirmed that the words were true. Phoebe and Nimbia had been transported safely to Palodad, but Gaspar now assembled all of his might to strike a final blow. Elezar had gone to direct his resistance, while Kestrel, carried by a broad-winged devil, led the wizards assembled from many realms.

As Astron slowly let the scrap fall back to the floor, a swarm of imps buzzed up from the stairwell, but he paid them no heed. The sky was almost as bright as day in the realm of men, so many djinns had Gaspar rallied to his side. With what meager forces Elezar had left, it was doubtful he would have any more need for his tiny entertainers.

Only if Palodad were swift enough to test the pollen and show it blazing in triumph would any who followed Gaspar pause and reconsider that the basis for the confrontation had indeed been won. Otherwise Elezar was lost, and, in the end, all who strove for him as well.

Astron looked at the sphere of bright lights converging on the darker knot of men and beings from other realms, now standing off in the distance and awaiting the strike. He reached out once with his empty hand, then pounded his sides in frustration. Astron, wingless Astron, the one who walked! In the end, he was reduced to being a mere spectator while others decided the fate of the realm.

Astron pushed against the tug of his stembrain. It continued to stir and boil. There was something that still bothered him, some additional conclusion that could be drawn from all that he had learned. He settled on the cushion, not bothering to bat away the imps as they swarmed about his head.

"Reality is a bubble," he muttered. "I have seen realms created, merged, and destroyed. Aleators like Centuron believe that such destruction is preordained. Either the will to believe decays the pressure within or the bubble is pierced from—"

Astron stopped. The already high state of agitation of his stembrain grew with a deep terror he had never felt before. Why the knowledge of fire in the realm of daemon held such power suddenly became clear. He knew why it was the ultimate precept, the greatest of them all.

Astron bolted to his feet and ran back to the open portal. "There is a reason why there is no fire in our realm," he shouted in panic, "a reason most profound. Fire breaks down the barrier that keeps a bubble whole; it creates an opening in the surface that protects it from the void."

Astron looked at the still brightening sky. He knew

that the distances were still far too great for his voice to carry, but he felt he had to continue on. The battle between Elezar and Gaspar suddenly was of insignificant consequence compared to what really was at stake.

"For all the other realms, the opening is to our very own," he yelled. "The pressure on both sides of the breach is the same. Except for creating a portal of transport, nothing else happens as a result.

"But a flame in the realm of daemon—think of it! When it pierces the skin of the bubble, where then will it lead? Not to another of the realms; other flames already provide those connections. No, it can only be to the void. Like the spheres of the aleators that surrounded the talismans, a small rupture lets out the essence inside. The realm of daemon would collapse into nothingness just as surely as if we had ceased to believe.

"It is not only our own universe that would wither away," Astron said. "All the other realms are connected to ours by the other flames. Like the merged realms of symmetry, they would all vanish as well, first oozing into ours and then following us into the chilling void. It would mean the end of everything, all of existence, all that there is."

Astron shook his head and tried to regain a measure of control. The battle of warring princes for supremacy in a single realm were only shadows of what confronted him. The death of a single realm or two was nothing compared to the end of them all!

"But who would wish such a fate on all of existence?" Astron wondered aloud. "Who could be so tired of living that he would succumb to the great monotony in such a fashion? Who would have the power to manipulate—"

He stopped and tried to look beyond the glare of the djinn light. "Oh, what have I done?" he shrieked. The greatest insight of all descended on him like a weight of the densest matter. "Nimbia, Nimbia," he moaned. "I have sent you to the worst possible place.

"It is Palodad." He whirled and explained to the buzzing imps. "Palodad, the one who reckons, is behind it all. I now understand it so clearly. He is the old one like Centuron whose only desire is to see the final end. He is the one who controlled events that combined two realms. He is the one that cut away the beliefs of all the aleators so that they vanished as well. Yes, who else but a demon would design an almanac with entries beyond the lifespan of a man. Who else but a demon would think it important to change the format of the entries so that the user would not get bored over such a span and succumb to the great monotony. Who else provided Jelilac with the calculation of where his spinner would come to rest.

"It is all part of his plan, the same one that he constructed to get harebell pollen to him for the final step. It is Palodad who has computed everything along the way. Gaspar's challenge, sending me on the quest, instructing Camonel merely to appear dominated by Phoebe while retaining allegiance to his prince—there was no other wizard involved at all. It is Palodad who must be stopped; Gaspar is merely a cog in his machine like the rest."

Astron looked at the converging djinns. Somehow Gaspar's rush must not only be halted but pierced as well. He had to get to Palodad's lair and stop the pollen grain from being ignited. Once it was ablaze, it would be the beginning of the end. He was the only one who knew the true peril. Not only Nimbia but all of existence was forfeit if he should fail.

He looked at the imps still swarming about him and grabbed at the thought that sprang into his head. "Servants of Elezar," he commanded. "Each of you, grab hold of my flesh where you can. Together you will transport me across the realm."

## CHAPTER TWENTY-NINE

# The Final Computation

KESTREL watched Gaspar's demons zoom in for their first attack and held his breath. His pulse raced. What he had chosen to do was right, but he could not keep the chilling reality of the most likely outcome from his thoughts. Even with a score of wizards from each of the realms of men, fey, and skyskirr, Elezar's forces were spread far too thin. The hastily constructed inner sphere of lesser devils that faced the lightning djinns was outnumbered at least three to one.

Kestrel pressed his foot down on the unseen blackness beneath him, still not quite believing it was there. He and the legion of reticulates stood in relative darkness on what Elezar had called an unoccupied node. Scattered throughout the realm were many such points, the prince has said, loci that remained fixed in the sky and did not fall toward whatever tugged on everything from below. On them, the djinns and lesser devils accumulated and weaved their meager treasures of matter, transforming the blank nothingness into elegant distractions that forestalled the great monotony. Kestrel pushed aside the wonder of it all. For now, although surrounded by Gaspar's forces like the rest, Abel and the others were ready to act in synchrony, and that was all that mattered.

Near the center of the spheres of converging attackers, not far from Astron's lair, Elezar blazed with a brilliant light, no longer hiding, but daring Gaspar to come forward. In the direction of Palodad's domain Kestrel had deliberately posted the fewest of the defenders in the hopes that, when the lightning djinns did swoop for the kill, their path would be directly through the middle of the two lines of waiting warriors.

The already-bright sky suddenly blossomed into splashes of intense color. Simultaneously, Gaspar's lieutenants unleashed bolts of searing energy at those who rose to fight them. Kestrel saw two devils and a smaller demon immediately enveloped in crackling tendrils of plasma, their shrieks of pain blotted by the rumble of the blow. He clenched his fists. Soon, one way or another, he would experience the fate of the hero.

More demons streaked outward, ducking past the spray of ichor and bone and launching strikes of their own. Behind them, broodmothers beat the air with heavy wings, carrying wizards in their outstretched talons. Gaspar's lesser devils swooped in behind their lieutenants, eyes wide with the choice of targets and sticky drool streaming from their chins as they contemplated the lust of battle.

Bursts of light flashed into incandescence. Kestrel had to shield his eyes with upflung arms. Three more defenders exploded in balls of boiling flesh, then a half dozen more. The deep booming laugh of Gaspar's lieutenants resonated with the rolling echoes of the explosions.

Still Elezar's defenders rose to meet the attack. The broodmothers climbed unrelentingly upward and the wizards they carried projected their wills. Kestrel saw the arm of one of Gaspar's lieutenants suddenly jerk in a spasm. A half-formed streak of energy sputtered and flew wide of its mark. The djinn scowled and turned his head to launch another bolt at the one who had interfered with his thoughts. Before he could, a brown-skinned devil soared past his outflung arm, blasting out with three sharp stabs of crackling pain. Elezar's smaller devils closed in on the mightier djinns. Even tiny imps harried them in vicious swirls, biting earlobes and cheeks when flailing hands could not keep them away.

But then a random blast ricocheted from a defensive shield and struck a wizard from the realm of the skyskirr squarely in the chest. One of Gaspar's minions shook his head at the sudden release from sluggishness. With a wild yell, he waved to the others, indicating whom they should attack.

All around the enveloping sphere, the word passed as fast as the bolts of plasma. Elezar's demons were ignored; the strikes were aimed at the broodmothers and the loads that they carried. The defending demons swooped to intercept the new focus of attack, but the first were blasted out of the way. One wizard fell, then two more. The others tried to maintain their concentration, but each misdirected bolt now did not stray as far from its intended target. The uprush of defenders halted. Gradually they began to give ground.

The warriors on the dark node stirred uncomfortably, but Kestrel indicated for them to be still. He glanced at Elezar and then back to the crumbling defense. Just as it looked as if the thin surface of protection would be pierced in a half dozen places, he saw the prince give the sign. The broodmothers and other demons along the deliberately weakened corridor suddenly turned in midflight and began to dive. With wings folded, they plunged toward Elezar, shooting directly between Kestrel and the two lines of reticulates.

For a moment Gaspar's minions hesitated. Then, with a shout of triumph, they came plunging after. The lieutenants saw the collapse. As Kestrel had hoped, they abandoned their own battles to join in the destruction of Elezar the prince. In an undisciplined riot, the mighty djinns circled to where the resistance had suddenly become nonexistent and poured down the corridor, striving to be the first to strike a blow at the one who waited below.

Elezar released two tremendous blasts of power of his own just as the first of Gaspar's devils sailed into Kestrel's midst, forcing them to stop and hastily throw up their wings to shield off the blast.

"Now," Kestrel shouted. "Demon of many heads, close your ranks just as we have planned."

The reticulates on the ends of the two rows nearest the djinns smartly heeled and rotated their lines inward. Like the lid of a box, in synchronized step they closed off the path to Elezar, presenting a perfect repetition of the lines that flanked the demons on either side.

More of Gaspar's lieutenants raced up in a flurry of wings. Crashing into one another, they looked puzzled at the silent lines of men linked together and marching in perfect step.

"And the bottom," Kestrel shouted when the last of a dozen had come. "Seal the one remaining means of escape and then they are ours. What can be the hope of a single djinn, no matter how mighty, against a foe with eight score heads and twice as many arms with which to unleash his awesome power?"

Kestrel bit his lip as he peered over Abel's shoulder. The lines of reticulates swung shut just as had the ones in front. For a precious moment, none of the djinns within the box moved or released any of their energy.

"Yes, eight score bodies all connected into one," Kestrel prattled on. "It must be so. Look at the unity in movement. Surely that would be impossible if each were somehow disjoined. One hundred and sixty torsos and hence one hundred and sixty times the strength. You have met your superior, minions of Gaspar. Surrender now so you can observe the extent of this power."

Kestrel reviewed his logic quickly. The demon mind freezes with the unusual, and it does not immediately consider the possibility of falsehood. With just a moment's more hesitation, a major part of Gaspar's strength would be neutralized.

"Inward with swords drawn," Kestrel commanded. "They will not resist one obviously mightier, one who cannot be brought down, no matter what happens to a single limb."

For a moment the lieutenants remained silent and unmoving, almost mesmerized by the cadence of the reticulates' march. Then one shook his head. What looked like a jagged bolt of blue lightning arched from his fingertips toward the warrior who was closest.

The reticulate exploded backward from the line with blood boiling from his chest, but he did not cry out. The line immediately closed and, in perfect cadence, resumed the march inward toward the puzzled djinns.

Another blast erupted and a third. Two more reticulates were hurled away, but their positions were again immediately filled, pulling the perimeter even tighter.

A fourth lieutenant raised his arm with sparks crackling between his fingertips but then hesitated. His eyes danced wildly as he tried to decide where to aim his bolt. Finally he slumped against the djinn next to him and let the plasma die away. Kestrel saw what he hoped was the beginning of despair begin to form in the devil's eyes.

"Who plays with the minds of my lieutenants?" A gruff voice behind Kestrel shot a sudden chill up his spine. He turned to see Gaspar hovering behind him, not quite touching down to land on the darkness of the node. The prince had not rushed forward with the rest.

Kestrel looked at the huge form of the djinn and shuddered. All the terror that man had for demonkind spilled over him in a crashing wave. Meeting Astron, Elezar, and even Camonel was one thing, but the presence of Gaspar was overwhelming. He saw the crackles of energy arching between the fingertips, the twitch of massive slabs of muscle barely under control, the swarm of mites about the bristly chin, and worst of all, the smouldering eyes that were focused on him alone.

"Who twists their minds?" Gaspar repeated. "Who has closed off even the suggestion that all they need do is fly upward and then they would be free?"

"It is the many-headed demon from the far reaches of the realm," Kestrel forced himself to say. "Palodad found him and instructed him in Elezar's defense. You may as well surrender as well."

"Palodad? Palodad helping Elezar, you say?" Gaspar tossed back his head and laughed. "Your words do not match the facts, mortal, and I have been warned there might be such as you." The demon looked about at the last of Elezar's defenders fighting his lesser devils. "Even without my lieutenants, the outcome is still determined—although it might take a little longer than had originally been calculated. And since you are the apparent cause of the delay, it is only fitting that you also provide my diversion until it is done."

388

Astron ignored the barbs of pain that stabbed his back and legs. It was better that the grips of the imps were sure, rather than comfortable. He did not like the heavy and labored sound of their buzzing wings, but what would happen if they faltered, he could not afford to dwell upon.

Astron looked back at the sphere of Gaspar's minions converging on his lair. He had half expected to be blasted out of the sky by one of them as he struggled away, but they all had rushed past in their haste to attack the prince. Evidently, one small demon in a cloud of imps was something that easily could be handled later.

The escape gave him little comfort. A few moments more of existence was all that he had gained, unless he could stop Palodad from lighting the harebell pollen. His stembrain bounced around the confines of his mind, unable to find peace with what it knew. He could no longer force it back into a quiet slumber. Only by straining with all his thoughts could he keep some degree of control on the impulses which threatened to fling his body into twitching spasms.

Inwardly focused, Astron did not note his passage through the darkness of the realm or the descent down Palodad's long entrance tunnel. Only by forcing his arm to move in clumsy jerks was he able to fling aside the barrier that opened into the interior that was blazing with light.

As the imps lowered him to the ledge that circumnavigated the huge globe, Astron froze for a moment, transfixed as he had been before by the enormous display of matter, the bizarre arrays of bound devils, the tugging fetters, and the booming cadence of whirling machines. Somewhere in the midst of it all was Nimbia— Nimbia and the pollen that had to be destroyed.

Astron ran to the first pulley-basket and climbed inside. He unwound the rope from its stay and began lowering himself hand over hand into the interior of Palodad's domain. His memories of the first visit were hard to keep in focus, but at each transit he was able to recall the direction he should take.

While he navigated the vast interior, Palodad's giant machine clanked onward, oblivious of his presence. The small, free-flying sprites darted from array to array, shuttling messages to the demons who were bound. The intricate lines of djinns who flipped from upright to standing on their heads paid him no heed when he passed.

Finally Astron spied the central platform that contained the plane of shimmering glowsprites. Huddled in front of the screen, clasping the pollen in his hands, was the ancient prince. Only hints of his raspy voice could be heard over the background, but Palodad was evidently waving his treasure about to two captives imprisoned in cages to his left.

Nimbia and Phoebe! Astron stopped his rush. They looked unharmed; but now that he was here, what exactly was he to do? Palodad could summon any of a hundred djinns to snare him like the others. How could a cataloguer, and one barely in control at that, stop a prince of demons who had plotted for eras before Astron was even hatched? What good was it to have guessed the answer to the riddle, if the final result was the same in the end?

Astron's panic grew. He felt his limbs stiffen. He knew that this time he would be unable to make them move. He strained to open his mouth and yell, knowing not what, but even his jaws grew rigid. Like a statue of inert matter, he watched Palodad cackle and preen with his prize.

The old prince seemed to babble randomly for a few moments. Then a motion on the screen caught his eye. He glanced upward and watched for a moment in silence. Finally he threw back his head and laughed raucously, his frail voice managing to be heard even over the clatter.

"It is time," Palodad burbled. "It is time for the final ingredient to come." He whirled and looked directly in Astron's direction. "Do not bother that your mobility is gone, cataloguer," he said. "Sprites are on their way to bring you to my presence." He waved his arm about the expanse of his domain. "You have come in duty to your prince, just as my calculations said that you would."

Astron should have felt shock at Palodad's awareness of his presence, but he did not. Only dimly was he aware of being lifted and brought to stand directly in front of the prince.

"It is about time," Palodad continued, a thick drool beginning to form down the side of his chin. "The ultimate precept is about time and nothing else. Time, time, time—of all the forces, it is the greatest, relentlessly pressing onward, unable to be turned aside by any of the other princes.

"But my power is by far more potent still—more so than Gaspar with his bolts of lightning or even Elezar and his keenness of mind. I will not merely harass time in its passage, but stop it altogether. The pollen at your feet, cataloguer, is the kindling, the great store of matter I have accumulated over the eons is the fuel. I will destroy this realm and all the others that connect to it. When I am done, there will be nothing left to measure the tick of time's passage. It will be gone. I will have been the one to see it finally destroyed."

Astron felt his eyes stiffly glance down at the pollen grain at Palodad's feet, a small shred of puzzlement tugging at the muscles in his face.

"You wonder why I have not already set it ablaze, do you not?" Palodad said. "Think, cataloguer! Besides the fuel and the kindling, what is the third ingredient for a flame?" Palodad's rheumy eyes widened. He pressed the metal ball in his hand against Astron's chest.

"It is the spark, the spark that ignites the kindling and sets the events on their way, a special spark that only a most unique demon can provide. That is the final ingredient, cataloguer. That is why I had to bind you to the quest, to manipulate things so carefully that in the end you would be here."

Astron tried to shake his head in protest, but Palodad ignored him and rambled on. "Yes, the spark cannot come from any demon; my calculations have shown me that just any shape and intensity of the energy will not do. It must originate from one for whose entire existence the stembrain has remained under control, a clutch brother of mighty djinns, but one who has repressed even the slightest hint of undisciplined thought."

391

Palodad pressed his face against Astron's own. "Now, cataloguer, to make the final calculation complete. Surrender, surrender at last to what has churned within you for so long."

Again Astron attempted to shake his head. He was merely a cataloguer, a stunted djinn without wings, one who could not weave. How could he provide the essence of what the mad demon sought? It could not be true, and yet— As the feelings churned within him, Astron could not deny what the prince had said.

Palodad was correct, the certainty swelled. He had been correct from the first. All the events had been calculated and there was no other outcome possible. The mad one's great machine, his incredible store of matter, and the pollen that would surely ignite—there was no logical way to resist. Not only would everything that existed vanish totally, but he, Astron, the one who walked, was to be the instrument for that destruction.

Astron tried to cry out, but he felt his final control slipping away. A ripping pain coursed through him, as if his very being were being torn apart. Thoughts exploded in all directions and bounced about his head. Through eyes wet with tears, he saw Nimbia's face contort with concern. He felt a strange tingling and then sharp nips of pain. His stembrain danced as it had never done before. Crackles of energy popped from his ears and raced down his arms. Purple and brilliant red streamers surged to his back and then onto his thighs. Helplessly, he saw Palodad kick the pollen grain between his feet, and the angry pulses of energy spurted and jumped to meet it.

Astron felt himself slipping away into a maelstrom of confusion. The lust for destruction within him grew. With the last shred of consciousness, he struggled to pull back the crackling power that radiated from him and keep it away from the prickly sphere waiting for its touch. But he could not hold back the flood. Past his knees, the sheets of plasma danced down onto his shins. White-hot sparks exploded out into the air. In a brilliant flash, globs of pulsing energy rained onto the floor.

\* \* \*

"I have let you agonize long enough in anticipation." Gaspar stepped forward into the darkness of the node. "Now you shall experience a hint of what truly is to come." He extended his arm and pointed at Kestrel's chest. A tiny arc of energy shot from the demon's fingertip and struck the woodcutter just below the throat.

Kestrel staggered to one knee as the stab of pain exploded across his torso and ran down his arms. He gasped, then gritted his teeth, determined not to cry out. For the longest while, Gaspar had stood silently taunting him while the battles behind the two of them still raged. Now only a few cries and bursts of light illuminated the darkness of the demon realm. Elezar's last defenders swarmed about their prince, but not even the most hopeful could now dispute the final result.

"What, no pleas for mercy?" Gaspar said. "No appeal to some better part of my nature to make the ending swift?" The djinn stepped forward and grabbed Kestrel beneath the arms and lifted him effortlessly to eye level. "You will grovel before I am done, mortal, grovel like all the rest when they feel the wrath of the prince whose power is the greatest."

Gaspar's hands started to glow with pulses of energy. Kestrel felt the fabric of his tunic shrivel and part. Waves of heat radiated into his chest. His skin began to blister and flake away. He shook his head from side to side, trying to find the words that would turn Gaspar's attention away— some clever stratagem that would misdirect even a prince of demons from his fiendish pleasure. He looked into Gaspar's eyes and saw only the twisted desire that would not be denied. In despair, he realized that there was nothing that he could say that would save him now.

Gaspar saw the expression on Kestrel's face and threw back his head with a booming laugh. Short stabs of plasma arched from the demon's shoulders and elbows and smashed into Kestrel's arms, adding rips of pain to the boiling heat that already was almost too much to withstand.

As the agony intensified, visions began to swim in Kestrel's mind. He thought of Phoebe and what would be her fate after he had gone, of Abel and the warriors behind him still faithfully confining the lieutenants as he had commanded them, and of Astron, a demon most unlike all the rest, of—

Kestrel reached out and grabbed at the thought as it flitted by. He closed his eyes and concentrated on where it was leading him. Astron would not challenge Gaspar with wily words. He would use whatever solid facts he could and from them determine what must be done.

Kestrel shifted his focus as quickly as he could through the numbing haze of pain. Gaspar—what was all that had been said about the prince in the times that Astron had spoken of him during the quest? He was a most powerful djinn with his weavings of matter, indeed perhaps the most powerful of all. But in Elezar's rotunda he had been chided for his lack of wit and unwillingness to challenge any wizard who sought—

Gaspar was a powerful weaver, it was true. Kestrel churned the thought in his mind. But what was Gaspar's strength of will? How well could he fare against the archimage, or Phoebe, or even—?

"Surrender," Kestrel yelled at the top of his lungs as he seized at the last chance. "Surrender to him who will be your master. It is dominance or submission. There can be no in between."

"You are no wizard—"

"Nor need I be. It is only a matter of will," Kestrel gasped. The pain in his sides became excruciating. He thought he could smell the burning of his own flesh. But he lashed out with his mind, seeking the essence of the demon that held him, ready to twist and turn with his last dying gasp. There was nothing else to try.

Kestrel's sight dimmed into hot glowing yellows. Blindly, his thoughts exploded, not knowing exactly what it was that he sought. He felt his awareness expand in all directions, pushing everything before it. All of his essence of being, his pleasures, his hopes, his fears, and everything of consequence boiled and churned, blasting all else aside.

Then Kestrel felt a resistance, something that slowed the outswell of thought that swirled midst the pain. Impulsively, he crashed against the barrier, at first skittering against the surface, but then striking it again and again. Visualizing mental arms and legs, he tore at the covering, trying to rip it asunder so that he could plunge inside.

The images whirled in his mind, but somehow even in the delirium of his pain, he stalked like a hunter, testing the seams of Gaspar's essence one by one. He jabbed a finger into a dark crevasse; when he felt something softer than the rest, he thrust in his hand. Whatever was inside attempted to wither away, but Kestrel was quicker and grabbed and twisted as savagely as he could.

"Your minions might have victory," Kestrel shouted, "but you will not share in it, Gaspar. I have come too far and changed too much to let it be so. I cannot weave, but it does not matter. My will is the greater because I fight for what I believe, not for some idle amusement to forestall an eventual dawn."

Kestrel felt his fist rip and tear. A shudder coursed throughout all his body. He reached with his other hand and pulled at Gaspar's being, spreading it open so that it was exposed. He felt a sudden wave of pleading protest, and then a smell of self-loathing that shook him to the core. Fear and submission flooded over him, drenching him in doubt and ultimate despair.

"Desist, master, desist," Kestrel heard Gaspar say. "Stop your smiting. I am yours to command."

Kestrel paused. He opened his eyes and blinked. He was lying astride Gaspar's chest as the demon sprawled on the inky blackness of the node. Kestrel looked at his bloody hands where he had been ripping at the djinn's face; the flesh of one jowl was hanging limp and oozing green ichor.

Tears sprang into Kestrel's eyes. Mingling with the lingering pain, he felt a deep catharsis wash over him. After all these years, the burden was finally lifted. His first deceptions and every one that followed he could finally put aside.

He started to speak, but the node beneath him suddenly rumbled. There was a flash of light that lit the sky from the direction of Palodad's lair.

"Ah, even in my defeat," Gaspar slurred through the

wreckage of his face. "Even in my defeat, it sounds as if my master has still achieved his own triumph, whatever it was that caused him to direct me so."

Astron's eye membranes snapped into place, but they did not help. The harebell pollen glowed with a white-hot intensity that was greater than any normal flame. Through a series of mirrors, the blinding glare ricocheted out of Palodad's lair and across the darkness of the realm in the direction of Astron's den, evidently a signal that the deed was done. Like a boiling sun, the sphere roared in incandescence, churning the air that surrounded it into waves of convective force. The metal platform on which it rested began to pool into a slaggy liquid. Nearby spars blistered and twisted. The wings of close-flying imps burst into flame.

But worst of all was the roaring hiss. Even though the air closest to the burning pollen had greatly expanded, it did not bubble away. Instead, scraps of parchment and small loose objects tumbled toward the flame, accelerating as they grew near. Then in a final rush, they vanished into the whiteness. The surface of the realm of daemon had been ruptured. Now its very essence was leaking away to the void of nothingness on the outside.

Palodad knelt down on his haunches and watched the sucking pressure increase its power. Oblivious to everything else and cackling at the top of his lungs, he snatched imps out of the air and cast them into the flame.

"The rupture is but a beginning," Palodad cried. He waved about the expanse of his lair. "As more fuel is consumed, the opening will grow. Stronger will become the force pushing every object into its ultimate dissolution. No matter where they hide, no one will be able to resist it. Eventually, all must tumble past Palodad, the one who reckons."

Astron felt the wind pushing against his back and rushing into the orb of destruction. His entire body was alive with dancing sparks, but he no longer cared. Despite his last futile efforts, he had been unable to stop the mindless rush of his stembrain and to restrain the power that gave rise to the all-important spark. Now all he felt was the compulsive desire to flee, somehow to shake off the rigidity that gripped him, and to hide from the growing suction as long as he was able.

He looked at Nimbia desperately, a small part of his mind dimly aware of how in the end he had not saved her from Palodad's fate. He saw Phoebe standing next to her, dumbfounded, her mouth open and watching the all-consuming energy of the fire.

Phoebe, Phoebe and Kestrel, Astron thought. If only the woodcutter had been along for the final confrontation. He would not have let his stembrain get out of control. Somehow he would have used its power instead, exploiting its irrationality rather than becoming its slave. But for himself, a demon, a cataloguer, Palodad's logic had been inescapable. There was no way that—

Astron gasped despite himself. Indeed, Kestrel would not fight the vagaries of the stembrain. He would not try to keep it under restraint. He would let it roam wherever it led him, seeking out solutions rooted in emotion that mere logic could never find. Astron looked a second time at Nimbia. With a shudder, he surrendered the last vestige of control. Totally unconstrained, he let his stembrain take over his body and do with it what it would.

Astron felt the sparks that raced over his body intensify. Like Gaspar, tendrils of blue and green flame filled the spans between his fingers. Glowing plasma danced over his lips and across his cheeks. The rigidity that held him melted away. Surrendering completely, he was able to sag to the ground with his legs trembling in mighty spasms and his head jerking from side to side. His tongue poked randomly out between his teeth. A meaningless cry escaped from his lips.

And inside Astron's mind the images swirled. The safety of his den, Elezar's beautiful spires, the mysteries of the realm of men, the constructions of the fey, the lust of the human body, the merging of two realms into one, the collapse of the universe of the aleators—they all danced and swayed. Colors fused and melted, the touch of smooth surfaces transformed into pungent odors and smells. He sensed his feelings for Nimbia grow into a passion that encompassed all of him and tasted heartbreak because none of her intimate mysteries would he ever experience. She would disappear like all the rest, a pleasure never sampled, a sweetness—

For an instant the tumble of Astron's thoughts jerked to a halt. He felt himself frown and pulled at the inconsistency that suddenly hovered just outside the reach of his consciousness.

Palodad had said he had come in service of his prince just as it had been calculated. That was certainly true, but the reason had been replaced by one far more powerful. In the end, it was his feeling for Nimbia, his concern for her safety above all else, his sense of—of possessiveness that had stirred in him so, and that was the motivator of his actions, far more than anything else.

Everything was not as Palodad had calculated, Astron realized in a rush. The irrationality of feeling, the concern of one being for another, the desire for sharing—the ancient prince had not counted on such things at all.

Astron glanced down at the pollen grain raging in front of his feet, tasting all the more strongly the natural impulse of any demon to flee. He looked a final time at Nimbia, while his stembrain churned and recalled the powers possessed by the fey. He felt his thoughts explode in one last desperate inspiration. Without trying to weigh its merits, he jerked to his feet suddenly and decided to act.

Palodad frowned at the sudden motion, but did not move.

"It will do no good to resist the tug of the void," he said. "Eventually you will be swept away with the rest."

"You wanted the essence of our realm and all others vented to the outside." Astron stumbled toward him. "It is only fitting that you should experience firsthand what it is like. It is totally irrational, but I will make the sacrifice. Come, together we will make one more journey through the flame—this time to what is truly nowhere."

Astron heard Nimbia scream behind him, but he paid her no heed. He reached out with both hands and grabbed Palodad in a viselike grip. The prince leaned forcefully to the side, pulling Astron toward the raging flame, and the

398

cataloguer did not resist. Instead, he added his own momentum to Palodad's thrust. Together they tumbled off balance. Holding the surprised prince tightly, Astron plunged headfirst into the center of the pollen grain just as if he were vanishing into a common fire.

The scene around Astron twisted and shimmered. He felt an immediate numbing cold and a total blackness, deeper than any he had ever seen before. Instinctively, he clamped shut his mouth to preserve what little breath he had in his lungs.

Astron felt Palodad twist free but he did not care. The feeling of numbing coldness began to grow. He felt his chest start to expand painfully and a sudden bubbling in his ears. His eyes bulged and he could not quite bring them into focus.

Astron whirled about and saw the feeble glow of the pollen grain sticking through from the realm of daemon into the void. The outrush of air batted against him, forcing him backward. He felt himself begin to drift away.

With a frantic swipe Astron reached out and grasped at the burning pollen, feeling a numbing pain that roared up his arms and into his chest. He was not sure that what he was going to try would work, but there was no other choice.

Palodad saw what Astron was attempting and banged the ball in his clawlike hand down on the cataloguer's elbow, trying to force him to release his grip. But Astron's senses were overloaded. The burning flesh in his hands, the numbing cold of the void, and the pressures within trying to dissipate him into the nothingness left no room for anything else. He wrenched at the pollen grain and felt it tremble slightly, like a giant root that would not quite pull free.

Tightening his grip and ignoring Palodad's rain of blows, Astron pulled himself to the surface that confined the realm. He planted his feet on its strange, spongy surface and arched his back. With a grunt that emptied his chest of any remaining air, he ripped the burning grain free and pulled it out into the void.

For an instant nothing happened. The light from Palodad's domain outwelled into the blackness. Astron could see the hem of Nimbia's tunic and behind her the rest of the prince's machine. He began to get dizzy from all of the churning impulses in his brain. He felt his thoughts begin to slow. His grip on the pollen grain loosened as Palodad scrambled to rip it free.

But as consciousness finally faded, Astron noted that the size of the hole into the realm of daemon began to shrink. He watched it close to the diameter of Palodad's metal ball, then to a coin in the realm of men. With a satisfying final rush, the rip vanished altogether and the realm was whole.

Almost absently Astron turned his attention to Palodad, frantically clawing away at what he possessed. For a second, the two demons wrestled with the sphere that no longer burned. Then with a final burst of energy Astron steadied himself against the outer surface of the realm and heaved the pollen grain as hard as he could deeper into the fathomless depths of the void.

Unable to surrender his most precious treasure, Palodad held his grip on the orb as it sailed away. He opened his mouth to scream a protest and no sounds came forth. In a spew of blood and foam, the prince arched into the nothingness and out of sight.

For a second Astron watched him go. Then he collapsed into a ball as he also began to drift away. He was ready to surrender to his fate; his job was finally done.

He had done it! Nimbia, the realm of daemon, all of existence, everything had been saved!

Only dimly was he aware of the transformation taking place around him, the formation of what looked like solid rock, shelves, a small pile of bones, pen and ink, a lock of hair, and three books and other artifacts from the realm of men.

The stembrain, he mused in misty incoherence—it was right even to the last conjecture, the slender chance that convinced him to take the risk. And she must have had deep feelings for him after all. For a mere subject, she would not have paid so much attention to the detail.

\* \* \*

"And so Astron gambled that Nimbia would be able to construct a new realm for him in time to save his life," Kestrel explained to the wizards who had assembled in the presentation hall of the archimage. Over a dozen score were there, sitting in precise lines and following each of his words with frowning concentration. The archimage sat in the first row, with his consort Aeriel robed in the deep green of the ministry of Procolon at his side. Crowded about the periphery behind them, scribes busily squeaked their quills across thick parchments, mingling with emissaries from Arcadia across the sea and other masters of the five arts. The setting sun cast long shadows through the high windows, and serious-faced pages began to light the sconces that would continue the meeting far into the night.

Kestrel glanced at the demon next to him on the dais, shyly clasping the hillsovereign's hand, and smiled. Behind the four of them, the fire that had brought them back to the realm of men flickered silently. "If her feelings had not been sufficiently strong, she might not have succeeded," Kestrel said. "But, as you can see, Nimbia was able to create a safe haven out of the void just in the nick of time."

"Astron's mind was never besotted by my—my external attributes." Nimbia's hand squeezed the one she held. "He alone judged me for my inner worth. Once I realized that, I knew that the quest that I had pursued almost unknowingly for so long was finally over."

"Then with Palodad out of the way, it was a relatively simple matter for the hillsovereign and me to bring the demons in his lair under our control," Phoebe said. "We dispatched scores to all corners of the realm to announce the answer to the riddle and to explain that it was Elezar who had won the contest. All the other princes stopped their struggle against him and, with the prince of lightning djinns himself defeated, brought Gaspar's minions under control. Now they all defer to Elezar's leadership—in fear if nothing else, so close was there almost disaster for all."

"So the golden one is back in command and I am still his master." Alodar rose from his chair. "The realm of men is safe once again." Holding a scarlet ribbon that pierced a large circle of gold, he stepped onto the dais. He cleared his throat and placed the medallion about Phoebe's neck. "The council of councils is unanimous in their vote," the archimage said. "Wear the logo of flame proudly, wizard. You have been accepted by all, the equal of any man."

"Far more important, I have accepted myself." Phoebe shook her head. "Man, woman, demon, hillsovereign of the fey—none of the opinions of the others really matter. Once a person has accepted herself, then everything else will follow."

Alodar turned to Kestrel and held out his hand. "To one who is not a true student of the five magics, the councils cannot convey any largesse," the archimage said. "But somehow I suspect that the fame of the master of lightning djinns will keep your pockets filled, nevertheless."

Kestrel shook Alodar's hand and his smile broadened. "I have gained what no amount of gold could ever buy," he said. He put his arm about Phoebe and pulled her tight. "Trust in one's fellowmen—a sense of belonging —is worth far more than even a treasure from beyond the flame."

Kestrel looked at Astron. "Of course I must admit, demon, to having learned a few other things as well. Before our journey together, lead balloons and pin-hole glasses I never would have suspected. Your use of them illustrated a powerful discipline. It was because of examining the facts of the situation that I found the way to defeat Gaspar when my glib words were sure to fail."

"Logic and calculations are indeed powerful." Astron pulled his eyes away from Nimbia. "When the quest began, it was for such knowledge of things that I hungered. Yet now that I ponder, it was knowledge of self that I gained the most.

"No logical demon would have rushed toward the burning pollen grain when every impulse was to flee. Not even the mightiest djinn willingly would travel through the fire into nothingness and then pluck away the one apparent means to return. None would think that they could pull matter through into the void if it were difficult for them to transport it between universes that are known. Without a demonstration, who could know for sure that a creature of the fey would have feelings intense enough to form a new realm in time.

"It was not logic but the freedom of the stembrain that gave me the plan, as irrational as it was. Palodad never suspected until it was all too late. We have both learned, Kestrel, from each other, you of things in the realms about you, me of the emotions that slumbered within."

Astron stood up and tugged on Nimbia's hand. "But enough of analysis after the fact. We should return to the lair that you constructed for me. We must give the tiny realm more thought and soon, so that it will grow. Together we can mold it into whatever we desire."

"After a moment, Astron." Nimbia did not rise. She pulled on the demon's hand to have him resume his seat. "I first wish to hear more of the legends that humankind have about the realm of the fey."

"But we have pledged to one another." Astron wrinkled his nose. "According to the sagas, the wishes of one are to be the other's command and—and I desire to go."

"You do not quite have it right." Nimbia smiled. "It is my desire that is the wish, your part is the command."

"But—" The wrinkle in Astron's nose deepened.

"Astron, there are still many more riddles in your future." Kestrel laughed. "And I think that you will find that Gaspar's was just one of the easy ones."

Astron looked quickly at Kestrel, saw Phoebe smiling with the rest, and then turned back to Nimbia. His stembrain told him that the words of the woodcutter were all too true.

# SECRET OF THE SIXTH MAGIC

BY LYNDON HARDY

## BEYOND THE FIVE MAGICS

The laws of the five magics were being set aside. First to go were those of the high art of sorcery. Then true magic, upon which the commerce of all Arcadia depended, had been voided. And now even thaumaturgy, the engineering knowledge of the world, was under attack.

Jemidon had traced the trouble to Melizar, the strange, cold being who had seemingly appeared from nowhere. Somehow, Melizar could alter or negate the laws that had always existed by using a mysterious metamagic – something which only he understood.

If the world was to be saved from Melizar, it was up to Jemidon to save it. But what could he do? He was only an outcast, unable to perform the simplest ritual without ruining everything.

ONCE AGAIN, AS IN *MASTER OF THE FIVE MAGICS*, LYNDON HARDY BRINGS US A STORY IN WHICH THE RIGOROUS APPLICATION OF LOGIC GIVES AN ADDED DIMENSION OF REALITY TO FANTASY.

0 552 126802

# MASTER OF THE FIVE MAGICS

BY Lyndon Hardy

TO MASTER FIVE GREAT ARTS OF MAGIC AND WIN A
QUEEN WAS NOT ENOUGH FOR ALODAR THE
APPRENTICE. HE MUST DO WHAT NO MAN DARED!

Alodar was a mere apprentice thermaturge, learning the least
of the five arts of magic. As such, he had no right to aspire to
the hand of the fair lady, Queen Vendora, not even when he
saved her during the demon-inspired siege of her frontier
castle. But aspire he did.

His quest forced him from one exacting branch of magic to
another, with the rewards he earned always going to others.
Finally, only the branch of wizardry remained – the great,
almost lost art of controlling demons.

It was then he learned of the ancient plot behind his rise –
and faced the greatest danger any man could dare!

ALODAR'S QUEST IS NOT ONLY A STIRRING TALE OF
ADVENTURE, BUT ALSO ONE OF THE MOST LOGICAL
DETAILINGS OF THE LAWS OF MAGIC EVER TO APPEAR
IN FANTASY.

0 552 126799

# A SELECTED LIST OF FANTASY
# AND SCIENCE FICTION AVAILABLE
# FROM CORGI BOOKS